SYMPHONY OF FATES

A LEGENDS OF TIVARA STORY

JC KANG

To Critique Circle
For all the help in teaching me to write.

TIVARALAN
IKSUVI
LIETUVI
ROTUVI
KANIN WILDS
TELE
CATHAY
DRAGON LANDS
KANIN
ANKIRA
MADURA
AYURI CONFEDERATION
LEVASTYAN
AKSUMI TRIBAL LANDS

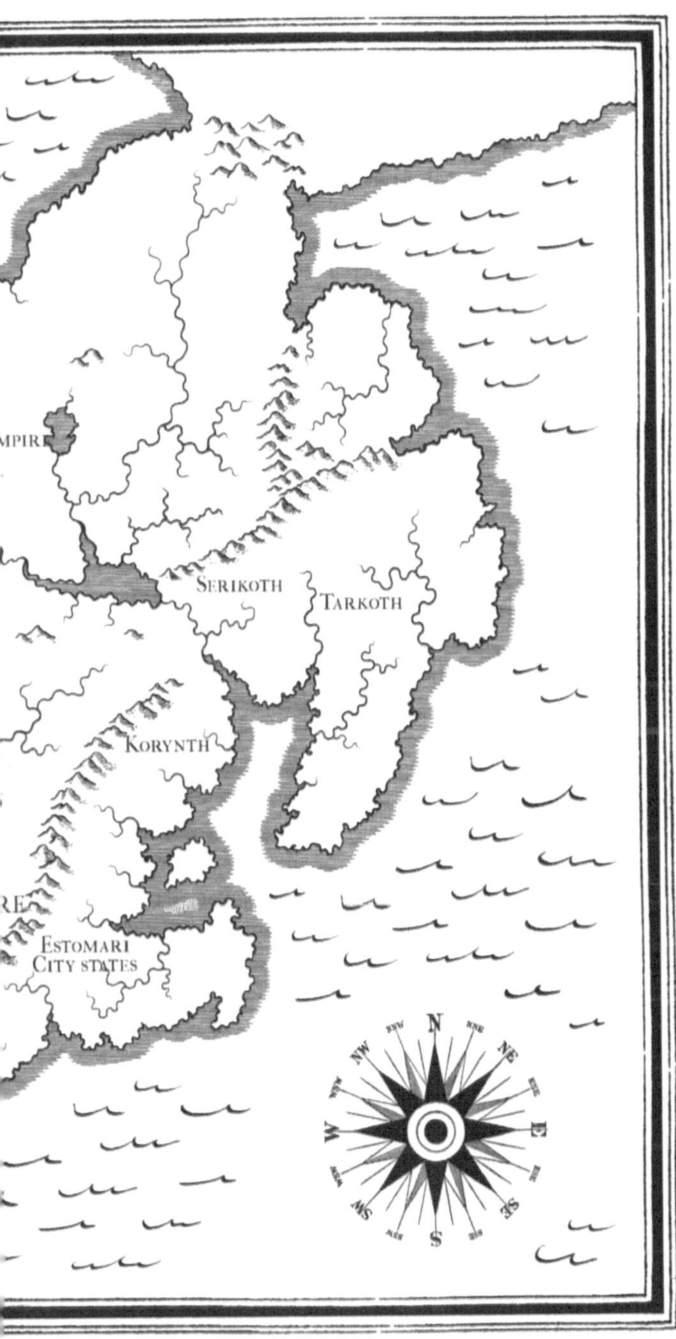

MPIRE
SERIKOTH
TARKOTH
KORYNTH
RE
ESTOMARI
CITY STATES
N
NNE
NE
ENE
E
ESE
SE
SSE
S
SSW
SW
WSW
W
WNW
NW
NNW

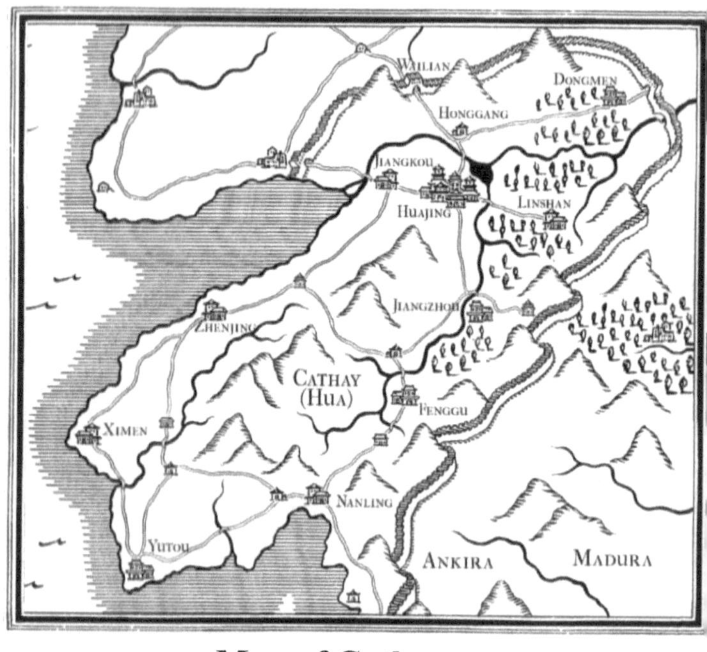

Map of Cathay

Who's Who in Symphony of Fates

Imperial Family
Wang Kai-Wu, the *Tianzi*
Wang Kaiya, princess
Wu Yanli, wife of Kai-Wu, from Zhenjing Province
Zhao Xiulan, wife of Kai-Guo, from Ximen Province

Kaiya's Friends
Ma Jun, Kaiya's imperial guard
Han Mei-Ling, Kaiya's handmaiden
Lin Ziqiu, Kaiya's cousin, from Dongshan Province
Wang Kai-Hua, Kaiya's cousin, married to the heir of Jiangzhou Province
Yan Jie, Black Fist spy, Kaiya's bodyguard

Kaiya's Mentors
Lord Xu, Elf Lord of Haikou Island
Doctor Wu, Taoist from Haikou Island

Royalists Lords
Du, Yu-Ming lord
Chen Qing, Yu-Ming heir
Han, Lord of Fenggu Province
Liu Yong, Lord of Jiangzhou Province
Liu Deying, Heir of Jiangzhou Province
Wu, Lord of Zhenjing Province
Zhao, Lord of Ximen Province
Zheng Han, Lord of Dongmen Province
Zheng Ming, Kaiya's main suitor, Heir to Dongmen
Zheng Lun, Third son of Zheng Han
Zheng Shu, Second son of Zheng Han
Zheng Tian, Fourth son of Zheng Han

Rebel Lords
Jiang, Lord of Yutou Province
Lin, Lord of Dongshan Province
Peng Kai-Long, cousin of the *Tianzi*, Lord of Nanling Province

Ministers
Fen, Council Minister
Geng, Treasury Minister
Hong Jianbin, Minister of Household Relations
Song Henglin, Minister of Foreign Affairs
Tan, Chief Minister

Insurgents
Liang Yu, former *Black Fist*
Song Xingyuan, Liang Yu's apprentice

Black Lotus Clan
Master Yan, Master of the clan
Huang Zhen, Clan initiate
Feng Mi, Clan initiate

Teleri Empire
Geros Bovyan, Emperor of the Teleri
Altos Di Bovyan, Teleri General
Leina, half-Ayuri from Ankira
Feiying, Master of the Nightblades

Wild Elves
Kiri, half-elf
Kala, half-elf
Nayori, Shaman
Dior, archer
Layani, warrior

Foreigners
Aelward Corivar, Prince of Tarkoth
Brehane, Mystic
Cyrus Estazadeh, Akolyte
Fleet, Madaeri Guide
Sameer Vikram, Paladin apprentice
Thielas Starsong, elf prince
Yuha, Maki Shaman

<u>**Legendary Figures**</u>
Aralas, elf angel
Avarax, Last Dragon
Celastya, Guardian Dragon of Hua
Yanyan, founder of musical magic

Prologue:
Of Gems and Dragons

Celastya had never seen a dragon transform into human form against its will before. From Avarax's shocked look as he swept his gaze over his now-tiny arms and legs, neither had he.

For millennia, he had forcibly mated with her and ate the resulting eggs to keep her energy low and enhance his own. Though she enjoyed a seven-hundred year reprieve as he dreamed through magically-induced slumber, Avarax had awoken on this night, when the heavens rained fire.

Thanks to her elf friend Xu transforming him into a human, she finally had an advantage. Her serpentine form now dwarfed Avarax.

The former dragon had little time to lament his frail new body. Xu thrust a thin sword at his chest.

The enchanted blade didn't even nick Avarax's soft skin. All three stared, wide-eyed.

Then Avarax looked up, bewildered expression transforming into a malevolent grin. He spoke a single word of power, sending the elf reeling to the sandy beach.

With Avarax's attention on Xu, Celastya dove at him. He was so tiny now, she'd rip him limb from limb with her talons. He met her first swipe with a punch to the claw. The pain rippled through her foreleg and into her core. The Pearl housed there shuddered. Undaunted, she swung her other claw.

She found only air. Avarax was gone.

Celastya snaked her head around. Neither elf nor dragon was anywhere to be found on the island beach. Before she could piece together what might have happened, Xu materialized out of thin air and collapsed into the sand.

"What happened, Xu?"

"We were lucky to take him by surprise. I froze time and transported him to the other side of Tivaralan. Though forced into human form, he still has all the vitality of a dragon. It took all of my energy to move him."

Celastya scratched her whiskers. She'd never imagined a mortal could be so powerful. "He will return."

The elf staggered to his feet. "Yes, but he will have to walk. It will take him years, unless he finds a way to regain his own form."

"And when he does?"

Xu sighed. "Let us hope I have time to teach someone with the right voice to sing him back to sleep."

Celastya's spine stiffened. The slave girl Mai, who had first accomplished the feat, died seven centuries ago. No one since had such a unique voice. It seemed hopeless. "Avarax will always find a way. He wants my Pearl, especially since he has not drained its energy for seven hundred years."

The elf searched her expression, and then pointed into space. "Tomorrow night, Ayara's Eye will be at its widest aspect this year. It will meet with the full White Moon and full Iridescent Moon in the God's Eye Conjunction. *Istrium* energies will wax to their strongest in three hundred years. With the power of this island and your Pearl combined, I can open up a rift in time and space. Pick a time and place, and I will send you there.

You can escape and never have to worry about Avarax again. Consider it and we can speak again tomorrow."

Celastya coiled herself around the rune-engraved arch that spanned the mouth of the atoll, allowing the vibrations of the island to resonate through her. She pondered the suggestion through the night.

How she longed to return to the last place where she had truly been happy. When she walked in human form. When she loved a human man; a man who died in a petty human struggle for mortal power.

The night brightened to dawn, and day darkened to night. Heavy clouds of ash from the previous night's devastation choked the atmosphere, blotting out the heavens. Though unseen, the celestial bodies rose to their inevitable meeting, low in the southern sky. The energy of the world resonated louder and louder to all who could feel it.

Toward dusk, Xu approached the arch. A young human woman accompanied him, dressed in tight-fitting black pants and a long black shirt, whose material and fashion looked out of place in this era. Her black hair and honey-toned skin marked her as Cathayi. She held a fist-sized globe of *istrium*, shedding a pale blue light. She gawked as her gaze swept across Celastya's serpentine form.

Xu bowed low. "Have you decided?"

Celastya drew a deep breath and coughed out her Pearl. The size of the elf's head, it swirled in colors like the Iridescent Moon.

Xu studied it, eyes curious. "When and where do you wish to go?"

Celastya recalled the moment she had fled the battlefield on her lover's orders, and held the image in her memories. She willed it into his mind.

With a nod, he chanted in the musical language of Deep Magic. Her Pearl's colors whirled faster, and the ground vibrated. The *istrium* sphere glowed brighter in the woman's hands as the island's energy coursed through Celastya and into the elf. The space under the arch wavered and flashed, and a wormhole opened.

Through the portal, the graceful eaves and wooden columns appeared familiar, as did the armor of the fighting men. A middle-aged warlord, ambushed and outnumbered, held a curved sword aloft. Yet it was not her lover, the one who had died two thousand years ago. When she saw silent flashes of musket fire, she knew it was the wrong era.

The human woman at her side gasped, nearly dropping the sphere, and looked from the portal to the elf and back.

Celastya shook her head. "This is the right place, but almost four hundred years too late."

The elf held the Pearl aloft. "I am sorry, this is the best I can do. Space is easy to traverse, but time is very hard to pinpoint."

Celastya's sigh sent waves across the atoll. It would be meaningless to go there; yet it would be a safe place to hide her Pearl against Avarax's return. She could remain here and, to some degree, even draw on her gemstone's energy across the vast distances.

The scene in the arch shifted, tracking the warlord as he retreated into a central building. Fires blazed around him. A wooden sign with *Original Mastery Temple* engraved in Cathayi script crashed to the ground.

Celastya had lived through that era, as wife to one of the warlord's most trusted vassals. The building would burn to the ground, killing the warlord. Her husband would usher in a new age in that nation's history. "I will take the Pearl and hide it there."

Xu raised a halting hand. "Without our combined energies to hold the rift open, the portal will collapse. You will be trapped in that time and place."

The Cathayi woman raised her hand. She spoke in a strange language, foreign to this world, but not to the one beyond the arch. "I will take the Pearl there."

As a dragon, Celastya could understand her words.

Xu apparently could as well. He shook his head at her. "Miss Wang, though you come from that world, it is a different time than you know. It is a dangerous task."

Wang patted a weapon at her side. "I am up to the task. Both that era in history, and that man there, have always fascinated me."

Xu and Celastya exchanged glances. If Xu trusted the woman, Celastya could see no reason to doubt her. In any case, the Pearl would be safe. Celastya nodded.

Xu's ageless brow furrowed. "I will see if I can move the aperture over to a safer place."

The scene shifted, pushing through burning temple halls. Flaming beams cracked and fell. At last, they settled on an interior courtyard, where some roof tiles had collapsed. The rubble partially obscured a well.

"There." Celastya pointed a talon toward the well.

The elf placed the Pearl into the woman's hands. She waded into the water and crossed through the threshold with a pop.

"Are you sure this is the right thing to do?" Xu regarded Celastya through half-lidded eyes.

"No. But when are we ever sure of decisions like these?"

Both turned and watched as Wang picked her way through burning debris. Reaching the well, she peered down. Then she dropped the Pearl into its depths.

Wang looked back through the portal for several seconds. However, instead of coming back through, she dashed through the halls.

"Turn around! Come back!" Xu yelled, though Wang would not hear him.

"She will alter the timeline of that world," Celaysta said, wondering about the consequences. Wang's weapon could turn the tide of the ambush, if she chose to interfere, and change the history of a nation. Maybe the world's.

Growling, Xu focused on the arch again. The image followed Wang as she ducked and weaved through fallen debris. At last, they saw the doomed warlord kneeling, katana in hand, preparing to disembowel himself. Behind him, a young warrior raised his sword, ready to behead the man.

Of course.

Their culture glorified honorable deaths. Celastya remembered it well, how her lover had charged into his enemies. She could have saved him, but it would have meant revealing her true identity as a dragon. He would have reviled her, and cursed her for denying him a glorious death. Celastya turned back to the portal.

In the land beyond, Wang drew her weapon. A light flashed, and the younger man collapsed.

The warlord looked up. He pointed his blade at Wang.

She gestured toward the portal. The man's gaze followed, and his mouth gaped.

The warlord picked up a musket that lay beside him as she helped him to his feet. They then spilled back through the temporal threshold, just as the room behind them burst into flames. The aperture snapped shut with a hollow popping sound.

Celastya's energy wavered as her connection to the Pearl stretched over time and space.

Xu jabbed an accusing finger at Wang. "What have you done? You cannot just change your history!"

Shrugging, Wang pointed at the man. "In our history, he died. His body was never recovered. They won't miss him."

The man spun around, wonderment written on his face. When he spoke, it was in yet another foreign tongue, one Celastya hadn't spoken in two millennia. "What is this place?"

Wang switched to a halting version of his language. "Far away, both in time and space."

Short of breath and limbs languid, Celastya's body shuddered. The pull of her Pearl was tentative, unable to support her mass. With the force of her will, she compressed her size, shrinking down and taking a human's frail form. She took a deep breath, and oxygen filled her newly-transformed lungs. Even at a distance, the power of her gemstone surged through her smaller body, awakening her with a renewed vitality.

Yet, faced with the prospect of living an eternity among mortals, regret overwhelmed her. Had she made the right decision? Whether or not she had the Pearl, Avarax would seek her out, if only for revenge.

Xu appraised her naked body, a wry smile forming on his lips. "Interesting choice. At least you will be able to walk among the Cathayi without drawing too much attention. Once you put on clothes." He turned to the real humans. "And what am I to do with you two?"

Wang stared into the elf's eyes. "Last night, you told me that this world is devolving into chaos." She gestured to the warlord. "Here is a military genius with the model for a superior weapon." She nodded toward Celastya. "Here is a *dragon*. We can restore order."

Xu rubbed his chin as he looked east toward the mainland. "We must protect this island at all costs. If not from Avarax, then from the Altivorcs. Very well, Wang Yuxiang. Tell me your ideas."

Chapter 1:
Deceptions

The setting sun outside the castle window taunted Kaiya, its descent marking one more day of concealing her pregnancy.

Though Doctor Wu's unparalleled acupuncture skills detected the twin boys in her womb, she couldn't discern their father. Was it the exiled spy she'd come to love during her escape from the frigid Northwest? Or the foreign tyrant who murdered him?

Neither was an appropriate match for a nineteen-year-old princess. Not when her unborn sons stood next in line to inherit the Dragon Throne.

"My choice is clear." Kaiya turned to her half-elf bodyguard, who was also her sworn sister and one-time rival in love.

Yan Jie sat on the wood floors of the guest suite's anteroom, sharpening a wicked knife that didn't match the softness of her plain, pink dress. She looked up, even as she continued to draw the knife across a whetstone in rhythmic swishes. Jie's childlike features had never appeared so forlorn.

Kaiya should've also been wallowing in grief. She'd ransomed her body and dignity to spare hostages from a brutal death and slow an invasion, yet couldn't save Father, Eldest Brother, or her beloved Tian. The experience would have broken her, if not for the mental block of Jie's *Tiger Eye* technique.

It gave Kaiya emotionless clarity. "Ming is Tian's brother and heir to a province. He's the best match."

Jie shrugged. Her usually perky voice droned. "You already rejected him once. No, twice."

"I doubt he'll need much convincing," Kaiya said. Ming would likely jump at the opportunity for social mobility, but she'd use the magic of her voice if necessary.

Now if he would only return home from his deployment before her flat belly started to swell.

The double doors slid open, revealing the castle steward. His green court robes rustled as he sank to his knees and pressed his forehead to the floor. "*Dian-xia*, Lord Zheng has returned and is on his way to greet you."

Well, that was serendipitous. At last, after five days of waiting in his family's castle at the border to the Wilds. A week since missing her period.

After conveying her permission with a nod, Kaiya turned toward Jie. "This is it. Try not to kill him."

Staring at the wall, Jie nodded absently. A sudden jerk of her hand revealed a trickle of blood on her finger.

"Are you all right?" Kaiya took a step toward her. For the meticulous Black Fist to nick herself sharpening a knife…

With a bob of her head, Jie thrust the bleeding hand behind her. "It is nothing, *Dian-xia*."

Kaiya peered at the girl. Despite the command to speak freely, Jie's tone and diction had reverted back to the distant formality of when they'd first met.

Someone cleared their throat at the door. Kaiya looked up, prepared to declare her intentions to Zheng Ming.

Lord Zheng *Han*, father of Tian and Ming, knelt on one knee, fist to the ground. His dark green travelling cloak, draped over his plain robes, smelled of a humid early spring. He must've come directly to meet with her. If only Ming travelled so fast.

"*Dian-xia*," he said. "Welcome to Dongmen Castle. I trust that my wife and steward have made your stay comfortable thus far?"

"They have, thank you." Kaiya motioned for him to enter.

Head bowed, Lord Zheng shuffled in and sank to a cross-legged position before her. "*Dian-xia*, I have just arrived from the capital. The *Tianzi* requests you return to Huajing."

Request.

An emperor didn't make requests, he gave commands. Second Brother had yet to understand his new role. Nonetheless, his wording gave her the leeway to remain at the border, ready to receive Ming when his army returned from the now-moot assignment of finding her in an enemy-infested wilderness. Surely her message would've reached him by now.

Kaiya would broach the issue of marriage in due time; first came the news she couldn't have delivered without the *Tiger's Eye* walling off her heart. She pressed her forehead to the floor and then looked up to meet Lord Zheng's wide eyes. An imperial princess would only bow so low to the *Tianzi* himself. "I regret to inform you that your fourth son, Zheng Tian, perished in his attempt to convey me through enemy lines."

Lord Zheng's lips quivered before he arranged his expression into stoicism. "Did he die bravely?"

More out of habit than sentiment, her hand strayed to Tian's lockpick pouch under her sash. Her only memento of him.

Revealing their secret marriage and pregnancy would've allowed her to console Lord Zheng as a daughter, let him know she understood his loss, even if the *Tiger's Eye* kept her from feeling it.

But no. Tian had been banished from the capital in disgrace, and his sons would be considered low-born bastards, if they were even allowed to live.

Kaiya straightened. "Zheng Tian performed admirably. I will never forget his service." Or his affection. If only she could remember what their passion *felt* like. The memories were detached, as if she had watched their love bloom from afar. Kaiya placed a hand over her womb, again wondering if her twins were Tian's sons, Lord Zheng's grandsons.

"Then it is my family's honor." Lord Zheng bowed again.

"I have one more request of your family. I would ask permission to marry your first son, Zheng Ming, at the earliest auspicious date. After the death of my father and brother, the realm needs both closure and hope."

Lord Zheng's eyes narrowed for a split second before his face blanked again. Did he suspect she was no longer a virgin bride? "While these are welcome tidings, it is sudden. Of course, we would first need the *Tianzi's* approval."

Drawing on the magic of her voice, which she'd once used to defeat Tivaralan's last dragon, Kaiya sang her next words of command. "Approve it."

Her voice came out melodic, but devoid of power. Her connection to the energy of the world sputtered in her chest. Instead of capitulating, Lord Zheng raised an eyebrow.

"Please," she added, as if it would change his mind. She must've looked like a fool, singing words like an opera diva. Why had she failed at such an easy invocation of power?

Lord Zheng's face betrayed nothing. "I appreciate your consideration, *Dian-xia*. I will convey to the *Tianzi* my desire to bind our families in the most auspicious of ties. With your leave, I must greet my wife and then make preparations for your departure."

Her departure.

He sat there, perhaps hoping she'd obey Second Brother's request, to rid himself of the responsibility. Or perhaps he suspected something. Why else would he hesitate at the great honor of marrying a son to an imperial princess?

Kaiya dismissed him with a slight dip of her chin, and considered the implications of her voice's impotence. The loss of emotions was a necessary compromise to make it through the most trying time in her life. The loss of her magic, on the other hand—

Jie let out a long breath as Lord Zheng's footsteps faded down the hall.

Kaiya turned toward the half-elf. "I've lost the power of my voice. It has always been tied to emotion. I think the *Tiger's Eye* is blocking both. You must unlock it."

"Are you sure that is wise?" Sucking her lower lip, the sprite-like girl hardly inspired the image of wisdom. Her elf blood made her appear no older than a thirteen-year old despite her thirty-two years. "After all, before you learned to use your voice, you relied on charm and intelligence. Please reconsider."

In the past, Kaiya's feelings might have prompted an impulsive answer, without considering the repercussions. "Yes, but that girl was manipulated by treacherous Cousin Peng and deceived by a dragon." And forced into bed with a dictator she could've slain before he even had a chance to capture her.

Six months made quite a difference.

She played with her hair. Magic came with the burden of coping with immeasurable loss. No magic meant relying on wits alone. "I see no other way. If I can't consummate a marriage to Zheng Ming soon, I'll have a hard time convincing him—and the empire—my sons are legitimate."

And while a prince's bastard could inherit the throne, her babies might be murdered or thrown out on the streets, and she'd be branded a harlot.

Heavens, she might as well be one. She harrumphed. Less than three months ago, she was still a virgin; if she slept with Ming, he'd be the third man in as many weeks.

There was no real choice.

For her sons. For the realm.

The half-elf sucked her lower lip again, her silence speaking louder than words.

Kaiya forced a chuckle she didn't feel. There was no love lost between Jie and Ming: she'd just as soon cut his manhood off and feed it to the carp; and since he knew it, he avoided her altogether.

In any case, it wasn't Jie who'd share the vain man's bed. Despite his weakness for women, Ming was the logical choice: a leader of men from a noble lineage, and uncle by blood to her sons—if they were indeed Tian's. "Do it. Unlock the *Tiger's Eye*."

Jie pursed her lips for a few seconds before nodding. "As the princess commands." She locked her gaze and formed a signal with her hands.

Kaiya stared at the shape of Jie's fingers. Soon, very soon, she'd have to cope with grief, but at least she'd have her magic. Then, influencing Zheng Han would be easy. The problem, quickly resolved.

"It is done," Jie said.

Nothing changed. No flood of emotion washing over to her. Kaiya's memories of Tian seemed just as detached and distant as before. She shook her head.

Jie sighed. "I feared this would happen. The effect on a Black Fist is unpredictable, since the *Tiger's Eye* is usually reserved for missions from which there is no return. You are not trained in our ways and the effect is even less predictable."

She'd said as much, when Kaiya first submitted to the technique.

"Will it wear off on its own, then?" A torrent of repressed emotions flooding back at an inopportune moment could be disastrous. When would she be able to draw on her magic again? Time was running out to legitimize her unborn sons.

"I cannot say." Jie shrugged.

So she'd have to live with the *Tiger's Eye* for now. Instead of the power of command, she had only wits and a pretty face.

In all objectivity, formidable weapons.

"Follow Lord Zheng. I need to know if he suspects anything, and if he will use the *Tianzi's* letter to force me to return to Huajing."

Jie dropped to her knee, fist to the ground. "As the princess commands."

Kaiya looked down at her belly. Even if she were his guest, she was still an imperial princess. Lord Zheng wouldn't dare force her to leave. She turned toward Jie, only to find the half-elf's dress crumpled on the floor.

Clad in a black stealth suit, Jie made plenty of noise as she trailed Lord Zheng's retinue through the castle halls. The glossy wood floors, specifically designed to counter spies, chirped like a nightingale with each of her steps.

Which was why Jie stepped in concert with the entourage.

One foot in front of the other. Each pace, masked by the huge guard in front of her. Though her feet were as light as ever, a heavy heart weighed her down. As if the shock of the affair between the princess and Tian weren't enough, she'd then lost her best friend. The man who almost became her lover until a war came between them. If only she could put *herself* into the *Tiger's Eye*.

Now was not the time for self-pity.

"*Jue-ye*," the steward said, using the formal address for a *Tai-Ming* lord. "Your wife awaits you in your chambers."

Zheng Han didn't break stride, facing forward as he spoke. "Yes, I will go there presently. Does she know of Tian's death?"

The steward hurried to keep up. "Yes, *Jue-ye*. The princess told her when she arrived five days ago. She is very distraught."

Like everyone else, except maybe the princess with her mental block.

Lord Zheng sighed. "I imagine so. Tian was always her favorite, her baby boy. She never smiled the same after his banishment."

"And she always hated the princess for her role in that," the steward whispered. "The hate has only grown, because the Lady blames the princess for his death."

"Indeed." Zheng nodded. If only his face was visible from here. Not like the lord had shown much up to now. He might as well have been a statue carved by the most inept sculptor in the world. "Now tell me, what has the princess been doing these last five days?"

"She has stayed in the guest wing the entire time. Her only visitors were her doctors."

"Her doctors?" Zheng Han stopped in his tracks and turned.

Jie ducked behind the guard. She peeked around to catch Zheng Han's expression. Still blank.

The steward nodded. "Yes, Doctor Wu and her disciple, Fang Weiyong."

"Why would she see doctors?" Zheng Han stroked his narrow beard. If he knew, there'd be no marriage, and the princess would be shipped back to the capital in disgrace.

Jie altered her voice to mimic one of the counselors and threw it with a *Ghost Echo*. "After the princess' trek through the wilderness, they wanted to check on her health."

A few of the men in the back looked around in confusion, but those in the front murmured and nodded.

Lord Zheng resumed his walk. "Maybe there is more. The princess travelled in the woods, with a group of men. Where are the doctors now?"

"I believe Fang Weiyong is in town," the steward said. "Doctor Wu left for Huajing already."

Zheng Han turned to one of his guards. "Find Doctor Fang and bring him to me. I do not want to make any decisions about Ming's future until I know more."

Jie had to delay the guard. Fang Weiyong had accompanied the princess on her escape and knew *everything*. He'd been the one to consecrate Tian and the princess' vows.

Before she could follow the guard, Lord Zheng motioned toward the steward. "Send word to Huajing. If Chief Minister Hong wants her back in the capital so badly, the *Tianzi* should order her to return. She has no choice but to acquiesce. It would buy us more time to make a decision on the marriage proposal. I will not have Ming raising some other man's whelp."

The steward bowed as they walked. "As you command, *Jue-ye*. I will draft a letter right now and stamp it with your seal."

"Very good." Lord Zheng turned to his military aide. "The situation in the capital is tenuous. The *Tianzi* has requested ten thousand of our troops to help in the pacification of Nanling Province."

"Why us?" the aide asked. "We are far away from Nanling, and if the reports are true, a Teleri army approaches, just on the other side of the Great Wall."

Lord Zheng threw his hands up. "The *Tianzi* has made nothing but irrational decisions. Chief Minister Hong has his ear, and neither have a mind for military strategy."

Jie had warned the princess about Chief Minister Hong's reliability in the past. He might be conniving and self-serving, but foolish? Moving an army away from a potential threat bordered on recklessness.

With more urgent matters than troop movements, Jie pressed herself against a shadowed wall.

Too bad Black Fist skills didn't teach one to be in two places at once. She'd have to choose between warning Fang Weiyong, or making sure a letter of her own got sent to the capital with Lord Zheng's seal. Leaving either problem unresolved meant the difference between Tian's children standing next in line to the throne; or being abandoned as a slut's bastards, just like Jie, herself.

Chapter 2:
All Warfare is Based on Deception

Zheng Ming rearranged himself on the hard cot, moving his head out of the blue ray from Guanyin's Eye. It peeked in through the poorly-thatched roof, returning his gaze wherever he moved. Yet it was neither the light nor the bedding which kept him awake.

He clutched Princess Kaiya's letter to his chest, rereading the contents in his mind. She'd made it through Teleri lines and now waited in Father's castle for him to return. Not only that, she wanted to marry at once, to heal a nation which worshipped the Imperial Family, after the death of the *Tianzi* and the Crown Prince.

At first light, he would torch this enemy fort he'd captured—it was little more than a half-completed palisade with a few ramshackle barracks and a bridge over a wide river—and return home with his victorious army. Then, into the arms of the realm's most beautiful, witty woman, who happened to be a princess.

A rap on the crude wooden door shook him out of his daydream. His jumpy second brother Shu must need guidance.

Again.

Ming had appointed him aide-de-camp, though the twenty-four-year-old had never seen battle until the day before.

Ming yawned. "What is it?"

Shu poked his face through the door. "Eldest Brother, our scouts report two hundred Bovyan heavy infantry, spears and swords, ten *li* to the east."

Two hundred? Ming had just routed over twice as many the day before, with his army of three thousand imperial musketmen. The enemy never even got close enough for his own province's two thousand spearmen to engage. "Any crossbows? Cavalry?"

Shu shook his head. "According to the scouts, no."

With the benefit of the fortress, shoddily built as it was, the Teleri didn't stand a chance. Though the palisade didn't reach the eastern side, the enemy would have to cross a shallow moat and charge up a steep embankment into his waiting guns. Not only that, it would take them at least three hours to arrive, even at a forced march.

Ming sighed at the decided lack of urgency. "Let the men rest another hour. After they have eaten, deploy them along the eastern embankment."

Shu bowed. "Forgive my ignorance, Eldest Brother, but with the princess safe, should we not make haste back to Cathay?"

"No. Let them come to us, tire themselves out. We will use their own fort to minimize our losses. Then we won't have to concern ourselves with pursuit. Send the scouts back to keep an eye on them."

"As you command, Eldest Brother." Shu bowed again.

By the time Ming emerged from the barracks an hour and a half later, the imperial musketmen stood in a line that wrapped from the north to east sides of the fort, three ranks deep.

His provincial spearmen, led by his third brother Lun, stood halfway up the embankment. They all turned and saluted, pressing their right fists into their left palms at chest level.

A chill of excitement ran up Ming's spine. *His* army. As a captain, he'd led a regiment of horse archers in defense of Wailian County. Now he was the *Dajiang*, Expeditionary Commander, ready to lead five thousand men to a second decisive victory. What had the Founder's Treatise on War said about morale?

Ming unsheathed his *dao* and cleared his throat. "Soldiers of Cathay! Yesterday, we showed the Teleri what men of Cathay are made of. We faced the stronger side of their fort and prevailed without losing a man. Today, we hold the higher ground with greater numbers and superior firepower. I do not want a single Bovyan to make it across the moat!" He pointed the tip of his sword at the tree line on the other side of the moat. "If any makes it to this side, make sure it is because they are walking over their own men."

The men roared in approval. An immoral warrior race had betrayed their princess and sought to invade their homeland. Now the Bovyans would pay.

***

By dawn the next morning, their enthusiasm wavered. Not from a blistering onslaught, but from boredom and a lack of sleep. Tired eyes all fixed on the spot where a road through the forest opened up into the clearing around the fort. Sweat gathered on brows as humidity clung to armored bodies. Not even the thick clouds and cool breeze did much to alleviate the heat.

Ming turned to Shu. "You said ten *li*?"

"Yes, Eldest Brother." Shu nodded.

"No word from the scouts?"

Shu shook his head.

The enemy should have arrived at this hour *yesterday*, and the ancient road they restored was the only way to move a large number of troops. The main river along the fort's south would be impossible for men to swim across— if historical records of the region were accurate; and the spring melt swelled the tributary river just to the west, leaving the fort's bridge as the only way to cross.

Ming looked back at the west side's palisade, now riddled with musket balls from two days before. "Shu, send more scouts out over the west side and turn north along the tributary to see if there is any place to ford. I want—"

A lieutenant pointed toward the opening in the forest. "Flags of parley!"

Ming followed the gesture.

Three light-haired Bovyan men, each standing a head-and-a-half taller than the tallest of the Cathay, strode into the clearing. Their chain tunics jingled beneath black surcoats emblazoned with the gold, nine-pointed sun of the Teleri Empire. One held a white flag aloft. Behind them, black cloth flashed between the tree trunks.

Along the Cathay lines, hands gripped musket barrels and spear hafts.

Ming motioned for Shu and another officer to accompany him. He grinned. "They want to negotiate terms for surrender."

Shu's jaw dropped. "Eldest Brother, we cannot trust them. They betrayed the princess in their negotiations."

Ming motioned for an imperial marksman who had distinguished himself two days before. "Xiao, I want you to target the big man in the center. If I give the signal or he shows any sign of treachery, shoot him."

Xiao pressed his fist into his palm. "As the *Dajiang* commands."

Ming edged his way down the embankment to meet the Teleri. They were even more intimidating up close. Two men with cropped brown hair flanked a man who radiated an air of importance and power.

His black mane, streaked with grey, hung loosely to the center of his broad shoulders and a scar on his right cheek marred his olive complexion. Eyes, one steel-grey, and the other disconcertingly blue, met Ming's as he spoke in perfect Arkothi, the common language of the North. "I am the First Emperor Geros of the Teleri Empire. You look familiar."

Geros, the turtle egg who betrayed Princess Kaiya and tried to capture her. Ming clenched his fists. He'd never seen a Bovyan leader so close before, let alone met one. He responded in his own halting Arkothi. "I am Ming Zheng, heir to the East Gate Province of Cathay."

Geros nodded, his expression registering recognition. "You must be closely related to the man I killed. I did not take him to be of noble blood, though he fought admirably and killed three dozen of my men. We sent his body downriver as is our custom for the honored dead."

The barbarism. Ming stifled a cringe and smirked instead. "Are you here to collect your dead from two days ago? Or to be added to the pile?"

Geros puffed his chest out. "I am here to make an offer. Surrender the fort as it is, then turn around and go back behind your Great Wall. On my honor, we will let you return unharmed."

Ming jabbed a finger at the Emperor. "I don't trust the honor of a man who reneges on his negotiations and tries to kidnap a defenseless woman."

"Renege? No, your princess attacked me by surprise, and we took her into custody to pay for her crimes against the Empire."

Ming clenched his fists. "You lie."

"I assure you, everything I said is true." Geros' grin widened.

Struggling to reach into his armor, Ming withdrew the princess' letter. He whipped it open and held it up for the emperor to see. "You never captured her. She made it past your blockade and is safe in my castle. She informed me, with her own words."

Geros' brow furrowed as his mismatched eyes flicked over the letter. "She forgot to mention she is now First Empress of the Teleri Empire, through marriage to me, and carries my heir in her womb. I only seek to reclaim what is mine."

Heat rushed to Ming's head, Geros' last words barely making it through the pounding in his ears. "Lie!"

Geros laughed. "So she did not admit to it in her letter? I wouldn't know, since I don't read your language."

The bastard was mocking him! Ming's fists clenched so tight, he might have been able to squeeze a lump of coal into a diamond.

The Bovyan's smug expression gave way to narrowed eyes. "You are taking the news quite personally. I restate my offer. Turn around and go in peace. When you arrive home, ask Empress Kaiya yourself."

"There are five thousand reasons for me to refuse your generous offer." Ming waved to the Cathay lines atop the embankment. "Sources tell me I have a twenty-five-to-one advantage in numbers, and an insurmountable superiority in weapons and position."

Geros tugged gloves off his hands and began counting his fingers. "I am just a simple soldier, and mathematics has never been my strong suit, but…" He raised a hand.

With a resounding thud, thousands of black uniforms stepped out from the tree line surrounding the north and east sides of the moat, heavy crossbows in hand. Behind them, ruddy-skinned natives whooped with bows raised in the air.

"…I think my odds are better than you think," Geros finished.

Ming smirked. He'd gotten Geros to reveal his numbers. Despite the poor scouting, he still had superior range. Once the Teleri emerged from the trees, they would already be within musket range.

If only he could wipe the patronizing smirk off Geros' face right here, right now. He drew his bow and nonchalantly tested the pull. "Consider yourself fortunate you are protected by the flag of parley. Once you cross back to your lines, my arrows will look for you."

"I give you until nightfall to reconsider my offer," Geros said. "A wise leader would not refuse it out of hand."

Ming did not care to hear lessons on leadership from a dictator who sacrificed his soldiers on a whim. Plans formulated in his mind. "If any of your men so much as step into the clearing, we will fire upon them."

Geros grinned. "I would respect you less if you did not." He spun on his heel and strode back toward the trees.

Ming turned and climbed the embankment. At the top, he summoned his command team. "How many days of food rations do we have?"

"Eight, twelve if you include what we captured here, Young Lord," the quartermaster answered.

Shu's voice trembled. "Are we going to fight?"

"No." Ming pointed back toward the west. "We did not establish supply lines. All they have to do is wait us out. However, we cannot leave the bridge or extra supplies for them. It will take us five days to return to Cathay at forced march. Dump excess food rations and the weapons we captured into the river. Set three kegs of firepowder on the bridge. Devise a plan to disguise our withdrawal."

And when they returned home, the princess would confirm Emperor Geros' words were all lies.

Geros studied the line of Cathayi soldiers glaring from the top of the embankment, muskets trained on the clearing's edge. If not for Princess Kaiya beguiling him, he would have visited the fort two weeks before and ensured the palisade surrounded the entire fort. How ironic that his own dereliction of duty made the fort easier to take back.

"Why did you give him until nightfall, Your Eminence?" Captain Mirin, who oversaw construction of the fort, kept his head bowed.

Geros locked his gaze on the man. "Because the savages tell me it will rain at dusk."

"Rain, Your Eminence?" Captain Mirin had a good mind for designing forts, less so for military tactics.

"Why do you think I slowed our march?"

Lines formed on Mirin's brow. "So that our vanguard could rest while more of our troops caught up?"

"And?"

Mirin's face blanked.

"Every move has multiple purposes. We sent the vanguard ahead to make their scouts believe they outnumbered us. They roused their troops early, and they have not slept for a full day. Also, by slowing our march, we will not sit idle waiting an extra day for rain. Rain will render their muskets useless and give our crossbows the advantage. Hand-to-hand, even with their superior position, a Bovyan is worth three of them. Despite what Zheng believes, the odds are very much in our favor once their guns are removed from the equation."

Mirin nodded enthusiastically. "Brilliant, Your Eminence."

"The brilliance," Geros said, "is in the strategies of the founder of Cathay's Wang Dynasty."

"Though what if Zheng accepts your offer?"

"Then we get your fort back intact. But he won't. He is a prideful man and I goaded him. Also, he is our key to breaching the Great Wall."

"What if he escapes?" The captain's eyebrows clashed together.

"He won't. Three thousand of our men are crossing the fords to the north as we speak, and will be behind them by dusk."

Chapter 3:
Loyal Men

Though spring sang its evening song outside her window, Kaiya didn't look up from her book until she heard Jie's quiet breathing by the door.

The half-elf dropped to one knee, fist to the ground. "*Dian-xia*, Lord Zheng suspects you are hiding a pregnancy. He sent his men to find Doctor Fang."

"I assume you warned Weiyong?"

Jie shook her head. "The legends of the Black Fists being able to be in two places at once are mildly exaggerated. I was forging letters. Lord Zheng wanted to ask the *Tianzi* to order you home. I swapped the letter out for one of my own."

"What did you say?"

Jie shrugged. "I expressed your heartfelt desire to marry Zheng Ming. Lord Zheng approves and asks for the *Tianzi's* blessing."

Heartfelt indeed. As if she could *feel* anything. Even grief over Tian's loss couldn't blunt Jie's sense of irony. Or perhaps her distaste for Ming stoked it. Kaiya snorted.

Regardless of the wording, the fake letter solidified her position. Second Brother Kai-Wu had always looked out for her. *Tianzi* or not, he would approve the marriage.

Hopefully.

Because if push came to shove, she wouldn't undermine his authority. His position in the eyes of the hereditary lords was already tenuous enough without a rebellious sister. "Then we can stay with the plan," Kaiya said.

Jie's expression, the sucking on her lower lip, said otherwise.

"What's the matter?"

"You are relying on Lord Zheng's loyalty to the Dragon Throne." Jie traced a circle in the air. "Realistically speaking, here in *his* castle, surrounded by *his* men, we are at his mercy. The local imperial soldiers will obey you, but they are garrisoned in other parts of the city."

Kaiya frowned. "So realistically speaking, it is just you and me."

"Do you wonder why the *Tianzi* did not send a complement of imperial guards? I think—"

Chirping footsteps sounded in the hall, seeming almost an affront to the pleasant birdsong outside. Kaiya quieted Jie with a wave of her hand.

One of the castle pages stopped outside the door and dropped to his knee. "*Dian-xia*, Lord Zheng wishes to see you."

Had he made a decision on the marriage proposal? Or had they found Fang Weiyong? The doctor would never betray her secret... would he?

The Founder extolled the virtue of preparedness. Only a fool would walk into a meeting uninformed. Kaiya raised an eyebrow toward Jie, who tilted her head at the tacit order.

In the meantime, Kaiya would stall for time. She nodded toward the page. "I will call on him once I have made myself presentable."

The page bowed. "*Dian-xia*, the lord will pay his respects here. He would never presume—"

"It is all right. I have been sequestered in the guest wing for so long. Go, apologize to Lord Zheng on my behalf for the delay."

"As the princess commands." The man rose, shuffled back several steps, and then headed back down the halls.

She turned back to Jie, who was already gone. No need for an order, just like the first time. Thank the Heavens for reliable retainers and friends.

Left alone, Kaiya rose to her feet and glided over the plush red carpet to the bloodwood make-up table.

Upon Kaiya's arrival at the castle, Lady Zheng had offered lip rouge, eyeliner, and other cosmetics, which now sat on the mother-of-pearl inlaid table, untouched. It wasn't for fear of contact poison in the cosmetics—though Lady Zheng had little love for her—but rather because there was no need for impractical vanities.

Until now.

In the mirror, a gaunt young woman with sunken cheeks and red-rimmed eyes frowned back at her. Where was the once-in-three-generations beauty, who'd bedazzled kings and generals? Or even the naïve and pimply girl who'd been duped by a dragon in disguise?

Kaiya blinked away a tear.

A tear. Had she just experienced an emotion? Longing? She tried to grasp at it, to hold on to it, but the feeling slipped through her fingers. She gazed back at the mirror. The perfect lines of her image were frayed by sleepless nights of plotting and calculating. That woman, while beautiful, couldn't coax a man to her bidding without the magic of her voice.

It was time to conjure a different type of magic. She reached for the eyeliner.

After half an hour, her transformation was complete. Kaiya experimented with a few facial expressions, which looked as artificial as the layers of cosmetics hiding the ravages of worry and fatigue.

Jie's reflection appeared behind her, eyebrows scrunched together. The Insolent Retainer's childlike beauty spoke of an innocence which had probably never existed in the half-elf. "*Dian-xia*, Lord Zheng is in his audience chamber with his wife. It pains me to say Lady Zheng does not hold you in high opinion."

Unsurprised, Kaiya nodded. "Go on."

"They questioned Fang Weiyong, who claimed you wished your health to be evaluated after your long journey in the wilderness."

Fang knew her story well, yet chose to protect her. His lie made her deception easier. Kaiya rose to her feet. "Come, let us see what Lord Zheng wants."

With Jie in tow, Kaiya walked through the halls. Unlike the lumbering men, she deliberately stepped to make the dark floorboards chirp in harmony with the symphony of spring. It was almost like the perfect melody of songbirds in the Kanin Wilds, on the frigid day when she'd fallen into a freezing tidal pool and tricked Tian into jumping in after her. She stifled a scoff at the coy girl and gullible spy.

She turned into the main audience room. A dozen provincial guards and a handful of silk-robed advisors sank into salutes on the forest-green carpeted floor. Several three-panel screens, lacquered and inlaid with shells and stones, lined the plastered walls. Behind one of the screens, someone breathed rapidly.

From where he sat on an embroidered silk cushion at the front of the room, Lord Zheng pressed his forehead to the ground. His dark green formal robes rustled, and his jade bead necklace clattered. At his side, his wife pursed her lips before bowing as well. Her blue gown, with its pink cherry blossom motif, was more suited for a younger woman.

"You may rise," Kaiya said.

Both looked up, and while remaining bowed, Zheng Han stood and surrendered his place to her. He then took several steps back and sat cross-legged facing the mat. "Thank you for seeing me, *Dian-xia*."

She glided up and knelt on the mat, placing her hands in her lap while Jie came and stood behind her. As protocol demanded, Kaiya tilted her head a fraction to show appreciation for his etiquette. "To what do I owe the pleasure of this meeting?"

From his seated position, Lord Zheng bowed low. "Forgive my insolence, but I have heard rumors."

Rumors. Unless Fang Weiyong revealed it, nobody within Zheng Han's earshot would know of her secret; and Jie had said Weiyong lied for her. Lord Zheng was baiting her.

"As I once told your son, Zheng Ming, rumors proliferate like weeds after spring rains."

Lord Zheng nodded. "Yes. But for every dozen weeds, there is an occasional flower."

Zheng Ming had once responded with almost the same line, what seemed to be a lifetime ago. Their conversation had been lighthearted in nature, a dance between man and woman. Kaiya had little interest in games right now. "What kind of flowers do we speak of?"

Zheng Han stared at the floor. "Hopefully, those that have not yet been despoiled."

He was questioning her virginity!

If not for the *Tiger's Eye*, Kaiya would've bristled at the audacity, despite the truth behind it. She feigned outrage, nonetheless, scowling and lowering her voice.

"Lord Zheng, given your many years of faithful service to my father and now my brother—"

He raised a hand. "One is dead. The other not only invites rebellion with weakness, but is also far away from here."

There it was, the first hint of mutiny. A stalwart supporter during Father's rule, even through the last unstable years, Zheng Han had never showed any signs of treason before.

And now, she was his virtual prisoner.

Jie fidgeted, eyes darting around the room and a hand inching into a sleeve. Yet even with her formidable martial skills, she wouldn't stand a chance against the entire castle garrison, let alone all of the provincial soldiers in the surrounding city.

It was time to persevere. Kaiya said, "So, what do you suggest?"

Lord Zheng pressed his forehead to the ground in a symbolic gesture that rang hollow, given his words. "My personal physician would like to confirm that the… uh… flower… is still… blooming."

Her younger self might have fainted from the suggestion. Instead, Kaiya pressed her hand to her mouth and widened her eyes for show, even as she weighed the alternatives. If she refused outright, Zheng Han would not dare force her; at the same time, he might hold her hostage.

On the other hand, the truth could give her leverage… *if* she could trust a hereditary lord who now questioned the authority of the *Tianzi*.

As Wang Xinchang, the founder of the dynasty, once said, *Ambitious men are easier to manipulate than loyal ones*. Maintaining a withering stare on the lord, she spoke. "Fang Weiyong, come out."

Lord Zheng straightened, and nodded toward the screen.

A guard emerged, leading a tall man whose head was covered by a black hood. The soldier lifted the cowl, revealing a gagged Fang Weiyong.

Zheng Han gestured toward his prisoner with an open hand. "Here is the source of the rumor: your doctor. I took him into custody for speaking ill of the Imperial Family. By the *Tianzi's* own law, I will have him publicly lashed. Unless he spoke the truth."

Eyes round, Weiyong tried to shake his head through the guard's grip on his hair. Knowing him, he must've been horrified not so much by the threat of a whipping, but by the notion he might have betrayed her.

He ceased his struggle when she flashed a smile at him.

Kaiya leveled her gaze at the lord. "Doctor Fang is not just my doctor, but my friend. One who would not and did not betray my trust. The question is, can I trust you, Lord Zheng?"

Zheng Han bowed again. "Of course, *Dian-xia.*"

Indeed. "Then send everyone but your wife, my handmaiden, and Doctor Fang out, so we might confer."

"Your handmaiden must go, too."

"I see trust only goes so far. You have nothing to fear from a girl."

Lord Zheng's eyes narrowed. "It would not surprise me if the girl had more weapons concealed on her than all of my guards here combined."

It wouldn't surprise Kaiya, either. Though how Zheng Han knew… "Very well." She nodded toward Jie.

Smirking, the Insolent Retainer bowed and padded toward the door.

"All of you, withdraw." Lord Zheng waved his hand. His men bowed and shuffled back out of the room, though one ungagged Fang Weiyong first. The double sliding doors closed behind them.

Satisfied, Kaiya bowed her head. When she raised it, she pressed her hand to her belly. "As you suspect, I am already pregnant."

Lord Zheng's lips twitched, his look one of vindication. He opened his mouth to speak.

She raised her hand, silencing him. "Doctor Wu confirmed they are twin boys. Your first grandsons."

Zheng Han's satisfied smirk slipped, replaced by a raised eyebrow. "How?"

"Your fourth son, Zheng Tian."

His jaw slackened, even as Lady Zheng sucked in a sharp breath.

Kaiya nodded away their shock. "Unless the *Tianzi* and his wife conceive, your unborn grandchildren are next in line to the Dragon Throne."

With a cough, Lord Zheng shook his head. "They may be my grandsons by blood, but they are illegitimate. They will—"

Kaiya raised a hand to quiet him again. "They are not." She tilted her chin to Weiyong. "As an imperial official, Doctor Fang consecrated my marriage to Tian. Were the rites and rituals carried out correctly?"

Fang Weiyong nodded. "Yes, *Dian-xia*. Your actions and corresponding vows followed ancient conventions, and are thus all legitimate."

Kaiya turned back toward Lord and Lady Zheng. "As you see, I am your son's widow. Yet his banishment would raise questions as to the validity of your grandsons' claim. That does not have to be the case, in the eyes of the realm. This is why I wished to marry your firstborn."

Lord and Lady Zheng exchanged glances, their expressions beyond Kaiya's skill at deciphering. If only Jie were in the room to gauge their reactions. Lord Zheng looked back at her, his face as blank as when he asked if Tian had died bravely.

"Timing is critical," Kaiya added. "Tian's seed has grown in my womb for three weeks now. If I do not consummate a marriage to Ming soon—"

He opened his mouth to interject, only to be interrupted by Lady Zheng. She rose to her feet, waddled forward, and pressed her forehead to the floor in front of Kaiya. When she rose, she extended a tentative hand toward Kaiya's abdomen. "Forgive me, *Dian-xia*, but may I?"

It was an audacious request, to be sure, but how could Kaiya deny it? The legacy of Lady Zheng's beloved, dead son grew inside of her. Kaiya took Lady Zheng's hand in hers and placed it against her abdomen.

Lady Zheng's tearful eyes met hers. Her voice cracked. "Are they really Tian's?"

Were they? Kaiya couldn't be sure, given the unfortunate circumstances. She contrived her most compassionate smile and nodded.

It was wrong to lie, not just on moral grounds, but also because the chance of exposure. The other potential father was just two weeks away, on the other side of the Great Wall. Emperor Geros didn't know she carried twins; he only believed the son she would bear was his.

He would spare no resource in the vast Teleri Empire to retrieve her. Fortunately, the Great Wall and a hundred thousand muskets stood between them.

Chapter 4:
Perfect Storms

From his place near the bloodwood dais, Chief Minister Hong Jianbin scanned the hundred-some men gathered in the Hall of Supreme Harmony. Whether it was his old eyes or the dozens of golden columns obstructing his view, he counted surprisingly few provincial lords kneeling among the blue-robed officials.

A messenger in dark green robes strode between the ordered rows of men, his boots clacking on the polished white marble floors. He dropped to a knee in front of the dais and bowed as he proffered a letter wrapped in rice paper.

Sitting on the jade Dragon Throne, the recently-anointed *Tianzi* gazed toward the tile ceiling mosaic of circling twin dragons high above. He probably would not have noticed if the messenger transformed into Cathay's guardian dragon spirit.

Hong expected no less from his puppet.

From where she sat on the smaller gold Phoenix Throne, the Empress Wu Yanli coughed. The *Tianzi's* head shifted from right to left, the dangling pearls on his hat clicking. His lazy comportment clashed with the regal yellow robes, which he rearranged more than once. At last, he looked down at the messenger and waved a hand.

A minister shuffled forward and received the letter in two hands. He unwrapped it and snapped open the note inside. In a high-pitched voice, he read, "A missive from *Tai-Ming* Lord Zheng of Dongmen Province. To the *Tianzi*, Son of Heaven and Enlightened Ruler of Cathay. Your sister, Princess Wang Kaiya, wishes to wed my son Zheng Ming. I approve, and ask for your blessing."

Hong's heart lurched into his throat. Despite his attempts to smear Young Lord Zheng in the princess' eyes, despite the two being separated for half a year, she still had feelings for the philandering lordling. How could he secure his own—

"It is an appropriate match." The *Tianzi* grinned and turned to the Empress. "I introduced them myself."

The Empress nodded, her own lips curving up into a radiant, if measured, smile. One of the realm's foremost beauties, she appeared much too young for the imperial yellow robes. Still, she wore the trappings of state with more dignity than her husband, and stayed disengaged from state affairs as a woman should.

Hong did not plan for her to remain Empress for long. However, if he could not stop the marriage of Princess Kaiya, the *Tianzi* would have to stay alive so Hong could still influence policy. Hopefully, the *Tianzi* would remember their private conversation from just a few days earlier.

"*Huang-Shang,*" Hong said, using the formal address for the *Tianzi*, "while Young Lord Zheng would make an excellent husband for the princess, the Zheng family is old and unquestioningly loyal. Perhaps you should use her marriage to reward an up-and-coming lord." Like him, after another promotion.

General Shan, bedecked in ceremonial dragon armor, stood and bowed his helmeted head. Doubt hung in his voice. "*Huang-Shang*, did Lord Zheng agree to send the ten thousand troops you ordered for the pacification of Nanling Province?"

The *Tianzi* raised his eyebrow at the minister. So unsightly for an emperor!

The official scanned the letter again. "No, General."

"Thank the Heavens," General Shan muttered.

The shortsighted man apparently did not see the danger of insurgency from those still loyal to Nanling's former ruler, the fugitive Peng Kai-Long. Hong pursed his lips. He knew all too well the threat.

A snake like Peng could wreak havoc, even from across the border in Rotuvi, where he enjoyed asylum after Princess Kaiya had failed to secure his extradition. It was time for Hong to share his brilliant idea, inspired by his lover's silly notions of chess strategy. In their last several games, the girl had kept her knight in reserve, saying that, like the imperial garrison in Wailian County, it could be deployed at any time.

As ridiculous as it sounded, she had won those games, just like all the others. "*Huang-Shang*," Hong said, "As the Founder emphasized, only the sword can bring order to a province in rebellion. Perhaps we should redeploy your most battle-hardened troops in Wailian to help contain the insurgency."

General Shan coughed. "*Huang-Shang*, such a move is not only unnecessary, but foolish as well. There is no insurgency. The lords of Nanling have already forsaken the rebel Peng and sworn fealty to you. Furthermore, Wailian County is outside of the Great Wall, protected from Rotuvi only by a shallow river and your armies. It is our main source of firepowder ingredients."

Hong shook his head. "*Huang-Shang*, until you finish replacing the lords of Nanling, the old guard will always be faithful to Peng and remain a threat. As for Rotuvi, they are embroiled in a war with their northern neighbors and cannot possibly divert attention toward Wailian."

The *Tianzi* looked from Hong to the general and back again. At last, he waved toward the crowd of officials. "What is the disposition of Rotuvi, Minister Yan?"

The aged man, who rarely came to court, bowed. "*Huang-Shang*, Chief Minister Hong is correct. Rotuvi is not a threat to Wailian. However, I agree with General Shan. I do not think we should leave it defenseless."

Hong laughed. "You are here to report, not to think, Minster Yan. Thank you for reporting." He turned from the minister and locked his gaze on the *Tianzi*. He had not worked his way into the Emperor's good graces for so long, just to have a few upstarts reject his brilliant ideas.

The *Tianzi* sighed. "General Shan, draw up the orders to redeploy the imperial garrison in Wailian. Ensuring stability in Nanling is our utmost priority. Even in exile, Cousin Peng may still try to interfere in matters there."

Peng Kai-Long, ruler of Nanling Province before his plot to seize the Dragon Throne failed, counted his men in the low light of dusk. Only thirty. It was still twice the number of imperial army troops stationed at the Great Wall's southernmost gatehouse.

A light flashed in quick succession from the top of the Wall, clearly visible from the mill where his men gathered. The signal meant his twenty loyalists on the inside of the gatehouse had taken control. If they suffered no casualties, he would command nearly fifty men. Just enough to hold off a counter-attack by imperial forces until his reinforcements arrived.

If Kai-Long's other assets in the countryside did their job, that counter-attack would never come, because the main imperial garrison, based out of *his* castle, wouldn't know about their loss of this strategic point until it was too late.

With a silent gesture, Kai-Long motioned his men toward the gate. It took three excruciatingly long minutes to cross the meadow. The doors to the gatehouse opened, allowing a column of light to escape the hushed crack.

Fools. They were supposed to keep the interior dark until he and his other men slipped in. If he weren't so shorthanded, the imbecile in charge might face punishment.

Inside, the provincial soldiers each dropped to one knee, fist to the floor. A dozen bodies lay against the walls, while three bound imperial soldiers gawked at him.

Kai-Long motioned to the doors. "Close them."

While one man jumped up to obey, his loyal shift captain looked up. "*Jue-ye*, we suspected the imperial army was testing our loyalty to the Throne when we received your secret orders. I am heartened to see that you are truly here in Nanling and not a refugee in Rotuvi."

Peng nodded at him. "Yes, rumors of my flight were greatly exaggerated. Or contrived, as the case may be."

The imperial officer spat. "You'll never succeed. You don't have enough men to hold the gatehouse."

Kai-Long knelt over him. "Word of my return spreads through the province as we chat. Despite their vows of fealty to the *Tianzi*, my loyal retainers and soldiers will side with me. We outnumber the imperial army garrison."

The officer laughed. "Maybe you could defeat us, but not without sustaining crippling losses. The *Tianzi* will quell your rebellion. With the nation's vast wealth and power at his command, he will send another army, and another, and another, until you are battered into submission."

Kai-Long turned his back on the man and motioned for his lieutenant. "Flash the signals on the other side of the Wall, to let the Madurans know we hold the gatehouse. They must arrive by daybreak, before the changing of the guard."

The provincial captain raised an eyebrow. "The Madurans?"

Kai-Long gestured him into silence, even as he looked back toward the imperial officer. "Tell me, what did the Founder write about facing an opponent who cannot be overwhelmed with force?"

His question was met with a gawk.

Kai-Long shook his head, laughing. "This is why the loyalist governor sits idly in *my* castle, unaware that I am about to take it back. Even the imperial officers have grown complacent with the nation's wealth, and have forgotten military lessons." He motioned toward the provincial captain. "What did the Founder write?"

"Avoid confrontations which lead to unacceptable losses..." The captain's eyes widened. "...have others fight for you."

Kai-Long grinned. Over the past several months, he had corresponded with Madura's Prince Dhananad. With the prince's unhealthy obsession over Princess Kaiya since she'd danced for him a year ago, he'd jumped at the invitation to invade.

However, instead of helping a foreign invader crush the imperial army, Kai-Long planned to keep his own provincial troops in reserve. Once he deemed both sufficiently weakened, he would close off the South Gate and cut Madura's supply lines. The Madurans would be caught between a hammer and an anvil, and he would do everything to ensure his enemies thinned each other out before crushing them both.

In the meantime, he had a dilemma. Cousin Kaiya was within reach of his agent in Dongmen Castle. He would like nothing more than to exact vengeance for her role in foiling his previous coup.

The only question would be how to keep Prince Dhananad motivated once she was finally dead.

Before Madura invaded and occupied her homeland, Leina had once been a dancer. Now she spent her days—and mostly nights—choreographing Cathay's unraveling from a small house in the capital's entertainment district.

A spring breeze wafted in through her window, brushing aside satin curtains and carrying in afternoon sun and the flitting laughter of coy Night Blossoms. In this high-end section of the Floating World, the ladies unwittingly heard secrets—either as they served rice wine to lounging officials or lay beside clients muttering in their sleep.

It was again time to harvest those secrets.

Leina knocked three times on the back wall of the pantry. When no response came, she pressed the dwarf-made trigger, and the wall opened outward, revealing the rear corridor of the adjacent Jade Teahouse. The sliding doors to private rooms stood ajar. All empty, as was to be expected at this early hour.

She brushed aside the dangling curtain of jade beads and pearls and walked out into the main room. There, a handful of Night Blossoms congregated among the bloodwood chairs and tables, sharing tea and gossip before dusk. Perhaps even the legendary Black Fist would never collect as much information as the girls in the Floating World.

Jasmine covered her mouth and laughed. Her sheer gown revealed the outline of the bloodwood chair she sat on, as well as her ample curves. Orchid lounged in a seat across the table, her eyes conspiratorially narrow.

Who came up with such names? Perhaps they took the term *blossoms* too literally. Or maybe feeding into the stereotypes excited the high officials and lords who sought them out.

Jasmine looked up and beckoned her over. "Lotus, Lotus, come!"

Leina chuckled. With a working name like Lotus, given for her half-Ayuri blood, she had no leeway to criticize floral names. She glided over and took a seat.

Orchid brushed a hand across Leina's sapphire-colored silk robe. "By the Heavens! This color brings out the walnut in your skin tone!"

Leina covered her mouth and giggled, imitating the irritating feminine conventions of Cathay. "Your gown, too. It emphasizes your dark eyes!"

Orchid batted her eyelashes. "That's what Minister Geng said, that lecherous old man. You know, he's looting the imperial treasury from beneath the *Tianzi's* nose."

Amazing to think how quickly the government fell into inefficiency, just with the death of the previous *Tianzi*. It almost made Leina's job too easy.

Jasmine sighed. "I wish some of the imperial treasury would find its way *here*. Many of my clients are tightening their belts instead of loosening them! Almost all of the officials and soldiers from Linshan Province went home."

A perky voice called from the entrance. "That's because Linshan's Lord Lin didn't want to be drawn into the Nanling expedition."

Purple Autumn. *Ziqiu,* in the local tongue. Now *that* was a clever name. Rumors swirled about the pretty young woman, like the lilac and silver gown she wore tonight. Supposedly only sixteen, she disappeared during the day, and only appeared some nights. Her clients were utterly secret, even to the other working girls' omniscient network of whispers. Perhaps like Leina, she had a powerful patron.

She sauntered over, swaying her thin hips, and took a seat at their table. With a lift of her chin, she tossed her rippling hair over her shoulder and then leaned in close. "Lord Lin has quite an independent streak. I wonder how long the realm will be able to rely on Linshan Province."

How could she know that? Could Lord Lin be her patron? Leina flashed a coy smile and threw out some bait. "I hear Lord Lin is quite virile."

Purple Autumn's pretty face contorted for a split second. Then her eyes flicked toward the entrance. When they returned Leina's gaze, her expression was unreadable. "As much as I would love to join you ladies for tea, I have an appointment to keep." She rose to her feet and strolled through the bead curtain and into the back rooms.

Orchid jerked her head toward the entrance and cringed. "Lotus…"

Leina looked in the long mirror behind the tea bar.

Her patron, Chief Minister Hong, hobbled in, shoulders slumped in a telltale show of defeat. Her stomach twisted.

"Until next time, my friends." Leina rose and nodded at the Night Blossoms. Of course they knew of her secret liaison with one of the most powerful men in Cathay. Nonetheless, what happened in the Floating World stayed in the Floating World.

Leina hastened to the secret door and back into her house, the one that Old Hong had bought just for their clandestine meetings. Little did he know of the other meetings she held there, with insurgents bent on toppling the Wang Dynasty.

Opposition to the *Tianzi* was the only thing certain about her visitor earlier in the day. She had kept Golden Fu at arm's length, feeding him a healthy mix of information and misinformation. The middle-aged spice merchant was likely much more than he appeared, but what he said rang true: the insurgency, while well-armed, would be too scared to act until the number of imperial troops in the capital declined. Maybe Purple Autumn's insights on Lord Lin could compel them.

Now, she had to clear the evidence of her meeting with Golden Fu before Hong limped in. A flash of gold in the parlor's red Ayuri carpet drew her eye. She snatched it up.

A pin.

It belonged to Young Lord Liu Dezhen, the heir to Jiangzhou Province. Married to the *Tianzi's* cousin,

Wang Kai-Hua, his baby boy had crept up the line to the Jade Throne. Or at least, that's what she told Young Lord Liu.

By the time Hong made it into her sitting room, she had cleared Golden Fu's wine cup from the carved rosewood table. She slid out the matching chair and invited him to sit.

He plopped down, and before she could kneel beside him, he took her arm in his worn, leathery hand and pulled her into his lap.

"A letter from Lord Zheng arrived earlier today," Hong said. "The princess wants to marry Zheng Ming."

Mention of the handsome young lord stirred memories of when she had slept with him, in a failed attempt to frame him for sedition.

Her heart fluttered at the reminiscence of their passionate lovemaking, but in this moment, Leina had other priorities. She had heard defeat in Hong's voice too often not to recognize it now. Without her subtle persuasion, he would have never become Chief Minister in the first place.

She reached out to stroke his leathery old skin, trying to avoid a shudder. "Dear Hong, you have the *Tianzi's* ear. All he has to do is order her to return before she has a chance to marry. She would never disobey her brother's direct command, especially with all of the hereditary lords questioning his fitness to rule."

Hong shook his head, his thin white hair ruffling the silken pillow cover. "But he won't force her to do anything. He is so fond of her."

Leina wondered if that were the case. After all, the *Tianzi* was actually considering allowing old Hong to marry Princess Kaiya. If only Hong knew that the princess was pregnant with—

Hong sighed. "I think the princess is lost to me."

If only he knew the whole story. Better that he didn't, because coveting the princess had kept him motivated for what, three years now?

To have the princess return to the capital would temporarily put her out of Zheng Ming's reach, thereby keeping Hong inspired. Yet it might also loosen Leina's hold on Hong, and therefore her indirect influence on the *Tianzi*.

Leina could not allow the latter to happen, at least not yet. Certainly not when the princess had demonstrated an ability to sniff out a conspiracy. Furthermore, from what Leina knew from the *other* letter she received earlier in the day, the princess' sudden desire to marry Zheng Ming showed she had a mind for conspiracy as well.

It was a gamble. Up to now, Leina had beaten the odds, using Hong as a game piece to outsmart and outmaneuver all of the other lords and ministers jockeying for power. Whether she decided to lure the princess to within reach of Hong's paws or her assassin's knife, the first step was the same: getting a message to her.

Now, she had to convince Hong the idea was his, something she did on a regular basis. She patted him on the chest. "It is a shame she does not want to come back yet. I am sure her brother's widow would like to see her."

Hong turned to her, his bright eyes gleaming in stark contrast to his wrinkled face. "Brilliant! Where would I be without your woman's intuition?"

Woman's intuition, indeed. Her plotting was masterful, worthy of the statesmen from the First Age of Empires. Nonetheless, she feigned delight with a girlish smile.

It was a look Leina had mastered in the three years since she arrived in Cathay in search of the Cathayi father who had left her behind in occupied Ankira. Using her mother as a hostage, Emperor Geros had given her a decade to undermine Cathay from the inside. His latest messenger bird came with a demand for immediate results, so he could claim Princess Kaiya and their unborn son.

Once Hong left tonight, Leina would contact her agent. Princess Kaiya would need to be harmed just enough to keep her convalescing at the border for when Geros arrived.

Chapter 5:
Luck Favors the Well-Prepared

Sitting on a bloodwood chair by her anteroom window, Kaiya strummed at a *pipa*. The pear-shaped, fretted instrument resonated in harmony with the birds outside, each note intertwining in the orchestra of spring sounds.

Yet even if her music was technically perfect, it lacked the passion she'd evoked in the past.

Kaiya had held crowds enthralled as emotions rippled through her music. Today, her only audience was Jie, and the half-elf seemed more interested in sharpening her knives. Kaiya continued strumming, despite the futility of trying to charm the Insolent Retainer. At the very least, her sons could appreciate it as they grew in her womb.

The *pipa's* melody shifted as it bent around a newcomer by the open door. Even if her music couldn't influence others, at least she could still sense how others' positions and motion influenced sound.

Kaiya's hands froze as she looked up.

A page dressed in dark green livery knelt near the door. When her gaze met his, he shifted his eyes down as protocol demanded. He proffered a letter in two hands. "*D-Dian-x-xia*, y-you have a message from the capital."

Without waiting for acknowledgement, Jie padded over to the young man and plucked the paper out of his fingers. She ordered him out with a perfunctory jerk of her head, and then delivered it into Kaiya's hands.

Her name was written on the front of the cover paper in a distinct script. Though she didn't have to, Kaiya flipped it over to confirm it was Sister-in-Law Zhao Xiulan's name on the back. The former Crown Princess before the death of Kaiya's eldest brother, Xiulan was like an older sister.

Kaiya opened the cover, unfolded the message within and read:

Kaiya, I was overjoyed to hear you were safe after your months stranded in the enemy-infested Kanin Wilds. The news has helped at least a little in numbing my devastation at the loss of the Crown Prince. I hope to see you soon.

Her eyes glided over the enchanted script, its Artistic Magic imbued by Xiulan's hand. The uncertain sweeps and melancholy whorls tugged at Kaiya's heart for a split-second. The sensation quickly disappeared, replaced only by an appreciation of Xiulan's technical mastery, as displayed in the perfect balance of characters.

Even so, Sister-in-Law's misery screamed out in her handwriting. Xiulan had suffered through five fruitless years of trying to conceive an heir. The late *Tianzi's* poor health had made the pressure all the more oppressive. Now, she'd lost her beloved husband, and her position as mother of the future *Tianzi*.

Kaiya scanned the letter once more. A return to Huajing would put another three days between her and Ming, further delaying a marriage. Yet a sense of duty prodded, urging her to comfort the one who had always given her encouragement. Maybe even confide in the sister who always supported her.

Yet without emotions, how could Kaiya possibly empathize with Xiulan's loss? And if she shared her secret pregnancy, wouldn't it just crush someone who'd tried so hard and so long without success?

Kaiya glanced over her shoulder.

Jie stood above her, her mouth drawn into a pout. A trickle slid down her cheek.

A tear?

Jie's eyes had not so much as glassed over at the death of Tian, her best friend and the man she loved. Now, she looked miserable for Xiulan, whom she was not especially fond of.

"What is it, Jie?"

The half-elf's voice choked. "I… I… The misery in the words. It's crushing."

Even if Kaiya didn't feel it herself, the power of Xiulan's script made Jie cry.

Jie never cried. Not only that, she'd proven immune to Artistic Magic ever since Kaiya started learning to focus it.

Kaiya rose and strode toward the door.

Whereas the letter's unhappy lines brought Jie to tears, it brought the princess to her feet. What did she plan to do now?

Whether the princess was charming dragons or enchanting dictators, Jie had learned that if anything was predictable about Princess Kaiya, it was impulsiveness. That meant constant vigilance.

Granted, under the *Tiger's Eye*, she'd been completely reasonable and logical.

At least up to now.

Jie wiped her eyes and trailed down the hall after her ward.

Yet the magic embedded in the miserable twists and turns of the former Crown Princess' handwriting continued to tangle through Jie's heart, yanking out bittersweet memories.

Her near-kiss with Tian, forestalled by duty. Then she'd lost him. First to distance, then to the princess, and finally to death.

Persevere. It'd been her mantra for the last week. She wore her discipline like armor, and took pride in her ability to focus. Then again, she had yet to be truly tested with anything beyond trailing Lord Zheng, forging a letter, and snooping on a meeting.

Now, even the thought of the letter's words hacked away at years of training, leaving her a quivering ball of pathetic emotion.

Just like any other girl. Just like the princess, before the *Tiger's Eye* transformed her into an efficient and practical dwarf clock.

Jie looked up. She'd been staring at her feet, lulled by the floor's rhythmic chirping.

Princess Kaiya was gliding down the halls a good seven paces ahead of her.

Just in front of the princess, the messenger from before dropped to his knee, left fist to the ground, the other hand—

The messenger.

When he'd delivered the Crown Princess' letter, beads of sweat had gathered on his forehead. His eyes had darted back and forth while he clasped and unclasped his hands.

"*Dian-xia*! Danger!" Hand on a throwing star, Jie surged forward, her short legs covering half the distance in just a second.

A second too late.

The princess stopped where she stood. She looked back. Her eyes widened like a startled doe's.

A short blade flashed in the messenger's hand. He sprang at her.

Even as the princess' turn opened a window for Jie to attack, the assassin's lunge on the other side of the princess rapidly closed it. Where was his knife?

Jie flung the star.

It whistled within a hairbreadth of the princess' ear, shaving off wisps of her hair and catching the man in the right breast.

He let out a shriek.

So did Princess Kaiya.

In a split second, Jie spun the princess out of the way and reached the messenger.

She spiraled out of his slow thrust and wrapped up his hand. With a quick twist of her wrist and jerk of her hips, she dislocated his elbow and shoulder.

He screamed again and the bloody dagger slipped from his fingers.

Jie silenced him with an elbow to the temple.

Even as unconsciousness quieted the would-be assassin, the rest of the castle roared to life. Provincial guards raced toward them with bared weapons, their feet kicking up a chorus of discordant chirps on the nightingale floors.

Heavens, that'd been close. Jie looked back toward the princess. "*Dian-xia*, are you unharmed?"

Though standing, Princess Kaiya's face paled and her eyebrows knitted together. She held her left hand to her right flank as she spoke through gritted teeth. "He… he grazed me. It hurts, but does not seem serious."

"Summon Doctor Fang," Jie called out.

They'd gotten lucky. Perhaps Princess Kaiya's inadvertent spin had turned her out of the path of a more dangerous blow. Jie beckoned the guards.

She glared at the shift captain, who now knelt before them. "Why was the messenger not checked?" No weapon was allowed near a member of the Imperial Family, unless in the hands of an imperial guard or a secret agent like Jie.

The captain bowed. "We *did* check him, at the entrance to the guest wing. He only carried the message, no weapons."

Bending over, Jie retrieved the curved knife. The imprint at the base of the blade showed it came from a provincial weaponsmith.

A weapon issued to a provincial soldier.

Her gaze raked over the assembled men as she held it up. "Is anyone missing their dagger?"

Two dozen hands checked their sides. A soldier rose, took a tentative step forward and dropped to his knees. He proffered a scabbard. "*D-Dian-xia*, it was m-my dagger. I s-swear, I didn't give it to him. I didn't even realize it was gone."

"You will submit to questioning." Jie snatched the sheath out of his hand and upended it. Fine white sand cascaded out. An old pickpocket trick, one used by her clan.

Could the assailant be one of her temple brothers? Until a year ago, she'd only known of one living renegade, the one she had been tasked with tracking down in the Eldaeri Kingdoms. Since joining Princess Kaiya's guard detail, she'd met two. She rolled the unconscious man over.

Probably no older than thirty, he didn't look like anyone she'd ever seen before, and she knew every Black Fist to pass through the Black Lotus Temple over the last three decades. He was too small for a Teleri Nightblade. Perhaps he belonged to one of the small, less reputable clans than pawned their skills to provincial lords. "Do any of you recognize him?"

Heads shook.

"Very well, bind him and let me know when he wakes."

The man was skilled enough to find a way through a cordon of guards, steal a knife, and attack the princess. He'd hesitated, and they'd gotten lucky.

For the Imperial Family, luck was not enough. Jie would have normally sniffed out such an attacker in her sleep, but in her current state, she wasn't fit to serve.

Though an imperial guard's response to failure would be to offer his own life, the Black Fist didn't live by such codes. She knelt. "*Dian-xia*, my skills are compromised. I must be released from your service."

"Jie, I—" Princess Kaiya tumbled to the ground. Her hand slipped, revealing a splotch of red, blooming out from the wound on her right flank.

Chapter 6:
Up In Smoke

With his brother Shu at his side, Ming peered through the darkness. Luckily, the dense clouds obscured the White and Blue Moons. The black of night, combined with the rustling of the river, covered his men's retreat. As he suspected, the Teleri would not launch a night attack, despite the expiration of their ultimatum.

A drop of cold rain plopped on his cheek, followed by another. He brought his hand up, feeling the wetness between his fingers.

A chorus of crossbows clicked and twanged, barely audible over the patter of rain in the moat.

"Take cover!" Ming threw himself into the dirt, dragging Shu down with him.

A few grunts and screams emanated from the embankment where the rear guard remained.

"Fire!" yelled an overzealous imperial officer.

"Hold your fire!" Ming barely heard his own voice over the disjointed roar of muskets. The sound would give away their dwindling numbers.

The second volley of muskets rang out, and then a third, each answered by shouts of pain in the moat.

Beside him, Shu struggled to his feet, pulling his *dao* from its sheath. All signs of his earlier nervousness disappeared.

Ming grabbed him. "Wait. Wait for the fourth volley."

That fourth volley, to be fired by the first line once they reloaded, never came. Only the clicks of triggers and snaps of hammers.

Ming strained his eyes through the darkness and rain to get his best view of the embankment. Nothing but dark shapes. Imperial musketmen shouted in frustration. Metal clashed on metal where his provincial spearmen stood.

He turned to Shu. "Fall back to the rendezvous point. At the first sign of Teleri on the bridge, blow it." Shu might not be much of an archer, but surely he could hit the firepowder kegs.

From among the spearmen, his other brother Lun yelled, "Fall back, fall—" A choke interrupted his command.

Ming strode forward, unslung his bow, and fit an arrow. Squinting, he tried to locate Lun in the fray. It was so hard to differentiate the dark shapes, even if the Bovyans were that much larger. Instead, he took aim at the figures slogging through the moat and loosed arrow after arrow into the Teleri surge.

The imperial gunnery officer nearly backed into Ming. "*Dajiang*, we can't hold the embankment much longer. We must sound the general retreat."

Ming clenched his jaw. This was becoming into a disaster. With a nod, he yelled, "Fall back to the bridge!"

A horn blared out, sounding the retreat.

As his own men ran past him, Ming worked his way backward, shooting arrows at Bovyan soldiers as they appeared at the top of the embankment. When he could no longer make out any of his own men in front of him, he spun and ran.

At the bridge, he withdrew a light bauble and dropped it among the kegs of firepowder to illuminate the area. Would a flaming arrow ignite the powder in the rain? If only he had been able to complete the evacuation on his own terms.

A cordon of his own spearmen at the other end of the bridge parted and let him through, then followed him in retreat. He raced to the opposite tree line, where Shu waited next to a burning brazier. He proffered an arrow coated with pitch and wrapped in cloth.

Ming dipped it in the brazier and it caught fire. He nocked the arrow, took aim at the bridge, and loosed.

His men all fell silent as the arrow arced through the clearing and landed in the middle of the bridge.

Nothing happened.

Ming loosed another half-dozen in quick succession, all with the same result.

Shu squeezed Ming's arm, his fingers trembling. "We must blow the bridge, take away their means to cross. Otherwise, the Teleri will be able to march right up to the Great East Gate."

"I know," Ming snarled. He looked among the officers and soldiers gathered around the brazier. The only alternative would lead to death or capture. "I need a dozen volunteers to follow me back, each bearing a torch and a spear. We'll fight our way back to the bridge and light the firepowder up close."

Several men stepped forward.

Shu's face paled in the flickering firelight. "But… Eldest Brother, that'll mean your death."

Ming frowned as his stomach tightened. As if he didn't know. He had much to live for: Marriage to the princess. Inheriting the province.

Yet the last time he was faced with dying in glory or living with cowardice, he had chosen the latter. Not this time. "You are now heir to Dongmen Province, Shu. Give Father my regards."

With a deep breath, Ming drew his sword with one hand and took a torch with the other. "Charge!"

He and his men had sprinted three-quarters of the way through the clearing when the first Bovyan appeared on the bridge.

The soldier's head raked back and forth before he spun on his heel and yelled back into the fort, "The Cathayi plan to destroy the bridge!"

They needed to reach the bridge before the Teleri reinforced it. Ming pushed faster, blinking rain out of his eyes.

He reached the western end of the span just as five Bovyans joined the first on the east side. Forming a line, they marched with lowered spears, their heavy steps sending reverberations through the wood.

Ming's hands trembled as he thrust the torch at the several lines of firepowder leading back to the kegs. He prepared to jump back, in case he could escape the blast. From his sides, his men surged forward, swords held high.

None of the firepowder lit.

It should have! The rain couldn't have possibly made it so wet so soon. Or maybe they had scattered it as they ran through it?

There was only one way. He abandoned his desperate game and started toward the kegs.

The Teleri vanguard crashed into his men.

He was almost to the first keg, just ahead of the enemy.

This would work, though it would mean his death. So be it. He reached out.—

A spear shaft slapped into the torch. The reverberation wrung his hands. The torch jerked from his grasp, flew over the side of the bridge, and sizzled and sputtered in the river. Another spear drove into his left shoulder, punching through his studded leather breastplate like paper.

Pain exploded in his shoulder before all went black.

The low murmurs grew louder, nudging Ming into consciousness. The throbbing in his temples intensified, screaming above the pain in his shoulder. It almost distracted him from the hard cot under his back.

He lifted his head and blinked away his fuzzy vision. It was the same roughshod officers' room as before. This time, he had guests.

Surrounded by four imposing officers, Emperor Geros stood above the wood table, pointing at what appeared to be a map.

Ming struggled to sit up, though his left shoulder, now in a sling, protested.

A Teleri captain cleared his throat. "Your Eminence, Lord Zheng has awoken."

Geros looked up from the table and grinned like a wolf. "Don't be rude, Captain Mirin, help the lord up."

The captain strode over and assisted Ming as he rose into a sitting position. Even an enemy deserved courtesy, and Ming nodded in thanks.

In two steps, Geros loped over and knelt, meeting Ming's bleary eyes. "I commend your efforts, Lord Zheng. Your ploy to escape on your own terms almost worked. However, you really should have accepted my offer."

Ming blinked several more times, then glared. "You were lucky it rained."

"Luck favors the well-prepared and the better-informed." After quoting the Wang Dynasty founder, Geros' smirk reeked of self-satisfaction.

A wry smile tugged on Ming's lips, unbidden. "I—"

Geros raised a hand. "I hope you have learned from your experience, because I am going to make you one more offer."

Another offer? What could the Teleri Emperor want that Ming could provide? He cocked his head. "I don't have much to give you, except maybe a tour of your own fort."

Geros laughed. "What did the Wang founder say about knowing your enemy? You do not seem to know what I want. But I know what *you* want."

Ming remembered the last time someone spoke to him in riddles: when Golden Fu had virtually mugged him in the streets of Huajing, after his secret liaison with the half-Ayuri beauty, on New Year's Day.

Just like then, this time would undoubtedly be some kind of set-up. He started to throw his arm up, only to be greeted by a stabbing pain. "You have it all figured out, then. What do you need with me?"

"I want you to open the East Gate of Cathay for my armies."

He wanted *what*? Not that Ming would do it, even if it were within his power to do so. He closed his gaping mouth. "Why would I betray my people?

Geros snickered. "Because I will offer you governorship over all of Cathay. You will be the link between the Teleri occupation and the Cathayi people. Oh, the first few months will be difficult, but we will engineer some way to make you look heroic."

"I am no collaborator." He had decided in his charge toward the bridge not to be remembered as a coward. He certainly had no intention of being denounced as a traitor.

"You can also marry Princess Kaiya." Geros stared up at the thatching.

Ming's eyes must have stretched to the size of tea cups before pinching again. "You want her for yourself."

"Yes—but alas, due to the Bovyan Curse, my preordained death is a year away. After I am gone, she is yours."

From what Ming had heard, the curse limited a Bovyan's lifespan to thirty-three years. The balance was forfeited to sustain the Orc King. Nonetheless... "I do not want from you what I could claim on my own."

Geros laughed. "You are in no position to claim anything. Except a grave plot."

Ming shrugged. Better to die a hero than live in infamy. "Nonetheless, I won't help you."

"Maybe not willingly. Your father might have a different opinion."

So he would be served up as a hostage. But Ming's father was too loyal to open the floodgates, even. Even if it meant the death of his firstborn.

Ming still had three brothers. Though that assumed Lun survived the battle. Nonetheless, he forced a confident tone. "My father will never be labeled a traitor for the sake of a single son."

A Teleri officer appeared at the door. "Your Eminence, we have cut off the retreating Cathayi. They are hunkered down three hours east of here. I request reinforcements to chase them down."

Shit. Ming's stomach clenched.

Geros flashed a toothy grin, which reached the kinks of his mismatched eyes.

Chapter 7:
Doubts

The stream rustled nearby, setting the rhythm for the chirping birds. Kaiya opened her eyes to the warmth of the midday sun. The orange blur of her eyelids gave way to a perfect blue sky. New spring grass caressed and cooled her back; her propped-up head felt warm. Something dug into her right side.

Kaiya started to dislodge whatever it was, when a round shadow encroached into her field of vision. She squinted, the image coming into focus.

Tian.

Upside-down. Her head was cradled in his lap, the cross of his legs a comfortable pillow. His intelligent eyes held her entranced.

He brushed an errant lock from her face. "Good afternoon, my love."

Kaiya's heart leaped so high, it might have joined the clouds outside. She pushed herself up, and tried to straighten out the wrinkles in her robe and untangle her hair. It would not do for her beloved to see her so disheveled. She looked up through her lashes.

He leaned in and took her cheeks in his hands.

She closed her eyes and parted her lips, inviting him closer.

Tian accepted the summons, pressing his lips to the divot between her collarbones. The heat of his breath sent a tingle down her spine, which intensified as he lavished kisses up her neck. Longing to feel his mouth on hers, she tilted her head forward to meet his.

But instead of meeting her lips, he leaned back. Kaiya opened her eyes. He grinned at her, the crooked smile emphasizing the defined curve of his jaw. "Not now."

She pouted. "Where are we? Did I join you in the world between death and rebirth?"

He shook his head. "I would be disappointed. I sacrificed myself so you might live. And our children."

Kaiya sucked in a breath and looked down at her belly. "They are yours?"

Tian's gaze followed hers. He placed his hand over her womb before lifting her chin. "It is not yet your time. You have much to do. He has much to do."

He? Not they?

She opened her mouth to protest, only to find Tian's lips against hers, his arms enveloping her. The energy drained from her body and she melted into him, all complaints forgotten.

Then his hand slipped to her right side. Pain seared in her flank.

***

Kaiya sat up straight on a bedroll, a kiss of warm spring air brushing across her face. Joy melted through her fingers like water, leaving only the ice of despair. Emotion, raw and uncontrollable, seized her breath.

Then pain tore at her right side. As quickly as they had come, her feelings disappeared. She blinked away the tears and brought her left hand to the wound.

"*Dian-xia*, rest easy," Fang Weiyong's voice called.

Rubbing her eyes, she found him in a chair by the window of her sunlit room. He slid down into a kneel.

She pulled her white sleeping robe tighter. Modesty seemed appropriate.

"*Dian-xia*." Jie sat cross-legged by the closed door. She rose onto her knees, head bowed.

Weiyong stood and shuffled toward her. "Please, rest. You lost a lot of blood, and were unconscious for two days."

Was that all she lost? Kaiya placed a hand on her belly. With all the doubts surrounding the pregnancy, perhaps it was for the better. No worries about who would inherit the Dragon Throne, no urgency to get married. At the same time, if they had been Tian's…

Oh, no. Her chest squeezed, a long-forgotten sensation.

A smile danced across Weiyong's face. "Do not worry, *Dian-xia*, your unborn sons were safe last time I checked. May I?" He gestured toward her wrists.

The sadness that came with the prospect of losing Tian's children slipped away as if it had never peeked out from under the *Tiger's Eye*. She offered her wrists to him, and he knelt over and felt her pulses.

Brow furrowed, he nodded several times. "Yes, you still feel very pregnant to me. Unfortunately, my pulse diagnosis does not compare with Doctor Wu's, so I cannot tell you much more than that."

Her dilemma remained.

"May I see the wound?" Weiyong averted his eyes, not that it mattered.

With a nod, Kaiya laid her arms at her side. "Please."

Jie crowded in behind him as he opened the right lapel of her robe and untied the dressing. "*Dian-xia*, please lift your breast." His voice sounded professionally sterile.

The breast felt full and sore in her hand, the nipple sensitive, no different from the day she found out she was pregnant. Surely her twins were fine.

Kaiya craned her neck to get a good look at the wound. Delicate stitches melded the thumb-length cut together, barely noticeable from her vantage point. "I can tell you did the sewing, Weiyong. I have seen Jie's handiwork. She is much better at cutting flesh than sewing it back up."

The Insolent Retainer's cheeks flushed, perhaps at the verbal jab, or maybe in memory of the same words the half-elf had once used to describe Tian's skill with needle and thread.

Weiyong smiled again. "I am honored by your praise, *Dian-xia*. Fortunately, the blade entered obliquely and glanced off your rib. It nicked your liver. I disinfected the cut with an herb wine wash. I have been treating it with a balm that should hopefully compensate for my poor stitches. I do not think it will leave much of a scar."

At least not a physical scar. If and when she ever broke free of the *Tiger's Eye*, this incident would be yet another memory that might keep her up at night. And why? "Jie, did you coax some answers out of the assassin?"

Jie sighed. "Yes, *Dian-xia*. However, the answers were inconsistent. At first he insisted that Lord Zheng ordered him; later, it was the bidding of the *Tianzi* himself. Another remote possibility is Peng Kai-Long, meddling from beyond the Empire's reach."

Unless Lord Zheng had suddenly decided to wipe his hands clean of her, he would have no motive. Her brother, even less. As for Cousin Peng… a hired knife taking her unawares reeked of his underhanded methods. To think she had trusted him for so long. "Did you find out anything else?" she asked.

"My throwing star punctured his lung, and he did not last long enough for more subtle interrogation." Jie dropped to both knees and hung her head. "*Dian-xia*, I was careless. I should never have let him get too close to you. I—"

"You were thinking of Tian, weren't you?" It was the only way to explain the Insolent Retainer's mistake.

Jie stared at the floor, the tips of her ears flushing deep scarlet. "It doesn't matter. I am of no use to you right now. We must arrange for a replacement."

A year and a half ago, Kaiya hadn't wanted Jie as a bodyguard. Now, she was indispensable. Not just for her skills, but also for her willingness to speak her mind. However, there was something she was not saying. Kaiya propped an elbow underneath her. "Help me up."

If Weiyong shook his head any more, it might very well come off. "*Dian-xia*, you must rest more. The stitches will tear if you move too much. If that happens, if you lose much more blood, you might very well miscarry."

Energy flagging just from that small effort, Kaiya collapsed back down on to the bed. "Weiyong, please leave us."

He knelt there, eyes darting from her to Jie and back again. At last, he rose. Holding a low bow, he shuffled backward out of the room.

Kaiya reached over and took Jie's hand in her own. She gave it an affection squeeze, or at least the closest approximation of how affection would feel. "You are my sworn sister and I trust you more than you can know. I order you to hold your post."

Jie's lips pursed, her focus on the floor. "As the princess commands."

It wasn't convincing. Kaiya squeezed her hand tighter. Jie would not openly oppose her order, but would find some way to skirt around it. There had to be some way to coax her out of her sadness. "I order—"

"No." Jie pulled her hand back. "A sworn sister doesn't give orders. A sworn sister doesn't steal the man her sister loves."

At last, the unspoken truth, finally verbalized. Yes, Kaiya had surmised Jie's love for Tian long ago. She'd even asked directly, only to receive evasive answers that confirmed her suspicions. In her heart, Kaiya had known, and she had wronged Jie. That much was clear now.

"We were caught up in emotion. I can see that now, with the *Tiger's Eye*—"

"Which I used on you, so you could cope with *your* grief. How do I cope with *my* grief?" Tears welled in Jie's eyes as she glared. "Because of you, I don't even know what I am mourning. The death of my best friend? Loss of a love that never blossomed?"

Kaiya closed her eyes, the accusations weighing her down more than the blood loss. "I am sorry."

"Being your support is in direct conflict with what I need myself."

"What do you need?" Kaiya opened her eyes and looked at a truly insolent retainer.

Jie's lips twisted into an ugly frown. "Distance. From you."

From her spot near the door, Jie cast a glance at the princess sleeping on her bedroll. Once the princess'

mind was made up, there was little anyone could do to change it. Her sense of right and wrong, combined with stubbornness, had put her in more than one unenviable position. Including the one she faced now.

Princess Kaiya was a worthy liege, and Jie now regretted her outburst.

Nonetheless, she could not perform her duties effectively until she had time to sort out her feelings. Letting an amateur assassin so close was proof of that. If only Feng Mi, who'd helped rescue the princess, had stayed here instead of returning to the capital to report to the Black Lotus.

Jie moved out into the hall, away from the princess' prying ears. She then wrote a letter encoded in the secret language of her clan. Her adopted father, the master of the Black Lotus Temple, would consider her request, even if the princess did not.

To Master Yan,

A rival clan sent an assassin to kill Princess Kaiya. Although they did not succeed, she was injured. I made several careless mistakes and failed in my mandate to protect her. I wish to be replaced by another Fist.

Yan Jie

She folded the letter, using a six-crease pattern which only one of her clan could open without ripping. When a castle valet came by to check on the princess, she slipped it into his hand along with the princess' messages. "When the next rider goes to the capital, have him deliver this one to the Cold Sun Bell Foundry."

The horse-relay messengers would reach the capital in four hours. A mute worker at the foundry, hired anonymously by the Black Lotus Temple decades before, would drop the message into a funerary urn at a specialty shop. A Black Lotus trainee would pick up all the items left there and deliver it to Master Yan. A replacement might be able to relieve her within three days.

The chirping of floorboards interrupted her self-pity. At the door, the castle steward himself knelt. "Please wake Princess Kaiya. We have news of Young Lord Zheng Ming."

Chapter 8:
Viper Awakened

Coming out of a coma on a funeral barge next to a dozen cold bodies wasn't as unsettling as knowing he'd somehow intentionally put himself into that coma. Though he didn't remember how he'd gotten on the log raft, or even who he was, he knew he'd awoken too early, before his injuries had stabilized.

The barge had come ashore, lodging in the rich-smelling earth. The river, swollen by spring melt, tumbled past, while the wind rustled in budding tree branches. A cool breeze brushed across his bare chest, causing his skin to erupt in goosebumps.

He groaned and pushed himself up into a sitting position. A warm sensation trickled down his back, emanating from the place where pain seared in his shoulder. That stab wound, unlike the numerous cuts all over his body, would bleed him out. Each heartbeat brought him closer to death.

Two lithe figures dressed in doeskin clothes stared at him with wide, almond-shaped eyes. With streaks of red-and-white paint across their faces and feathers in their hair, they looked as wild as the untamed forest around them. They were... elves.

How he knew that, he wasn't sure.

The silence lasted only a few seconds. The brown-haired male, with sharp features and a sharper dagger put his hands on his hips. When he spoke, the flowery language belied the threat in his voice. *"Amane esaya na!"*

How to respond to such gibberish? He cocked his head and shrugged, sending a surge of pain through his shoulder.

The girl with chestnut-colored tresses had rounded features that spoke of human blood. Her high-cut doeskin skirt revealed toned thigh and calf muscles. Appearing to be about twelve human years, she evoked an unsettling sense of familiarity. Had he met her before?

She poked her companion in the back, thankfully not with the steel dagger at her side. *"Esala iyani na."* Even if the language remained unintelligible to him, her tone dripped with sarcasm. She then turned to him. "Bow before the messengers of the gods."

Messengers of the gods? He had to suppress a laugh; not just because the two carried daggers and all he had was the broken sword in his lap, but also because it hurt too much. At least he understood her words, though they were not his mother tongue.

He fumbled with a response in the language the girl spoke. "You are not messengers of the gods. You are just…" He frowned, trying to dig the word out of the cobwebs entangling his mind. The term translated to *spirit*. Perhaps the native speakers of this language considered elves to be angels? He switched to his own native tongue: "…elves."

The two elves exchanged glances and spoke animatedly in hushed voices.

He took the opportunity to survey the surroundings. Large men lay dead around him on the beached raft, their hands folded across their chests. All had suffered wounds delivered with surgical accuracy from swords, knives, and throwing stars. Two smaller bodies with black hair and honey-toned skin seemed familiar. Flies buzzed over the stinking, bloated corpses. Hopefully, he didn't smell as ripe.

He looked back up at the arguing elves. "I'm bleeding to death."

They both turned and stared at him. At last, the male extended an open hand, hopefully to help him to his feet and off the raft, and not to pull him into a gut stab.

His wounds complained as he took the elf's hand. Though small in his own, its callouses spoke of years of use, likely with a weapon.

When he lurched onto shore, the female pressed on his shoulder wound, sending flares of pain up and down his back. She started wrapping strips of cloth around his chest. "Hold still. We need to slow this bleeding until we can get you to a healer."

"I am Dior," the male said, the sound rolling of his lips like cherry blossoms dancing on the wind. "What is your name?"

His name. His brow furrowed as he tried to remember. "I don't know."

The female harrumphed. "We have to call you something."

"Munikai." Dior grinned.

She rolled her eyes. "In our language, that means *Sleeps With Dead.*"

Not-Munikai cringed and shook his head. "Maybe something else?"

Her eyes brightened as a cute smile blossomed. "*Feneyas.* The Awakened."

Feneyas nodded. "Better than *Sleeps with Dead.* What is your name?"

"Krztsh." It was more a grunt than a name, and could not have possibly belonged to the beautiful language they sang. She studied her feet.

Feneyas tried to repeat her, but his mouth couldn't imitate the sounds. He shrugged, sending another jolt into his shoulder and evoking an involuntary wince. "I am sorry, but your language—"

With a violent shake of his head, Dior clucked. "It's not *our* language. We call her Kiri."

Kiri. Now that was more manageable. Feneyas bowed, right fist in his left palm. "I am honored to meet you. Dior and Kiri."

Both stared at his salute until Dior met his eyes. "Kiri, do you think Feneyas can move without returning to sleep with the dead?"

She nodded. "I have slowed the blood loss, but he'll need to see Nayori if he stands a chance of living."

"Then let's get moving. Blindfold him."

"Blindfold?" Feneyas stepped back, raising his hands defensively—as if he could defend himself in his weakened state. Pain erupted in his shoulder again, forcing a wince.

Kiri grunted. "Hold still, or you'll start gushing again."

"Yes." Dior nodded. "You're a stranger, and while you don't look like one of the Metal Men, we need to ensure the safety of our village."

The large warriors must've been the Metal Men. Feneyas sighed and bent over to allow Kiri to cover his eyes.

"Don't worry," she said. "I'll point out any obstacles along the way."

A bumped head and a dozen near-stumbles later, they came to a stop. Yet despite their attempts to conceal the path to their village, the sounds and smells and the number of paces and turns told him they were just two *li* north-northeast of where they found him, high in the trees. At least seventy-three distinct voices whispered around him.

Dior's hands pressed on his shoulders, easing him down to sit on gnarled wood. Kiri's slender fingers worked the knot of the blindfold. It slipped off, the soft light of dusk blurring his vision.

Feneyas blinked, allowing everything to come into focus. Greywood tree limbs meshed together to create a broad platform towering high above the forest floor. Several male and female elves trained arrows on him from where they stood on branch bridges to other trees. Not like he posed much of a threat, with his energy flagging.

Kiri and Dior bowed as an older elfwoman alighted on the platform, from the ramp of branches that wound around the tree. She appeared to be forty. Her face paint formed circles and dots along her cheeks and forehead. Dark hair scattered down bare shoulders. A doeskin dress with tassels and shells hung down to her bare feet. She regarded Feneyas with large, dark eyes that spoke of both beauty and wisdom.

Dior raised his head. "Nayori, this is Feneyas." He continued in their own language, with the Metal Men mentioned twice.

Feneyas bowed, placing his right fist in his left palm, again attracting snorts and stares.

Nayori's nod wasn't reassuring. "Your salute is not of the Metal Men, nor of the Kanin humans who worship us as messengers of the gods. You look a little different, too." She pointed at him. "The eyes, the skin tone. You belong to the People Beyond the Wall. Your kind has not ventured here for centuries. How did you come to our lands?"

Memories drifted in the distance, beyond Feneyas' reach. He shook his head. "I don't remember."

Nayori's studied him. "Were you fighting with or against the Metal Men?"

His aversion to the large men and recognition of the other two bodies suggested they were foes, yet why would he have been lain with his enemy's honored dead? "Against. I think."

She flashed a smile. "Dior, bring blankets and lay him down. We shall see if Ayara favors him enough to allow me to channel her divine healing. Feneyas, do you submit to will of the gods?"

Feneyas nodded. "I don't have a choice. I will die. Without your help."

"Very well. After hearing my prayer, you will sleep. You will dream. You will share dreams with those who care about you. When you awake, it will either be before the throne of Koralas to receive judgment, or back among us. "

When Dior returned with blankets, Feneyas lay down. He closed his eyes, perhaps for the last time.

Above him, Nayori's voice lifted in song. Though he couldn't understand the words, the sounds were beautiful, like angels singing. Maybe that was why the Kanin humans thought the elves were messengers of gods. For him, it stirred fleeting memories of an onyx-haired beauty, which disappeared before he could grasp them. If this was the last sound he ever heard, he would die happy.

"Now sleep, Feneyas. You will dream. Of the past. Of the future. They may very well remind you of your life before you slept among the dead."

Chapter 9:
Unsavory Options.

The low buzz of murmuring soldiers addled Kaiya's mind even more than the loss of blood. At Fang Weiyong's insistence, she'd been carried on a litter to the audience room. It now took all her energy to remain upright and seated on the cushion at the head of the chamber.

Her face must've been quite pale, given the gawking of the provincial ministers and officers when they saw her. Lady Zheng, in particular, wrung her hands and hyperventilated. She'd fussed and ordered Kaiya to return to her room and rest, though Lord Zheng had insisted on her presence.

He sat perpendicular to Kaiya, his expression stoic as a carved stone. Unlike the other men, who fidgeted and shared whispers, he remained absolutely quiet.

Sitting motionless across from him, Jie shared his silent stoicism. Beside her, Weiyong's eyes raked back and forth among the people present, occasionally meeting her gaze with a compassionate look. Thank the Heavens for reliable friends.

Two soldiers marched in, both with dirt-streaked faces framed by disheveled hair. Their torn uniforms rustled as they approached. One was an imperial army officer in royal blue, the other a Dongmen provincial solider in dark green. Both dropped to their knees, fists to the ground.

The imperial officer spoke first. "*Dian-xia*, I bring regrettable news. Almost our entire army of five thousand was killed or captured by the Teleri."

All five thousand! Lost because of her.

Lady Zheng sucked in a sharp breath. "What about my sons?"

The provincial soldier raised his head. "My Lady, I regret to inform you that Young Lord Lun was gravely injured while leading our spearmen. He might not survive. Young Lord Shu was captured. We are unsure of Young Lord Ming."

Lady Zheng wobbled in her place. Her husband placed a supportive arm around her, although his expression didn't change.

Kaiya made her best attempt at a sympathetic gaze. Nonetheless, all she could think about was Ming going missing. If she couldn't marry him, what was the next best option for legitimizing her sons? "Tell us what happened."

"*Dian-xia.*" The imperial soldier bowed again. "After we captured the Teleri's westernmost fort, our scouts reported a small army rapidly approaching by forced march. *Dajiang* Zheng Ming ordered us to deploy immediately. However, the enemy did not appear until a day later, with significantly larger numbers than originally reported. *Dajiang* ordered a general retreat under the cover of darkness, while he stayed back to destroy the fort's bridge. He never rejoined us."

Lady Zheng's shoulders heaved as she raised a hand to cover her mouth. Her eyes glossed over.

Lord Zheng patted her shoulder, but nodded toward the solider. "Did he succeed in destroying the bridge?"

The man bowed. "No. The Teleri main army was able to cross."

"Continue." Lord Zheng's voice remained steady.

The imperial officer looked up. "The enemy cut off our retreat, and though we fought valiantly, we did not have much firepowder. Young Lord Zheng Shu surrendered. They sent the two of us back with a message: Emperor Geros will arrive by dusk today to negotiate terms for our prisoners' release."

Dusk! Despite Kaiya's mental haze, two things were clear. First, the chance of an expedient marriage to Ming had dwindled, along with the chance of legitimizing her sons. Second, Geros was close by.

Oh, to get back to her room, close her eyes and think.

Lady Zheng jabbed an accusing finger at her. "You. It is *your* fault. My sons went to rescue *you*. Now one might have already joined his youngest brother in the grave, while another is a prisoner of war, and the eldest is missing. You are a curse on our family."

There was no denying the accusation. Kaiya was the cause of the Zheng family misfortune. If only she could *feel* the remorse as she bowed her head, contrite, as if it would make her any less a monster.

Yet it was the least of her concerns at the moment. In a castle whose lord contemplated rebellion, her standing had just become more tenuous. If she weren't pregnant with Tian's sons, Lord Zheng might just as soon use her as a bargaining chip. If he knew just how valuable she was to Emperor Geros…

Still holding her bow, she found Lord Zheng in the corner of her eye.

He stared at her, expression empty. If only it was easier to read him, to know what he was thinking. Beside him, Lady Zheng glared, lips pursed and brows furrowed.

At this point, Kaiya's only worth to Lady Zheng was as a womb for her grandchildren.

If they were her grandchildren at all.

Lord Zheng waved a hand toward his guards and councilors. "Everyone, out."

The men exchanged glances, but rose all the same. They bowed and filed out of the room in a rustling flash of court robes.

"You too." Lord Zheng nodded at his wife, whose eyes widened. He then jerked his head at Jie and Weiyong. "Them as well. Princess Kaiya and I have matters to discuss in private."

Lady Zheng rose, hesitantly, keeping her eyes on her husband. Kaiya nodded to Jie and Weiyong.

Once they were gone and the doors to the audience chamber shut, Lord Zheng shifted to stand directly in front of Kaiya.

He bowed low, then rose and made direct eye contact. "I am afraid my wife is too emotional. All she can focus on now is her sons. As lord of this province, I must look beyond that."

With a nod, Kaiya quoted the Founder's consort: "'At times, the ruler must make personal sacrifices for the good of his people.'"

He sighed. "Yes. I have been thinking your situation over. It might very well be that in order to protect all of Cathay, I will lose my sons. You realize what this means for your sons, my grandsons?"

Kaiya nodded again. "I—"

"I have a solution." He bowed low. "Forgive me for proposing this: if I take you as my wife, the realm would think the boys were mine."

What? He couldn't be serious. That solution was even more unpalatable than marrying Ming. Thank the

Heavens for the *Tiger's Eye,* allowing her to stay objective.

Lady Zheng had no such objectivity. Her gasp could be heard from outside the room. The doors flew open, and she stomped in with several guards on her heels.

Jie, face flushed scarlet, slipped in behind them.

"Don't you dare." Lady Zheng pointed an impertinent finger at Kaiya. "Conniving whore! You will spread your imperial legs for anyone to get your son on the Dragon Throne."

It had been Lord Zheng's suggestion, and she was getting blamed! Even with the objectivity of the *Tiger's Eye*, her moral compass could never allow her to do such a thing to another woman.

She shook her head. "I did not agree. I do not care about the throne, only that Cathay survives."

Lady Zheng spat. "Cathay will survive whether or not a Wang sits on the throne."

Kaiya shifted and bowed low to Zheng Han. "I must decline. The Edict of Marriage, as promulgated by Queen Regent Wang Yuxiang, ended polygamy in the Empire three hundred years ago. I would not have you discard your wife of three decades. There must be another solution."

Lord Zheng eyed her, his expression blank again. "At least consider it. We must have a contingency plan if Emperor Geros demands more than we can offer in return for my sons. Now return your room and rest. You will need all your energy when we meet with him this afternoon."

That was the worst possible scenario. Up to now, only a handful of people knew she'd been Geros' prisoner, pressured into his bed to guarantee the safety of hostages.

If he saw her, he'd demand she be turned over as part of any prisoner exchange. If he told others that she carried his child, then Lord Zheng would trade her for his sons without a second thought. Lady Zheng might push her out the gates herself.

No; whatever else one could say about Geros, he was a smart man. He would downplay Kaiya's value so that he could demand more for the Zheng brothers. Though a new problem occurred to her.

Would the emotional armor of the *Tiger's Eye* hold strong if she faced her rapist?

Jie had figured out many ways to get around without sending the nightingale floors into a chorus of chirps. Stepping in the right spot, pop-vaulting at corners and other acrobatic tricks made the castle a virtual playground.

Of course, going through windows and climbing along the outside walls bypassed the chirpy corridors altogether. She now hid just outside of Lord Zheng's bedroom antechamber, eavesdropping.

He wouldn't find comfort in Lady Zheng's arms tonight.

"You Turtle's Egg! How could you even consider abandoning me?" If Lady Zheng's voice were any sharper, Jie's knives would be jealous.

"Calm down, my love," Lord Zheng said. "It would be in name only."

"Liar! You just want a pretty young princess in your bed."

His silence was damning. Well, that would explain Ming. The shit didn't fall far from the bull's ass.

At last, he spoke. "It was your idea to gain power for myself, to declare Dongmen independent. This is our chance—"

"Not at the expense of my sons. You have already given up on them, too. That little harlot is wrapping her tentacles around you."

Lord Zheng sighed. "Our sons are lost anyway. What they will ask—passage through the Wall—will mean the end of our province, the end of Cathay."

His footsteps approached the window, and Jie crouched lower. He pushed open the shutters. When he spoke again, she heard the smile in his voice. "What I propose will make us rulers of all of Cathay. Tian's son, legitimized by my name, will sit on the Dragon Throne with the Mandate of Heaven, and we will rule as regent."

"And this has nothing to do with your desire to bed the princess?"

"Of course not!" His answer was much too quick, much too defensive. Would Lady Zheng see through it?

A bell tolled, indicating the fifteenth hour of the day. When Lord Zheng left the window, Jie crept back along the walls toward the princess' chambers. With the Teleri arriving in two hours, the princess would have to make some difficult choices about her future.

And also, perhaps, the future of Cathay.

Chapter 10:
The Doe-Eyed Girl

Sitting cross-legged in the cool grass, Feneyas leaned back and lifted his head to the warm rays of the spring sun. They danced in orange hues over his eyelids. Silky tresses brushed warmth across his lap. He opened his eyes and looked down.

A stream of black rippled across his legs, pillowing an ethereal face. The perfect lines of a delicate jaw accentuated high cheekbones and the slim nose of the young human woman as she slept.

The beauty opened her eyes.

Those eyes! Large and liquid like a doe's, they met his. Unbidden, his heart pounded.

"Heavens!" Her voice could have been an angel's, and she spoke in a language whose familiarity could only be his mother tongue.

A cool breeze blew a tendril of hair across her cheek, and he brushed it out of the way. Who was this girl, and why did she seem so familiar?

She sat up with the grace of a willow branch in the breeze. She swept delicate hands over her robe and through her hair before turning back to him. Chin down in a pout, she looked up at him through her lashes.

All the racing thoughts jolted to a stop. When he bent forward and cupped her face in his hands, she closed her eyes and parted her lips.

Thus invited, he brought his lips to the hollow between her collarbones. He pressed several kisses up the smooth skin of her neck.

She tilted forward to meet his lips…

***

Feneyas sat straight up on a soft fur blanket. The Doe-Eyed Girl was gone. His chest ached as if someone had torn his heart out.

He looked around, and paused where a little elf girl sat, staring at him. Just like Kiri, her rounded features spoke of familiarity and human blood. On closer inspection, she might have been his rescuer's younger sister, or perhaps even a younger version of the half-elf.

"You awake," the girl squeaked in the foreign language he understood.

He shook out the sleep and his strange dream, blinking his eyes. Sun filtered in through the tree canopy, dappling the platform in light. The elf woman who'd prayed for him was gone; though, as he rotated his shoulder, so was the pain. A male stood on a branch nearby, bow in hand.

The little girl scrunched up her nose and pointed at him. "Come. You stink. Bath."

Feneyas eased himself up, his joints complaining from lack of use.

She beckoned him, then skipped down the stairs of branches.

At the bottom of the tree, she turned south. The rustling sounds of the river grew louder. Nobody else was around, yet eyes followed him from up in the trees. Even when he gazed directly back, there were only treetops with sun peeking through leaves and branches.

"Come, Feneyas." The girl tugged at his bare arm and they slipped through a gap in boulders.

On the other side, a small waterfall tumbled into a circular pool, about three times as long as a man's height. Above, the canopy of trees opened to allow sunlight to filter in.

Standing in waist-high water near the waterfall with her back to him, Kiri looked over her shoulder to acknowledge his arrival. Long, thin scars crisscrossed her toned back. A large blotch marred the vertebra at the base of her neck. She beckoned him. "Come in."

Something felt wrong about a grown man bathing with a—

"What's wrong?" Kiri turned all the way around, exposing smooth, unscarred skin. Feneyas averted his eyes.

"*Ish oklerk krazt sho, grztck.*" Kiri's ear-splitting words sounded nothing like the flowery language she spoke among the other elves. Nonetheless, they had a familiar ring to them.

The younger girl nodded. The tilt of her head revealed a similar scar at the base of her neck. She slipped through the gap in the rocks, leaving Feneyas and Kiri alone.

"Get in. You stink so bad, I can smell you from here." She took a step back, closer to the waterfall. "I am not going to hurt you. If I had ill intentions, I would have left you to bleed out among the Metal Men."

Wherever he was from, they must have different conventions. Keeping his eye on the water, Feneyas eased half a toe in the pool.

Kiri giggled. "Aren't you going to take off your pants? They need washing, for sure, but…"

Heat rose to his cheeks. He spun around, loosened his pants' drawstrings, and stepped out. Covering himself, he turned back around. He focused on her forehead.

Her expression stiffened and she placed a hand on her chest. "I'm sorry. I didn't realize you were injured *there*. Did *they* hold you prisoner, too? Was it punishment?"

Injured? Punishment?

Why did she emphasize *they* and shudder? Feneyas shook his head. "I am *not* injured or punished. At least, I don't think so. It's just that… well, where I'm from… men and women don't bathe together."

Her face brightened and her mouth opened in a contagious smile. "What? So silly." She took a step to the side, which elevated her. The water now came up to the middle of her thighs. "To think I was concerned about you. Now get in and wash off your stench."

Feneyas looked back down. Maybe the heat in his cheeks would cause the pool to boil. Still concealing himself, he waded in. Through the cold, clear water, his feet squished into the bluish sand of the pool's floor. Several smooth rocks rose out of the sand. Only when he was submerged to the waist did he lift his hands and hug himself to counter the chill. He faced away from her.

"You *are* funny." Behind him, Kiri's hand plunged into the pool with a splash and came out with a rush of water. Something swished through the air toward him.

Without conscious thought, Feneyas shifted to the side and caught a wet cloth as it passed above his shoulder. He turned and glared.

"Wow…" Kiri's eyes rounded like river pebbles for a split second. "Use that to scour the dried blood off." Her surprise transformed into an ear-to-ear grin, reminiscent of a temple guard dog.

Temple?

The memory of a knee-high, white-furred dog flashed through his mind. If only he could step back and see the sign by the temple door, maybe it would spark more recollections.

"Hey, you there?" Kiri asked.

He looked up and nodded.

She chuckled. "What did you dream about in the realm between life and death?"

"A beautiful girl with doe eyes." He scrubbed vigorously, turning his honey skin pink.

Kiri cocked her head. "Did you know her?"

"She seemed familiar."

"Maybe someone important to you. A sister, perhaps."

He shrugged. Kissing a sister felt as wrong as bathing with a girl. "Maybe."

"Here, let me help you with your back." She waded over.

Feneyas flinched, and then froze up when her warm hand pressed on his back.

With her other hand, she reached around and pried the washcloth from his fingers. "Wow, you have quite a few scars."

"So do you. Where did you get them from?" Perhaps having something to talk about would keep his mind off the awkwardness of having the girl wash him.

She froze in place, and he turned around. Tight lips and a faraway gaze replaced her usually mischievous expression and flippant demeanor. Apparently, he was breeching taboo territory.

"No need to—"

Without looking at him, Kiri dropped the washcloth in his hand and sloshed to the edge of the pool. After brushing the water off with her hands, she snatched up a towel on the bank and dried herself off.

Feneyas waded toward his own clothes, still shy about covering himself. By the time he got one foot through the pants legs, Kiri had already thrown on her clothes and was disappearing through the crack in the rocks.

"Kiri!" Feneyas hurried after her, nearly tripping on the second pant leg.

When he made it through the gap, Kiri was crouched by the opening, looking outward. She held an open palm behind her in the universal sign to stop.

Feneyas slid forward and knelt, craning his neck just above Kiri's shoulder.

A human woman in a deerskin dress ran on the path below, her feet crunching in the dry underbrush as she clutched a bundle of cloth to her chest. Her long dark hair, braided back in a single queue, indicated she was married.

How did he know that?

Heavier footsteps cracked and thumped after her. Not far behind, two large men gained ground with loping strides. A golden nine-pointed sun embroidery blazed on the left breast of their black surcoats. Longswords and daggers thudded against their hips and thighs.

Feneyas started to rise, but Kiri pulled him down. She glared at him with eyebrows ferociously knitted together. He stopped in place and evaluated the scene unfolding below.

One of the soldiers dashed past the woman and stopped to cut her off. She skidded to a halt, just as the other came up from behind and seized her shoulder. He whipped her around with a sneer.

"Come back quietly, and your punishment will be lenient." His words were in yet another foreign language, one Feneyas also understood.

Apparently, the woman didn't. She tried to twist out of his grasp, screaming in a language similar to the one Feneyas used to communicate with the elves. "Let go, stop!"

The first man snatched one of her arms and yanked. The swaddled package she held started to wail.

Every instinct screamed to observe. It wasn't his fight.

A small voice tugged at him, reminiscent of the Doe-Eyed Girl's, from his dream. *You must help.*

But with what? He looked down at his hand to find Kiri's knife, though it was barely large enough to skin a rabbit. Nonetheless, it felt right in his hand, and the voice prodded him out into the open.

"You!" Feneyas emerged from the gap, speaking the same language as the men, though it came out haltingly. "Let her go."

Soldiers and woman all stopped and gawped, the baby's crying and Kiri's hiss cutting through the sudden silence.

"The ghost of the Warrior From Beyond the Wall," the woman whispered in awed tones.

The solider on the right smirked as he slid his sword out and pointed it. "This doesn't concern you. Go back where you came from and we will let you live."

"I have a dozen archers. Their arrows are trained on you." Feneyas pointed behind them. "Go back where you came from. We will let *you* live." Would they believe his bluff?

"Then shoot." The second man spread his arms wide, inviting an attack.

When nothing happened, he jerked his head back up the path. "Come on, let's take her back."

Kiri whispered through her teeth, "What are you telling them?"

One man seized the crook of the woman's arm, spun, and started to walk away. The other kept his sword pointed at Feneyas and backed up. When he turned his head toward his comrade, Feneyas hefted a stone and flung it.

The rock smacked into the soldier's temple, sending him tumbling to the ground.

Feneyas picked up another and hurled it. The other man released the woman and covered his face. The stone slammed into his arm.

Staggering back, the soldier rubbed the wound.

Feneyas landed on the ground in a crouch, not even remembering his jump.

What was he thinking? Armed only with a small knife, he didn't stand a chance against the angry soldier who now brandished a longsword.

Hack, chop, thrust—Feneyas turned out of the line of each attack as he closed in. Up close, he yanked his opponent's dagger out of its sheath with his left hand, joining his own knife in a crossing arc. The blades sliced through the flexor tendons of the man's sword arm, causing his fingers to go limp.

Sweeping out with the knife in his right hand, he slashed the enemy's left wrist, while cutting through the tendons in his right knee. The man's weight buckled and he collapsed to his knees.

"Look out!" Kiri yelled from her spot on the boulders.

Feneyas twisted to the side, just avoiding the other warrior's downward chop. The blow clove through his comrade's shoulder, shattering the clavicle and at least two ribs.

Finishing his spin, Feneyas set the edge of the dagger flush against the soldier's radius, halfway up his forearm. As his opponent yanked his sword free of his companion, the dagger sliced through flesh and nerves, severing the thumb tendons.

The man's bellow carried through the forest, cut short when Feneyas drove the knife into his neck.

The native woman huddled over and covered her mouth, her shoulders heaving. The baby continued wailing.

Kiri jumped down, appearing not the least bit fazed as she surveyed his handiwork. "Wow."

Feneyas stared at the dead men and then at his own hands. Killing felt wrong, even if these soldiers might've deserved it.

Everything had happened so fast, and he'd acted so instinctively. Somewhere in his lost memories was combat training. He brushed his hands on his pants and paced over to the woman. "Are you okay?"

Her ruddy complexion faded green, hand still over her mouth. She looked first at him, then at Kiri. After a few deep breaths, she spoke. "You must be the Warrior Beyond the Wall. Brought back by a Messenger of the Gods." She nodded toward Kiri.

Straightening, Kiri cleared her throat and took on an authoritative tone. "Yes. Now go back home and tell your people of the gods' glory."

"Wait." Feneyas held a hand up to Kiri while he held the woman's gaze. "You said the Warrior Beyond the Wall. I don't remember him."

The woman shook her head, her eyes sad. "It *must* be you. Poor man. It is said that the reborn forget who they are."

Kiri nodded vigorously. "Yes. The spirits have said as much. Now, hurry home before more of the Metal Men return."

Feneyas glared back at her. "Wait. Tell me more."

"Our shamans," the woman said, "have told stories that you came from beyond the Wall and dwelled among the Maki tribespeople. Taught them how to fight. But then you were killed rescuing the Willow Beauty from the Castle of Trees. So the stories say."

Kiri looked him up and down. Apparently, she didn't believe the story any more than he.

"Where is the Castle of Trees?" Perhaps he could learn more about his identity by backtracking. Maybe find out who the Willow Beauty was.

Forehead crinkled, Kiri shrugged. "Never heard of it."

The woman, however, pointed back down the trail. "Maybe five days' walk, that way. The Metal Men defiled the forest and built the Castle of Trees by the Great River's north bank."

Feneyas followed her finger. "Is your home in that direction? May I accompany you?"

The woman's eyes widened. "The village would be honored—"

"No." Kiri rose up to her full height, admittedly only up to Feneyas' chest, yet she projected an air of authority. "First, your shaman must perform the correct rituals, and the spirits will determine whether or not he will go."

Feneyas met her gaze and she winked. He rolled his eyes with a sigh.

The woman placed a hand on her chest and headed up the trail. Somewhere, in that direction, he would find out more about his life.

Chapter 11:
Victory Without Fighting

The sweet evergreen forest below the Great Wall's East Gate obscured the invading army. Still, the low rumble of drums told Kaiya exactly where they were. The beat carried above even the roar of the spring-swollen waterfall half a *li* away.

Soon, too soon, she would see Emperor Geros again.

She only hoped the stifling lamellar armor hid her identity as well as the *Tiger's Eye* buried her emotions. The steel helmet would've weighed her head down if she'd been in perfect health; still recovering from her wound, it might as well have been a dwarf anvil. It was the price she paid for the T-slit which exposed only her eyes.

The drums stopped. Black flags emblazoned with the Teleri's gold sun emerged from the tree line, almost a sixty feet below, borne by a dozen soldiers. A single white flag of parley fluttered alone among the swaths of black. A man, larger than all the rest, marched at the head of the procession.

Even though his features remained obscured by distance, his confident gait and sheer size announced the arrival of Geros.

Memories of his muscled mass pinning her down, taking, sent a chill down her spine. He'd violated her body and crushed her soul. The recollection was too close, too personal compared to her other memories. She faltered back a step.

A hand, Jie's, pressed between her shoulder blades. The small gesture served as a reminder that Kaiya was not alone.

Around her, provincial musketmen trained their weapons on the unwelcome visitors. Lord Zheng Han stood by her side, accompanied by officers and lords, and fortunately not his emotional wife. Imperial soldiers from the local garrison were also conspicuously absent.

Geros wouldn't be able to pick her out from all of the men, not from this distance. The fear disappeared just as quickly as it had appeared. Kaiya straightened, squaring her shoulders as well as her energy allowed.

The enemy formation came to a halt. A single officer stepped forward and yelled, "I present Emperor Geros of the Teleri Empire."

If only she had the power of her voice. Conventions and rules of parley be damned, she would command the musketmen to fire on him.

Geros strode to the fore. "Great Zheng Han, Lord of East Gate Province, open the gates and swear loyalty to me."

Lord Zheng burst out laughing. "We Cathayi believe a man can only have one master. I already owe allegiance to the Son of Heaven, *Tianzi* Kai-Wu Wang. He happens to be on this side of the Wall."

Though truth be told, Lord Zheng had not acted as such over the last couple of days.

Geros' voice boomed loud in Kaiya's ears despite the distance and elevation between them. "And what has that allegiance gained you? New lands? Rewards of gold and silver? Auspicious marriages?"

"The Teleri Empire cannot offer me lands," Lord Zheng said. "Nor does the Bovyan race believe in marriages. Only a traitor, who would be reviled until history ends, would take treasure to betray his lord."

Geros shook his head. "I offer you all of Cathay. You will be governor, to administer the will of the Teleri Directori. You will rule your own province as an allied independent state. All you have to do is give me control of the East Gate."

Murmurs erupted among the gathered lords. Kaiya was among those who turned to gauge Lord Zheng's reaction.

After his indecent proposal and Jie's report, she'd expected him to reject any offer—at the cost of his sons—and then take her to his bed, by force if she refused. This new proposal might be too sweet to decline.

He remained silent, face blank.

Emperor Geros, on the other hand, grinned. "Consider this, Lord Zheng. Cathay rots from the inside, with corrupt ministers and greedy lords undermining the nation for their own gain. Multiple enemies wait on the outside, ready to invade. We will restore order and prosperity, and defend your borders."

The weasel! Kaiya bit her lip. Cathay's belligerent neighbors acted only on Geros' bidding. It would not be surprising if he had somehow meddled in Cathay's internal affairs as well.

Lord Zheng echoed her suspicions. "I imagine our neighbors would behave differently if you ordered them to. I—"

"I have offered them generous rewards, as I will to you. Your title as Governor shall pass to your sons and grandsons."

Kaiya shuddered, knowing what would happen next.

The Teleri ranks parted and two soldiers pushed forth their gagged prisoners.

A shaky young man, his steps faltering.

A man almost entirely wrapped in bandages, dangling between two large Bovyans.

And Ming. Now accounted for.

He kept his chin high and walked tall. Despite his proximity, a marriage seemed farther away than ever. It was past time to consider a new course of action. For now, however, it remained to be seen how the events would play out.

With their resemblance to Ming and Tian, the other two prisoners were undoubtedly Shu and Lun. Lord Zheng's stoic expression wavered for a split second.

Remaining motionless to avoid drawing Geros' attention to herself, she spoke. "Lord Zheng, if you open the gates to the Great Wall—"

"Silence," he hissed through gritted teeth. When he spoke out loud, it must have been for her benefit. "My family has defended the East Gate for three hundred years. This is not a decision I can make without the counsel of my vassals and advisors."

"Do not deliberate too long." Geros reached over and yanked Shu's arm, eliciting a yelp from the young man. "I will remove one of your son's fingers each hour that I do not hear a satisfactory response. You have ten hours before I remove his head."

Lord Zheng's shoulders slumped. "You will have my answer within an hour."

When the flags of parley retreated back into the forest, he turned around and strode toward the stairs. His advisors followed close behind.

Kaiya tore off the helm and stumbled to keep up with him. The armor might have well been a ship's anchor.

"Lord Zheng, I never took you to be a collaborator. If you do this—"

Her jerked around and planted a finger in her chest. "If I do this, then my sons will live and pray for our ancestors and my own repose."

Since when had the great lords of mighty Cathay given up so easily? They must have grown complacent after three hundred years of peace. With the armor of the Great Wall and a hundred thousand rifles pointed out, the nation's soul had rotted within.

She took Lord Zheng's sleeve in her feeble grip, not believing what she was about to say. Despair crept in through her emotional armor, nearly breaking her resolve. "Please, wait. Marry me, take my sons as yours so that they might one day rule. Just keep the Teleri out of Cathay."

He wiped her hand away and turned. "I already have sons. I will rule, and so will they."

"Only as slaves to the Bovyan scourge. I—"

"Guards, take her to my family temple."

She reached for him again, using all her energy to lift her arms, to no avail. Her voice failed her, coming out no louder than a whisper. "Offer me. Offer me for your sons, but don't let them in."

He didn't acknowledge her. Perhaps he hadn't even heard her plea over the jangle of armor.

Then, he snorted. His stride lengthened and he disappeared behind a wall of trailing soldiers.

The truth. It was time to admit the truth. Surely Geros would trade Zheng's sons for her. Kaiya's lips moved, but no words came out.

She couldn't even speak, let alone channel the power of her voice. Unable to keep up with Lord Zheng's brisk pace without losing her breath, Kaiya had no hope of changing his mind. She hunched over and gasped for air as two guards came to either side of her.

The fleeting emotions rippled and eased enough for the *Tiger's Eye* to focus her. There was another way to keep the Teleri out.

Kaiya straightened and lifted her chin. Even if her voice held no magic, it still carried the tone of imperial authority. "Wait. Withdraw and give me a moment with my handmaiden."

Both soldiers took several respectful steps back and bowed their heads.

She beckoned to the Insolent Retainer. "Jie, scout out the Teleri army's numbers and weapons."

"What should I do if I find the Young Lords and cannot expedite their escape?" Jie stared at her feet.

The underlying question spoke more loudly than if Jie had yelled it out at the top of her lungs. The only leverage Geros had was Zheng Han's sons. Remove the sons from the trading block…

The dilemma gnawed at Kaiya's conscience. Could she trade the lives of three men for the livelihood of millions? The *Tiger's Eye* might have stifled her emotions, but her moral compass remained.

Yet she was forced to admit the real reason behind her order to scout out the enemy. The half-elf would not have the same compunctions toward taking away Geros' bargaining leverage, and Kaiya could wash her hands of the decision.

Until Jie asked.

The *Tiger's Eye,* battered by hopelessness, crumbled around her. Despair and guilt threatened to keep her from verbalizing what she must. Tears blurred her vision.

"Take away Geros' leverage."

As much as Jie disliked Young Lord Zheng Ming, the thought of murdering him didn't sit well in her stomach. It was the logical decision, one which the princess had forced through the crumbling wall of the *Tiger's Eye*.

It had reformed almost as soon as she choked the words out, standing as strong and steadfast as the Great Wall, which Jie climbed down before sneaking up on the Teleri camp.

With a skillset geared toward urban operations, each step on the uneven forest floor made her cringe. A twig here, dried pine needles there, all ready to crackle and reveal her location. Not that she would have to worry, since the Bovyans made enough noise to disturb the dead.

The sentries, placed every thirty feet along the perimeter of their camp, jingled in their chainmail. Other soldiers sat and sharpened weapons, the metal on whetstone whispering loud enough to mask her steps. Most soldiers leaned against trees and slept.

Jie skirted the edges of the encampment, taking count. About six thousand heavy infantry in the vanguard. In the field, they might overwhelm Dongmen's provincial armies if they were able to close to melee range without taking devastating losses from musket fire. They would never stand a chance trying to breach the Great Wall.

Using trees and marching soldiers as cover, she then made her way into the heart of the army. Sixteen officers gathered around a fallen tree, discussing options in the event the cowardly gate lord refused their passage.

Ming and Lun were nowhere to be found. Zheng Shu however, sat at the end of the log, hands bound with rope. Sweat trickled down his brow, despite the cool afternoon breeze. A guard stood cross-armed beside him.

While Tian had always worshipped his eldest brother Ming, and admired his second brother Lun, Shu was more of a peer. Like Tian, Shu preferred painting over swordplay. From the way his eyes flicked nervously about now, he didn't seem suited as a warrior. The poor man didn't deserve death at her hands.

Jie could kill the guard, but not without drawing the attention of the officers just a few feet away. The camp would rouse, limiting her options. She needed to find Lun and Ming and reevaluate the feasibility of killing all three.

Creeping back through the enemy's camp, she happened upon the supply van. With the last leg of the ancient highway yet to be restored, the Teleri had relied on porters: a thousand Cathayi prisoners of war, connected to each other with rope around their necks. It must have been a nightmare trying to traipse through underbrush at a quick pace while carrying packs of supplies.

A hundred enemy soldiers stood watch over her countrymen as they rested against trees. There was little she could do for them by herself. Lun lay flat, breathing heavily.

Still no sign of Ming among them. Smart, keeping the most important hostages separated. The minute she rescued or killed one, the Teleri would secure the others. The mission was hopeless.

Jie leaned against a tree and stifled a sigh. When had she ever been so defeatist? Just over a week ago, she'd stormed an impregnable fortress against overwhelming odds to rescue the princess. Before that, she would've never dismissed a task as impossible out of hand.

Ming's grating voice hissed from beyond the camp. "Do three of you really need to watch a man squat and empty his bowels?"

Jie shook the image out of her mind, even as everyone else within earshot snickered. She then worked her way toward the source of his voice.

On the outskirts of the camp, three bareheaded Bovyans surrounded him. Their sheer size obscured Ming's bent-over form, much to Jie's relief. Imagining him in the act was bad enough; she would've never been able to scrub the actual sight from her memory.

Plans formed: Draw the guards away and ambush them one at a time. Use the prisoners as a diversion. There wasn't enough time for either, unless Ming suffered from constipation. Besides killing Ming, that left only one option — a direct attack.

A single armored Bovyan would have little trouble beating her in a fair fight. Three would be suicide. Which was why she did not fight fair.

She crept from tree to tree until she was just a few feet from the back of the closest guard.

Modulating her voice to imitate Geros', she used a *Ghost Echo* technique to throw her voice behind the other two guards. "Men, over here!"

As soon as their heads started to jerk toward the source of her trick, Jie leaped onto the closest man's back and lodged a knife into his throat. His legs wobbled, and she dragged him down to his knees. When the farthest guard glanced down at his fallen comrade, she sent a throwing star whirling into his face.

Even before the second skidded into a convulsing pile, Jie slipped behind the kneeling man as he clutched his throat and choked up blood.

Turning back and forth, the remaining guard yanked his longsword from his sheath. Ming, pants down around his ankles, swept his gaze left and right, his mouth gaping. His right shoulder hung in a sling.

Jie threw her voice again, behind the remaining enemy. "Intruders, over here!"

He looked over his shoulder.

She darted across the spot, careful not to step in Ming's business, and lunged into a scissor-kick.

He toppled onto his knees and fell back in a jingling heap, while she used her momentum to spring up. She landed mounted on his chest and drove her knife into his eye socket.

Too much noise, so sloppy on her part. She turned to Ming and immediately averted her eyes. "Come on, come on, pants up, on your feet! You can wipe later!"

Ming wiggled his pants up with his free hand. "Jie! You came for me."

For him, indeed. "Princess Kaiya sent me." To kill him. "Now come on." Jie broke into a run, pulling Ming deeper into the forest. She took care to pull his sleeve, not his hand.

Behind them, the Teleri camp roused to life.

Chapter 12:
In Search of Self

Ming shuddered at the prospect of being stuck with the impertinent half-elf for the rest of his life. Their last journey together had involved a pyramid, two magic gemstones, and a hundred belligerent charlatans; and it hadn't been the charlatans who came closest to killing him.

A certain half-elf had.

He stepped on a branch, sending a loud crack echoing through the woods.

She pulled him down into the brush, then poked her head up and looked around. The last jerk of her head put those evil eyes directly on him.

She hissed at him in a low whisper, "If you're going to make so much noise, then stop clinging to me like a wet leaf. Go home."

Go home. If only he could; but that choice evaporated days ago. It wasn't like he could have waltzed through the Bovyan horde to the gatehouse, or scaled the Wall like she suggested. Especially not with his shoulder still hurting. He brushed himself off with his good arm, avoiding eye contact with his tormentor.

And provider.

She opened up that magic pouch of hers, the one with infinite space that the elf hag Ayana had given her, and pulled out some jerky.

His stomach rumbled at the aroma. He flashed his most smoldering gaze, the one which had charmed many a woman into his bed.

Jie rolled her eyes and thrust the dried meat into his face. Ah, the smell of home, the special spice mix that the castle chef made. All the food she pulled out of that pouch undoubtedly came from Dongmen Castle, so technically it was his, anyway.

She had left prepared. They had followed the Kanin River upstream for what, six days now? But why? He mumbled out his words as he chewed. "So where are we going?"

"I've told you." She threw her hands up. "We—I mean, *I* am looking to sabotage the Teleri supply lines."

She *had* told him. Each of the dozen times he had asked. However, he knew women, and Jie's focus and determination went beyond duty. There was more, and eventually she would relent and tell him.

Jie stared at Ming's sleeping form, curled up on dried leaves, and sighed. Why hadn't she followed Princess Kaiya's orders and just put him out of his misery?

Because he was Tian's brother.

Tian didn't even like to kill enemies, and would be even less pleased if she'd murdered the brother he'd once adored so much. Of course, no matter how many times she threatened Ming over the last year, she'd never really intended to follow through.

Which didn't explain why she hadn't just left him behind after the improbable rescue. She pulled the blanket up over him. The last thing she needed was for him to catch cold and slow her down.

He'd already slowed her down enough. At least on their quest in Selastya, he could swing a sword and shoot a bow.

Well. *Really* well, if she had to grudgingly admit it. He had dropped fake Akolytes, Bovyan shock troops, and an altivorc who nearly killed her.

She pried back the dressing on his shoulder to inspect the wound. Whatever else she could say about the Bovyans, they knew battlefield medicine.

Even so, Ming might never pull a bowstring again, and they didn't have a sword for him to swing with his good arm. Even with the knife she loaned him—well, gave him, because she sure didn't want it back after he put his paws on it—he didn't stand a chance against a ten-year-old version of herself in a knife fight.

And the incessant questions.

Question.

Where are we going?

The one which she answered with the same half-truth.

Out. There.

Away from princesses and responsibilities and intrigue and wars. Pick a direction and walk, until the food and supplies she'd appropriated from the castle halved. Which was much faster with Ming's appetite.

Jie stared out into the forest, her elf vision picking out the hues of green.

Somewhere out there, she would find herself again. Ming would provide the semi-intelligent human interaction she needed to remain sane, or at least be a practice dummy to keep her tongue sharp. And if he got them both killed first, so be it.

Though the wild elves didn't forbid Feneyas from leaving, he didn't know the first thing about surviving in the wilderness. When a search for his identity meant a slow death by exposure and starvation, the treetop village became a prison. If he wasn't their prisoner, he was their virtual pet, performing tricks in return for their generosity.

At least the tricks kept him occupied.

He sidestepped a sword thrust and dumped the young elf man to the ground with a clip of his arms.

Another elf stepped into the ring of warriors, spinning a quarterstaff in rapid circles. As the weapon swept in a broad arc toward his knees, Feneyas leapt over it with a butterfly twist and landed up close. He seized his opponent's hand in one of his, and the end of the staff in the other, and rotated it so that it put his opponent into a wrist lock.

How could he do all this? No matter how, he was living up to his reputation as the Warrior Beyond the Wall.

Whatever that meant.

From what his new friend Dior had said, an enormous Wall rose up along the western edge of the Wilds. Humans who looked like Feneyas lived on the other side. Perhaps the mysterious Doe-Eyed Girl walked among them.

He could go east to the Wall, or west to the human village, and find out more about himself; yet here he was, trapped in a village in the trees. Spending each day sparring with elves who wanted to see if he was as good as Kiri said.

At times, he'd accompany Kiri and her little sister Kala when they gathered spring shoots and searched for mushrooms. Perhaps eventually, he would know enough about safe food to set off on his own, but in the meantime…

Wait, his hosts said.

Wait for what? Feneyas swiped an arrow out of the air and tracked it back to its origin.

Dior grinned. "I was aiming to miss, anyway!"

Perhaps. No matter what good hosts the elves were, they still made him wait, all to maintain a charade.

Proper channels, Kiri had said. The elves fed the native humans' superstitions, tricking them into believing they were spirits. It seemed like a dishonest means of control, but Kiri claimed it was for everyone's protection. The elves stayed out of sight, while the local humans, who called themselves Kanin, made regular requests to the messengers of the gods.

Over the last several days, the requests had multiplied. Small forest animals came by, visiting Nayori, the older woman who had healed him. Powerful in magic, the elf was the closest thing to the wild elves' leader, at least as far as he could tell. The birds and squirrels apparently delivered requests from Kanin tribal shamans.

Feneyas snorted. As if animals could talk.

He used the arrow he'd caught to barely brush aside another sword thrust. A woman this time, who moved faster than any of the men thus far. He punched and thrust and tried to grab her, but Layani avoided all of his attacks with effortless grace. Her blade swirled in elegant twists and arcs, all of which missed.

On purpose. He raised his hands in surrender and bowed.

She was better. Maybe not in overall technique, but her speed and reflexes were like… memories of a brown-skinned man with a curved, guardless sword flashed in his head.

There was a name to the handsome face with its pointed beard. It taunted Feneyas' conscious mind, just out of reach.

He looked up at Layani, her expression as mirthless as always. "How do you move so fast?"

She shrugged. "You are just slow."

The spectators all burst out laughing, though none of them had even presented a credible challenge.

Kiri shook her head, even as the sides of her eyes crinkled. "No, Feneyas, it's her gift."

"Gift?"

"Martial magic," Dior said. "Some of us have it, some don't. Unlike our supposedly *civilized* brethren, we can't use all forms of magic."

Layani glared at Dior, then offered Feneyas a rare smile. "We are among the tribes which didn't believe Aralas was an angel sent by Koralas. Our ancestors didn't answer his call before the War of Ancient Gods. Nor did we leave our forest homes when his son became king of Aramysta and his daughter queen of Aerilysta. Unlike our kin, who have idle time to pursue a vast array of skills, we spend many of our waking hours providing for the village."

The fairy tale, or perhaps history, sounded familiar. A half-sized man with scruffy hair and mischievous eyes dashed through Feneyas' memory before he could catch it.

Nayori's voice danced in the tree tops. "Feneyas, come."

Yes, he was a pet. The fluffy white temple dog barked in his memories, but still gave him no sense of who he was or why a temple was important to him.

On instinct, he looked up to the voice. Just as each time before, there was nothing but the sun peeking in from the budding branches of countless trees.

Magic, Kiri had said. Bending limbs to the elves' fancy and creating an illusion for the rare passerby who glanced up.

She took him by the hand, as was her wont. Hers was warm and moist, her grin perky. She was always jovial, with a tongue as sharp as a *dao*, at least if he didn't try to bring up her past. She seemed so familiar; just being with her invoked a sense of comfort and contentment. The Warrior From Beyond the Wall must've had a younger sister in his former life.

Kiri pulled him toward the tree, the one with invisible stairs encircling it. He could only climb it with his eyes closed, lest he trip and fall.

Seventeen steps above the ground, the tree branch steps materialized around him. No matter how many times he climbed the stairs, the transition from nothingness to solidity was disconcerting.

At the top, on the village gathering platform, Nayori sat on a gnarled knot, holding a haughty chipmunk in her palm. As it chattered away, she nodded.

Feneyas exchanged glances with Kiri, who just added a shrug to her mischievous smile.

Nayori's gaze then lifted to meet his. "Feneyas, the eyes and ears of the forest have told us the Metal Men are marching in greater numbers than ever before, heading west. The village shamans have all requested the gods to send the Warrior Beyond the Wall to teach them to fight."

Feneyas nodded. "I want to go west. I want to meet other humans. Maybe they can tell me who I am."

Her eyes, seas of liquid brown, searched his. She hefted the chipmunk, who afforded Feneyas a smug look. "My little friend here comes from the Maki tribal lands. He tells me there is a shaman who claims he can tell you who you are."

Chapter 13:
Resolve

The roaring falls of the North Kanin River poured into the Cathay basin, drowning out all other sounds as Kaiya climbed from the palanquin. Along with Fang Weiyong and six provincial soldiers as *escort*, she made her way up the cliff path toward the Zheng family temple. The late afternoon sun danced in the falls' mist, forming a shimmering rainbow above the rocks.

Even with Fang Weiyong's support, her chest heaved as she fought for each breath. Pregnant, anemic, she struggled to climb the trail. If this short trip drained her, how could she hope to escape and make the three-day journey to the capital?

Weiyong apparently shared the same doubts. "*Dian-xia*, perhaps you should continue in the palanquin."

It was a sound suggestion, but Lady Zheng apparently wanted to make her trip as difficult as possible. The palanquin bearers waited at the bottom of the cliff. She shook her head and continued toward the flat bluffs halfway up.

Like the road, Zhengguang Temple was carved into the cliff face. Grateful to reach the waterfall pool overlook, Kaiya paused under the sloping tile eaves, which sparkled with condensation and sunlight. Heads turned and lips moved among the couple dozen common folk, and like a wave, they all sank to their knees.

It would not do to let them see her so haggard. Kaiya straightened her back and lifted her chin. She turned to the provincial soldiers. "Wait here. Weiyong, come with me."

The soldiers all bowed and held back.

Summoning all her grace, she glided through the red columns and into the temple. Trickles of smoke wafted from burning incense, cloying the air with a sweet fragrance. Light bauble braziers stood partially shuttered, casting the central chamber in a warm golden glow.

Several priests knelt and chanted before the Zheng family altar. Kaiya approached them, passing between two enormous statues holding silent vigil at the sides of the broad chamber. On the left stood Lord Guan, patron saint of warriors and guardian of the East Gate Province. Chest jutted out, he held a halberd whose haft touched the tiled ground and whose blade tip reached the vaulting ceiling. Wu-Long, the Dragon Protector of Cathay, faced him, coiling up from floor to roof.

One of the priests met her gaze. Word of her arrival passed among them, and they all turned in place and pressed their foreheads to the ground.

Kaiya's voice caught in her throat, and she had to clear it. "Rise." Her own voice sounded weak in her ears.

They all came out of their bows. The abbot rose to his feet and approached with his eyes politely averted. "*Dian-xia*, thank you for gracing us with your presence in this trying time. Did you come to pray for our soldiers?"

Kaiya nodded. "Yes. And while I pray, bring me the tablet of Zheng Tian, fourth son of Lord Zheng Han."

The abbot looked at her, his eyes searching hers in a display of impudence.

In the past, she might have feigned anger. Instead, she kept her voice level. "That is my command."

The abbot bowed and disappeared down a passageway behind the altar, hustling into the temple's depths.

She took several steps forward and bowed before the altar. All this time, she'd played games, planning and plotting ways to legitimize her children. She was no better than the ambitious lords and ministers who jockeyed for power back at court. Perhaps the gods were punishing her.

It was time to make things right. After praying for the Cathay soldiers' safety, she silently asked for forgiveness of the gods, and also of her true husband, Tian.

Outside the temple, at the edge of her hearing, a commotion broke out over the din of chanting monks and the raging waterfall. Before she could turn to see the source, the abbot returned with a hand-sized tablet.

Kaiya received it in two hands with her head bowed. All it took was a cursory scan to see Tian's birth name engraved. Was that a clenching of her stomach as she ran a finger across his birth and death dates?

In the only twelve days since he'd sacrificed himself so she could escape Geros, she'd abandoned his memory. She looked up and met the abbot's gaze. "You are not to tell anyone I have this."

"As the princess commands." He pressed his palms together and bowed.

Soft footsteps behind her drew her attention. She turned around to find Lady Zheng, dressed in silken riding robes, kneeling on the tile floor. Weiyong bowed low in apology.

"Lady Zheng," Kaiya said, "please rise."

The woman's eyes focused on Kaiya's hands. "You have Tian's tablet."

Kaiya bowed. "Yes, Mother."

The hard lines of Lady Zheng's face softened. "I have arranged for a regiment of imperial soldiers to escort you back to the capital."

That couldn't be right. How quickly an attitude could change. Kaiya raised an eyebrow. "You would betray your husband?"

"I have faith you will not betray yours." Lady Zheng offered a sad smile. "I cannot allow Teleri hands to sully the mother of my grandchildren and raise more questions about their legitimacy."

"Thank you, Mother." Kaiya kept her expression warm and grateful, despite the irony of Lady Zheng's words. As Father once said, sometimes half-truths and misdirection accomplished more good than the truth.

"You do not have long before my lord surrenders the gate. Make haste."

Kaiya bowed, then glided out of the temple, running her hand over the cool surface of the tablet as she did. Tian, her husband, jettisoned in the last few days for the sake of convenience. Her love, even though she couldn't feel it.

She'd take the tablet back to her family temple in Huajing, and have Fang Weiyong vest it with hers to formalize Tian's marriage into her family. She tucked the tablet into an inner pocket of her robe.

Outside, dozens of imperial soldiers dropped to one knee. "*Dian-xia!*" they proclaimed in unison. Around them, commoners pressed their foreheads to the ground.

Her energy flagging, Kaiya straightened. "Rise."

The soldiers rose and stepped to the side, revealing the palanquin and kneeling porters. She stumbled with her first step toward it, but Weiyong caught her by the arm. Both he and a captain helped her in.

Once the doors slid shut, she slumped into the padded chair, grateful for the chance to sit. Whereas the tight confines would usually send her into a panic, the *Tiger's Eye* kept her calm.

"Where to, *Dian-xia*?" Weiyong asked from outside.

"To the capital."

"If Emperor Geros finds out you are near, there is no way we can stay ahead of them."

Especially in her condition. The objectivity of her thoughts suggested the *Tiger's Eye* still held her emotions firmly in check. "Lord Zheng may betray Cathay, but I do not think he will betray the mother of his grandchildren."

"In any case," Fang Weiyong said, "enough people have seen you here. We cannot just leave by the highway."

"A diversion, then. Send the palanquin down the main highway with my guards, while you, Jie, and I will take a riverboat."

Weiyong's silence outside perhaps echoed Kaiya's own misgivings. Strategic diversions like this had failed her at least three times in the past. What would make it work this time?

"Weiyong," she said. "I don't think we have any other choice."

"Yes, *Dian-xia*." His voice wavered.

"Captain, send a runner to Count Du, telling him to expect us soon."

"As the princess commands," the captain said.

On her command, the palanquin set off toward the town bordering the waterfall's lake. The narrow confines, which in the past gripped her with terror, now provided a screen to hide her exhaustion.

After catching her breath, she slid the window open to see the ancient buildings, shrouded in mists. Even from a few *li* away, the commotion of worried townsfolk carried over the waters.

The noise grew as they made their way into the town. Commoners cleared the road for the palanquin. Perhaps the imperial soldiers drew the many points and murmurs.

"Fang Weiyong," she called through the window. "Make sure they know it is me."

He bowed in acquiescence, and then moved out of her line of site to the front of the palanquin. His usually timid voice rose, though its shyness remained. "Make way for Princess Kaiya."

A hush fell over the crowd. Like a wave, they sank to their knees, foreheads to the ground, rising with excited whispers as the palanquin passed. In a land where the Imperial Family was revered, hopefully her very presence gave them a sense of calm against the impending invasion.

Before long, they arrived at the villa of Count Du, the local *Yu-Ming* lord. She'd rejected his first son two years before, but he'd always been faithful to Father in the past. Then again, so had Lord Zheng.

As they approached the gates and passed through, Count Du's soldiers all dropped to a knee, fist to the ground.

The palanquin doors slid open, and Kaiya climbed out. The imperial soldiers serving as her escort and the villa guards all dropped into a salute.

Head bobbing, Count Du shuffled out to meet her. "*Dian-xia*, welcome. Had I known sooner, I would have made sure the entire town was out to greet you with waving banners of the Empire, and prepared a meal fit for the *Tianzi*."

Kaiya nodded. "I appreciate the sentiment all the same. Now, I ask that you allow me to stay here for an hour."

Count Du bowed. "It would be my honor."

Kaiya beckoned the captain of the imperial soldiers. "Leave eight of your best men to protect me. The rest of you, escort the palanquin down the highway toward Huajing."

Fang Weiyong startled from a dream and sat up straight on the thick blanket. Sweat clung to his neck and head, making the chill air of the guest room seem colder. Yes, he was near the great waterfall of Cathay, not back in his recurring nightmare.

He rubbed his neck, where then-First Consul Geros had held him aloft in Iksuvius Heights. To think the giant Bovyan and his cohorts gathered outside the walls, just half a day away. The more distance between them, the better.

Weiyong clambered out from beneath his covers and padded over to the carved wooden bed where Princess Kaiya slept. Her chest gently rose and fell, even as her brow furrowed and she hugged herself.

He pulled the covers over her, and her body relaxed. At least the stubborn young woman had listened to his suggestion, to rest at Count Du's pavilion until early morning. Much to the count's and his own chagrin, she insisted he stay in the room with her.

Now if only she would stop calling him by name. Weiyong might be a priest, her doctor, her Maki tribe brother, and her friend, but he was still a man.

A man who had no business wondering what it might be like to feel her lips against his.

Such a fool! He shook his head and stalked off to the window. Throwing open the shutters, he pushed his face out into the night air.

"Weiyong, is it already time to go?"

He turned around to find the princess sitting up on the bed. He dropped to his knees and bowed. "No, *Dian-xia*. We still have another hour before we set off for the docks. Please go back to sleep."

"You, too." She flashed a demure smile and eased herself back down.

His heart pounded in his chest, and he stared out the window. Once they returned to the capital, he could put more distance between her, too. But where to?

"That is my command."

He turned back and bowed, then shuffled back to his bedroll. Sleep did not come easily, and he spent the rest of the time staring at the ceiling tiles, trying not to think about beautiful princesses.

Hurried footsteps across wood floors jolted Kaiya out of sleep. Even so, she stayed buried beneath the covers, protected from the dark and cold.

"*Dian-xia*," an imperial soldier called from outside of the door. "We must reach the docks in an hour. Please get ready."

Groaning, she kicked off her blanket and sat up. Surprisingly, rest had done her good. Weiyong's herbal medicine probably helped, too.

She tightened her gown around her shoulders. "Any news of the Teleri?"

"No, *Dian-xia*."

"Very well. I will be ready in ten minutes." Kaiya dangled her feet over the edge of the bed and set a foot down. The wood was cold. Poor Weiyong. He must've been freezing.

She pushed her feet into slippers and glided over. Kneeling by his side, she placed a hand on his shoulder. "Wake—"

He bolted upright, nearly crashing his forehead into hers. His gaze met hers before staring at the floor.

Kaiya giggled. It seemed appropriate for his faux-pas. "We leave in ten minutes."

"Yes, *Dian-xia*." He pushed himself to his feet, avoiding eye contact. Was he *that* embarrassed?

Kaiya returned to the bed and picked up the hooded travelling cloak hanging over the footboard. Draping it over her shoulders and pulling up the hood, she walked to the door. "Come, Weiyong."

Though he responded immediately, hesitancy weighed down his words. "As you command, *Dian-xia*."

Why was he so tentative? A walk to the quay should be nothing compared to their harrowing escape from Iksuvius. She flashed him a reassuring smile. "We will be all right."

He simply nodded, still avoiding eye contact.

In the courtyard, her eight new guards waited with Count Du. They all knelt as she emerged.

She nodded to her host. "Count Du, I thank you for your hospitality. My handmaiden Yan Jie will come here searching for me. When she does, tell her that I have taken a river boat to the Huajing. Do not tell anyone else."

He bowed. "As the princess commands. I wish you safe travels."

They set off. The waxing gibbous of the White Moon Renyue and the almost-open Blue Moon Guanyin's Eye shone bright, providing little cover. They both hung close to the Iridescent Moon, also nearly full.

Before long, all three would join in the Godseye Conjunction, a rare omen of great change. At this moment, that change didn't look good.

The windows of homes were all shuttered, and they encountered no one in the streets. Only the roaring of the waterfall and the owl calls accompanied them. If Count Du planned on betraying them, he had yet to make a move.

They arrived at the lakeside docks in short time, where sailors worked at preparing a riverboat for departure. A fresh-faced young man with broad shoulders approached and bowed. "I am Captain Su. I understand we are to take you to take your unit back to the capital?"

"Yes." The highest-ranking solider dropped a purse in the captain's hands.

Captain Su hefted the bag and then stepped aside. "We are almost ready to embark. Go ahead and board."

Not wanting to reveal her identity, Kaiya prodded Weiyong with a poke in his arm.

He flinched at her touch. "Captain Su, is there any news about the Teleri army?"

Captain Su sighed. "Yes. Lord Zheng will surrender the East Gate to them today, at first light."

Chapter 14:
Misinformation

Liang Yu looked past his tea cup at Chief Minister Hong Jianbin's cinnamon-skinned lover, Leina. The light blue gown emphasized her striking blend of Cathay and Ayuri blood, and every movement spoke of grace—like the Black Lotus clan's Steel Orchids, who'd once been deployed here in the Floating World. Or maybe even like the Beauty from his own team, three decades before.

The pleasantly nostalgic feeling floating in his chest disappeared. To think the hideous old man had this exotic beauty warming his bed. Or rather, *her* bed, since he always met with her in this house he'd bought..

Ah, the perks of wealth and influence. Though if Hong knew Leina also entertained Young Lord Liu of Jiangzhou from time to time…

Smiling, Liang Yu set the cup down and placed his white *weiqi* piece on the board. Since helping Hong become Chief Minister, the old man had avoided him. Not as if it would be that hard to pay an unannounced visit; but sometimes a predator let his prey believe he had given up.

Especially if there was another way to get information. If Hong knew how loose Leina's lips were, he might not share state secrets with her. Secrets that Liang Yu could coax out. "The Night Blossoms tell me that fewer officers are coming to the high end of the Floating World."

"Oh, Golden Fu, I can't tell you how hard it is on everyone." Her accent flitted. With a dainty motion and tilt of her head, she played her black piece, setting a subtle trap. Clever; but with his eye for conspiracy, easy to see. "So many provincial and imperial troops went south to put down that rebel Peng. Many of the Night Blossoms are spending their nights alone."

So he'd heard. Now, only the most untested armies defended the North. Luckily their northern neighbor was preoccupied with a regional conflict and couldn't pose a threat.

If only he'd succeeded in tracking down Peng, Liang Yu's knife could have prevented the civil war. Thirty years ago, his team wouldn't have failed. His own planning, the Beauty's wiles, and the Surgeon's scalpel would've vivisected Peng's rebellion before it could spread.

What had she said? Something about Night Blossoms? He pretended not to see her trap, and placed his piece to make it seem he was attacking. "Well, there are still the ministers and officials."

"Fewer of them, too." She lowered her voice. "The new *Tianzi* does not inspire confidence. Many of the hereditary lords are concerned about their own domains and have gone home. Almost the entire Linshan provincial legation is gone."

This last piece of information he knew. His pupil, Lin Ziqiu, was the daughter of Linshan's *Tai-Ming* lord and had told him as much. Liang Yu swirled the tea around in his cup. "Once the imperial armies crush Peng, things will come back to normal. Hopefully, it won't be too long."

The wistfulness of her sigh could have inspired poets. "Tonight wouldn't be soon enough. Maybe all the revelry when Princess Kaiya returns will help—"

He almost spit his tea out, but choked it down. "Princess Kaiya?"

She placed a hand on her chest and sucked a breath in. With a conspiratorial look in her eyes, she leaned in and whispered, "Yes, she left Dongmen by river barge two days ago, in secret, with only a light guard."

That couldn't be true. Princess Kaiya's half-elf bodyguard would have sent word to her Black Lotus superiors, and Liang Yu had been intercepting their correspondence. There was no way Hong could find out about the princess' imminent arrival before the clan. If he did, however, Leina's slip was a good lead. He shifted in his seat. "Yes, the citizenry will be happy to have their princess back."

He, on the other hand, needed her to stay away from the palace. If her past gave any clues, the princess would likely try to find a peaceful resolution to the South's rebellion. She might even beg for clemency for Peng, despite his many attempts to manipulate and kill her.

It was time to pay a visit to the funerary shop to confirm this rumor.

Leina held a low bow as Golden Fu departed, his gold-threaded robes swishing out her side door. As much money as the avaricious spice merchant lavished in the Floating World on prostitutes, he probably spent even more funding the anti-imperial insurgency.

To what end, she could only surmise. He was just one of a dozen horrible men she had to deal with. Conflict and uncertainty increased demand for his other import: weapons. Like so many of the rich and powerful in Cathay, he profited on suffering and broken dreams.

Collecting up the tea set, she gave herself a mental pat on the back. The information she'd fed him would embolden the insurgents, and hopefully wreak havoc in the capital ahead of Geros' arrival.

She lifted one of her cups to the light bauble lamp. A barely perceptible crack stretched across the surface. It would split it in two if mishandled. Cathay's cracks and fissures were far more evident, and deservingly so. Yutou Province had aligned itself with Peng's Nanling Province in rebellion. Linshan Province stood at the side, waiting to see where the pieces would fall.

With a cursory glance at the *weiqi* board, their game unfinished, she sighed. Golden Fu was good, much better than Old Hong at strategy games. Still, he was too concerned with surrounding her pieces; he didn't notice the weakness in his inside lines.

In Cathay, that weakness was the semblance of unity among the Royalists. Jiangzhou Province's soldiers marched with the imperial army, but nobody else knew their *Tai-ming* lord, Liu, had plans of his own.

Plans she'd planted in his unimaginative brain, much as she did with Hong.

Golden Fu would learn that, and the other information she'd withheld, soon enough. The armies of evil Madura, at Lord Peng's behest, already trampled on Cathay's soil. Lord Zheng in Dongmen Province had surrendered to the Teleri. Soon, Rotuvi would attack Cathay's source of firepowder in Wailian, and from there, maybe even storm the now lightly defended North Gate of the Great Wall.

With armies in motion across three fronts, there was nothing keeping the capital from falling.

Except Princess Kaiya. That woman had proved resourceful, and if anyone could rally Cathay, it would be her. Hopefully, Golden Fu's insurgents would act on the information of her imminent—and more importantly, unprotected—arrival.

The plans of ambitious men were coming together in a perfect symphony of chaos. Now it was time for the climax to the opera she'd written. Leina opened a drawer in her altar table and withdrew a silk brocade box. The silver brooch inside, engraved by a master craftsman to evoke magic, ostensibly protected her against hooligans. To think a piece of Cathay's unique Artistic Magic would be used against its own people.

Even if Old Hong had outlived his use in sowing seeds of havoc and pushing the imperial court into disarray, he still served one last purpose. He had the *Tianzi's* trust, and she had his.

She sighed. Poor man. He wasn't that bad, really. Kind, even. But she was so close to getting her mother freed. Geros would surely keep his word, as Bovyans did, and it was going to happen years earlier than she could've ever hoped.

The secret entrance from the Jade Teahouse into her house whispered open. Old Hong had arrived.

Peng Kai-Long stood on the hill, flanked by his secret Water Snake bodyguard and several officers. In the stretch of farmland below, the Maduran invaders, thirty-thousand strong, braced against the onslaught of the imperial army.

No doubt the Maduran Prince Dhananad would be infuriated. The original plan had called for Kai-Long's own army of ten thousand musketmen to draw in the imperial vanguard of fifty thousand, and then for the Madurans to fall on their right flank.

Kai-Long grinned. He had sent one of his men, disguised as an imperial scout, to feed misinformation. Now, the Madurans would bear the brunt of the imperial army attack, while his own men, held in reserve, would attack the imperials' left flank. Well, once both sides had weakened each other.

Muskets roared in staccato, and firepowder smoke drifted across the plain. An hour in, and the *Tianzi's* troops seemed satisfied to keep out of range of Maduran archers. At this rate the Madurans would be too sapped to face the bulk of the imperial army, now marching through Cathay's central valley.

He turned to his aide-de-camp. "Form up the musketmen on this hill in ranks of three."

"But *Jue-Ye,*" the aide said, "that would reveal our position."

If only there were another way. In the corner of his eye, a young officer edged forward. Peng snapped his fan shut and pointed with it. "The Madurans are pinned down. At this rate—"

"Look!" The officer pointed.

Kai-Long followed the gesture. Below, a dozen Madurans broke from their entrenched positions and zigzagged through the barrage of musket balls.

Not a single one fell.

Kai-Long tried not to gape. These were undoubtedly the vaunted Maduran Scorpions.

Real ones. Not the boogiemen from the stories he'd manufactured over the last few years to instigate war. In seconds, they crashed into the imperial army's orderly ranks, breaking the long line in at least ten places. A couple of the Scorpions fell as hundreds of imperial spearmen surged in to relieve the musketmen.

"Hurry! Deploy!" Peng waved his fan emphatically. They had to make a show of attacking, lest even the dimwitted Dhananad suspected—

"*Jue-ye!*" The aide yelled.

Kai-Long turned, just in time to see a man chopping at him with a broadsword.

"A message from Prince Dhananad!" the assassin shouted. No time—

The weapon clashed against another sword, wielded by Kai-Long's bodyguard. The instrument of his death stopped just a finger-length from his neck.

"Take him alive!" Kai-Long fell back as his other men swept in to surround the would-be assassin. Blades flashed in the sun.

A few more swords clashed against the assassin's. With a quick jerk, the man raked the blade over his own throat. Blood sprayed out as he collapsed.

Dhananad had sent him? Kai-Long rubbed his neck. Perhaps the prince wasn't so stupid after all.

His bodyguard, from the Water Snake Clan, dropped to a knee. "*Jue-Ye*, the assassin was Black Lotus *Black Fist*. You can tell by his technique."

To everyone else, *Black Fist* were only rumors, tools for mothers to keep unruly children in line. No more real than the Guardian Dragon of Cathay. Still, Kai-Long had to keep up pretenses in front of his officers. He favored the man with a raised eyebrow. "There is no such thing."

The bodyguard bowed. "Of course not, *Jue-ye*."

Kai-Long nodded. The slip could be forgiven, especially now that the Water Snake Clan had saved him from one of Cousin Kai-Wu's agents. "You will be rewarded."

The man bowed again. "Protecting my lord is my honor."

His honor, as long as Kai-Long kept paying the clan. They'd turned on Lord Tong during his rebellion three years ago, only recently resurfacing. Perhaps even after he gained the Jade Throne, he would keep them around.

He looked back at the battle, which his own men now joined, firing at the imperials' flank. The Madurans had suffered significant casualties and would need reinforcements if they were to face the brunt of the punitive expedition.

He motioned to his bodyguard. "Inform your superiors to keep the South Gate open. We can't blow it yet. Not until the Madurans weaken the imperial army more."

Soon. If the battles all worked out like today, the Madurans and Imperials would devastate each other, leaving the road back to the capital open and the North relatively undefended.

Hong Jianbin waited at the arching stone bridge between the castle and the rest of the palace grounds, clasping the jewelry box Leina had given him.

A present for the *Tianzi*, one which would ensure Hong stayed in good graces despite the failed policies he suggested. The girl had exquisite taste, and undoubtedly it was a work of art. His hands tingled in excitement.

The rhythmic beat of a dozen footsteps approached. He looked up to see a contingent of imperial guards, surrounding the *Tianzi's* golden palanquin. Sunlight reflected off its dragon and phoenix carvings.

When the first guards reached him, Hong sank to his knees and pressed his forehead to the ground. "*Huang-Shang*, might I have a word?"

"Halt," the *Tianzi's* voice called from within.

The porters came to a precise stop and set the palanquin down. One slid the door open. Inside, the *Tianzi* leaned back on the cushions, his eyes soft and friendly.

He waved an open hand. "Chief Minister Hong, rise. Are we not finished with official duties for the day?"

"Yes, *Huang-Shang*." Hong looked up and presented the box. "I would like to present a token of my appreciation for your benevolent rule."

The *Tianzi* raised an eyebrow. In retrospect, it was strange for a minister to give something to the ruler, who had all. What had he been thinking? He started to return the box to the fold of his cloak.

"Well?" The *Tianzi's* eyebrows now scrunched together.

He wanted to see it! Hong bowed and rose again. His heart pattered like summer raindrops as he opened the—

The silver dragon pendant within glared at him with ruby eyes. It uncoiled in clouds of black smoke, clogging Hong's lungs. The flesh of his wrinkled hands withered to grey. What was left of his hair thinned and fell out. His manhood shriveled, and all energy seeped from his limbs.

His worst nightmare! Debilitating age and dotage.

"Ghosts!" yelled a man.

"Centipedes, crawling all over me!" screamed another.

Around him, the vaunted imperial guard fell into disarray. *Dao* rasped out of sheaths. The porters fled in all directions. A female servant looked about, bewildered.

"Retreat, retreat!" the *Tianzi* yelled. "Fall back to the castle and seal the gates. All the hereditary lords are rebelling! Hong, find the empress and make sure she makes it back to the castle."

"Yes, *Huang-Shang*!" Despite using all his energy to speak, Hong's voice came out a whisper. He wobbled to his feet, even as his shriveled arms and legs weighed him down like ship anchors. One foot in front of the other, he staggered back toward the palace grounds. After a few steps, he hazarded a glance at the demonic pin in his hand.

It was just a silver brooch, formed in the shape of a dragon. Exquisite, really. What had happened?

He looked back. The *Tianzi* had disappeared into the winding alleys of the castle, leaving his own palanquin behind. Imperial guards watched over the bridge. Horns blared.

Those horns… the ones that indicated an enemy had breached the palace walls. Once the castle gatehouse closed, the *Tianzi* would be sealed off from the rest of the world.

Who would lead now?

Liang Yu huddled by a tree, just outside the pottery shop where the Black Lotus leadership received secret reports. If the old adage about information winning wars was true, the clan might rival the Floating World in strategic value.

He unfolded the first missive from the agent in the South and deciphered the coded language. Peng had let the Madurans through the Wall.

The fool! At least an assassination attempt on Lord Peng was in the works, and the *Black Fist* were particularly adept at such operations. Thoughts of the Beauty and Surgeon, long banished to fond memories, surfaced yet again. Liang Yu was growing soft and nostalgic in his old age.

He refolded the message and sighed. With dumb luck, all the idiotic army deployments Chief Minister Hong had been whispering into the *Tianzi's* ears would avert disaster. The combined imperial and auxiliary provincial forces should have little problem repelling the Madurans, and that would send a warning to the independence-minded Lord Lin in Linshan.

What a fool Liang Yu had been. The nation was on the brink, and he had put them there. His plans to unite the hereditary lords in the call for war against foreign neighbors had instead weakened Cathay. Some Architect he was. He sighed again and unfolded another note.

Liang Yu's eyes widened. A missive from the *Black Fist* guarding the palace. The *Tianzi* had barricaded himself inside the castle, insistent that the *Tai-ming* had risen up against the Jade Throne. The confused hereditary lords had declared the *Tianzi's* second cousin, a babe of just four-months, as acting *Tianzi*. His grandfather, *Tai-Ming* Lord Liu of Jiangzhou, would be his regent.

What had happened? The *Tianzi* was weak-willed and incompetent, to be sure, but insane? If anyone were more weak-willed and incompetent than the current *Tianzi*, it was Lord Liu. It couldn't all be a coincidental perfect storm. At the same time, anyone who could orchestrate so many parts was more of an Architect than he.

Harrumphing, Liang Yu almost tore the last message while trying to unravel it. A message from Princess Kaiya's *Black Fist* bodyguard. The princess had been injured in an assassination attempt, and the half-elf requested a replacement.

Standing, he stashed the note into his robe. With a quick glance to make sure no one was watching, he returned to the funerary pot and dropped in the other two messages. The Black Lotus leadership needed to know about the unholy alliance between Peng and the Madurans, as well as the chaos inside the palace.

As for the half-elf's... That one, he would keep. If Hong's mistress was right, Princess Kaiya would be arriving at the river docks sometime tomorrow, expecting a new Black Fist bodyguard.

Liang Yu could play that role. She would need it, since even though Regent Liu was incompetent, he would still see her as a threat to his grandson's claim to the Jade Throne.

By protecting her, Liang Yu could control someone with a legitimate claim to the Mandate of Heaven. Or make demands of the Royalists who supported the Wang family.

He just needed to get to her before the imperial guard. That might not be hard, since they apparently had their hands full in the palace.

Geros shifted in the bloodwood chair, not trusting the spindly struts to support his weight. He must look ridiculous, but better that than sitting on the floor like these uncivilized Cathayi. His own officers and soldiers stood at attention behind him, likely dubious of the other seats brought to the Lord Zheng's audience chamber.

If his sour face was any indication, the castle chamberlain had been none too pleased to bring one chair, let alone scrounge up a dozen. All the other assembled Cathayi councilors and officers appeared equally bewildered and angry.

Lord Zheng, on the other hand, revealed nothing in his expression. He sat cross-legged across from Geros, a sheathed Cathayi broadsword in front of him. "Where is my eldest son? Or have you gone back on your word?"

Geros snorted. "Viceroy Zheng, I only said that if you did not open the gate, I would start removing your sons' body parts. I have been generous and given two of them back." Of course, he would have returned Ming, if only for good will, had the slippery lordling not escaped.

"Where is he, then?" Neither Lord Zheng's face nor tone had changed. The most dangerous man was one who could not be read.

It was time to find out just how much his newest vassal knew. Geros laughed. "Let's stop playing games.

You know, of course. Princess Kaiya's half-elf rescued him."

Now Zheng's expression did twitch, if only for a split second. He knew nothing of the escape, apparently, which meant…

In Geros' fury at the escape, he had missed the logical connection. His heart leapt as he leaned forward in his chair. "If the half-elf was here, where is Princess Kaiya?" If she had not yet fled to Huajing, he could delay the assault until Leina could thoroughly undermine the government.

"She returned to the capital." Lord Zheng's mask and glib tone had returned.

"When?" Geros kept the urgency out of his voice. Yet if had been recent, he could send some officers on horseback to chase her down.

"Three days ago, as soon as she was well enough to travel after the assassination attempt."

Geros sucked in a breath. She must have reached Huajing by now, into the nest of snakes vying for power. One of those had likely sent the assassin in the first place. Geros had to protect his love. Unless Lord Zheng lied. "So why was the half-elf still here?"

"I don't know," Lord Zheng said. "It was not my place to question the princess. However, she had expressed interest in marrying my son, so perhaps she had left her bodyguard here to greet him. Or facilitate his escape."

Geros scratched his chin. As soon as Princess Kaiya reached the capital, Leina would surely send a messenger bird to let him know. The intelligent Eldaeri-bred birds gave the Teleri a significant communication advantage over the horse-relay systems which most other nations used. "Make sure all imperial horse relays are cut off, Viceroy Zheng. You are dismissed."

Bowing, Lord Zheng collected his sword. He stood and backed out of the room, followed by his own men.

Geros motioned toward a shadow near the wall. "Was Lord Zheng telling the truth?"

Master Feiying stepped into view and bowed. "He is hard to read, Your Eminence, but I suspect he did not lie."

"Follow him and make sure he executes my commands faithfully." Geros beckoned the officer in charge of communications, a Bovyan of Kanin stock. "Lieutenant Espios, prepare a messenger bird bound for Leina in Huajing. Tell her that Princess Kaiya may be walking into a trap, and to arrange protection."

A familiar, annoying laugh erupted from the entrance. A sinking feeling settling into his stomach, Geros looked up.

The Altivorc King, with none of his usual retinue of vile guards, leaned against the door frame, twirling that wand of his. "Geros, Geros, since when did you care about a woman so much, you would forget all about military strategy?"

Heat rushed to Geros' face. How dare the king mock him in front of his men? "The princess has important strategic value. The people adore her, and our son will legitimize Teleri rule over Cathay."

Yawning, the altivorc strolled down the middle of the room. "As you say. It doesn't matter to me, as long as you hold up your end of our deal."

Geros waved him off. "Yes, yes, the Cathayi pyramid is yours."

"There are two more things I want." With a flourishing twirl, the King sheathed his wand. "Inside the Temple of Heaven in Huajing, there is a chunk of a fallen star. A token, really."

Right. Geros grinned. Anything the lizard wanted had to carry some importance. "This was never part of our deal."

"Of course not," the Altivorc King said. "Which is why if you bring it to me, I will start ending the Bovyan Curse, beginning with you."

An end to the curse. Geros gawked in spite of himself. He had promised Ming Zheng the hand of Princess Kaiya once he died, but now it seemed his death would not come so soon. All of the plans and timetables to secure his legacy, now less relevant.

No; hope must not replace resolve. Even still… "And the second thing you want?"

"Information. I overheard something about the princess' half-elf. Where did you see her last?"

Chapter 15:
Many Unhappy Returns

The sloshing waves changed in frequency and mingled with the nearly inaudible buzz of the Fallen Star in the Temple of Heaven, letting Kaiya know that she had reached the Songyuan river docks in Huajing.

She afforded herself a silent scoff. If the *Tiger's Eye* allowed her any sense of nostalgia, her inner voice might've waxed poetic about that naïve girl who had set off from these quays just over a year before.

Tested by conspiracies, dictators, and a dragon, she was no longer that girl. At what cost, though? Four of the five imperial guards who'd accompanied her that morning had died in her defense. Her beloved, also as dead as her emotions. Her beloved's brother, perhaps needlessly sacrificed.

She scanned the dockside. Dockworkers and sailors bustled about, seeming no different from the last time she'd been here.

Did the imperial court know of the impending invasion? It didn't appear so. It had taken them three days by boat, but the horse relays should've brought news of the Teleri breaching the Wall within just a few hours.

Unless Lord Zheng had managed to silence every loyal imperial soldier… Impossible.

If that *were* the case, the imperial armies would have three less days to mobilize. She had to warn Brother Kai-Wu.

Though herbal medicine and rest had helped her regain some energy, her legs wobbled as she rose. Weiyong came to her side and helped her disembark with a firm hand.

She offered him a grateful nod, then turned to the captain of her escort. "We must make haste to the palace."

"*Dian-xia*," Fang Weiyong said, "For your safety, we should not travel through the city without a contingent of imperial guards."

He was right. She pursed her lips. Plenty of people in the capital would recognize her. If just one spotted her, news of her arrival would spread faster than she could walk. Who knew if the insurgents had been completely pacified?

Still, Brother Kai-Wu needed to know about the imminent Teleri attack. Withdrawing the pouch containing Tian's tablet, she proffered it in two hands to Fang Weiyong. With Lord Zheng's and Tian's names inscribed, it could only come from Dongmen. "Weiyong, take this to Sun-Moon Palace. It is proof. Tell them—"

"Wait, *Dian-xia*," a weathered male voice called.

Her guards all placed hands on their broadswords, their eyes shifting left to the source of the voice. She followed their gazes.

A middle-aged man knelt, one fist to the ground, the other hand clasping a walking staff. He bowed, exposing streaks of silver in his long hair.

Who was he? She lifted her chin. "Rise."

He raised his head, revealing an average-looking face with no defining features. Had she seen him before? If a foreign artist were to sketch a Cathay male, this would be him—one who could melt in with the faceless crowds.

"*Dian-xia*," he repeated. He shuffled forward and held up a creased sheet of paper. The gibberish was likely Black Lotus code, written in Jie's unmistakable scrawl. "Your black lotus asked for a replacement."

Black Lotus? Unless he was describing Jie's dark heart and pretty looks, only a *Black Fist* would know the clan name for the *Tianzi's* spies and assassins. Most of the select few people who'd even heard of the name would assume it referred to an order of cloistered monks who kept historical records and accounting ledgers. The half-elf must've disobeyed the order to hold her post, and asked for a replacement.

If not for the *Tiger's Eye*, Kaiya might have taken it personally. Instead, she nodded. "What is your name?"

"Fu, *Dian-xia*." He bowed. "My cover name is Golden Fu."

Where had she heard that name before? Perhaps someone Zheng Ming had mentioned when the Black Lotus rooted out the former Chief Minister Tan as a conspirator. She stared at him. "You knew of my arrival."

He straightened and grinned. "Of course. It is our business to know things."

Definitely *Black Fist*. No telling what kind of weapon the walking staff was. But… "If you knew, why did the *Tianzi* not send a contingent of imperial guards to greet me?"

Fu's gaze darted to her guards, then settled on hers. He edged closer, cupped his mouth, and whispered in her ear. "*Dian-xia*, we are not going to the palace. It is not safe right now."

Not safe? She leaned back and narrowed her eyes. "There is no place in Cathay more defensible than Sun-Moon Castle."

He whispered again, his words barely audible. "The danger I speak of is inside the palace itself. Your brother never fully recovered from Peng's poisoning. He went mad and sequestered himself in the main keep. There has been no contact with him."

Could it be true? Gentle Second Brother, driven insane? "Who rules?"

"Lord Liu of Jiangzhou rules as regent, and plans to ship you off to a nunnery. On his command, the imperial guard will apprehend you the instant you step into Sun-Moon palace."

Never. Lord Liu's absolute loyalty came from an utter lack of ambition. The imperial guard would side with her, anyway. Keeping suspicion out of her voice, she summoned her most incredulous tone: "How did Lord Liu become regent? Why would he capture me?"

"His son is married to your cousin, Wang Kai-Hua. Her son, now four months old, was next in line to the Jade Throne. You are a threat to his grandson."

Kai-Hua, a mother. To an unwitting usurper, no less. She'd never willingly be part of such a plot. Had Lord Liu hidden his ambitions like Cousin Peng? "If you are loyal to the *Tianzi*, why are you helping me?"

"The imperial guard is loyal to the Jade Throne. Our clan is loyal to the Wang family. There are several of us here to protect you." He pointed a subtle thumb behind him to his right, then to his left.

A mirror flashed from a warehouse, then another from a tea shop. Both in the directions he had indicated. Six black-garbed faces bobbed up from a third rooftop.

Even if he wasn't who he claimed, they were surrounded. Perhaps by dozens of soldiers. But he'd flashed Jie's letter, so perhaps she could trust him. Though that would also mean Brother Kai-Wu was mad, and yet another cousin had betrayed her. "Where are we going, then?"

"One of our clan's safehouses." Fu handed her a travelling cloak. "Please cover your head." He turned to her guards and spoke up. "Soldiers of Cathay. You are now the imperial guard. Your first duty is to the princess."

Kaiya pursed her lips. These men, while serviceable, were not imperial guards. It seemed like an insult to Chen Xin, Zhao Yue, Li Wei, and Xu Zhan.

The soldiers all snapped to attention. Golden Fu beckoned them to follow.

Never had Liang Yu been so close to the supposed once-in-three-generations beauty, and for the first time his old eyes could appreciate her gorgeousness. He guided the princess and her small entourage into an alley, grateful he'd been able to convince her to follow.

Her suspicious questioning, hidden behind a decent semblance of shock, suggested she was no longer the gullible girl he remembered stalking a year ago. Even then-Household Minister Hong had manipulated her.

Liang Yu glanced around to make sure they weren't being followed. For the time being, he held a potential claimant to regent. The sooner he took care of her eight guards, none who appeared formidable—

"Fu," she said. "Everyone seems so calm. Life goes on as usual. Are the imperial armies ready to repel the invasion?"

Fu nodded. "Yes, *Dian-xia*. A combined force of imperial and provincial soldiers, three hundred thousand strong."

"Which provinces march with the imperial army?"

So idealistic. She was undoubtedly trying to think of a peaceful resolution to the rebellion. Her leadership would make Cathay stronger… but only after they crushed Peng and his Maduran allies. "Zhenjing, Ximen, and Fengu Provinces all obeyed the Mandate of Heaven."

"And the others?" Her authoritative tone showed the slightest hint of worry.

He only had to keep her trust a little longer. He tilted his head toward a passerby. "We are almost to the safehouse. Let us speak more of this in private."

"Very well." Her passive expression would make a Black Fist envious.

After a few more minutes, he brought them to a warehouse and opened the door for her. "In here. Imperial guards, the princess is safe for now. Wait here and one of my men will come and take you to a nearby inn."

Or rather, to a temporary prison, but they didn't need to know it.

The captain stepped forward. "Our duty is to the princess. We must accompany her."

The man took the title a little too seriously. Well, soldiers would be soldiers. Nothing he hadn't planned for. Liang Yu raised an eyebrow at the princess.

She nodded. "They will enter as well."

No matter. He had prepared for this contingency, even if he had hoped to prevent any bloodshed. Had the Surgeon been here, he'd already be killing. Liang Yu cast a quick glance around to make sure they'd not picked up a tail. "Come along, then. This is not our final destination."

He guided them through some twists and turns until they appeared thoroughly bewildered. At last, he came to his trading company's warehouse. He held the door open for the princess.

She nodded and stepped in. The doctor and the eight guards followed close behind. Inside, the light baubles illuminated the middle of the spacious empty room, but not the sides, just as planned. The guards and doctor looked around, taking in the new surroundings.

The princess' head swept from one side of the room to the other, before her gaze settled on Liang Yu. Her nose scrunched up. "This was not exactly what I expected…"

She wouldn't expect what happened next, either. He closed the door and edged forward, ready to separate his walking stick into a knife and spear. "Now."

Shrouded in the darkness of the mezzanine above, dozens of repeating crossbows cocked.

Taking advantage of the imperial soldiers' initial shock, Liang Yu slipped between them. They backed into a circle around the princess, but he was already close. He pushed the doctor to the side and hooked his knife around her throat. The doctor took a step toward him, but Liang Yu placed the tip of his spear at his chest.

"Don't try to sing any commands," Liang Yu said. No, after falling victim to the power of her voice a year before on New Year's Day, he'd taken precautions.

"Some of my men's ears are covered, and they await signals."

She raised her hands. "What is the meaning of this?"

How could she show no signs of fear? Liang Yu pressed the blade obliquely into her neck. "You are in no position to ask questions. You are all trapped. There is no need for anyone to die. Tell your men to stand down."

"We…" the captain said, "we are willing to… die for you, *Dian-xia*."

The lack of enthusiasm in his voice was depressing. Liang Yu snorted. Perhaps these men weren't worth keeping around.

Lowering her hand, the princess spoke in a steady voice, "Captain, order your men to surrender."

The captain's words trembled out of his mouth. "Men, drop your weapons. Hands on your heads."

The imperial soldiers wasted no time in obeying. There would be no need for bloodshed, at least not yet.

Liang Yu beckoned his own men with his spear. "Bind them. You, *Dian-xia*, come with me."

"Fu, if only three provinces stand with the throne, I must go to the palace to convince the others to join. Cathay's survival depends on it."

Perhaps he misread her, if she wanted to unite the nation against the rebel. Still, her military acumen left a lot to be desired. He chuckled. "Only Yutou Province stands with Peng. They hardly constitute a threat. Even with the Madurans—"

"Madurans?" The shock in her wide eyes had to be genuine.

He cocked his head. "Who did you think was invading us?"

The princess pointed north. "The Teleri army, led by Emperor Geros himself, occupies Dongmen."

Dongmen? His men erupted in murmurs. She was pointing in the wrong direction, but still. It must be a trick, to throw him off-guard. The bonfires on the Great Wall and fire towers would have brought news within an hour. Even if no one heeded the signal, they would listen to the daily couriers out of Dongmen.

Still, if she were telling the truth, nothing stood between Dongmen and Huayuan. The entire North was virtually undefended, while an incompetent ruled as regent.

A perfect storm, caused in part by his own past actions. The Beauty would've been laughing at him right about now. She'd always predicted he would make a huge mistake. "Are you certain? There has been no such news."

The princess glared at him. "Of course I am certain. Lord Zheng was about to let the Bovyans in when I left."

A collaborator! That would explain it. Lord Zheng must have waylaid the imperial couriers and made sure the fire signals remained unlit. "Very well, *Dian-xia*. I will have one of my men send a warning to the palace now."

"You must let me go to the palace myself. I will take the risk. I will make them listen."

"Not so fast." First, he needed to confirm it. "We must talk first. Come along."

"Allow Fang Weiyong to accompany me."

Liang Yu evaluated the man with a quick glance. The doctor had shown no signs of fighting skill, and probably wouldn't pose a significant threat. He also had the imperial plaque. "Very well. Your men are my hostages. Any sign of disobedience, and I will kill one of them, starting with your doctor."

Her eyes shifted from him to the doctor and back.

Snapping his spear and knife back together into a walking stick, he held an open hand toward the warehouse office. "Please."

She cast him a scathing glare. "Who are you?"

No sign of worry. He blanked his own expression. "I will answer your question, but in the privacy of that room. Please walk. The doctor first."

The doctor looked at the princess, and she nodded. He turned and led her to the office. Liang Yu followed one step behind. At the door, he darted to the side and opened it for them.

Kidnapping her had made so much sense before. However, if what she said was true about the Teleri invasion of the undefended North, maybe she was the only one who could bring the country together.

Without the least amount of fear, she walked into his office. It was time to ascertain if she was telling the truth.

Kaiya took a deep breath. She'd walked blindly into a trap, duped as if she were Avarax's fool again. Her hand strayed to Tian's lockpick pouch. For now, at least, her escort was safe. If she could only figure out who these people were and what they wanted. She stepped into a small room, with a single window that bathed the room in afternoon light.

A silhouetted figure stood on the other side of a bloodwood desk. He cradled what appeared to be a repeating crossbow in his arms. At least he didn't point it at them.

Fu gestured her toward the two bloodwood chairs in front of the desk. She glided over and settled on the edge of one, while Weiyong stood on her left.

Seemingly unconcerned about the Teleri invasion, Fu walked by them and took a seat behind the desk, next to the other man. With the sun at his back, she couldn't read his expression; not that she was good at it in the first place.

"Now, to answer your question," Fu said. "I am a spice merchant with the nation's best interests at heart."

And a *Black Fist*. Perhaps the renegade who had perpetrated all the attacks a year before. She pursed her lips. If he really had the nation's best interests at heart, he had a strange way of showing it.

She adopted a tone of command. "Then send a message to the palace. At least let them know of the Bovyan invasion."

"Of course." He bowed, and then gestured toward the doctor. "You gave him an imperial plaque earlier. Give it to me."

The imperial plaque? What was he talking…

The doctor cocked his head. "I—"

She held up an open hand, silencing him. Fu must have mistaken Tian's tablet for the imperial plaque. Now it was bargaining leverage. Blasphemous, all the same. "Weiyong, give me the plaque."

"But *Dian-xia*—"

He was sweet, but he could be so dense sometime. Of course, she didn't know where the real plaque was any more than Weiyong. In her frightened younger self's haste to escape Iksuvius, she'd forgotten it. Maybe Emperor Geros had recovered it. She suppressed a shudder as a twinge of fear sparked, only to be smothered by the *Tiger's Eye*.

Keeping her focus locked forward, she extended her hand to the doctor. "You won't be taking it to the palace now."

Understanding bloomed in Weiyong's eyes. He bowed and proffered the pouch. Kaiya turned and received it in two hands. Fu's henchman took a step forward with an outstretched arm.

Fu barred his way with the walking staff. "*Dian-xia*, Little Song here needs the plaque to prove he is your messenger."

She glared at him. "I will not have an insurgent—"

"Patriot," Fu said. "Little Song cares about Cathay. He is the son of the former Foreign Minister Song Henglin."

At Song's new angle, she could see his face clearly. Yes, it was Song Xingyuan, the son of Minister Song, who'd held the Chief Minister title for a single day… before it was revealed his son was an insurgent.

Song dropped to one knee, head bowed. Fu, too, nodded in respect to the supposed plaque. Apparently, he still recognized the symbol of the *Tianzi* and the Mandate of Heaven.

Summoning her tone of imperial authority, though not as effective as the power of her voice, she said, "For now, I will keep the plaque."

Fu smirked. "What keeps me from taking it from you?"

"Mutual benefit. I could have sung the order for your men to kill each other." She tucked the pouch into the fold of her robe. He believed she still had her power; would he believe her bluff now? If her frightened younger self could trick a dragon, her older self, armed with the *Tiger's Eye*, could deceive a man. "However, if you are a patriot and the information about Lord Liu is true, then I will need you."

She kept her expression impassive as his eyes searched hers.

At last, he leaned back in his chair. "I will bring a friend of yours here, one who can get into the palace with no proof of identity."

Kaiya pursed her lips. Who was he speaking of? "I do not want any more people kidnapped."

Fu grinned. "She will come of her own free will. Little Song, go to the Linshan legation and tell Lin Ziqiu I have a mission for her."

Apparently the *Tiger's Eye* couldn't suppress surprise, because Kaiya's mouth must have been gaping. Had Ziqiu been spying on her in the past, using flightiness as a disguise?

Chapter 16:
Cherry Pairs

Thirty-three days. Feneyas estimated more than a cycle of the White Moon would pass before he ever learned his identity, just because the wild elves insisted on maintaining pretenses with the humans. He could've gone straight to the Maki village himself; instead, the woodland messengers would go and deliver instructions for the shaman to come visit the sacred pool.

Sacred, indeed.

As if blue sand and exfoliated elf skin made the pool magic. It was almost a joke among the elves. Dior laughed, recounting how he had tricked a shaman and his two young children when they had visited a half a year before, by whispering in the wind and tossing rocks into the pool.

In the meantime, life went on. More weapons practice, more hunting and foraging. Though restless, Feneyas at least had a chance to learn a little about woodcraft from Kiri and the others. Dior taught him the finer points of archery, though it did little more than earn the laughter of the elves when they watched.

Well before dawn on the eighth day, Feneyas jerked out of sleep and nearly tumbled from his hammock.

Kiri stood just ten paces away, frozen in her approach. She flashed him a mischievous grin. "No one can sneak up on you, even in your sleep. Now come, there's a dawn-blooming everblossom I want to harvest."

Feneyas shook the fog out of his mind and lumbered to his feet. Following Kiri through the other hammocks of sleeping elves, he made his way down the tree steps to the ground.

Little Kala beamed at him from the bottom, while Dior yawned. The bow and quiver strapped across his back did not seem suited for the task at hand.

Feneyas poked Kiri in the back. "Do we really need four of us to pick flowers?"

She batted her eyelashes. "No, but eight baskets carry more than four."

They set off down a path, with the three others barely making a sound. It helped that *they* could see in the dark. Then again, that was no excuse. He made plenty of noise traipsing across the forest paths in broad daylight.

"What are the everblossoms for?" Feneyas asked in a low whisper.

Kiri chuckled, but didn't answer.

Dior leaned in. "Women's issues."

Before long, they arrived on a low ridge overlooking a clearing in the trees. Broadleaf plants covered the ground. Kiri motioned for them to stop, and pointed at the shrubbery. Kala crouched and stared at the closed sepals.

The sky began to fade from black to dark blue, and the forest erupted with birdsong. Pink formed on the horizon, heralding the arrival of the sun. The groundcover burst forth in an explosion of yellow and white blooms.

Kiri squeezed Feneyas' hand, looking up to meet his gaze. Her smile was refreshing and happy.

His stomach fluttered. Perhaps who he was didn't matter, just that he belonged somewhere. All sounds of the forest quieted in that moment.

Yes. He could forget—

In the distance, metal jingled.

Feneyas spun in that direction, then back to meet Dior's eyes. The elf's ears twitched. His bow was already in hand.

As the sounds grew louder, Dior motioned them off the ridge and into some bushes. Huddled by Kiri's side, Feneyas lifted his head and ventured a glance out.

A squad of Metal Men, all wearing black surcoats over chainmail hauberks, pushed through some brush and paused on the path Feneyas and the elves had taken. They stood just fifteen feet away.

At point, a Kanin tribesman took a step and squatted, pressing his hand to the ground. The soldiers, eleven in all, gathered up behind him. Some passed a flask around and took swigs.

One, with spiked shoulder guards and a steel breastplate, pushed forward toward the front of the column. He stood only as tall as his companions' chests, but might have been just as broad and muscular. Shaggy black hair jutted out from beneath his half-helm, setting him apart from the others' close-cropped coifs. Unlike his comrades' longswords, this one had a wicked broadsword hanging at his side.

He turned in Feneyas' direction, revealing turquoise-colored skin in the early morning light. His squat, blocky face was so ugly, Feneyas probably would've remembered had he seen a more hideous person in his past life.

Kiri dug her fingers into Feneyas' arm as she shrank behind him.

The guide bobbed his head over and over again. "Sorry, sorry," he said in the Metal Men's language. "I lost the half-elf's trail."

Half-elf... they were searching for Kiri. Feneyas shifted over, as if it would protect his friend.

Turquoise Man turned back and smacked the guide across the cheek, sending a loud crack echoing through the woods. He let out a series of foul syllables that could only be a curse.

One of the Metal Men shoved the guide in the back. "If you don't pick up the trail, we'll chop your children to pieces. See if your legendary tracking skills can find them all."

The tribesman's voice trembled. "Only two, not easy. And dark. Too dark to see."

"But fresh." Turquoise Man seized the guide by the shoulder and yanked him to his feet. So strong.

Kiri tugged at Feneyas. He looked at her.

Let's go, she mouthed. Her eyes glistened with tears. Her other hand clutched Kala's hand. Kala's free hand covered her mouth, and her eyes were squeezed shut. Dior... Dior was nowhere to be found. Kiri let go of him and started to stand.

Feneyas grabbed Kiri's wrist and shook his head. Fleeing would give away their position. She squeezed his wrist back.

The guide pointed toward the forest floor. "A track. Smaller human. Went that way." He now pointed past Feneyas and the others, toward the ridge.

The Metal Man shoved him in the back. "Then lead us."

Kiri's grip tightened as the column jingled and clanged single-file past their hiding place.

Feneyas held his breath.

Kala burst into tears. She jumped up and bolted in the other direction. Kiri scrambled to her feet and ran after her.

"Look! The half-elf!" More armor clinked as bodies turned this way and that, swords sweeping out of their scabbards.

Turquoise Man jerked his head in Kiri's direction, then lumbered through the underbrush after her. Despite his short legs, he moved fast. Two Metal Men followed.

A bowstring twanged somewhere to the left. An arrow thwipped through air and lodged into a nearby Metal Man's throat. Another brute collapsed into a heap nearby with an arrow through his eye. The fletching marked it as Dior's.

"Trap! Take cover!" the first Metal Man blurted.

His comrades had already broken toward the cover of the trees, heads twisting every which way to find the source of the arrow. One poked his head out, only to take an arrow through the mouth.

Three enemies fallen, the others pinned down by Dior's marksmanship.

And three in pursuit of Kiri and Kala.

Feneyas leaped up and took off after his half-elf friends. Turning a corner on the path, he nearly tripped over one of the Metal Men, throat slashed with blood gushing out.

Kiri's scream tore through the forest from down the path. Oddly calm despite the chaos, Feneyas broke into a run.

After several seconds, a trail of black blood appeared. The sounds of metal on metal clashed louder. Then, there they were.

With his right arm hanging at his side, Turquoise Man leaned against a tree. He swung his broadsword in vicious arcs, keeping Kiri at bay.

How had Kiri gotten the upper hand against an armored warrior?

Not only that, she had changed her clothes? Gone was the doeskin dress, replaced by tight black clothes. At least, they might've been black if not for all the mud splattered on them. She'd apparently found time not only to change her clothes—and where had she kept the new ones stashed?—but to roll around in the dirt as well.

"You can drop your weapon and answer some questions," Kiri said, "or you can die."

She could speak the Metal Man's language! And speak it *well*, even better than her proficiency with Kanin. Had she been keeping that a secret the whole time?

Still brandishing his sword, Turquoise Man burst out laughing. "Come on, Orc Slayer, see if you can get close enough to make good on your empty threats."

"Okay, have it your way." Kiri reached into the fold of her shirt and whipped out three stars.

Stars? The name came to him unbidden, foreign and familiar at once. They whistled through the air and lodged into Turquoise Man's face, neck, and gut. With a squelch, he collapsed to the ground.

Feneyas coughed. Where'd Kiri gotten the clothes and the foreign weapons?

Kiri met his gaze. Her eyes widened as large as greywood tree leaves, and she stumbled back two steps. "*H-Heavens!*"

She could speak *his* native tongue.

From Feneyas' right, another man crashed through the bushes, longsword raised. Feneyas spun to his attacker's right, and would have broken the man's arm had the assailant not skidded short, mouth hanging slack.

"Heavens!" His would-be attacker's voice sputtered in shock and awe. Gawking, he lowered his sword. Apparently, the People Beyond the Wall enjoyed invoking the Heavens.

The man had also spoken in Feneyas' native language, and at cursory glance, he had the same honey skin, black hair, and almond-shaped eyes. He held a Metal Man's sword.

"Heavens…" Warrior Kiri took a tentative step toward him, hand trembling.

The second Metal Man burst out behind Yellow Man and hacked down with his longsword.

Feneyas reached out and raised Yellow Man's arm, angling his sword so that the Metal Man's clanged into it. The weapon jarred from Yellow Man's grasp.

Feneyas caught it underhanded by the hilt, and swept it up into the arc of the Metal Man's back stroke. Its edge smashed into the flat of Feneyas' sword with a clank.

The reverberation wrung his hand, but he kept hold of the weapon. He butted Yellow Man to the side with his hip and drew his knife with his left hand.

The Metal Man transitioned to a strong thrust.

Brushing it to the side with his own sword, Feneyas spun in and slashed down with the knife, across his enemy's throat and to the inside of his left wrist. On the upstroke, he cut the inside of the Metal Man's right wrist.

Yellow Man lunged and tackled the Metal Man from behind. He pushed himself up, favoring his right arm, climbed on the Metal Man's back, and ripped off his helm. He then repeatedly bashed the hapless soldier's head into the ground.

Apparently satisfied with his handiwork, Yellow Man looked up, his mouth agape. "Heavens! You are alive!"

Yellow Man must have known him. On closer inspection, they had similar features. Unlike the diversity of elf faces, maybe the People Beyond the Wall all looked the same? Feneyas found his tongue, his native language stumbling out of his mouth after an eternity of non-use. "Who are you? Where did you come from?"

Yellow Man rolled his eyes. "*Heavens*! Stop being silly. I am bright—"

Dior appeared on the path, prodding the Kanin tribesman along.

Then, *another* Kiri peeked through the bushes. She took a tentative step out, pulling Kala along with her. She wore the same doeskin dress as before.

Warrior Kiri spun and held her knife aloft. Then her gaze met the real Kiri's.

The two looked exactly alike, even more similar than Yellow Man and Feneyas. Like the fruit dangling in a cherry tree, always in pairs, they mirrored each other.

Heads shifted from person to person, eyes widening and brows furrowing.

Both Yellow Man and Dior pointed back and forth at real Kiri and Warrior Kiri.

Warrior Kiri's stare fell on Feneyas', and then shifted to her twin. The knife slipped from her fingers, and she stumbled back several steps. "This can't be happening. This can't be real."

With mouth half-open, the real Kiri appeared surprised, but not nearly as dumfounded as Warrior Kiri. Clearing her throat, she gestured toward Dior. "Shoot, shoot!"

"Wait!" Feneyas took a step to interpose himself between Dior and Warrior Kiri.

Too late.

Dior had unslung his bow, nocked an arrow and loosed it at Warrior Kiri.

Chapter 17:
Limited Information

With Weiyong at her side, Kaiya sat serenely in Golden Fu's office. Footsteps and clanking weapons out in the warehouse indicated at least twenty rebels, while the cloying scent of a myriad spices roiled her stomach. Perhaps Fu was indeed a spice merchant.

An evasive one at that, whose questions begot more questions, and whose answers answered nothing. Apparently, the *Tiger's Eye* could do nothing to control impatience, even if she hid it. Every hour they waited meant Geros and the Teleri army approached unopposed.

Though if what Fu said was true, there was little the imperial court could do. Only a skeleton army remained in the capital, as a precaution against Lord Lin in Linshan attacking with his provincial soldiers.

Out in the warehouse, a set of lighter footsteps approached. Fu's attention flicked to the entrance, then returned to her. As the door opened behind her, Kaiya kept looking past Fu, at the glass window. Its muted reflection revealed a young woman in a grey commoner's dress, whose eyes met hers.

Her supposed friend, Lin Ziqiu.

Fang Weiyong lacked any discretion, and turned to see who it was.

The woman padded in and stopped a few steps behind. "Master, I had a hard time sneaking out of my home. I came as quickly as I could."

The voice belonged to Ziqiu, yet the tone lacked its past capriciousness.

Fu motioned toward Kaiya with an open hand. "An old friend of yours, Little Ziqiu."

The girl shuffled a few steps over and leaned in.

Shifting in her seat, Kaiya met her gaze.

Ziqiu looked so different after just a year. Gone were the carefree smile and eyes dancing with mirth, replaced by serious intent.

Then her expression settled into the flightiness Kaiya remembered. "Kaiya! *Dian-xia.* I thought you were in Dongmen. When did you get back? And what are you doing *here*?" She cast a sidelong glance at Fu.

Kaiya pursed her lips. "I would ask the same of you."

"Fu teaches me about information gathering." Ziqiu bowed to Fu. "He is my master."

Kaiya shook her head. "*I* am his *prisoner*. Or hostage, perhaps." As for information gathering… Ziqiu had only ever seemed interested in trivial gossip. The girl might've been spying on her all this time.

Ziqiu turned and slapped a hand down on the desk. "Master, how could you kidnap Princess Kaiya? I thought you cared about Cathay."

Fu leaned back in his chair. "I do. The princess would have walked into a trap at the palace. Surely you know of the coup."

"Coup?" The incredulity in Ziqiu's voice sounded convincing enough. "I haven't been to the palace since my father returned to Linshan. Our villa is surrounded by imperial troops."

Fu scratched his chin. "There is another threat. A Teleri invasion through Dongmen."

Ziqiu faced Kaiya, her face pale. "Is it true?"

Kaiya nodded. They didn't need to know Geros was coming for her, to claim the twins she carried.

"True or not—" Fu said, "and I am not convinced the princess speaks truthfully—a foreign invasion will force the hereditary lords to reunite." He nodded toward Ziqiu. "Go to the palace and inform them."

That would do little to improve Kaiya's situation, and it also put Ziqiu in danger. Kaiya stood. "No. With doubts of Linshan's loyalty, they will take her hostage. We cannot endanger her. Let me go instead."

Weiyong shuffled his feet. Placing her hands on her hips, Ziqiu opened her mouth.

Fu held up a hand and chuckled. "You are just as much at risk as Little Ziqiu, unless you can absolutely convince Regent Liu of the invasion."

"And," Kaiya said, "you would just as soon keep me here."

Ziqiu's eyes flicked back to Fu's. "Forgive me, Master, but she is the princess. You can't do this."

"I can." Fu stared Ziqiu down, and then shifted his glare to Kaiya.

She held his gaze. He wasn't exactly wrong. Still… "The palace must be warned."

"How do you propose to do that?" Fu steepled his hands together.

How, indeed?

The door opened, and Song entered. "Master, the imperial couriers bring bad news from the South."

And how did these misguided rebels have access to the imperial couriers?

Fu motioned for Song to continue.

Song sighed. "Still no news out of Dongmen Province. Also, the Madurans have pushed into the central valley. When Ximen Province sent the bulk of its soldiers east to flank Peng's army, traitorous Lord Liang in Nantou attacked them from behind and occupied Ximen."

"The stupidity!" Fu slapped his hand on the desk. "If not for incompetent commanders, the imperial armies and their provincial allies should have crushed the rebellion and the Madurans in two weeks."

Summoning a map in her mind, Kaiya closed her eyes. Even with her poor sense of geography, she saw Cathay faced imminent collapse. Traitors gobbled up the South. Foreign enemies trampled over the North, unchallenged. Three hundred years of peace and prosperity, over in two months. Jobless scholars who knew the secret of firepowder would find new employers, ushering in a new age of warfare. If only they could find a way to just let Regent Liu know—

Opening her eyes, she found everyone staring at her. She composed her expression into regal aloofness. "Fu, how are you intercepting the imperial couriers? And how did you get my half-elf's letter?"

"I have my ways."

If not for the *Tiger's Eye*, his roundabout non-answers might've been infuriating. "Then use those ways. Drop a message into the courier bags, if that is how you do it. However you got Jie's message, send another on. And..." why hadn't she thought of this before? "...what would it take to capture a message tower?"

Fu's face blanked.

Lin Ziqiu clapped her hands together. "Three *li* outside the north city walls, there is a horse relay station and a message tower."

"Yes." Fu turned to Kaiya. "Do you know the light tower codes?"

How would she? Even the *Tianzi* himself probably never concerned himself with such minutia. Well, that went without saying in her brother Kai-Wu's case, but certainly Father had too much to worry about to learn flashing light signals he might never see with his own eyes. Then again, Fu didn't need to know that. "I am surprised the Black Lotus don't know them."

Ziqiu's ears quirked. "Black Fist?"

Fu laughed. "Imperial soldiers, not boogeymen, control the light towers. Those towers have not been used since the last time an enemy breached the Great Wall."

As in, never. Kaiya snorted. Still, this was a chance to escape from her captors. "Then you will need me to go with you."

"Or you can tell us." Fu's eyes narrowed again.

"And if I refuse?"

Fu laughed. "*You* were the one who wanted to warn the regent."

Kaiya looked out the office window. The Iridescent Moon waxed to its mid-crescent. Already late afternoon. Less than three hours of daylight. So much wasted time! "If you are truly a patriot, then you would see the need as well."

Fu stroked his chin, a gesture reminiscent of Tian. "I also see the need to keep an eye on you."

His motives, clearly stated. Kaiya frowned.

Lin Ziqiu sighed. "Master, you can't keep a Scion of Heaven prisoner."

Fu held a finger up. "We do not know if her brother still lives or not. If the grandson of Lord Liu sits as *Tianzi*, then Miss Wang Kaiya is no longer a Scion of Heaven."

It was true. How easy it would be not to carry the burden of responsibility. But no. The Teleri Empire would relegate Cathay men to second-class citizens, and do much worse to the women. Someone had to do something. She opened her mouth to speak.

Fu opened his hand, stopping her. "Which is not to say she can't be Scion of Heaven. We must time her *return* carefully. Now, we must plan the capture of the light tower."

Which would mean unnecessary killing. There had to be another way. "Wait."

Fu looked up at Song, apparently ignoring her. "Inform our asset that we need to insert a message into the imperial courier network."

Song shook his head. "He'll share information, but I don't think he would pass fake messages."

"Even in an emergency?" Fu scowled.

Kaiya stood. "There is an easier way, one that can avoid any casualties. Allow me to go with you, and I will command the couriers and light tower to pass the messages on."

"With your voice, or imperial authority?"

She might not have either, but Fu didn't need to know. "Whichever it takes."

"And how do I know you will continue to accept my protection?"

Kaiya flashed a disarming smile. If he could mince meat as well as words, he might actually be useful. It was a matter of convincing him of her own worth. On her own terms, of course. With two hands, she raised the pouch containing Tian's tablet and bowed her head to it. "I swear on this."

The tablet might not have been what Fu thought, but it was just as important to her. She wouldn't break a promise. As she had learned from the Bovyans, an oath without specifics could be twisted. How long she would *accept* Fu's protection depended on how long he remained useful.

Fu bowed to the tablet. "Very well. Now, we have another problem. The thirty men out there are all anti-imperial insurgents, originally funded by your cousin Peng Kai-Long, before I took over. They aren't about to let you leave."

Liang Yu knew a thing or two about playing two sides, and had already planned a means for getting the princess out. Still, as long as she believed she needed him, he could control her.

Though she might no longer be so naïve, the princess would have a difficult time winning over hardened soldiers who wanted to oust her family from the Jade Throne. Surely her voice could not affect them all.

He just had to redirect their anger once she failed. No telling what they would do to her otherwise. He held the door to let her out of the office.

Back straight and chin lifted high, she stepped out into the warehouse. That wouldn't endear them to her! Her head immediately turned to her bound guards and the men guarding them. Murmurs broke out in the darkened mezzanine.

"Soldiers of Cathay," she said, voice mellifluous. "I understand your grievances."

Or so she thought. Liang Yu grinned. He had told her just enough that she would still need him.

She placed a hand on her chest. "My father always had the nation's best interests at heart, even though you might not have agreed with his decisions."

"Cathay stagnated!" a voice from the mezzanine called, followed by a chorus of agreeing murmurs.

"The lords got rich," another said, "while we soldiers were forgotten when we got older."

"We never got the rewards we were promised."

"There were no wars to fight."

Amid the barrage of complaints, the princess looked at Liang Yu, an eyebrow raised. She was already at a loss. She needed him, just as he planned.

He came to her side and opened his mouth. "Fellow patriots—"

"Soldiers of Cathay." With dexterity rivaling the Surgeon, she slid in front of him and bowed low at the waist. It was unheard of for a member of the Imperial Family to bow to a solider, let alone an insurgent. "We now suffer the consequences of our complacency. Foreign invaders trample on Cathay's soil."

"Madurans." One of the soldiers next to her guards spat on the ground. "They have no chance."

"No." The princess straightened. "The Teleri Empire has captured the East Gate and marches unopposed on the capital."

"A lie!" A crossbow cocked above. Liang Yu tightened his grip on the staff, just in case he had to knock a bolt out of the air. If his old eyes could see it in time. Alas, if only he were as good as the Beauty at it! Surely they wouldn't shoot at the princess. Would they?

"We would have heard."

"They can't just march an army down the highway in secret."

Liang Yu hid his grin. He had trained some of these men to think for themselves, and it showed now.

The princess raised a hand. "Lord Zheng has betrayed the realm and silenced all news coming out of his province. Once the Teleri Army reaches his borders, it will be too late to mobilize and save everyone between here and there."

The same story she'd told him. Plausible, but not likely. Liang Yu gauged his men's reactions, at least the ones he could see. Most looked to him for approval. He shook his head. Truth or not, she needed to know he was her only way out of the warehouse.

The princess swept a hand toward the mezzanine. "Duty to your nation calls. Only with your help can we save the North. I am conscripting you all as my personal guard, under the command of Golden Fu."

The mezzanine lit up. Robes rustled as several men dropped to a knee, fist to the ground. Others followed, more tentatively.

Liang Yu stared at her. *That* was unexpected, like the Beauty going off-script with his plans. The princess hadn't even used the power of her voice.

Well, let her play her games, because when it came down to it, honor and promises didn't feed hungry mouths. He was the one paying these men, and she had no access to the dwindling imperial coffers, anyway.

She turned to him. "General Fu, prepare for our march on the way station."

He bowed. "As the princess commands."

Now, how could they make it through the city without alerting the general populace of her arrival?

Chapter 18:
Existential Crises

The two arrows speeding toward Jie's face effectively delayed her existential crisis.

The first she caught as she spun out of the way of the second. A third, just loosed, she knocked out of the air with the first in her hand.

"Stop!" Tian, or Tian's doppelganger, stood between her and the elf, arms splayed out.

The girl who looked exactly like her, save for the doeskin dress, spewed out several unintelligible syllables. The male elf fitted another arrow and pulled the string back again.

Jie palmed a throwing spike. As soon as Tian, or whoever he was, got out of the way…

The elf circled, but Tian moved to stay between them. He repeated the same word over and over again. At last, the elf lowered his bow.

Tian turned around and stared at her. "Who are you?"

This couldn't be right. They must be in some bizarre land of dread sorcery, inhabited by mirror images of people she knew. Would the princess' facsimile burst onto the path next?

Her own doppelganger sidled up to Tian, stood on her tiptoes and whispered something in his ear. Not breaking his gaze, Tian leaned into her.

Think, think. There was no such magical place. They were still in the Kanin Wilds, harassing Teleri supply lines. She'd just killed a Bovyan and an altivorc, and then avoided a swift death by elf archery.

Which meant, if this was reality…

That man *really* was Tian. He had used a *Black Fist* knife technique to defeat the Bovyan. Now, he tapped his chin, just like always. He whispered something back at her twin.

This couldn't be right. Tian had died—she'd watched with her own eyes as Emperor Geros shot him with a crossbow, then kicked him into the dirt.

Unless. Unless.

Jie sucked her lower lip, dredging up painful memories. Just before the Emperor struck, Tian's expression had melted into one of calm acceptance. It looked nothing like the confusion written on his face now.

Her mouth gaped. He'd lost the *Tiger's Eye*, and then must have put himself into the *Viper's Rest*, which would have slowed his heartbeat and breathing to imperceptible levels.

Which also meant he might not have any idea who he was. *Black Fist* masters practiced the technique with utmost care, to prevent memory loss. Only the legendary Architect had mastered the *Viper's Rest* to the point that he would not lose his sense of self, and some stories suggested he bordered on insane. Jie shuddered to remember her own experiences with the technique.

So that probably explained Tian, whose eyes now moved from her to the half-elf girl.

Who apparently wanted her dead. Who was she? An identical twin, separated at birth? The princess had mentioned something about twins, and a berry that grew in the Wilds. But then her lazy dastard of a father would've abandoned both of them at the temple, right?

Was the arrow-happy elf their father? Like a weed, perhaps he had scattered his seeds farther than imagined. That could possibly explain the little girl, who was sucking on her lower lip.

Except Cathayi people never came out here, and she *did* look a whole lot like the ten-year-old version of herself who could've beaten Ming in a knife fight.

Apparently, just thinking about Ming prompted him to break the shocked silence. "Tian, I am glad to see you alive. Jie told me that Emperor Geros killed you."

The floodgates opened, with questions erupting from all over the place. Everyone spoke at once. Fingers pointed. The elf. Her twin. The little girl. Tian, trying to silence them with frantic gesticulations. Only the enemy Kanin savage hung back, not saying a word.

Ming took a few steps toward Tian, arms outstretched. Everyone quieted.

Tian backed off. Awkward.

"Uh…" Ming stopped in his tracks. His attention fell on Jie's twin. "…interesting company you keep, I—"

The half-elf silenced him with a glare. If anything good came out of this, it would be that Ming could now be terrorized by *two* half-elves.

Though Tian's eyes flicked in Ming's direction, they instantly returned to meet hers. Dark and intelligent as always. Jie's heart hammered in her chest.

Ming's brow furrowed. "Tian!"

Tian's eyes again flashed to Ming before settling on her. He must not even know his own name. Certainly a possible side effect of the *Viper's Rest*.

"Ming, he has lost his memories." Jie wobbled forward a few steps.

With a frown, Ming said, "Apparently. And filled them with swordsmanship. Last time I saw Tian with a sword in his hand, Princess Kaiya beat him with ease."

Her again. Jie's stomach knotted. There was no escaping the princess.

Yet Tian didn't react to the name. He looked from Jie to Ming and back again. "How do you know me?"

Ming spoke loudly enough to scare away the forest animals, enunciating each word with deliberate slowness, as if Tian had lost his hearing and not his memories. "Because. I. Am. Your. Brother."

Tian's nod could only be described as tentative. "You bear a resemblance to me. I agree. But I don't know either of you. I don't even know my own name."

"Tian," Ming said. "Tian. Fourth son of Zheng Han, *Tai-Ming* Lord of Dongmen Province."

Jie drew the character for his name in the air. "Tian, as in sky; Tian as in heavens."

Tian's expression brightened. Did he remember? "That's what the Doe-Eyed Girl called me. In my dream."

Doe-Eyed Girl. That could only be…

"And you." Tian lifted his chin at Ming. "You called me that, too. I thought you were invoking the Heavens."

Ming snorted. The elf archer in deerskin clothes blurted out a few halting syllables.

Tian nodded at the elf. "Tian," he said.

"Tian," her twin repeated. She then jabbed a finger at Jie and unleashed a tirade of foreign words.

He turned back to Jie. "Kiri wants you to show the back of your neck."

Kiri, eh? So she had a name, and an elf-sounding name at that. In order to get answers to her growing number of questions, Jie dropped to a knee. It was safe; the elf had lowered his bow and stowed the arrow. Even if he could nock it pretty fast, Tian wouldn't let the elf shoot her. Hopefully. And she would hear Kiri approaching in time to defend herself. Unclasping the frog ties at the front of her blouse, she shrugged her shirt down to her shoulders and bent her head forward.

Kiri let out a long breath and said a few more words.

"So who are you?" Tian asked.

Who was she? Best friend. Jilted lover. Maybe a twin sister, all of a sudden. Some things were better left unsaid. Jie stood and turned around. Maybe everything was better left unsaid. She flashed their clan hand signals at him. *You Black Fist.*

Brow furrowed, he returned a sign. *What Black Fist?* His ability to respond left absolutely no doubt it was Tian.

The others' heads jerked back and forth, following the exchange. Kiri threw her hands up and blurted out a string of unintelligible words. Tian shrugged.

Jie pointed a finger at her nose. "My name is Jie. You and I belong to the same clan of warrior-spies."

"What?" Ming's mouth slackened.

Kiri tugged at Tian's sleeve, while he shook his head, slowly, and eased back.

Jie stepped toward him and shot her hand out. He lifted his in defense, and their wrists met. The elf's bow was in his hand, an arrow nocked, while Kiri stumbled back a few steps.

Ignoring them, Jie lowered into a broad stance and pressed her wrist against his. His body melted into the same stance as he turned at the waist and redirected her force to the side. He twisted his hips back and leaned into her center of gravity. Sinking deeper into her stance, Jie unleashed a flurry of preset patterns. Tian reacted with prearranged responses, the pressure at the point of contact between their hands remaining constant.

She disengaged, pirouetting back in a flourishing end to the form. She settled into the final pose, a single arm outstretched, wrist bent and palm upturned, her other hand arced above her head.

A few steps away, Tian mirrored her. His Yang to her Yin, they were meant for each other.

Maybe the *Pushing Hands* game of *Supreme Ultimate Fist* had jolted his memory.

Black Fist. The word meant nothing to Feneyas, beyond Jie's explanation of warrior-spies.

However, there was no doubting the veracity of her claims after their martial dance. His every technique harmonized with hers, an orchestra of offensive and defensive energies. Now, there she stood just six feet away, her pose mirroring his exactly.

He looked up and stared at his arms. At least *Black Fist* explained where the fighting skills came from. No telling what those hands had done in the past.

If he and Jie belonged to the same clan, it might explain the sense of familiarity Kiri stirred in him. Though how did Kiri and Jie look exactly alike? Identical twins?

He turned to Kiri. "Why did you want to see the scar on her neck?"

Her brows scrunched together and shook her head. "She doesn't have one."

"She has a few marks, like yours." Though in truth, unlike Kiri's ugly long scars, Jie's had been masterfully stitched. Except one on her right shoulder, whose jagged lines looked like a sailor had knotted them together with rope.

"Not like mine. And not one here." Kiri turned and tapped the blotch on her back, at the base of her neck. "She's not one of us."

"One of you?"

"Vrztchkrn."

Feneyas cringed at the strange sound. "I don't know what it is."

Kiri pointed at Turquoise Man's body. "*Their* language. I don't know how to translate in Kanin or Elvish. Maybe *sisters*. Exact sisters."

"Twins," Feneyas used the word from the Kanin dialect. Though the term, at least as he understood it, didn't exactly mean the same as *identical twins* in his native language.

Dior pointed at Ming. "And what about you and the other Man From Beyond the Wall? Is he your twin?"

"A brother, at least," Feneyas said, shrugging. One he didn't remember, and who seemed more like Jie's comic sidekick.

Jie cleared her throat. "What's Kiri saying about the altivorc?"

Altivorc. The race of non-human mercenaries, Feneyas remembered now. Kiri didn't even understand the language spoken among the Metal Men, yet the very sight of the altivorc sent her into a panic. She could also speak the altivorc language. He shook his head and locked his gaze on Jie. "Nothing really, just told me a word in their tongue. *Identical twins.*"

Ming nodded. "They look exactly alike, like two cherries from the same tree." His smile then melted and he muttered something inaudibly under his breath.

Jie shot him a glare, and he stared down at his feet. Harrumphing, she shifted her gaze to Kiri. "That must be it: we are identical twins." She took a hesitant step toward her twin and stretched out her hand. "May I?"

Kiri stared at the hand, then looked up. "I'm sorry I had Dior attack you. I thought you were someone else."

The two just talked past each other, neither understanding their counterpart's language. How strange that a man without memories would most likely end up as translator between long-lost sisters. Jie's hand touched Kiri's shoulder, making the girl flinch.

Jie looked up at him. "I never knew I had a real sister. An identical twin, no less." Her eyes bent toward Dior. "Is the elf our father?"

Feneyas almost choked. "Dior? No. Just a friend."

"What did she say?" Dior stroked an arrow's fletching.

"She asked what your relationship was to Kiri."

Dior chuckled. "Guardian. Conscience."

"And what about her?" Jie tilted her chin at Kala.

Feneyas scratched his chin. Their relationship had never been explained, since Kiri refused to talk about her past, and Kala barely spoke Kanin. He had always assumed that from the way Kiri cared for Kala, and their similar appearance, they must be sisters. "Sisters, maybe?"

Ming nodded. "Just like us, brothers."

"Can you ask?" Jie's stare bored into him.

Tian nodded, then turned back to Kiri. "Are you and Kala sisters?"

"Vrztchkrn."

That word again, which sounded like a pack of angry dogs fighting over table scraps. Tian looked back at Jie, nodding. "Sisters."

Jie and Kiri peered at one another, sizing each other up.

He would have to mediate. But first, he had a lot of questions, one which pricked at him more than the others. "I want to ask you something. I have dreamed about a beautiful Doe-Eyed Girl. She seems to be an important part of my past, but I don't recall how. What can you tell me about her?"

Chapter 19:
Smoke Signals

The last time Kaiya marched at the head of an army, it'd been a contingent of Paladins and her imperial guard, to face down Avarax.

Today, she led a ragtag militia of forty-two insurgents and eight green imperial soldiers, commanded by a middle-aged spy. Who walked with a staff.

Not to mention he held Weiyong hostage back at the warehouse, to ensure her good behavior. Apparently, trust only went so far.

At Fu's insistence, she kept her hood up as they travelled in small clusters through the capital, where the crowds went about their daily lives. Little by little, they wasted precious time regrouping on the road by the way station, three *li* outside the city walls as Ziqiu had said.

Kaiya found the Iridescent Moon, now waxing to half. Not long until dusk. Soon, the light signals would be visible for several *li*. She turned her attention to the tower.

Cut from blocks of stone, it rose some sixty feet into the air. Beside it, several imperial soldiers lounged outside the stables and barracks. Some gambled over dice, while one read. More than a few afforded her army a cursory glance, yet made no move to approach or warn the rest of the garrison. The martial discipline Father had once inspired was gone.

Kaiya looked to Fu. "We do not want to make them nervous with so many armed men. You and Song accompany me. There will be no need for violence." She hoped.

Fu smirked. "And if you do take command of the tower without drawing a sword, what is to keep you from ordering the imperial soldiers to arrest us?"

"I swore on this." She held up Tian's tablet, still hidden its pouch. No need to mention that Weiyong's safety depended on it, since they both knew it.

"Very well, *Dian-xia*." He bowed and stretched a hand toward the tower.

Tired and wearing commoners' travelling clothes, she hardly looked the part of a princess. Without the power of her voice, convincing the imperial soldiers of her identity might prove to be difficult. Perhaps she should ask Fu to come up with a backup plan, just in case…

No; he probably had a plan ready anyway, most likely involving the killing of loyal men. With a deep breath, she took several steps toward the tower. Fu and Song followed just behind.

The imperial soldiers watched their approach with disinterest, most turning back to whatever they were doing.

Unacceptable.

With such poor discipline, they didn't stand a chance against the Teleri. Lifting her chin and straightening her carriage, Kaiya lowered her hood and shifted her hesitant gait into a delicate glide. The soldiers now murmured and pointed, and many squared their backs and shoulders.

She stopped by the tower. The two sentries' roving eyes served as a reminder that her beauty alone was formidable weapon against gullible men. Infused with magic or not, her tone carried imperial authority. "Summon your commander."

The soldiers glanced among themselves, their confusion clear in their expressions.

Fu slammed the butt end of his staff into the ground. His voice flared with anger. "Princess Kaiya gave you a command!"

The men dropped to a knee, fist to the ground. "Yes, *Dian-xia*," the shouted in unison.

"Rise." She lifted a hand. Thank the Heavens for Fu's impeccable timing.

The sentries stood and held rigid stances. One ran into the tower. Hopefully, the commander would be just as compliant.

Presently, a middle-aged man with oil-coifed hair and an impeccable uniform emerged. His insignias marked him as a captain. His eyes fell on her and widened.

He dropped to a knee. "*Dian-xia*."

"Rise, Captain," she said, "and tell me the latest news out of Dongmen Province."

Standing, the captain's attention shifted from her to her companions and back. "The last message out of Dongmen was four days ago. The palace has not sent any couriers in this direction in days."

Four days ago. Right before her escape. Lord Zheng must have cut communications soon after. She cast a sidelong glance at Fu. Hopefully he'd be placated.

She turned to the commander, who returned her gaze instead of averting his eyes as protocol demanded. "A Teleri army marches on the capital from Dongmen. Send a rider through the relay stations to confirm that."

He shook his head. "*Dian-xia*, this is highly irregular. I must have official authorization."

"I am the sister of the *Tianzi*. Do it." She drew herself up to her full height and glared at him, sending his eyes downward.

He, along with his fellow guards, dropped to a knee, fist to the ground. "Yes, *Dian-xia*."

"Send another courier to the palace to inform them of the invasion."

The captain looked up, his mouth agape. "Before we confirm it?"

"Time is of the essence. Do you not believe a Scion of Heaven?" She squared her shoulders.

"Of course I believe you." He bowed again. "However, this is just a relay station. I don't have the official correspondence seals."

Kaiya placed a hand on her chest. "Have your scribe write it, and I will sign." Would the relay stations believe it? While the nations of the Arkothi North used signatures and wax imprints, Cathay only used such means for personal correspondence. Probably no one outside her circle of friends and the rebel Lord Peng had even seen her handwriting before.

"Yes, *Dian-xia*." The captain beckoned one of his men. "Prepare for a dispatch, both inbound and outbound."

As the soldier ran off to the stables, she peered west, where the hazy red sun peeked just above the horizon. With an open hand, she waved toward the tower. "Now captain, let us alight the tower and prepare a message."

If the captain's mouth could open any wider, he probably still wouldn't be able to fit his equally large eyes in it. "The light tower hasn't been used in… in…"

"Never." Kaiya composed her most grave expression. "My ancestor erected the towers, and since then, Cathay has never suffered an invasion. She does now."

"Yes, *Dian-xia*. Please follow me." Holding a low bow, the captain beckoned them into the tower.

Kaiya placed a hand over her belly, where her twins grew. It was a long climb up those steps.

With Little Song flanking him, Liang Yu eyed the princess, who sat at the captain's wooden desk, panting. Surely, a short trip up two flights of spiraling stone stairs should be easy for such a young woman, a dancer no less. Nonetheless, her brow furrowed with unmistakable fatigue. She had not so much as whiffed the tea and egg custard pastry the lieutenant had offered.

Still, tired or not, her poise and authority had captured the tower with only words, and prevented needless bloodshed. Perhaps she was worth much more than any of the nearsighted hereditary lords had thought.

The captain reappeared at the office door and bowed. "*Dian-xia*, I have sent couriers toward Dongmen."

Eyes narrowing, she stood and walked around the desk, interposing herself between Liang Yu and the captain. "What about the capital?"

"Yes, that too." He scratched his nose, a telltale sign of a lie.

The princess pointed up. "Then let us climb the tower to send the signals."

"Forgive my impertinence, *Dian-xia*." His eyes darted from her to Fu and Song and back. "I will wait until a courier returns before I send the message."

Such a waste of time. The relay couriers would take at least two hours to reach the border of Dongmen. Not to mention, they weren't scouts, looking out for enemies. Even if they didn't get caught, the message to the capital would be delayed for four hours.

The princess had already gotten them inside, past the bulk of the garrison. The rest was easy. It was time to channel his inner Surgeon. Shuffling forward a step, Liang Yu grasped both ends of his staff, ready to expose the spear and sword. They didn't need this capt—

The princess shot her hand back, barring the path to his intended victim. "Captain, I understand your concern. However, every hour we wait gives the imperial armies one less hour to mobilize."

Chewing on his lip, the captain's attention shifted from Song to Liang Yu and back to the princess.

Her head tilted, and she ran a hand behind her ear. When she spoke, a breathy, sultry tone replaced her imperial voice. A trick the Beauty had used time and time again. "Please. I will accept full responsibility."

"I… uh, as the princess commands." Pupils dilated, the captain sucked on a lip and bowed.

What had the nation and its soldiers come to? Apparently, a beautiful woman's charms could work better than imperial authority these days. The man straightened and strode to a bookshelf. He pulled out thread-bound book and dusted it off.

Liang Yu frowned. If only his old eyes could make out the title on the cover before the captain opened it. "This is no time to read."

The captain held it up. "These are the codes for the light signals."

Incompetence! They should know these codes by memory. "I am sure it is not every day that royalty strolls into a watchtower, but—"

The princess shot him an angry glance, one that demanded silence. Why? She could just tell him the sequence of signals.

Unless she had lied about knowing the codes. Not only that, if she were in such a hurry, why did she waste time making requests instead of just using the magic of her voice?

Kaiya fought to stay upright, hands on her knees as she huffed for air. The climb to the top of the tower had proved even more daunting than it initially appeared. It didn't help that the pungent pastries had sent waves of nausea roiling through her stomach. Hopefully, Fu hadn't noticed.

She looked up. His narrowed eyes relaxed and his expression blanked. Flashing a smile, she straightened and gazed through dusk's cloak over the surrounding farmland. A courier horse clopped in the distance, heading toward Dongmen.

Of course, the light signal would arrive sooner, if only the captain could get the shutters to work. He fiddled with the metal slats. "*Dian-xia*, the hinges have rusted."

Rusted! Perhaps the Expansionist faction had been right all along. The realm had fallen into complacency, too secure with a hundred thousand guns pointed out from behind the Wall. The great lords, Father included, never considered the possibility of fighting an invading army on open ground.

She frowned. "Hurry."

He bowed. "Sorry, *Dian-Xia*."

Fu sidled up to the captain, who in turn nudged Fu to the side. With a graceful twist which belied Fu's age but lent credence to his claims of a Black Fist background, he spun around to the other side of the captain, right next to the shutter mechanism.

He snorted. "*Dian-xia*, the hinges are fine." He pulled on a lever, and the dozen slats whispered open. Bright light flared from the crystal globe within.

Blinking away the orange glare in her visual field, Kaiya gasped. Had the crystal carried a magical enchantment all this time, for three hundred years? Glowing unknown in perpetuity, until this very moment? Maybe the elf lord Xu had infused them himself.

"Look!" Song pointed into the countryside.

In the indeterminate distance, small orbs lit up in slow succession, forming a dotted line to the north. Kaiya turned in the other direction. A light glowed on the main gatehouse of the north capital walls. A couple dozen seconds later, another one flashed from a tower inside the city, followed not long after by one on Sun-Moon Lake.

The palace knew! What must they be thinking? What about the general populace? The lights had never been seen before, after all.

Kaiya's heart fluttered with excitement before the *Tiger's Eye* stifled that emotion. "Captain, hurry. Send an encoded message."

The captain licked his lips, and shifted on his feet.

Something wasn't right. She exchanged glances with Fu, who jerked his head toward the light with a look of askance. Of course, he believed she knew the codes. She'd implied as much.

She glowered at the captain. "I order you to send the message."

"As the princess commands." He bowed and placed his hands on the lever. With several pushes and pulls of varying lengths, the light blinked and flashed.

She squinted back toward the palace, some thirty *li* away. As far as she could tell, the dots of light blinked the same sequence… Followed by a new one?

Fu apparently noticed, too. "What was the response?"

The captain's face contorted. "That they received the message, and for the towers to await further orders."

With a rasp, Fu separated his spear and sword. One, he placed across the captain's throat.

Song's hand took her wrist in a strong grip and wrenched her arm behind her back.

"Now, captain," Fu said, "what did the response *really* say?"

"Just what the princess commanded. That a Teleri army has breached the Walls at Dongmen."

Fu snorted. "And why did you only send a horse toward Dongmen, but not to the capital?"

Kaiya listened again. Yes, a horse clopped north, but none headed south.

The captain shouted, "Men, surround the tower. Don't let anyone in or out."

Chapter 20:
Old and New Scars

Though she'd spent a year blindfolded during her training, Jie had never excelled at blind techniques like her human clan brothers and sisters. With elf vision, she rarely needed them. Now, however, she tripped and stumbled on numerous occasions as they traipsed through the forest, each time bruising her ego as much as her body.

All Tian's fault. If he hadn't decided to be alive, maybe she wouldn't be so bewildered. The simultaneous discovery of a missing twin, now holding on to her arm and doing an awful job of guiding her through obstacles, didn't help matters.

What was her twin's story? Did she know their father? She could apparently speak the altivorc language and was scared of Jie. There was an unbelievable story somewhere in there, even beyond the improbable reunion with an amnesiac Tian.

Meanwhile, the Teleri moved supplies through the Wilds unhindered, to support their invasion of Cathay.

Crack! She stepped on a dry branch, and would've fallen on her face if Kiri hadn't supported her.

Brushing off her hands, and also what was left of her dignity, Jie sighed. "Is the blindfold necessary? I'm lost."

"It's not that bad," Ming chirped from somewhere behind her.

How humiliating. Shown up by Ming, of all people. However, it seemed like Tian was doing a better job at leading him through the forest compared to her own guide.

"We're almost there." Tian's voice bore into her back, his unanswered question undoubtedly still weighing on him. Amnesiac or not, his need to know, and know *now*, remained.

A wife and unborn children, possibly his, were more than he needed to learn about in his state. Right? Yes. There'd be a better time and place for that.

Heavy boots clomped on pavestones in the distance. A hand pressed on her shoulder and pushed her down. The underbrush rustled as Tian, Kiri, Kala, and Dior sunk to the forest floor.

"Ouch!" Ming hissed as he clumsily fell into a shrub. "The shoulder!"

"Shh," Tian said.

The blindfold came off, and Jie's eyes adjusted. She peered through the trees in the direction of clopping boots and jingling chainmail. Light glinted off metal, with the occasional flash of red feathers.

At least thirty Bovyan soldiers guarded over a hundred natives and ten horse-drawn provision carts. They headed west to supply the Teleri invasion of Cathay.

She and Ming—or rather, *she*—had been harassing these convoys for over a week now, first on the overgrown paths near Cathay, and later on the restored roads. With an elf archer and Tian, it would be even easier. She started forward to get a better view, only to be restrained by Tian's hand.

He shook his head and flashed the Black Lotus signals, *Stay down, keep quiet.*

Why?

Too dangerous. He grinned for the first time, the crooked smile that sent her heart pounding.

She glanced back at the others. The elf watched their hands dance with a look that could only be described as bored. Ming gawked, while little Kala huddled low, oblivious. Kiri, on the other hand, scowled, her lips tight enough to crush a walnut.

Jie knew that expression. Her own, when jealous. Used with alarming frequency while in service to the princess. Perhaps her twin shared expressions *and* an attraction to a not-so-dead man.

The sound of marching boots and creaking wheels faded in the distance, and with it, the opportunity to wreak havoc on the Teleri supply lines. Dior motioned them up.

"We could've slowed them down." Jie put her hands on her hips. "I've been doing it for over a week now. I—"

"*We*," Ming inserted.

Jie raised her voice. "*I* have sabotaged their supplies, and made their lives miserable. We need to get back to that."

Ming snorted. "You couldn't have done much without my help." If *help* meant distracting the Teleri with incompetence...

The elf faced Tian and spoke in a string of syllables that sounded not much different from the secret Cathay imperial language. Tian pointed in the direction of the men, then Jie, all the while fumbling through the same language. Kiri apparently added her opinion as well, leaving Ming and Jie to exchange glances.

With a shake of his head, Tian turned to her. "Their village is close by. The elves don't want the Metal Men to even know they exist. It's the best way to protect their home."

Jie sucked on her lower lip. "What about *your* home? The Teleri march on Cathay, and your own father let them in."

He stared back at her, expression empty. Ming studied his feet, sharing Tian's guilt.

No, she wouldn't let their guilty feelings cow her into silence. Not when the realm and all its women relied on their help.

She continued, relentless, "Think of what they did to the natives here. They will do the same, if not worse, to your *own* people. What Emperor Geros himself did to—" no, better not to bring *her* into the conversation, for Tian's own good, "—so many women."

Dior poked Tian in the back and they exchanged more words. Kiri joined in, her frown and tone evidently conveying her opinion in no uncertain terms.

Tian turned back. "That's not the elves' concern." Apparently, he'd gone native.

"It will be." Ming kept his voice low. "The Wilds lie between Cathay and them, and they will eventually connect it all. No one on the plateau will be safe, not even these elves."

Jie studied Ming. Someone had swapped out the bumbling buffoon for a *Tai-Ming* heir. She nodded at Tian. "Translate."

His gaze shifted from Ming and settled on her. He then spoke again to the elves.

After a brief exchange, Tian nodded. "Dior says your argument has merit. He will present your case—"

"*Our* case." She glared at him.

"—our case back at the village for the people to discuss."

Great. More elves, and from the look of it, more blindfolds, too.

Tian. His name was Tian, even if the revelation didn't jar any memories.

Now he couldn't get back to the treetop village soon enough. Whoever this Jie was, whatever his relationship to her, she remained tight-lipped about the Doe-Eyed Girl from his dreams. So many questions about his past, and yet, Jie cared more about the future. Namely, the threat of the Metal Men to a homeland he didn't remember.

"Were you looking for me?" He pulled Ming to the side, just avoiding a limb that would've smacked his supposed brother in the face.

"Ow! The shoulder!" Ming winced. "No, I thought you were dead."

"Then how'd you come to be here?"

"The insane half-elf." Ming pointed in the wrong direction. "We were stuck on the wrong side of the Wall, and instead of trying to find a way back in, she took us deeper into the Wilds."

Insane didn't quite seem to do Jie justice. But Ming was leaving something out. Tian frowned. "Why?"

"Ask her. I'm still trying to figure it out." Ming threw his hands up, but then immediately grimaced and grabbed his left shoulder. "Though I am pleased we found you."

"What happened to your shoulder?"

Expression souring, Ming rubbed it. "A Teleri soldier stabbed me. It will be a miracle if I ever draw a bow again."

Miracles apparently happened around here. Tian removed his brother's blindfold and pointed up the tree. "Here we are. Perhaps the elves' shaman can help you."

Ming looked up the circling branches. "It's just a tree canopy."

The others gathered around the base of the tree, except for Kala, who pranced up the branches. Jie tracked the girl, then met Tian's gaze. She raised her eyebrow and quirked her lips in the cutest manner.

Her question was clear. Tian nodded. "Yes, the village. You'll be surprised."

With a shrug, she followed Kala up. Kiri's glare was sharp enough to shear cured leather, yet she said nothing as she joined her unexpected twin. The rest of the group followed.

At the top, dozens of elves gathered, many gazing with curiosity at Jie. Ming's eyes rounded as wide as walnuts. Jie's expression blanked, but her irises drifted across the platforms and bridges, pausing on any elf with a weapon. Just like Tian himself had done the first time.

Dior called out, "More strangers, and even more mysteries." He pointed to Ming. "Feneyas' brother, coming to search for him." As attention drifted to Ming, Dior shifted an open palm toward Jie. "And her."

The elves murmured among themselves in a low hum of musical voices. Though their language escaped him, Tian could guess the general sentiment from their nods and gestures: she and Kiri looked exactly alike. Jie stared back at them, her brow wrinkling.

Layani, the elves' best warrior, spoke with Kiri, their voices getting louder with each exchange. Kiri shook her head vehemently before snapping her lips shut and staring out into the forest. Oh, to be able to speak their language.

Tian sighed. What was it with these half-elves withholding information? Kiri apparently knew more about her relationship to Jie, yet refused to explain. Jie would not speak of the Doe-Eyed Girl.

Sidling over as the elves' debate reached a crescendo, Ming whispered in Tian's ear, "What are they saying?"

"I'd surmise they have the same question. As you and I." Tian jutted his chin first at Kiri, then at Jie.

"And me." Jie crossed her arms. "I hate that they're talking about me and I have no idea what they're saying."

"Enough." Using the Kanin dialect, the shaman Nayori's voice cut through the animated discussion, bringing the treetops to silence. She sang several words, and a wind whistled through the village.

When she spoke again, her elf words echoed back in the Cathay tongue. "Feneyas, you wished to learn who you are. You have been reunited with those who know you."

The unspoken message left no doubt:

He should go.

To the elves, he must be like a wolf that scavenged on the edge of a Kanin village. Tolerated, amusing to watch, yet not loved like the tribe's dogs. They would not miss him if he left.

Yet how could he, with so many questions left unresolved? Only Kiri could answer some of those, if they could coax her to talk about something so obviously painful.

"Wait," Tian said. "The Metal Men come in greater numbers."

Nayori nodded. "Headed west, to your home beyond the Wall."

Jie raised an open hand. "Not if we sabotage them here. Their army needs supplies, transported across the plateau."

At least until they established a foothold in Cathay and ravished the lands there. Tian's eyed edged toward the shaman.

Nayori regarded Jie with a frown. "You would turn *our* home into a battleground."

Muttering under his breath, Ming said, "The elf's got a point."

Jie's glare immediately cowed him into silence. "If the Teleri occupy Cathay, they will engulf this area from two sides."

"Just like the stories." Dior sounded strange speaking in the language from beyond the Wall. "Our grandparents lived through the first human empires, who cut down the sacred trees and carved up our homeland."

Kiri chimed in, her voice's similarities to Jie's more than a little disconcerting. "Until the Heavens rained fire."

The elves murmured, their voices swirling around them like ghosts of the people from beyond the Wall. A shiver crawled up Tian's spine.

"Allow us to stay just a little longer," he said. "Until the shaman who knows me arrives." It would not be much longer, maybe only four or five days.

Nayori's gaze met each of the elves'. Some nodded, others shook their heads. None seemed completely convinced.

"We will consider it," she said. "Eat and rest. I will inform you of our decision tomorrow."

Perhaps that would be enough time to get Kiri to reveal what she knew of the half-elves' shared past—and in turn, get Jie to shed some light on the Doe-Eyed Girl.

Ming jerked straight up in his hammock, the bizarre dream yanking him from much-needed sleep. Princess Kaiya. His father. An unenviable choice. All slipped from his memory before he could process the meaning.

Bright light filtered in through the tree canopy, the dappling falling right across his face and waking him for good. Apparently, everything in this forest taunted him. He blinked the gunk from his eyes, and the little half-elf girl came into focus next to him.

Pointing down, Kala babbled something in a melodious language and beckoned for him to follow.

What was her rush, so early? Ming stretched his arms out… and his shoulder *didn't* hurt. His eyes must be round as imperial jade medallions. He stood and followed the girl down the trees. At the bottom, he looked up. Like before, there was no sign of the treetop village.

A tug on his sleeve brought his gaze back down. Kala held out some dried berries and lifted her chin to him. An offer. Ming extended his hand and she dumped them into his palm.

Chewing on the sweetish-sour berries, he followed the half-elf through twists and turns between the trees. Birds chirped and animals scuttled through the branches above, yet there was no other sign of intelligent life.

He tapped Kala on the shoulder. "Where are we going?"

She turned and cocked her head, but then pointed. "Friend. There."

Ming scratched his chin. Apparently, the girl could speak a few words of the Cathay tongue. After a few minutes they emerged into a clearing.

A dozen elves were gathered, practicing archery. Ming skidded to a halt, even as Kala continued walking. His shoulder felt great; maybe he could draw a bow.

With all the women so beautiful, he sauntered over to the most scantily-clad. The brunette's top, made of finely-stitched animal skin, exposed her midriff and revealed more than a Cathay bust binder.

"May I?" He extended a hand toward her weapon.

She stared at him with liquid brown eyes that sent a tingle up his spine. Speaking a few words in what didn't sound like Elvish, she patted the shoulder of a boy and proffered her bow and a quiver of arrows.

Kala appeared at his side. "She challenge."

Challenge? A woman? All Ming wanted to do was test the draw. He pointed to the maiden and raised an eyebrow.

Kala shook her head, then tilted her chin toward the youth. He couldn't be much older than the equivalent of twelve human years, and his bow looked like a toy. "Son."

The insult! Ming fit an arrow and pointed at the rotting stump at thirty paces.

Shaking her head, the mother pointed in the distance.

Ming squinted. Apparently, she'd chosen a cone hanging from a sweet evergreen twice as far away as the stump. A difficult shot with his own weapon, and the weight and tension of the elf bow felt all wrong. At least his shoulder didn't hurt at all. Just a little stiff. The shaman's magic was nothing short of miraculous, despite the bizarre dreams that accompanied the healing.

He took aim at the cone. A little left. Up a little… and loosed.

The arrow flew between the gaps in the trees and lodged deep into a trunk just a few hands from the target. So much power! And close. Still, a sinking feeling settled in his gut. Could this kid hit such a small target, so far away? If he did… Oh, the embarrassment.

At his side, the boy drew the bow and shot in a quick, smooth motion. The arrow sailed true, dislodging the cone from the branch. He met Ming's gaze, eyes curious, with no hint of maliciousness or gloating. Many of the elves afforded Ming a sympathetic, if patronizing nod. He looked back down.

The boy was gone.

He glanced around the clearing to find himself alone. The birds had stopped chirping. A chorus of chainmail jangled somewhere not far away.

Chapter 21:
Homecoming

Sword still held at the captain's throat, Liang Yu stared at the princess. After claiming her allegiance, it looked like she had betrayed him. If that were the case, she'd join a long list of betrayals, which started with his own master and comrades thirty-three years before.

Unlike the others, she'd earn her comeuppance now. He pointed the spear tip at her. "What did the light signals say?"

For good measure, Little Song twisted her arm.

The princess yelped. Gritting through her teeth, she said, "I don't know. I swear." Her gaze shifted to the captain. Pleading?

"Your oaths aren't worth much." He used the spear to lift the pouch containing the imperial plaque from the fold of her robe. "You swore on this."

She nodded. "To accept your protection."

"You lied."

Eyes narrowing, she shook her head. "I did not lie. I never said I knew the codes, just that I was surprised the Black Fist didn't."

True enough. Or at least, a half-truth. Liang Yu pursed his lips. "Then why?"

"So you would bring me here. So I could get my message sent to the capital, and you wouldn't kill anyone."

Her voice sounded sincere, and there were no signs of lies in her expression. Then again, leaders regularly manipulated their underlings with pretty words. If she truly cared about the lives of anonymous soldiers… there was a way to test that.

"I will kill someone now." He pressed his sword into Captain Zhou's neck.

Zhou went rigid.

"No!" She reached out with her free hand and struggled forward. Little Song wrenched her arm up, sending her to her knees with a squeak. "No, please. You don't have to kill him. Captain Zhou, please tell us what your message was." Her hand strayed to her belly, even though she had fallen to her knees.

The captain let out a long breath. "That this tower was commandeered by insurgents, led by someone claiming to be Princess Kaiya." His pulse remained rapid beneath Liang Yu's grip, no other physiological sign of a lie.

"And?" the princess said. "What was the response?"

"The palace commanded me to detain you until they arrive."

Of course. The unprecedented use of a tower light. If Regent Liu believed it was the princess, he'd see her as a threat to his grandson's claim to the throne. A cavalry unit could mobilize and reach the tower in less than an hour. Liang Yu pulled the captain to the edge and looked down. Below, the way station garrison formed up in defensive positions, maybe thirty men in all.

He could get out of this trap, but not with the princess, maybe not with Little Song. Not unless he let his men fight against imperial soldiers. Toe-to-toe, his partisans wouldn't stand a chance against regular soldiers. Better to live and fight another day. If only he'd thought that way in his youth, maybe the Surgeon and Beauty would still be alive.

The princess, still on her knees, bowed low. "Let the captain go. We gain nothing by killing him."

Liang Yu shoved the captain toward the others and snapped his weapons back into staff form. "Little Song, surrender. Do your best to protect the princess." With one last glance at her, he swept out of the door and into the stairwell.

Shocked murmurs erupted among the armored cavalrymen as Kaiya emerged from the tower. Hands folded in front of her, she straightened her carriage and swept her gaze over the hundreds of people. Light bauble lamps illuminated their faces and cast shadows over wide eyes and gaping mouths. Sent from the palace, they were here to take her into custody. Nonetheless, their expressions suggested they recognized her. Many looked down, as protocol demanded.

"Here are the insurgents we captured. The rest retreated back toward the city." Captain Zhou prodded Song forward, hands bound in front of him. He then placed a hand at the small of her back and pressed her forward. "This one claimed to be Princess Kaiya."

The cavalry commander dismounted from a black imperial stallion. Reaching back, he received a lamp from a lieutenant and held it up to her face.

Kaiya squared her shoulders and locked gazes with him.

He sank to his knee, fist to the ground, and bowed. "*Dian-xia.*"

Captain Zhou gasped. Then he shuffled back two steps and dropped to his knees. He pressed his forehead to the ground. "Forgive me, *Dian-xia*."

"Rise," she said. "There is nothing to forgive. You made the correct choice, but now we must warn the regent of the impending Teleri invasion. Release my aide." She gestured toward Little Song.

"No." The cavalry commander rose in a jingle of armor. "I am sorry, *Dian-xia*, but Regent Liu has ordered us to take you into custody."

Taken into custody! Then what Fu had said was correct, Liu Yong saw her as a threat to his grandchild. And where was Fu? He'd disappeared down into the tower. With just one exit, he was certainly trapped inside… or was he? Jie had escaped from worse situations.

Was it for the better, or worse? Though an invaluable resource, Fu was a tenuous ally at best. A dangerous bedfellow. By the glint in his eyes, he'd been about to kill the captain. Her plea must have persuaded him. Hopefully, he wouldn't do anything to Fang Weiyong.

"Hurry, then. We must return to the capital to warn the regent of the pending invasion." She presented her hands, palm up, for the commander to bind.

He shook his head. "That is not necessary. You upheld the honor of our captain Xie Shimin, and for that we are grateful."

Kaiya's heart stirred from beneath the *Tiger's Eye*. It was just over a year since Xie Shimin had tried to assassinate Tarkoth's Prince Aelward. Such a short time, yet she was no longer the naïve girl who'd convinced Xie to reveal clues to the conspiracy.

"Are you well enough to ride?" The commander motioned to the horses.

Kaiya nodded.

The commander beckoned to an underling. "Bring the princess a mount."

A soldier rode his horse forward and swung out of the saddle in front of her. He dropped to all fours and bowed. "Please, *Dian-xia.*"

Grabbing the pommel, she stepped onto the man's back and pulled herself into the saddle. The smell of horse sent her stomach into rebellion. She covered her mouth.

Curse this morning sickness. Would it be safe to ride? If only she'd paid more attention to Doctor Wu's physiology lessons. She beckoned toward Song. "Allow my guard to accompany me."

The commander nodded and waved for another horse. Even with his hands tied, Song swung into the saddle with nonchalant grace. Mounting up, the commander gazed out over his men and then gave a signal. With expert precision, the horsemen peeled off in ranks of four and trotted back toward the capital with rhythmic clops.

The ride jostled Kaiya in the saddle. She kept a hand over her belly. Hopefully, her babies would be all right despite the knocks and bumps.

And what would happen when she faced Regent Liu? Would he believe her news of the impending Teleri invasion?

She'd find out soon enough. In ten minutes, they reached the city's open north gate. Soldiers pounded on drums, the combination of low beats signaling the arrival of an Imperial Family member. In the distance, the same pattern repeated.

Even at this late hour, windows and doors opened as they rode by. Excited commoners whispered and pointed. Most bowed low. Several shouted out.

"Princess Kaiya has returned!"

"The princess!"

"*Dian-xia.*"

Before long, her return after half a year would be on everyone's lips.

Had her emotions guided her, the sights and smells of the city might pique nostalgia. Now, the blooming plum blossoms did little to bring back memories of an innocent youth.

"What do the tower lights mean?" one woman yelled.

The crowds nodded and repeated the question over and over again, each time with more urgency. What had she done? Instigated mass panic? Of course, no one had ever seen the tower lights actually in use, and nobody knew what the signals meant.

The cavalrymen formed up around her, insulating her from the amassing city folk. Kaiya glanced over her shoulder. Where had Song disappeared to? She looked from side to side. Nowhere to be seen. Pointing and waving, some of the cavalry discussed his disappearance.

Another drumbeat echoed, its deep bass marking it as a palace drum. She gazed up to see the gates of Sun-Moon Palace up ahead.

They dismounted at the first moat. Flanked by a commander and several of his men, they crossed over the arching marble bridge. In the plaza on the other side, twenty imperial guards in blue robes and burnished breastplates dropped to a knee.

"*Dian-xia,*" they all shouted in unison.

The cavalrymen stepped back and sank down as well, leaving her halfway between the lines of soldiers, in the moons-cast shadows of the palace walls.

An unfamiliar imperial guard—the commander, by his insignia—rose and stepped forward. "Welcome back, *Dian-xia*. I am General Jin. Please accept my apologies that I must present you to the regent as a prisoner."

A prisoner, in her own home. Her supposed bodyguard Song had also disappeared. When?

Kaiya suppressed a wry smile. Another wave of nausea threatened, but she squared her shoulders. Eschewing feminine grace, she purposefully strode toward the open main gates. The imperial guards formed up behind her.

Keeping her attention forward, she asked the general, "Is there any news of my brother, the *Tianzi*?"

"No, *Dian-xia*. He has sequestered himself in the main keep, with no communication in or out. For all intents and purposes, he has abdicated. Liu Yong is acting *Tianzi* until we can confirm the previous *Tianzi's* fate."

Kaiya stifled a sigh. Despite the well-organized ministries and official bureaucracy, the nation was paralyzed unless someone at the top gave those first orders. Now, that person was a baby boy.

She looked up, to where the nearly-full White Moon, near-open Blue Moon, and waxing Iridescent Moon floated inexorably toward their conjunction.

A crier yelled out. "Princess Kaiya has returned."

On the other side of the main gate, the moonlight bathed the central courtyard. Boasting their spring blooms, hundreds of espaliered fruit trees formed a path to the Hall of Supreme Harmony. Up a hundred and sixty-eight steps, tiring enough when she was *not* pregnant *and* wounded.

General Jin abruptly turned off the central path.

"Where are we going?" Kaiya stopped in her tracks, sending the imperial guards behind her into a rustling halt. There was no time to waste; Regent Liu had to hear the news of the Teleri invasion immediately.

The general faced her, though he kept his eyes averted. "The Hall of Bountiful Harvests, *Dian-xia*."

"Not an audience with Regent Liu?" She gestured toward the Hall of Supreme Harmony.

The general shook his head. "No, *Dian-xia*. The regent has already retired for the night."

Gone to bed! Rebels in the South, an invasion to the North, and the regent was more concerned about his beauty sleep.

"Where is the regent staying?" Her eyes strayed toward the residential section of the palace grounds. If the castle itself was barricaded, there would be no other place for him to stay.

General Jin extended his hand. "Please, *Dian-xia*. To the Hall of Bountiful Harvests."

"I command you to take me to the regent."

The general bowed. "I am sorry, *Dian-xia*. You may be an honored prisoner, but you are still a prisoner."

Fire flared in her face before fizzling out under the *Tiger's Eye*. Liu Yong considered her an adversary. Though why did they bother to bring her to the palace? Kaiya glared at General Jin, whose attention remained fixed on the ground. Even with a weapon, she was no match for him. Without the power of her voice, there was little she could do about her situation.

"Very well," she said. "Please take me to the Hall of Bountiful Harvests."

The general let out a long sigh and raised his head. His wrinkled brows looked nothing like the imperial guards' ubiquitous stoicism. "Again, I am sorry, *Dianxia*." He extended his hand toward the hall.

With a nod, Kaiya resumed her stride. Apparently, Fu had told her the truth about one thing: the imperial guard were loyal to the Jade Throne, no matter who sat on it. She tilted her head and assessed General Jin out of the corner of her eye.

Tentative, nothing like his predecessor. Tian's grizzled cousin, General Zheng, would certainly have sided with her in this matter. Unfortunate that he, along with a hundred of the finest imperial guards, had perished in her escape from Iksuvius.

After three turns and a flight of marble steps to a veranda, they arrived at the Hall of Bountiful Harvests. Its blue-tiled eaves glistened in the light of the moons, reminiscent of so many nights spent here as a starstruck sixteen-year-old.

This was where it all started, where she had met a dragon in man's clothing. That magically-induced infatuation had been a prison of a different sort.

Servants opened the doors and dropped into kneels. Inside, light bauble lamps revealed other servants preparing cushions and blankets for a makeshift bed on the marble floor. A sleeping robe lay folded at the side. They all stopped their frenetic activity, sank to their knees, and pressed foreheads to the floor.

"Rise." Kaiya lifted her chin.

The servants returned to their duties, though more than one flashed an apologetic nod. An older man, dressed as a chamberlain, shuffled forward, bowing. "I am sorry for the poor accommodations."

Kaiya nodded. It wasn't his fault. Liu Yong was sending a message: she didn't even warrant a guest room in a pavilion.

General Jin cleared his throat. "We will leave the princess to rest."

"Wait." She bowed at the waist.

All the guards and servants dropped to their knees in a rhythmic swoosh of armor and robes.

"Please wake the regent. Let him know the Teleri army, led by Emperor Geros himself, is headed this way."

"As the princess commands," the general said. Holding low bows, the servants all shuffled backward out of the room, taking all the light bauble lamps. The doors closed behind them.

The lack of conviction in the general's voice didn't inspire confidence. She closed her eyes and listened. Outside, at least six imperial guards stood at the door. She might be light on her feet, but she was no Black Fist. There would be no secret forays into the palace, like that night three years ago when she sought out Prince Hardeep in the Nine Court. For now, with the Teleri marching on the capital unopposed, she was stuck here, alone.

And tired.

Her arms and legs weighed her down as she slipped out of the travelling robe. At least the nausea had subsided. Bust binder untied, her breasts felt swollen, the nipples sensitive. Still, her belly remained flat. With a sigh, she slipped into the robe and wrapped the sash around her waist.

Kaiya settled into the cushions and pulled a cover over to protect herself from the dank chill. How long would they keep her here? Would she be able to present her case to the regent?

The sounds of guards shuffling outside settled. A nearly-imperceptible breathing hid in the voice of the night. Kaiya bolted upright, heart in her throat. Apparently, the *Tiger's Eye* did little to prevent surprise.

From behind, a hand clamped down over her mouth, and warm steel pressed into her neck.

Kaiya froze in place. Perhaps the regent wanted to be done with her altogether. Though if that were the case, this interloper could've already killed her.

"*Dian-xia*," a girl's voice whispered in the dark. "I am letting go. Please keep quiet."

Jie? Had she made her way back?

No.

The voice was wrong. Kaiya nodded.

The hand and blade withdrew. Kaiya turned and squinted through the darkness.

A wisp of a shadow knelt there, her expression unreadable in the dark. "I—"

"—rescued me from the Teleri Fortress. Your name is Feng." Her skin tone was distinctively lighter than most Cathayi.

The Black Fist girl nodded. "Yes, Feng Mi."

Likely a code-name, since it sounded like the word for *honey*. A moniker suited for spies in the Floating World. Yet Feng had come to rescue her. "Have you heard from Jie?"

"She is not with you?"

Apparently, the Black Fist didn't know *everything*. "I sent her on a mission, and then we were separated by the Teleri invasion."

Feng's scowl, while not visible, was clear in her tone. "Young Master Yan was responsible for you."

Kaiya nodded. *Just leave it at that.* There was no need to revisit that drama. "It looks like you are my new bodyguard. Can I rely on you, even if Regent Liu rules?"

"The Black Lotus is loyal to the Wang Family." Feng bowed and placed a fist on the ground.

"Good." It seemed Fu was correct about the Black Lotus Clan. "Now, how do we get out of here?"

"*We* don't. I can't get you past six imperial guards, and I can't fight them. Their breastplates' aura is too strong."

Kaiya stared at the doors, picturing the palace layout in her mind. "Are there other clan members around?"

"No. All the others nearby are in the castle proper with the *Tianzi.*"

"Can you contact them?"

Feng's lips pursed. "Our clan designed the castle defenses to prevent one of our own from being able to penetrate it."

Kaiya sighed. Even with a Black Fist, she was still a prisoner in her own home.

"There is another way." The coldness in Feng's tone might have sent a shiver down Kaiya's spine if not for the *Tiger's Eye.* "The regent's power comes from his grandson. Kill—"

"No." Kaiya shook her head emphatically. There had to be another way than slaying her cousin's infant son. Though, if it might save more people...

A commotion erupted outside. The doors swung open.

Hong Jianbin's heart rattled in his chest as he stepped through the doors. At long last, after over half a year, he would see Princess Kaiya again.

Though perhaps his chest ached from his precarious situation. For now, he was in the regent's good graces; but if the real *Tianzi* emerged from the castle, Hong might very well lose his head for his role in accidently deposing him.

Unless he convinced the princess to marry him. Though even then, if the regent retained power, he would find a way to remove her from the picture.

Ah, that petty little tyrant, having power drop into his lap by virtue of noble birth and a freak accident. Not like Liu Yong had the brains to harbor any traitorous thoughts beyond which rice-wine merchant to stiff.

Hong raised the light bauble lamp, which filled the room with a gentle white glow.

The princess sat, one hand clasping a sheet to her body, the other shading her eyes. Was she naked underneath?

If Hong's heart beat any faster, he would faint. Leina might be exotic and charming, but none could rival Princess Kaiya's beauty.

Hands trembling, he lowered the lamp and creaked into a kneel. "*Dian-xia*, I am relieved to see you are home safe."

"Chief Minister Hong." She ran a hand through her hair and lowered the cover. The top of her cleavage peeked out from beneath the sleeping robe. Had her breasts grown since he last saw her? To think in this very room, three years ago, when they had greeted

Avarax in human form, she had been a plain bean pole. Now, she was the most desirable woman in the realm.

"I am sorry to disturb your sleep, *Dian-xia*." He raised his head and met her smile. Had she lost weight? Her face seemed thinner than several months before. No doubt her winter in the wilderness had taken its toll on her health. He lingered a few more seconds on her plump breasts. To be able to cup them…

"I am happy to see a friend," she said. "What brings you here?"

Hong looked back to the doors. Closed, safe from prying eyes and ears. "*Dian-xia*, I have come to warn you. Even at this late hour, Regent Liu is meeting with the hereditary lords. He plans to brand you as a traitor." The news would crush her. He leaned forward, ready to provide support after the shocking revelation.

"I see." Her expression remained… impassive? Too shocked, maybe. Still, she didn't back away, despite the inappropriate distance. Maybe…

Hong edged even closer. "There is a way to protect you." Something he could do.

"How?" Her tone wasn't desperate, more…disinterested.

Hong took a deep breath. "Avoid a political marriage to a provincial lord. Marry a commoner, ideally in Regent Liu's good graces."

"There is no time before my audience with the regent." The stoicism in her face could rival that of an imperial guard.

She did not even seem to be considering his reasoning. All of that shock—betrayed by a tyrant, forced to wander in the wilderness, coming home to be branded a traitor. Poor Kaiya. The Dragon Charmer had faded, replaced by the naïve girl from years before.

He reached forth with a trembling hand and placed it on her shoulder. So soft and warm. A tingle jolted up his arm and settled in his chest. His other hand extended of its own volition, coming to rest on her other shoulder. He opened his mouth to speak, but only a croak came out.

Clearing his throat, he said, "*Dian-xia*, I will marry you. I have always had a wonderful relationship with Lord Liu."

Her eyes studied his. Her plight must finally be dawning on her.

This was his chance, at long last. It might never come again. Time to banish all timidity. Heart pattering like a rabbit's, he drew her forward and leaned in. If she returned his kiss—

The princess turned and cast her gaze down. Not an outright refusal. Shy, just like an appropriate maiden should act.

He pecked her on her cheek. So smooth and soft, it sent heat coursing through him. Waves roared in his ears. At long last, after three years of planning and maneuvering, the princess was his.

Chapter 22:
Black Fists and Stone Arrows

Exhausted from his harrying trip back from the light tower, Liang Yu stumbled to his warehouse just as a predawn line of black-blue appeared on the eastern horizon. Even at this hour, the capital buzzed with rumors of Princess Kaiya's return and a possible invasion.

He rapped out a code on the door, which whispered open a crack. It was Little Song. He had done what a Black Lotus Fist, trained from youth, could not: escaped with the princess from a heavily armed escort.

No, impossible. Keeping his expression blank, Liang Yu slipped past Song and into the warehouse. "How did you get back here?"

"The imperial cavalry allowed us to ride horses. When we arrived in the city, I used the citizenry's confusion to escape."

Impressive, but, "Where is the princess?"

Little Song slouched over. "I am sorry, Master. We were separated, and she was too heavily guarded."

"Unacceptable." Liang Yu slammed his staff into the wood floor. "My order was to stay close to her."

Song hung his head. "Forgive me, Master."

Liang Yu snorted. A warrior might atone for such a transgression by taking his own life. In the bureaucracy, from which Song's family came, failure was met with demotion or forced retirement. Song's talented father had failed only once—raising a son who became an insurgent, exposed by Liang Yu himself—at the cost of his short tenure as Chief Minister.

A Black Lotus Fist's failure, however, was met with greater challenges. Liang Yu pointed out the door. "Intercept the imperial couriers, find out what they know."

Song raised a hand. "First, there is other news. I sent a scout out on horseback to verify the princess' claims. She was telling the truth." He unfurled a map. "A Teleri army, fifty-thousand strong, marches along the main highway, a day away by forced march."

Fifty thousand!

A day away. With the bulk of the imperial armies engaged with Peng and the Madurans, there couldn't be more than ten thousand soldiers in the capital. The only other army nearby... he looked up at Song. "Seek out Lin Ziqiu. Inform her of the situation. Ask her to return to Linshan Province and ask her father to mobilize his armies."

Watching Song dart out the door with youthful exuberance, Liang Yu headed back to his office. The princess' doctor slept in a chair, right where Liang Yu had left him, hands bound to the armrests. Liang Yu started unravelling the knots.

Doctor Fang's eyes shot opened. "Where is the princess?"

"The palace, I believe." Unless the regent had locked her away in a secret dungeon somewhere.

The doctor rubbed his wrists. "The regent will treat her as a traitor." His voice spoke of adoration, like the Surgeon's unrequited love for the Beauty.

Liang Yu laughed. "Maybe. Don't worry. The princess is hardly a damsel in distress. She is quite resourceful, actually."

"What are you doing with me?" Doctor Fang stood.

Liang Yu blindfolded him. "Go to her. One of my men will guide you out of the warehouse district. If she has need of me, she can tie her command to the second branch of the third tree on the path to Jianguo Shrine."

Once the doctor departed, Liang Yu leaned back in his chair. Resourceful indeed, that princess. His hand found the imperial plaque inside his robes and he withdrew it from its pouch.

He sat up straight. It was no imperial plaque, but a jade funerary tablet. The princess had tricked him yet again, swearing on the name of Zheng Tian, fourth son of Zheng Han: *Tai-Ming* lord and now Teleri collaborator. If his sources were correct, Zheng Tian had been banished from the capital, then eight years later appeared at the Cathay embassy in the Northwest as a clerk for a trade official.

Liang Yu snorted. Not likely. Zheng Tian's resume, or lack thereof, screamed of Black Lotus Fist. Now dead, like so many of his former clansmen, his spirit roaming the netherworld until he was reborn.

Tian threw his hands up in exasperation, barely avoiding a low-hanging branch. Playing translator for two twins who didn't understand each other was hard enough. Kiri refusing to speak of her life before joining the wild elves made the task even more frustrating, since that was all Jie asked about.

"It's not important," Kiri said. "I'm here now."

Jie prodded him in the ribs. If she were really a *sister* in their clan, she was a mean one. "What did she say?"

Tian shook his head. Kiri had repeated the words so often, Jie must certainly know what they meant by now. "She doesn't want to talk about it."

Sighing, Jie drew circles on the forest floor with her foot. "All my life, I wanted to at least know who my parents were."

It was a different, less open-ended question. Perhaps Kiri would answer. Tian asked, "Do you remember your parents?"

Kiri sucked on her lower lip. "No parents."

Tian turned to Jie and shook his head again. "She doesn't want to talk about—"

The wildlife quieted. Both Kiri's and Jie's pointed ears twitched like a temple dog's, their noses sniffing as they turned to the north. Tian followed their stares.

The river rustled in the distance, but other than that—chainmail and boots, marching down the main path, not far away.

Jie pulled him down, almost on top of her. The closeness and heat at once felt comforting and *right*.

Dropping into a crouch, Kiri put hands to her mouth and called out like a wild bird. At other points in the forest, birdcalls responded at quick intervals. The idea seemed familiar, even if the specific calls did not.

Kiri met their gazes and twirled her finger in a big circle. Then she held up two fingers, closed her hand, one finger, then six. Tian exchanged glances with Jie, who quirked an eyebrow up. She wanted a translation.

How should *he* know what Kiri meant? Even if he knew what Jie's expression did. He flashed his best guess back in hand signals. *Two altivorcs, sixteen Teleri.*

Jie nodded, then started to crawl forward. Kiri placed a hand on her shoulder. With wide eyes, she shook her head. She held both hands up, thumbs and fingers forming crescents, then brought them together into a small circle. Were the Teleri surrounding them, drawing the noose tight? Sixteen wouldn't stand a chance against the elf village, unless…

A voice boomed out from a distance, speaking in the Kanin dialect. "We know the messengers of the gods are here, around the sacred pool. We have the area surrounded. Surrender now and you will be spared."

Kiri paled. With her eyes, Jie prodded him to translate.

Surrounded, he signed. The elves, with their forest dexterity, could likely get into the trees and their hidden village two *li* away before the Metal Men could entrap them. He and Jie, on the other hand… and Ming, wherever he was, with his bad arm.

Hunching low, Kiri beckoned for them to follow. Elbows in the dirt, Tian crawled after her, with Jie close behind. Shouts and curses in the Metal Men's language erupted nearby, but there was no sound of clashing swords or men felled by elf archery.

Ming's voice rang out from closer to the village. "Help!"

Stranger or not, Ming was a brother. Tian rose next to a tree and peered around the corner. Nothing.

"Down," Kiri hissed through her teeth.

Tian glanced at her. Shaking his head, he darted from tree to tree.

Jie was on her feet just behind him, crackling just as many leaves and twigs despite her smaller size. Not like the enemy would hear; they were making even more noise with their boots and armor.

He skidded to a stop at the edge of a clearing where the elves sometimes practiced archery, close to the sacred pool.

Seven Metal Men lay dead or dying with arrows through impossibly small openings. Arrow nocked and bow drawn, Ming took aim… at the edge of the clearing, where a Metal Man hid behind a tree, hand clamped over an elf boy's mouth. At least thirteen other Metal Men ducked in the cover of the trees. So much for there only being sixteen of them… Had Ming killed those seven? With an injured shoulder, no less?

One at Ming's back jumped out, sword raised. Ming spun and loosed his arrow into the attacker's throat. At the same time, two more arrows struck the man. Ming turned back to the kidnapper. Apparently, Nayori's divine magic had healed him.

"Ming. You protected. Watch first man." The words were in the language from Beyond the Wall, and the speaker was…

Little Kala.

Ming nodded, then spoke in the language of the Metal Men. "Let the boy go, and we will allow you to leave here alive." It wasn't likely the elves would let that happen, even if they understood Ming's words.

"Attack!" one of the Metal Men yelled.

Eight—eleven—no, fifteen of them charged into the clearing from different angles, longswords raised. Arrows zipped in from all directions. Three men fell. Ming took deliberate steps toward the hostage-taker, seemingly oblivious to the enemies closing around him.

Tian surged in. Swiping a dagger from one of the fallen soldiers, he ran up behind another. Heavens, they were huge. A leap put him on the Metal Man's back. A yank on the helm's T-slot jerked his head up. Tian thrust his weapon into his victim's eye. As he crumpled to the ground, Tian landed on his feet.

Two more steps toward the Metal Man with the boy, and Ming loosed his arrow. He cursed.

It struck the man right in the chest. His hands clawed at the shaft as he stumbled back. The boy bolted deeper into the woods.

A heavy boot crunched on pine needles behind Tian. A sword swooped down. He twirled and sidestepped out of its arc, then ducked under the follow-up. A backward handspring took him out of range, but the Metal Man pressed his attack. An arrow zipped in from the side, skewering the man from flank to flank.

Tian stared at the stone arrowhead protruding from the collapsing soldier, then looked up to reassess. There…

Jie danced through five enemies, her moves familiar yet blurred at impossible speeds.

Like the elf woman Layani. And the brown-skinned man that plucked at Tian's memories. Slipping thrusts, ducking hacks, and lodging knives into impossibly small spots. If combat were poetry, Jie would be a master poet; her enemies, rice paper anchored by a weight stone for her to write on with impunity.

Pain exploded in the back of Tian's head, and everything went black.

In the heat of battle, Jie had seen Tian's attacker.

Ever since training with the Master Paladin on the Shallowsea skiff, combat automatically slowed in her perception, whether she wanted it to or not. Her opponents might as well have been slogging through honey. Even so, she could do nothing to save Tian from his own inattention. With all her energy channeled into fighting, words died on her lips.

He should've been able to sense the hulking brute. Even a Black Lotus trainee could detect someone sneaking up from behind. Yet a Teleri soldier had lumbered up and slammed him over the head with his sword pommel.

"No!" Kiri yelled from the trees, using the only word Jie recognized in the Kanin language. Her twin raced to Tian's side.

More Bovyans poured into the clearing, streaming past Tian's inert form. Arrows flew in from the sides, but not nearly enough to stem the tide. No! Jie couldn't let them capture him. Not after she just found him.

Butterfly-twisting between two enemy slashes, she landed on her feet and ran toward him. Disorientation jolted her as time returned to normal for six steps before slowing down again.

Exposed targets, which once blinked open and closed in a split second, now remained gaping wide holes in the warriors' armor. Duck under one sword, stab to the unprotected knee tendons. Dodge right and slash another's wrist. Leap over a spear thrust and drive a knife into a third's eye slot.

Stop short of an elf arrow. Lean back under the sweep of another sword. It was almost too easy. Behind a wall of three men, Kiri shielded Tian's body with her own, clinging to him while another Teleri tried to pull her off.

Jie spun around the wall of men, leaving them swinging at air. On the other side, a short, thick soldier chopped his broadsword down at Tian, with no apparent regard for Kiri being in the way. They were no longer interested in taking prisoners.

She leapt into the arc of the attack her knife extended. If she caught it just right, maybe her weapon could alter the broadsword's path.

The force of impact sent a jolt up her arm. She had misjudged the angle, and the broadsword ricocheted up instead of down. It travelled slowly, so slowly, heading right to her neck… and there was nothing she could do to get inside of the attack, no leverage to change her direction and get out of the way.

The blade caught her in the collarbone. Pain blossomed from the site. She looked up through her tunneling vision to see…

An altivorc, mouth locked in a snarl.

The sword was yanked out. He raised the blade with two hands and chopped. She started to lift her knife, but her arm barely rose.

Ming had missed! He knew as soon as he loosed the arrow that it would miss the T-slit of the Teleri's helm, and instead bounce harmlessly off his chainmail. Somehow, the stone arrowhead not only penetrated the metal, but went all the way through to the other side.

He stared at his next arrow, its head glittering in a ray of sun. Other than the sparkles, it seemed like ordinary stone. Though perfectly smooth and razor sharp, it still shouldn't have been able to penetrate metal.

Several Teleri shouted, Kiri yelled, Jie screamed.

Ming turned to see yet another altivorc ready to decapitate Jie, whose arm hung limply at her side. He nocked and loosed two arrows in quick succession. Both found their mark, knocking the brute on his back. The half-elf owed him her life one more time, for saving her from the orcs *yet* again.

He raked his gaze across the clearing. Tian lay on his back, breathing but unconscious. Kiri was sprawled on top of him, and Jie over her.

A virtual threesome with identical twins! One of Ming's daydreams—albeit with statuesque beauties in place of a homicidal smart-mouth and her taciturn sister.

Several more able-bodied Teleri looked up from the half-elf heap and met his eyes.

He only had two arrows left. He nocked and loosed both, dropping the closest and slowing the next. Behind them, an amorphous gaggle of enemies charged. In the back, the elves ventured into the clearing and pulled Tian and the half-elves into the trees.

Someone tugged at his arm. He looked down to find little Kala, her gaze intense.

"Run!" she said.

Not daring a glance back, he took off down some random path. There was no way they could outrun the long-legged Bovyans, especially not his diminutive guide.

Who'd just spoken in the Cathayi tongue.

Twigs and needles crunched under Teleri boots behind them, yet the sound grew distant. They burst out into another clearing, where tall boulders rose out of the forest floor. Somewhere, water tumbled over stones. Kala pulled him along the edge of the rocks, then turned sharply back into a crevice.

Where had that come from? Rounded steps rolled up the rock formation, blending in seamlessly with the surroundings. Another cleft opened into a small basin with a pool, whose waters glowed a luminous blue. Just like Guanyin's Teardrop in Fenggu Province, which he'd visited several times as a youth. Its waters supposedly had healing powers.

Kala covered Ming's gasp before it escaped. She pointed down, where the Teleri soldiers jogged by. Nine in all.

One stopped right near the crevice. He looked left, looked right… But never up. Another voice called from the distance. "We've lost them!"

"Go find one of the native trackers," another voice said. "Bring them here."

The man at the base of the boulders turned around and jogged back the way he came.

Ming let out a long sigh and faced Kala. Something was wrong here; things didn't quite add up on a broken abacus. "How do you speak our language?"

Kala's eyes rounded, but then she cocked her head and raised an eyebrow. Unintelligible syllables spilled out of her mouth, replacing her broken Cathay.

Chapter 23:
Indecent Proposals

Thank the Heavens for the *Tiger's Eye*. Without it, none of Kaiya's discipline could've kept her from recoiling from Chief Minister Hong's attempted kiss. He was old enough to be her father, maybe even grandfather.

Still, his literal proposal might be a viable option if no others presented themselves. She maintained the shy girl façade, drawing back before he kissed her neck, and pulling her sleeping robe tighter to completely cover her breasts.

"I… I appreciate your willingness to make such a sacrifice. Please, it has been a long day. Let me consider it over sleep." She bowed low, like a potential bride at the matchmaker's.

Still kneeling, Hong waddled back and bowed. "*Dian-xia,* no matter what you choose, I will do everything I can to protect you."

"Thank you, Chief Minister." She bowed again. Undoubtedly, he was squinting at her cleavage again. Jie had said something about him obsessing over her. Perhaps there was quite a bit of truth to that.

His knees and spine creaked as he rose to his feet. Retrieving a bauble lantern, he held a bow as he tottered backward to the entrance. He knocked on the doors, which opened, and backed out.

When the door closed, plunging the room in darkness, Kaiya snorted. Hong was old, and marriage to him would likely not last long. It couldn't be any worse than what Geros had done to her, and as long as the *Tiger's Eye* pent up her emotions, it wouldn't matter anyway.

Though if Hong couldn't perform in *that* ministry, then her babies would still not find legitimacy. Unless he died before their births.

None of it would matter if Geros captured her, and as of yet, nothing stood between the enemy army and the capital.

Feng Mi, forgotten in the drama, cleared her throat from up in the eaves. "You should rest, *Dian-xia*. There is a lot to think about." Her voice couldn't be much more disdainful.

Kaiya smiled at her, even if she probably couldn't see it. "I always insisted Jie speak freely. Tell me, what do you think?"

"The Chief Minister keeps a half-Ayuri concubine in the Floating World. He is unfailingly careless whenever he visits." That explained the disdain, though her tone now hinted at something more.

"There is something else you want to say."

"That would not be appropriate." Feng's voice sounded like a raging torrent behind a dam. It wouldn't take much to get her to speak.

"I command you to speak your mind."

Feng harrumphed. "I cannot believe you are actually considering marrying Hong. Especially after you ruined things between Young Master Yan and Zheng Tian."

Kaiya sighed. It couldn't be safe to have so many Black Fists resentful of her. Yet how could she explain it? She remembered what love felt like, but her logical mind still wondered what she ever saw in Tian. Handsome and sweet, to be sure, but still a banished fourth son.

It didn't matter. Tian was dead, only rarely visiting in her dreams.

Kaiya stood at the edge of Huajing's largest market, usually noisy and vibrant during the daylight hours. Not today. Flags and paper lanterns hung lifelessly over deserted city streets.

She was utterly alone. Where was everyone?

A distant chorus of yells and shouts broke out behind her. She turned around to find herself on an abandoned river dock, looking out over the angry waters tumbling by. Dark clouds gathered above, sending streaks of lightning across the sky. Sunlight bathed the opposite bank, where crowds of her people beckoned. Some pointed at her.

Or maybe behind her, where war drums pounded and boots clomped on Huajing's paved city streets.

She whirled back around. A sea of Teleri heavy infantry, with Geros at the fore, marched in perfect ranks through the marketplace. His eyes locked with hers, and a grin formed on his lips.

That cruel smirk, the one he wore each time he... Kaiya's heart seized. Her chest constricted, denying her even a single breath. She had to flee—right, left, back, anywhere—but her legs seemed made out of lead, her feet fused to the ground.

Several of the advancing soldiers fell, breaking the Teleri's perfect formation. They collapsed, driving an approaching crevice through their ordered lines, each time punctuated by grunts and groans. The gap opened up in the front phalanx, and a lithe figure spilled out.

Jie! The half-elf spy, bloodied *dao* held in two hands, studied Geros for a split second, then turned and ran toward Kaiya. A rescue! If anyone could help her, it would be Jie. Their gazes met. Or did it? Jie looked past her, at...

Kaiya twisted around, as best as her heavy legs would allow.

Tian. He stood just a few feet away, looking... past her.

Kaiya turned back around to find Jie closing. Behind her, the Teleri marched at double time, the holes in their ranks now closed. Geros sheathed a sword and loped over. Kaiya watched as Jie sprinted by and into Tian's outstretched arms.

Tears blurred Kaiya's sight. He should be embracing *her*. Protecting *her*. She raised a hand to wipe her eyes.

A huge, gauntleted hand seized her wrist. Geros.

Not again. Kaiya screamed.

***

Kaiya jerked up in her bed, her body wracking with sobs. Tian had abandoned her, in favor of Jie. Her sleeping robe was soaked.

The *Tiger's Eye* took hold, scattering all the unpleasant thoughts. It was only a dream. Tian was dead.

Kaiya wiped away her tears just as the doors swished open. Squinting through the light of dawn, she brushed out the creases in her robe. Shadows at the door began to take shape.

The weight and length of the footsteps sounded familiar. Her sister-in-law, Zhao Xiulan, knelt beside her. Her beautiful hair, gone. Extravagant gowns exchanged for the robes of a Praise Spring Temple nun.

No longer was she the paragon of beauty and grace whom Kaiya's younger self had idolized. More concerning was how thin her face looked.

"Eldest Sister." Kaiya bowed.

Xiulan shook her head, expression serene. "I have taken the temple name An-Guo to represent my hopes while I pray for Kai-Guo's repose."

An, for peace; *Guo* for nation, the same character as Kai-Guo's. A beautiful double entendre, but nonetheless, the kind and thoughtful sister-in-law would always be Xiulan, *Extraordinary Orchid*, in Kaiya's heart.

If she could ever find her heart under the blanket of the *Tiger's Eye*. Kaiya leaned forward and wrapped her arms around Xiulan. "I am so sorry for your loss. I so wanted to come back as soon as I got your letter."

Xiulan nodded. "Chief Minister Hong asked that I write it."

Hong again. Apparently, this unlikely suitor had been thinking of her for a while. "Thank you for visiting me, though it might not be wise to call on a potential traitor."

Xiulan beamed and shook her head. "I asked to be your attendant."

Again, the *Tiger's Eye* didn't block Kaiya's surprise, even if it prevented her from feeling mortified by the proposition. She waved her hand. "I could never face Kai-Guo in the afterlife if I allowed you to do that."

"I could never face him if I didn't." Xiulan squeezed Kaiya's hand, then turned and waved toward the door. "And you will never live down the embarrassment of presenting yourself to the regent dressed in a sleeping robe or travelling rags."

A servant shuffled in, holding a low bow. She extended a blue court gown in two hands.

"Leave us," Xiulan said, receiving the dress.

The servant backed out and closed the door, leaving the room illuminated with a light bauble lamp.

Clambering to her feet, Kaiya straightened the covers on the makeshift bed.

Xiulan sucked in a sudden breath. "Since when do you make your own bed?"

"The testy half-elf handmaiden never helped in my travels."

Xiulan nodded. "She was poorly trained."

At least as a handmaiden and in court etiquette. In other ways... Kaiya smiled. "Hopefully, I will come back to a bed and not to the executioner's block."

"I will pray for your exoneration." Xiulan bowed. Apparently, Liu's intentions were no secret, at least in the court. "If Heaven fails you, I will slit my own throat." She reached for the sash's knot at Kaiya's waist.

Fighting off her hands, Kaiya undid the binding herself and shrugged out of the robe. Exposing herself might be out of character, or at least from what Xiulan knew from their past, but it wasn't like they hadn't soaked in hot springs together before.

Nonetheless, Xiulan coughed. "You have lost weight, except..." She shook her head and presented the inner gown.

Kaiya received it in two hands. She slipped it on and wrapped a white sash around her waist. It squeezed around her pregnancy-swollen bust.

"I thought I knew your size." Eyes narrowed, Xiulan cocked her head. "Perhaps I was wrong, and unfortunately, your wardrobe is in the sealed-off castle."

Those dresses likely wouldn't fit, either. Kaiya stretched an arm into the hanging sleeve of the outer gown. Perhaps it'd been a bad idea to undress in front of Xiulan. She'd tried to conceive for so long. If she deduced—

A wave of morning sickness rolled through her. Covering her mouth, she heaved, but luckily, nothing came up. She glanced up.

Xiulan's eyebrow rose, though her lips squeezed tight. "Come, the regent awaits."

Kaiya nodded and followed Xiulan out of the hall. Outside by the steps knelt a dozen imperial guards, and several familiar faces. Among them, Chief Minister Hong's gaze met hers, perhaps searching for an answer to his question. Doctor Wu, as well, looked at her through her unique blue eyes. Or maybe not so unique; the luminous color seemed familiar somehow. Where—

"*Dian-xia.*" One voice out of the chorus stood out. Fang Weiyong's. How had he gotten here? The bright robes of Yang-Di and meticulously coifed hair felt strange after all these months of seeing him dress like a Kanin tribesman.

"Fang Weiyong," Kaiya said. "I am glad to see you safe. Your hair."

He bowed. "Yes, *Dian-xia*. I came straight away from… but yes, there was no time to shave my head."

It might have been faster to shave it than to put the effort into coiffing it. In fact, Weiyong never appeared so gentlemanly. And he was somehow here, out of Fu's clutches.

"You did not find time to keep it cut during your time in the wilderness?" Eyes slitted, Xiulan looked from Kaiya to Weiyong and back.

He bowed. "Unfortunately, my razor dulled, and we also tried to blend in with the natives."

"*Dian-xia*." Doctor Wu's voice silenced everyone. "I came to the palace as soon as I heard you had arrived. Everyone in the streets is talking about it. Luckily, I was able to get Weiyong in. Now come along, we mustn't try the regent's patience."

Without waiting, she turned and walked down the steps with the speed and grace of someone a quarter her age. However old that was.

Kaiya followed her and the rest of the entourage fell in behind. Despite the hour, when the palace grounds would normally be awash with ministers and servants, the walkways and courtyards were nearly deserted.

At the foot of the one hundred and sixty-eight steps to the Hall of Supreme Harmony, Kaiya looked up. Sleep had done little to refresh her. After the climb, she'd be exhausted again.

Weiyong's eyes followed the steps up as well. "Allow me to help you, *Dian-xia*."

Minister Hong bowed. "I will assist you, as well."

Kaiya nodded, and they proceeded up the marble steps. Weiyong kept his firm hand in hers, pulling her with encouragement when she slowed. Minister Hong offered a tentative hand on her elbow as well. Behind them, imperial guards and other officials muttered at the breach of decorum.

At last, they arrived at the top. Her legs protested as she stepped over the ghost-tripping threshold, but with Weiyong's help, she made it across without an embarrassing tumble to the ground. The room quieted as soon as she stepped in.

How could there be so few people? Whereas the ministers, officials, and hereditary lords used to cover almost every foot of the floor, today there couldn't be more than sixty. The Jade Throne at the front of the hall stood empty, though Regent Liu sat at its right hand. Beside him knelt an old man… Treasury Minister Geng.

Kaiya took a deep breath and straightened her carriage. Murmurs surfaced again as she glided down the central row between the thin ranks of men.

Just before the throne, she stopped, stretched out her arms to straighten her sleeves, and knelt. How low to bow? Maybe if her baby nephew sat on the throne, recognized as *Tianzi*, it would warrant her forehead to the floor. A regent… no one had held that position since the Founder's consort, over two centuries ago; and in any case, an imperial princess' rank stood only a rung lower than a prince.

Whether Liu Yong considered her an imperial princess or not was another story. Either way, playing the role of demure woman would more likely win him over. Waiting until Chief Minister Hong took his place on the dais, she set her hands in front of her knees and bowed low. Whispers rumbled through the assembled men.

"Rise." The regent waved a dismissive hand. Behind him, Minister Geng whispered something in his ear.

She raised her head. "*Jie-xia*, I—"

"—are trying to incite a revolt against my grandson's rule, I hear." He scowled.

At least Chief Minister Hong had warned her, so it didn't come as a surprise. "No, *Jie-xia*. I have come with dire news of a Teleri invasion."

The lords and ministers broke out in a low murmur of confusion. Minister Geng leaned in and whispered something to Liu again. Chief Minister Hong tried to approach the regent, only to have Minster Geng box him out. Perhaps Hong had less influence than he thought.

The regent slapped his hand down on the armrest. "A distraction, making use of the light towers to scare the populace and rally the troops to you. You cannot fool me. No army can breach the Great Wall."

Kaiya shook her head. "I assure you—"

"What you say does not agree with what you did." Minister Geng wagged his finger at her. "The way station claimed you approached with a ragtag militia of insurgents and imperial soldiers. I think you were raising an army of your own."

It was clear who was in charge. A baby might act as *Tianzi*, a fool might be regent, but ultimately, it was an ambitious minister who pulled more than purse strings.

Kaiya placed a hand on her chest and faced Liu Yong, whose bewildered expression did not bode well for Cathay. "*Jie-xia*, I only wanted to warn the capital as quickly as possible."

Brows furrowed, the regent looked at Minister Geng, who in turn stared at her as if she were a commoner.

Chief Minister Hong cleared his throat. "Princess Kaiya has always had the realm's best interests at heart."

Minister Geng counted on his fingers. "Misappropriation of imperial resources. Fomenting rebellion. *Jie-xia*, you must ascertain her loyalty to your grandson, the *Tianzi*. Allow me some time with her, alone, for questioning." A lurid smile formed. No surprise, given his lecherous reputation.

Hong's complexion blanched. "*Jie-xia*, I have always been loyal to you. I will retire. Please allow me to marry

Princess Kaiya, and I will ensure she does not meddle in your affairs."

The assembled ministers and minor lords all broke out into animated discussion.

Kaiya suppressed a scoff. No one believed the Teleri were invading. The nation was on the brink of collapse, and two old men were fighting to bed her.

A smirk formed on Regent Liu's face, his eyes narrowing. That was an idea forming, and if the current proceedings were any indication, that idea would have nothing to do with bolstering the capital's defenses.

He raised his hand, and the room ebbed into quiet. He turned and grinned at Chief Minister Hong. "I seem to remember a promise you made me a year ago, when you were Imperial Household Minister. It was at Lord Peng's pavilion, the night he tried to assassinate our beautiful young princess and frame the Madurans."

Apparently, Lord Liu was much more aware of things than he let on, or at least he remembered this particular detail.

Minister Geng leaned in to the regent's ear, only to be rebuffed with a wave of the hand. On the other side, Hong's leathery face flushed an interesting shade of crimson as his eyes met Kaiya's. He opened his mouth, but no words came out.

Lord Liu's stare fell on her as well. "Imagine how differently things might have been if Peng had succeeded. You would be dead, and it would be him sitting here," he nodded toward the Jade Throne, "instead of leading some insignificant rebellion."

Kaiya looked from the regent to Hong and back. Where this was headed was anyone's guess, though it likely had little to do with mobilizing the army.

Liu beckoned Chief Minister Hong off the dais with a jerk of his hand. "I accept your resignation, since I had to fulfill your promise on my own. You," Liu said, pointing an obtuse finger at her, "will marry my second son, Liu Deying, who will serve as Chief Minister."

Chapter 24:
That Which The Spirits Brought Together

Jie hid behind a vacant street vendor stall as Teleri soldiers marched through Huajing's busiest marketplace. Storm clouds hung high above, while wind blew through flags and paper lanterns in the deserted city streets. Crushed squashes and fall greens lay scattered about, strange to see during the spring.

Time to sit and wait. Once the Teleri column passed, she'd resume her search for… Tian? No, she'd found him. She was searching for… her parents? What a strange notion.

Somewhere down a side street, a woman spoke with frantic urgency, in the feeble voice of a dying person. "The elves won't protect her. My father will."

That voice! Familiar. It plucked at the primordial chords of Jie's very existence. Teleri army be damned, she had to find the speaker. She rose and picked the most likely side street. Her shoulder hurt as if Yanluo, God of Death, was yanking on her arm from down in Hell, while leaving the rest of her in the world of the living.

At least the Bovyans didn't seem too interested in her. They kept their eyes forward, marching inexorably toward the river docks. The woman had spoken somewhere nearby, but Jie scanned several side streets to no avail.

A male voice rose in song, each note perfect, rising and falling like the hymn the gods sang to create the world. Its beauty rivaled Princess Kaiya's singing.

Ears perking, Jie froze in place. That song! A lullaby. A wave of calm washed over her. In a daze, she ambled forward, one foot in front of the other, heading toward the music like a moth toward a flame.

There! By an abandoned shop, near stacked crates, the singing man knelt, cradling the dying woman. His golden hair tumbled behind a pointed ear. Even though distance and shadows obscured their faces, their love resonated in the man's music and the woman's dying breaths.

Jie took several more steps, moving to within a throwing spike's toss away. The man looked up and met her gaze with large violet eyes. He had to be one of the most handsome men she'd ever seen, and yet, even thinking that felt wrong. With a smile, he proffered an arrow. Silvery impurities veined in regular patterns through its transparent crystal point.

A gift? From an elf?

Jie stopped mid-stride. To receive it seemed like accepting that part of herself, the one she denied. No. She faltered back.

A regiment of snarling altivorcs streamed out from between two buildings, blocking her view of the elf man and his arrow. Glaring at her, they parted to make way for a leader who stood a head taller than the rest. Dressed in a dapper military uniform, he was handsome, even more so than the altivorc prince she'd killed in Iksuvius. He spun a magic wand around his finger.

Jie drew her *dao*. Refusing the gift from the elf was one thing; being denied by some pretty altivorc prince and his henchmen was another. She took a long stride forward.

With a grin that exposed his fangs, the prince thrust the wand into a sheath on his belt. He stepped aside and yanked on a chain. A little half-elf girl... Kala... stumbled forward. A short, cloaked figure emerged on the other side of her.

An unknown variable.

Jie paused. A prince and foot soldiers already posed a challenge. How could she rescue Kala—

The cloaked figure lowered its hood.

Jie gasped. She might have been looking in a mirror. Kiri? Her twin gazed back with a killer's eyes, so unlike her usual sadness. Drawing a shorter version of an altivorc broadsword, Kiri charged.

Metal clashed against metal, the reverberation sending vibrations through Jie's hand. The pain in her shoulder flared. Combat, instead of slowing, seemed to speed up. Kiri moved blindingly fast, like the Golden Scorpion Jie had faced in Vyara City. That encounter hadn't ended well.

Jie fell back under the onslaught of slashes and hacks. There was no way to win this, not with her shoulder. Heart hammering in her chest, she turned and ran.

In seconds, she caught up with the crowd of Teleri heavy infantry. With their huge size, they offered a perfect place to hide from Kiri. She picked her way through the ranks, slaying Bovyans who blocked her. One, three, six—they fell before her, opening a path of escape. She had to get away.

One collapsed, and a ray of light sprayed in the opening he left in the orderly lines. In her blind fear, she'd reached the front! Maybe it would be safer to keep running.

Jie burst out of the line of soldiers, not far from the river docks. Only one man stood ahead of her: Emperor Geros. If she killed him, the invasion of Cathay would surely falter. An uneasy feeling settled in the pit of her stomach. No, that felt wrong. Killing Geros felt like killing Tian.

Yet another strange notion, in a day of strange notions. She ran around him instead. On the other side, Tian stood, beckoning her. Jie raced into his embrace. Warm, protective, comforting. They could stay like this forever...

Jie's eyes fluttered open. Fluffy and cool, the bed beneath her back might've been made of clouds, while a puffy fur blanket covered her to the chin. A warm hand clasped hers outside the blanket. She craned her neck to see.

Tian. Sitting on the treetop floor, he leaned against her bed. His head rested in the cradle of one elbow while his other hand held hers. Eyes closed, his back rose and fell.

An elf with gifts, altivorcs, murderous twins, and Teleri emperors. It must've all been a dream. A very real dream. Yet, just like at the dream's end, here she was, with Tian.

Pulse racing, she squeezed his hand.

His eyes popped open and he sat up straight. "Jie! I'm so glad you are okay. You were unconscious for several hours."

"No thanks to you." She pouted at him.

He grinned sheepishly. "Yes, so Ming told me. I owe you my life."

"Again. So, are you all right?" With her free hand, she beckoned for him to lower his head. "The Bovyan hit you pretty hard."

"Yes, just a lump." He rubbed a spot on his scalp.

She giggled. "Apparently, amnesia claimed your sense of awareness." To sit up, she brought her elbows up under her... Her right shoulder moved, pain-free, but inordinately stiff. Like it wasn't her own arm. She freed her hand from Tian's grasp and tried to stretch it out.

Tian lifted a quizzical eyebrow. "What's wrong?"

"My arm." Though it didn't hurt, everything felt bound up around the wound. Her heart stuttered. If she couldn't use her arm, what use was she as a Black Fist? "My arm," she repeated, panic rising in her voice.

"Let me see." Tian started to pull back the fur blanket.

No, he would see her boyish figure, so flat compared to Princess Kaiya's curves. Jie pressed the blanket down, only exposing her shoulder. She twisted to get a look herself, but the wound was too close to her neck.

He shook his head. "Nayori bandaged the cut. Let me get her."

"No." She pulled his hand as he started to rise. "Stay with me, please."

Tian searched her eyes, and with a nod, settled onto the floor beside her.

Jie tested her arm again, yielding the same result. Though painless, her shoulder seized and her arm refused to move. Her very identity laid in her Black Fist skills. If she couldn't use her arm, she would be... normal. Tears threatened to overcome her, but she blinked them away and buried her face in her left arm.

The elf shaman Nayori's voice rode on the wind, in the language of Cathay. "You have woken from your dreams."

Jie wiped her eyes and peered up.

Nayori flashed a grim smile. "Sit up."

Clasping the blanket at her neck, Jie sat up. Cool air brushed across her shoulders, but her back seemed covered. She pulled the covers forward and peeked… and let out a sigh of relief. A long dress of animal skins passed under her arms and wrapped around her chest.

"Kiri's," the shaman said.

It would make sense that her twin's clothes would fit. Still… memories of Kiri from the dream sent a shudder through her.

Nayori leaned in and pulled away the bandage, which stank of pungent herbs. She smiled. "It is completely healed."

Crowding in, Tian nodded. "There's no sign of an injury at all."

No injury at all? Jie tried to move her arm again, and again, the shoulder locked up. "Then why can't I move my arm?"

Nayori sighed. "The grace of Ayara has healed your body. Your spirit, on the other hand… perhaps only Aralas himself could channel the energy to repair that."

Tian tapped his chin. "You said you didn't believe Aralas was the Angel of Koralas."

"We don't. It doesn't mean he wasn't powerful in magic."

Now was not the time for a history lesson. Jie's voice cracked. "How do I heal my spirit?"

Nayori searched her eyes. "What did your dreams tell you?"

The dreams didn't make sense, and certain parts remained better untold. Jie shrugged, but even then, her shoulder refused to obey her brain's command. "I was chased by Kiri."

"Then maybe you will find answers with Kiri." Nayori's gaze swept along the other trees before returning to Jie. "With those answers, you might regain use of your shoulder."

It wasn't like she hadn't tried to get Kiri to talk. It was hopeless. Tears again welled in Jie's eyes.

Tian leaned in and enveloped her in his embrace, pulling her close. It was so soothing, and Jie buried her head into his shoulder. He stroked her hair and pressed his chin into the crest of her head. It felt so right, the way things had been meant to be before the princess had come back into Tian's life.

She looked up and pressed her face into his neck. She had found him, alive. Perhaps spying and killing didn't define who she was any more than the elf blood she never wanted. Maybe as long as she had him, they could reinvent themselves and she wouldn't need her arm.

Nayori cleared her throat. "Tian, the human shaman you lived with awaits you at the pool."

Tian held Jie's hand as they headed to the sacred pool, the memory of her lips on his neck sending shivers through him. It felt so right.

She felt so right. No wonder he'd felt so close to Kiri, her identical twin, in such a short amount of time. Maybe the Doe-Eyed Girl was just a figment of his imagination, some fantasy, while Jie was here and now.

Had they been more than just clan brother and sister? It might explain the way she looked at him. Yet she was holding back, not telling him everything.

Her palm felt cold and clammy in his. Each of her steps was tentative. Maybe she felt as excited as him about meeting this shaman. Maybe it would spark memories where his reunion with Ming and Jie had not.

Heart racing, he turned to glance at Ming, just a few steps behind. His brother stared at Tian and Jie's clasped hands, his expression alternating between bewilderment and relief. No doubt, whatever history lay between Ming and Jie would make for an interesting tale.

They climbed up the rocks to the gap between the boulders. On the other side, voices spoke in the Kanin language. What would the shaman say? Tian's legs wobbled beneath him. With a deep breath, he entered.

Two men stood by the pool, gawking at him. One wore the feathers and shells of a Kanin shaman; the other dressed like a tribesman, though his face was from Beyond the Wall. Neither sparked a rushing back of repressed memories. On the other hand, beyond the expected disbelief in their expression, there was something else… anger, perhaps? Such a strange response.

"Brother," the shaman said in the Kanin language. "The spirits did not deceive us with their most unbelievable news, that your own spirit had returned to the land of the living."

The man from Beyond the Wall nodded. "Several people saw you die."

"A skill from our clan." Tian squeezed Jie's hand, drawing stares. "However, it has cost me my memories. I'm sorry, I do not even remember you or your names."

The shaman's mouth formed a circle. Then he placed a hand over his chest and spread it out in an arc. "I am Yuha, shaman of Swiftrun Village."

"Ma Jun, imperial guard of Cathay." The other put his right fist in his left hand, and also exchanged nods with Ming. "Young Lord Zheng."

Ming grinned. "It has been a long time since we all assaulted the Levanthi pyramid." He cast Jie a sideward glance.

"Evidently, you've forgotten more than our names." Lips pursed, Yuha pointed at their joined hands. "You do not belong to this woman."

Jie's palm clasped his tightly, sending his stomach fluttering like a dragonfly's wings. No, it couldn't be. Certainly they were meant for each other.

Nodding vigorously, Ma Jun said in the language from Beyond the Wall, "Jie, you know Tian's choice."

His choice?

Jie turned to Tian, her glassy eyes searching his. "Tian is reborn. The choices of his past were forgotten, by Heaven's will."

She was being evasive again, avoiding talk of whatever his choice had been. As much as he wanted to know, he couldn't bear to hurt someone who already wore such a pained look. Ma Jun leaned in and whispered into the shaman's ear. Jie's own ears twitched, and a scowl formed on her face.

Yuha spread out his arms. "You cannot simply undo what the spirits have brought together. You swore by the rituals of our people and your own."

Tian shook his head. How could he live by an oath he didn't even remember? "Who do I belong to?"

"Kaiya!" Ma Jun and Yuha said it together, and Jie recoiled as if slapped across her face.

"Kaiya!" Ming's jaw slackened, and then his eyebrows clashed together.

Kaiya.

The name meant nothing to him, even if the three men spoke it as if invoking the gods. He shook his head again.

"We called her the Willow Beauty," Yuha said.

Tian slowly nodded. The Kanin woman he'd saved from the Metal Men had mentioned something about the Warrior From Beyond the Wall rescuing the Willow Beauty. Still, the moniker meant nothing more now than it had at the time.

Yuha made two circles with his fingers. "With eyes like a doe."

The Doe-Eyed Girl.

Tian's heart jolted.

Sniffing, Jie stared at the ground. Ming coughed. Ma Jun nodded emphatically.

Tian lifted Jie's chin. "It was another life; it doesn't matter." The words felt like a lie, even as he spoke them. An urge deep inside fueled his need to know who he once was, even if it meant that Jie was not *that* part of it. Still, after she'd sacrificed her arm for him...

"The spirits' wrath will come down on you," Yuha said. "If you are to break your commitment to Kaiya, then you must do so with the correct rituals."

Jie met his gaze. Her lips trembled. "You must make your decision based on all information. That is who you are, who you have always been. What I loved in you from the time we first met."

"It obviously wasn't his good looks," Ming muttered under his breath.

"Emperor Geros wants to occupy Cathay." Jie pointed west. "However, he is even more focused on capturing the princess. He thinks she carries his child."

Ming choked.

Tian's head spun. If the Doe-Eyed Girl was his, and yet might carry the child of the Metal Men's leader…

"When I left her," Jie said, "your father was holding her prisoner."

"You didn't tell me that!" Ming's eyes widened.

Jie shrugged. "He was also about to surrender the East Gate of the Great Wall."

Ming threw his hands up. "And you sent us deeper into the woods?"

"Go to her," Yuha placed his hand on Tian's shoulder. "I will come with you to undo your vows if that is your final choice."

Shouldering his pack, Ming kicked the dirt. A day which had started with him winning the well-deserved respect of the elves now ended in despair. His father, a traitor. The woman he was supposed to marry, already married to his kid brother. In addition, it appeared Emperor Geros' claims were true, that he'd indeed despoiled her.

Ming sighed. Now their ragtag group was heading back to Cathay, something he would've welcomed the day before.

What was Jie thinking? It would be so much better if she and Tian just stayed here and made quarter-elves, and left the princess for… no, did he really want to be third in line?

Several of the elves gathered to bid them farewell, or rather to see *Tian* off. Dior grinned and gesticulated, each motion graceful like a lady. The elf shaman gave him trinkets. Kiri clung to him like a burr to horsehair, while Jie pursed her lips at the contact. What was it with him and half-elf girls?

Wait, one half-elf was missing. Ming scanned the crowd a couple of times. "Where's little Kala?"

Heads turned every which way, and Dior disappeared up into the trees. That would take some time getting used to, the idea that entire village was up there, hidden.

A tug at his sleeve drew Ming's attention down. The little boy he'd rescued grinned. Beside him, his beautiful mother bowed and spoke in mellifluous tones. A well-deserved thanks, no doubt. She handed him a quiver of arrows, each head ground from stone.

"Made by their master craftsman," Tian chimed in. How had he snuck up like that?

The stone heads that could penetrate metal. Ming bowed to the woman. "Thank you."

She nodded again, flashing an alluring smile. If only there were more time…

"There's Kala." Jie pointed with her left hand, the one she could still move.

The young half-elf looked at Jie, and then cast her eyes down.

Ming frowned. "You spoke our language. How?"

Kala raised her head. "*They* taught me."

They? Ming's brow furrowed. Tian, Jie, and Ma Jun all stared at Kala.

"*They* trained me in many things. Once I grew up, I was supposed to hunt down my sisters. But Kiri rescued me and we fled."

"Sisters?" Jie gawked at the younger half-elf.

Kala exchanged nods and words with Kiri before facing Jie. "Kiri says you aren't what she expected. She hopes you succeed."

"Succeed?" Jie shook her head in slow turns. "At what?"

"Killing *him*."

Chapter 25:
I, Regent

Surprised conversations filled Kaiya's ears as she stared at the floor, feigning acquiescence to Regent Liu's order. Perhaps it would work for the better. Marriage to Liu Deying would legitimize her babies and keep her close to the throne.

Hong, former Chief Minister, plodded by her. His defeated gait suggested his head must be hanging quite low.

The other supplicant for her bed, Minister Geng, hissed in Liu's ear. "*Jie-xia*, only someone who has passed the civil service exams may serve as a minister, let alone Chief Minister. Your son—"

"—will preside over your execution for insolence," Liu said, "if you do not quiet down."

Minister Geng's immediate silence set the tone for all other conversations coming to a sudden halt. Kaiya looked up to see the old lecher's gawk.

The regent beckoned the imperial guards. "As of today, Mister Geng is stepping down from his position as Minister of the Treasury. He will be reassigned to Nanling Province, as stablemaster. Remove him from the palace."

Nanling Province! Currently in rebellion under Cousin Peng. If this was the way Liu would rule over

Cathay, the nation was doomed. No matter how corrupt former Minister Geng was, someone had to remonstrate the regent.

As the imperial guards strode forward, Kaiya rose to her feet. "*Jie-xia*, if you remove everyone who disagrees with you, sooner or later there will be no one left."

The regent's eyes narrowed. He'd started to lift his hand, when someone cleared their throat and stood in a rustle of robes.

Kaiya glanced back.

There stood Young Lord Chen Qing, *Yu-Ming* heir to a county in Jiangzhou Province. "The classics assert that a wise leader listens to diverse opinions and builds consensus, lest the nation fall into disorder."

Several of the hereditary lords voiced their agreement; unlike the ministers, their positions didn't depend on the *Tianzi*.

Kaiya settled back into her kneel. Young Lord Chen had been one of her early suitors, one whom she had dismissed as dumb as a rock. Perhaps clouded by the dragon Avarax's enchantment, she'd failed to see Chen's potential.

Regent Liu jumped to his feet and pointed at Lord Chen. "Insolence. I order you to cut your throat."

Tiger's Eye or not, Kaiya gasped. Though it was certainly the regent's prerogative, Father had never given such an order. Wouldn't have, even if a hereditary lord had spat in his face. She rose again, the sudden motion sending her stomach into rebellion. She swallowed the words on her lips along with the rising nausea.

And now, she stood before everyone in silence, looking like a fool.

Fool or not, even without the power of music, she'd apparently struck a chord. Behind her, court clothes shuffled and armor jingled. She turned her head.

Several hereditary lords marched to her side, many with hands on their shortswords. She glanced to the dais, where imperial guards now drew their *dao*.

Young Lord Chen dropped to one knee at her side. "I stand with Princess Kaiya."

"I stand with Princess Kaiya." Lords crowded in around her and knelt, reminiscent of their salute to Father when he recovered from Peng's first poisoning attempt. Perhaps if she could feel emotions, it would be moving.

Lord Liu's shoulders huddled, and he took several steps back. Then he straightened and wagged a finger at all of them. "Then you will all die, traitors to the Dragon Throne! Guards!"

Weapons rasped from sheaths, for perhaps the first time ever in the Hall of Supreme Harmony. Imperial guards formed up in front and back, while ministers cowered on the floor.

Even with *dao*, the lords wouldn't have stood a chance against imperial guards. It'd be a slaughter, at a time when the realm needed to come together. There could be no more internal fighting if the nation hoped to withstand a rebellion in the South and an invasion from the North. Submitting to the regent would buy them a temporary reprieve, though it had to be on her terms.

She lifted her chin. "Stand down."

Even without the power of her voice, she could still imitate Father's imperial tone. The guards halted their advance, though their swords remained drawn.

Kaiya stretched out her arms to smooth out her sleeves, and then folded her hands in front of her as she bowed.

It was time to expose her secret, portraying herself as a mourning widow. Prevented by convention to marry for a year, she was still available to be *protected* by the all-powerful, yet easily manipulated regent. He'd protect her sons, believing them to be his. She'd influence policy by making the regent believe the ideas were his own.

It wasn't much different from sacrificing her dignity to Geros to protect seven hundred prisoners—save for the higher stakes and the *Tiger's Eye* which made the decision all the more logical. Straightening, she tilted her head to expose her bare neck and pressed her arms inward to flaunt her cleavage.

As expected, Regent Liu's stare dipped. Minister Geng, pressed between two imperial guards, craned his neck as well. If she'd been less naïve years before, and knew how to use her blossoming tools, perhaps she could've prevented Cousin Peng's conspiracy and the ensuing upheaval.

"*Jie-xia*, I am afraid I cannot marry your son." She paused to let it sink in, ready to deliver her veiled offer at the right moment.

The room fell into silence again, the collective surprise mirrored in Lord Liu's expression. Still, his gaze remained firmly focused on her chest.

"Instead," she said, "I—"

Booted footsteps stomped across the tile floors. Robes swished and heads turned. This inopportune interruption was ruining the precise timing of her offer.

Kaiya cast a sideward glance toward the entrance.

An imperial messenger dropped to his knee just a few steps behind her. "*Jie-xia*, the messengers sent by Princess Kaiya to scout the countryside have returned with urgent news. A Teleri army, at least fifty thousand strong, now march down the highway. They are a day away."

Gasps echoed in the hall. Eyes turned to the regent, whose face blanched. His hands trembled like a maiden's on her wedding night.

Like hers, on *her* wedding night. Kaiya studied his panicked look. The poor man, he was playing mahjong without money to back his losses. When accepting the position, he probably thought the imperial army would vanquish Cousin Peng in short order, and he would win all the glory. He would reap the rewards of future peace and prosperity. Now, confronted with an actual crisis…

Around the room, ministers, guards, and lords muttered in bewilderment. If there was a time to unify them all, it was now.

She cleared her throat. "Men of Cathay. I am Daughter of the Dragon Throne. Hear me."

Young Lord Chen dropped to his knee before her. "What do you command, *Dian-xia*?"

Eyes shifted from the regent to her. Most importantly, the imperial guards sheathed their swords, and their commander, General Jin, looked at her with an expectant gaze.

What should she say? Warning the regent of impending invasion was one thing, taking command, something completely different. Somewhere, Jie was laughing at her expense. No, leave strategies to the military leaders, provisioning to the experts.

Tilting her head, Kaiya extended an open hand to the messenger. No, too feminine. She squared her shoulders and tightened the hand into a fist. "Send messengers to all imperial barracks in and near the capital, ordering them to mobilize. Summon all our generals to the palace at once."

She took four steps and alighted the dais, then turned to face the assembled officials and lords. Someone among them had to know something about provisions and administration. Chief Minister Hong was nowhere to be seen. "Who is the senior-most official present?"

The ministers looked among themselves, and several inched back. Not a single one stood. All these officials had passed civil service examinations, yet apparently none had ever endured true adversity.

In matters of hardship, she had much more experience. She nodded to a page. "Summon former Chief Minister Song to the palace to resume his post." A post he'd only held for a few days, but he'd proven his administrative skills during his tenure as Foreign Minister.

The hall burst into quiet whispers. Minister Geng, still staring at her chest, said, "Minister Song's son was an insurgent."

She shook her head. "It doesn't matter. In these desperate times, a man's capabilities overshadow the sins of his family."

"But the classics say—"

She scowled at him. "The classics teach a ruler wisdom, but they do little to repel invaders."

Young Lord Chen cleared his throat. "I nominate Princess Kaiya to replace Lord Liu as regent."

Kaiya stared at him. Was that even possible? Removal of a sitting regent? And how was a regent appointed? There was no precedent: in the three hundred years of the Wang Dynasty, only the Founder's consort had ruled as regent before Lord Liu, and she'd pretty much assumed the position.

She looked at Lord Liu's cushioned chair. Whoever sat there in these trying times had to contend with bickering lords, corrupt officials, and perhaps an assassin's knife. Only a fool would want the position.

Yet right now, the realm needed her. "I proclaim myself Regent of Cathay."

The hereditary lords followed Lord Chen's lead, dropping to their knees and bowing. "*Jie-xia!*" they shouted in unison.

Officials pressed their foreheads to the floor, repeating the chorus.

The imperial guards all faced her and dropped to a knee, fist to the ground. As the only ones with the swords, their acquiescence mattered the most.

"*Jie-xia,*" General Jin said.

Eyes glazed over, Lord Liu staggered back into his chair. "I resign as regent. *Jie-xia,* please take care of my grandson until he comes of age."

Kaiya swept her gaze over the bowing men. The trust of the lords and ministers might very well be misplaced. If the imperial armies couldn't mobilize in time, her reign as regent might be short-lived.

Reduced to riding a rickshaw. Hong Jianbin bounced in the seat, each joint between the pavestones sending a flare of pain through his old spine. Now forced into retirement, he had lost the perk of riding in a palanquin, protected from the masses by a wall of guards.

Instead, the rickshaw offered him a front-row view of the panicked citizenry, all rushing to the markets to hoard supplies. The buzz of hushed whispers all repeated the same thing: the Teleri Empire had breached the Great Wall and now marched on the capital.

The driver stopped in front of the Jade Teahouse. Unlike the rest of the city, the Floating World seemed calm as always. If one thing remained constant, regardless of whether the *Tianzi* or a foreign conqueror sat on the Jade Throne, it was a man's need for entertainment.

Tripping over his robes, Hong stumbled out of the rickshaw. He straightened himself and offered a silver ring to the wide-eyed driver, though it was worth much more than the cost of the trip. Hong carried no money. He never had to in the palace. Without looking back, he trudged into the teahouse.

The proprietress bowed as he walked through the common area and into the back hallway. He pushed open the secret entrance to Leina's house. His house. Now stripped of his title, he would probably never see his official villa ever again.

Inside the parlor, Leina sat, studying a *weiqi* board. A white stone danced between her delicate fingers, but the other seat across the table was empty. Hong creaked into the vacant chair, and Leina looked up. Sucking in her breath, she stood and bowed. "My lord, I did not hear you come in. Let me get you some tea." She turned toward the kitchen.

"Wait." He cast her a bitter smile.

"My lord, why so glum?" She placed a hand on his shoulder.

Why, indeed. Because his dreams were dead. He would not become a hereditary lord, not marry Princess

Kaiya, nor become regent. Years of planning, all for naught.

They were Leina's dreams, too, and he had failed her as well. A tear threatened to cloud his vision, but he blinked it away. "I was forced to resign."

Her hand pulled back and she stared at him, mouth almost agape. "What happened?"

"Regent Liu no longer had need of my services. I am sorry, you will not become the second most powerful woman in Cathay, as I promised."

"My lord." She sighed. "It doesn't matter. You have already given me so much. We still have each other. Come, have some tea. Tea makes everything better." She glided across the room with a grace of a dancer and disappeared into the kitchen.

Did she really not care about their forfeited dreams? If so, perhaps it was not a total loss. He was a fishmonger's son, yet had once risen to the most powerful office in Cathay. An exotic young woman loved him. He still had her, this house, and plenty of money in a bank.

He studied the *weiqi* board. A game of simple rules, yet so complex in strategy. Who had she been playing with? Black stones controlled the board, with her remaining white pieces all in precarious positions. Whoever it was appeared to be thoroughly beating her, something beyond belief in itself. Though Leina might be naïve, without a mind for real strategy or politicking, she excelled at these kinds of games.

Leina reappeared and placed a tea cup in front of him. She flashed a demure smile.

Beaming back at her, he drew in the sweet scent and took a sip. A comforting warmth trickled down his throat. "Who were you playing against?"

She cocked her head. "Myself."

"You did not give yourself much of a challenge."

Leina grinned at him. "Much earlier in the game, the white side had a seemingly insurmountable advantage. Unfortunately, it left insignificant gaps in its lines. Black was able to exploit what appeared to be white's strengths, but were ultimately weaknesses."

So confusing! How could she see all of it? Hong took another sip of the tea. "Does white stand a chance now?"

"There is always a chance, no matter how improbable." She giggled. "I guess if we bent the rules so white could play four pieces at once… just like when I swapped some white pieces for black earlier."

Hong laughed. "But that's cheating."

"Nobody said life was fair." She shrugged. "As it stands, a fool leads white and black is relentless."

He took a deep swig of tea as his brows furrowed. The silly girl, rambling again. "What *are* you talking about?"

She stared at him, her cheerful demeanor darkening. "You really never saw it, did you?"

"What?" Perhaps his unemployment had driven her mad, despite her earlier claims otherwise.

Pointing at the board, Leina said, "Cathay is white. It rotted from the inside while its enemies gathered strength."

He shook his head. "Impossible. How could that happen?"

"You. *You* made it happen. The troop movements *you* recommended left strategic areas undefended. *You* alienated loyal hereditary lords so that they turned their back on the Jade Throne." She blew out a long breath. "And then *you* used magic engraved in art to depose the *Tianzi*."

Thoughts bouncing in his skull, Hong squinted at her. All these things, ideas she had inadvertently given him. Or maybe it hadn't been inadvertent. Maybe… "You… *you* planned all of this!"

Her smile appeared more sad than triumphant. She nodded.

All this time, he had looked down on her. Now… "Why?"

"In its greed, Cathay sold muskets and firepowder to Madura, which allowed Madura to conquer my homeland." Tears trickled down her cheeks. "Then, the Madurans let the Bovyans in. Sharing your bed was nowhere near as bad as being used by a dozen of them a day. When First Consul Geros released me and gave me a chance to free my mother, I took it."

All her hate and bitterness! Never was it so evident. Hong's head spun. "Why did he do that?"

"Because my father was a trade official from Cathay, and I could use that as a connection to meet a benefactor like you. Someone who could weaken Cathay from the inside with the right manipulation."

Just as he tried to backtrack her winning moves in games, he now connected the events *she'd* set in motion.

He was a fool, tricked by a woman. Still, she had made a mistake in revealing it to him. Once he told Regent Liu, he might be reinstated and she would be executed. He rose to his feet.

Then collapsed back in the chair.

His vision began to darken, and each breath took more effort.

She faded out of focus, and her words cracked beneath her sobs. "You won't be telling anyone. The poison in your tea will give you a merciful death."

Poison! Death! Murdered by his own concubine. The one who had engineered Cathay's downfall with him as a pawn. He could have prevented it at any time, if only he had seen it coming.

"Goodbye, Old Hong."

Leina wrung her hands. She had wished for Old Hong's death time and time again, and yet, now that it had come to pass, her heart ached.

He sprawled in the chair, lifeless eyes seemingly locked on the *weiqi* game, the one they had played in real life for the last three years.

He wasn't a bad man, just a misguided one. He had cared for her, which was more than she could say about the father who abandoned her or any other man in her life. Most of the time, he had been sweet, albeit patronizing.

Out in the city, sonorous bells tolled a foreboding chorus. Not for Hong's death, but as a warning of impending danger.

Leaning over, she closed Old Hong's eyes with a gentle sweep of her hand. She kissed his forehead, and with one last look at him, turned and left.

It was time to initiate her final plan, the one which would leave the city defenseless.

Chapter 26:
Reunions

From the clearing's edge, Ming stared at the site of both his greatest success and greatest failure as a leader. Still incomplete, the Teleri peninsular fort he'd captured and lost bustled with activity. Natives and Bovyans alike worked at packing and moving weapons and supplies, their activity visible across the moat through the unfinished palisade.

Ming leaned in to Jie and whispered, "We must be lost. We didn't pass this on the way."

The half-elf harrumphed. "Can't you picture a map?" The shoulder wound made her even testier than before. Now she knew how he felt when he couldn't draw a bow.

He would take the high ground and not rub it in. Plus, even with one good arm, she could still slash his throat in the night. He shrugged.

She pointed east, along the moat which spilled into the Great Kanin River. "We forded the tributary several *li* to the north."

Right, north. Probably where the Teleri had cut off his army's retreat, as well. Still, they were stuck. "We can't wade through the shallows, because the Teleri would see us." He pointed at the wide river, which flowed past the fort. "And it's too wide to swim." For Jie, at least, with her arm, but some things didn't need to be said.

"Can we go the way you came?" Tian's gaze shifted from the fortress back to the group.

Ming cringed. It was a wet, bug-infested walk through swamp to the fords. Not all that much easier than just wading across the moat, walking through the fort, and over the Teleri-made bridge.

"Wait," Ma Jun said. "If we can sabotage their supplies here, it might slow their invasion of Cathay." The erstwhile imperial guard turned and spoke in the jumbled native language to the shaman Yuha. Tian nodded and pointed, while Yuha shrugged.

Ming had some good ideas about sabotage, but they were leaving him out of the conversation. He grunted at Jie. "I wonder what they are saying."

The irritable half-elf snorted. "Probably that four and a half of us don't stand a chance."

Half? Even after saving her miserable life, *again*, she still insulted him. He jabbed a finger at her. "I am not a half. I would bet—"

"*I* am the half." She studied the ground.

Such pessimism. Ming sighed. It had to be more than the arm stifling Jie's irrepressible nature. He opened his mouth—

"Shh, get down." Jie crouched, ears twitching.

Though alert, her expression still looked forlorn. His snappy comment about her worth as a watchdog died on his lips.

She exchanged a few hand signals with Tian, who nodded and whispered something in Yuha and Ma Jun's ears. Yuha sunk low to the brush and crawled northward. Ma Jun crept east.

Ming rolled his eyes. All the secrecy, and he was left out, again. To think there'd been a time when he, Jie, Ma

Jun, and his imperial guard comrades had helped those Southerners assault a pyramid. They—

"Don't move, you are surrounded," a shrill voice called from deeper in the forest.

Ma Jun and Yuha froze in place on the ground. Tian pressed his back to a tree, a Teleri longsword in hand. Jie jerked her head and peered somewhere to the west. Even with a bad arm, she still had amazing senses. Ming drew his bow, nocked an arrow and aimed in that direction.

A mop of shaggy brown hair ventured out from behind a tree, and Ming loosed and nocked another arrow. Whoever it was ducked back out of the first arrow's trajectory, and peeked out again. "Hey, I come in peace. You aren't really surrounded."

Tian gaped at the half-sized man who skipped out from behind a tree, Ming's arrow in hand. Too mature-looking to be a child, too short to be a human. The word for the newcomer's race flitted at the edges of his addled recollections. Even more disconcerting was that this same little man appeared in his memories when he watched Layani and Jie fight. Him, and the brown-skinned warrior with the pointed beard.

"Fleet!" Mouth agape, Ma Jun rose and dusted himself off.

"Fleet…" Jie droned in monotone, as if she'd just seen a spirit.

Fleet. The name sounded no more familiar than Kaiya.

"My, my, Ma Jun and Tian." Fleet eyed the rest of them, nodding in turn. "A Maki shaman and Princess

Kaiya's bodyguard. And you—" he pointed at Ming, "—the princess' former beau."

The princess' former beau? Tian's eyes bulged. He looked to Ming, who cast his gaze downward. How much more awkward could this get? A woman who he had apparently loved but couldn't remember, stolen from a brother.

"Halfling," Ming said haltingly in the Metal Men's language, "who are you, and how do you know me?"

The madaeri—that was the term— sauntered over and grinned at Ming, twirling the arrow between his stubby fingers. "Your notoriety precedes you. You shouldn't waste an elf-sharpened arrowhead."

Cheeks flushed, Ming snatched the arrow away and shoved it back into his quiver. Jie's lips twitched upward, the first sign of a smile since they'd set off from the wild elf village.

Fleet bent over, revealing a scar on the back of his neck, and rummaged through Ma Jun's pack. He withdrew some dried berries and tossed them into his mouth. "So. My friends in the local tribes speak of a Warrior From Beyond the Wall. I assume it is one of you?"

All eyes turned to Tian. More awkwardness. The locals revered the Warrior From Beyond the Wall, but his exploits were tales Tian had heard but didn't remember experiencing. He shook his head. "I don't remember anything."

"That explains the blank look, despite all the good times we had together." Fleet pulled on his ear. "Then again, you weren't the sharpest sword in the armory to begin with. Maybe some familiar faces will help jolt your memories. Follow me."

Familiar faces? Tian started to speak, but the madaeri disappeared into the woods without a sound. The others exchanged glances and shrugs. "Who's that?" Tian said.

Jie's voice rang with awe. "He helped me track the Water Snake *Black Fist* clan in the Eldaeri Kingdoms."

"He guided us through the hills of Iksuvi," Ma Jun said, "during Princess Kaiya's escape from Iksuvius."

Yuha beckoned them to follow. "The Traveler brings good luck. He's visited our village in the past, and always the spirits bless us afterwards."

Probably coincidence, but Yuha hurried after Fleet, so unlike all the caution he'd exhibited over the last several days of travel. With a sigh, Tian followed, and the rest trailed after him. The madaeri moved quickly, oftentimes stopping to wait for them.

The tumbling of water over rocks grew louder, and a *li* to the east, they arrived at the river bank. A canoe lay partially hidden by shrubs, and the underbrush had clearly been disturbed.

Fleet whistled.

Three faces of varying brown shades popped out from behind different trees. The darkest, a pretty woman with a chocolate complexion and coarse hair, smiled broadly. Dirt streaked her white dress, and its band of colored patterns across her chest was faded. One of the men bowed his shaved pate, and a gold disk hanging from his neck spilled out of his ascetic robes. The third… was the other man from Tian's memories. Flowing black hair and a pointed beard, a curved sword in hand.

Ming and Ma Jun hurried forward, exchanging excited greetings with the newcomers, though Jie hung back.

Yuha sidled up to Tian. "It looks like a reunion of old friends."

Tian nodded. "I'd wager there is a story behind this."

"Involving a pyramid," Jie said. "And charlatan priests and magic gemstones."

Pointed Beard strode over. "Well met, Tian," he said in the Metal Men's language, though with a thick accent. "I didn't expect to meet you here."

Tian didn't expect to be here either. He stared at the newcomer. "I'm sorry..."

"He lost his memories," Jie said, her tone acerbic. "He doesn't know who you are, Sameer."

The man's lips formed a ring. He pressed his hands together and bowed. "I am Sameer. You have saved my life, and I have saved yours." He pointed his chin toward the others. "I, and my comrades Cyrus and Brehane, owe your brother, Ma Jun, and Jie a favor we can never repay. Come."

Frowning, Tian followed Sameer. All this interpersonal history, lost to him. Only Sameer's fighting skill made any kind of impression, and that was through dreams. Up close, the other two looked no more familiar than almost everyone else he'd met since waking from the *Viper's Rest*. Brehane held both of Ma Jun's hands.

"...going to Cathay," the bald man, apparently Cyrus, was saying.

Ming cocked his head. "Whatever for?"

Sameer chuckled. "Princess Kaiya offered to take us to your pyramid."

The image of a four-sided pyramid, by a large lake with blue waters, flashed in Tian's memory.

"Princess Kaiya is in no position to offer anything," Jie said. "And you would have to get through the Teleri army to reach her."

Ming snorted. "Just like us."

Fleet whistled. "I'd warned the princess that the Teleri were heading that way. I didn't expect it to be so soon."

"So what's your plan?" Tian asked Sameer. Maybe they had a better idea.

"We still need to visit the pyramid," Cyrus said.

Sameer pointed at the dugout canoe. "We were waiting until dark to row past the fortress."

A boat. Tian smiled to himself. Why hadn't *he* thought of that when they left the wild elf village? Too bad this canoe wasn't big enough for an extra five people. At least— "Could you ferry us, too?"

"Wait." Ming held up a hand. "The Teleri invasion is supplied from this fort. I know firsthand. We need to destroy the bridge on the other side of the fort."

Fleet stroked his chin. "Sameer and his friends must make haste and can't risk capture by the Teleri."

"However," Brehane chirped in, accent thick, "We can take care of the bridge."

As they drifted by the fort under the cover of darkness, Jie peered at the soldiers on the bridge with her elf vision. Earlier in the day, her heart had raced as she approached the napping Akolyte Cyrus. If he felt the same as Sameer about returning her a favor, surely he would invoke the healing powers of his One God.

She had shaken him awake, and his eyes fluttered open.

"Can't you let a man sleep?" He groaned and turned back over again.

"I need your help." The pleading in her voice sounded pathetic, but maybe this was her only hope. "You *owe* me."

"All right." Grumbling, Cyrus sat up. Sleepy eyes wandered to her injury. "It's about your arm, right?"

She nodded. He had always been perceptive.

"You never believed Athran was the One God," he said.

In fact, she'd mocked Cyrus at the pyramid in Levastya when he had lost his power, but... "I will convert to your faith."

"Right." Cyrus snorted. He withdrew the golden disk hanging from his neck. Clasping it, he placed a hand on her shoulder and chanted in his language.

Warmth flooded through her shoulder, and her pulse skipped a beat. Perhaps she had better invest in a gold disk.

When Cyrus finished his prayer, he opened his eyes and looked expectantly at her.

She reached for her dagger and... nothing. Her shoulder remained just as frozen as before.

"I am sorry," Cyrus said, his voice sincere.

Despite her best efforts to control them, tears had filled her eyes then.

They did again now, blurring the shades of grey and olive of her elf sight as Fleet poled the boat to shore. She wiped her eyes with her good arm and cleared the lump in her throat. To think the only things making her useful were the exceptional senses from the elf blood she hated. Still, she couldn't let Tian see her cry.

Ming, Yuha, Ma Jun, and the Southerners waited on the banks. Ma Jun took her hand and helped her disembark, while Tian and Fleet jumped off with ease after her. She ripped her hand from Ma Jun's. Her arm might not work, but she was no invalid.

Ming pointed at the bridge over the great river's tributary, some hundred feet away. "Logs lashed together with rope. We tried to use gunpowder to destroy it, but it wouldn't light in the rain."

Or Ming had been incompetent. Jie snorted. She'd imploded Wailian Castle and obliterated a quarter of the Cathayi embassy in Iksuvius with firepowder.

"We could slash the ropes now," Tian whispered. "From underneath."

Jie shook her head. "It would take too long by yourself. I can't help you, and you are the only one who stands a chance at succeeding without them seeing."

"I'm standing right here," Fleet muttered.

Brehane raised a silencing hand. "We need to get closer. I will use magic, but it will tire me out. I will need you to help me back to the boat."

Jie stared at her. The most impressive magic Brehane had mustered a year ago was putting a bunch of fake Akolytes to sleep, and even that had left her on the verge of collapse from the fatigue.

Yet Sameer and Cyrus nodded at her confidence now.

Fleet pointed a chin at Ming. "You provide cover with your bow. Tian, Sameer, and Ma Jun, come with me just in case we run into some baddies when we approach."

"What about me?" Jie would've thrown her arms up if both had worked.

Fleet grinned. "You guard the boat with Yuha. Cyrus, wait in the boat so we can make a quick getaway."

Guard the boat, indeed.

More like, *don't get in the way*. Jie sighed as the others shuffled off toward the fort, making plenty of noise as they did. She tracked their progress as they stepped on pine needles, fallen branches, and dried leaves. It'd be a miracle if they didn't rouse the entire garrison.

Brehane stopped them with an open hand, just thirty-some feet from the bridge. She barked out several guttural syllables. The men in the fort turned and pointed—

An explosion blossomed out from the center of the bridge, erupting in brilliant streaks of sparks and flames. Jie shielded her eyes against the sudden brightness as the ground trembled beneath her. Men screamed, and the fortress descended into chaotic cacophony. The bridge lay in charred ruins. Burning logs sizzled in the water.

Since when had Brehane grown so powerful? Jie met the Aksumi's eyes as she staggered back, panting, supported by Tian and Ma Jun. Sameer followed them, backing away from the fortress with sword in hand.

"Hurry!" Fleet zipped past her toward the shore. "There might be patrols on this bank."

They gathered on the shore, and Sameer helped Brehane into the boat.

Fleet waved. "We part again. Perhaps we will meet again, in Cathay."

Jie stared at the madaeri. How would the three Southerners get past the East Gate? How would *they* get past the East Gate?

Chapter 27:
Loose Threads

Stomping boots, swishing robes, and garbled conversations in the palace grounds below interrupted Kaiya's fleeting moments of quiet and peace. With just a couple of hours before the generals and Chief Minister Song arrived, she had cleared the Hall of Supreme Harmony in hopes of collecting her thoughts.

It was not to be.

The double doors opened, revealing Cousin Kai-Hua. With husband Liu Dezhen and a pair of imperial guards in tow, she cradled the new *Tianzi* in her arms. Asleep and innocent, beautiful as only a baby could be, he was an unwitting pawn in a power struggle which promised to continue despite all the oaths of loyalty and pledges of support.

Kaiya relinquished the central dais and knelt on the floor before it. Her cousin stepped up and, bowing deferentially to the Jade Throne, took a seat. With the dizzying shifts of fortune, Kai-Hua must have been bewildered. Nonetheless, she had always been a close confidante. If not for the awkward circumstances, the two would likely have hugged.

"Cousin… Queen Mother," Kaiya said. "It is good to see you again."

Kai-Hua nodded. "Yes, Kaiya… *Jie-xia.*"

"*Jie-xia*." From his place next to his wife, Liu Dezhen bowed low. "Forgive me for my outburst earlier. I am grateful for your patience and confidence."

Kaiya waved a hand. "There is nothing to forgive. As far as I am concerned, until we ascertain the fate of my brother Kai-Wu behind the castle walls, your son is *Tianzi*."

Liu gaped.

She pressed her forehead to the cool marble floors. "I swear to defend him and faithfully administer affairs of state in his stead until he comes of age." Perhaps her maternal ancestor had prostrated herself and spoken the same words to her adolescent son three hundred years before. Unlike the Founder's consort, Kaiya would relinquish her position. She raised her head.

Liu Dezhen and Wang Kai-Hua bowed. She smiled when she straightened, but the glint in *his* eye didn't inspire confidence. Kaiya's spine pricked. Perhaps a knife in the back awaited her later. Queen Regent Wang Yuxiang had faced several challenges to her rule, all underhanded and life-threatening.

Kaiya held a low bow as they left the hall.

"*Dian-xia*," a female voice called from the entrance.

Rising, Kaiya returned to the bloodwood chair beside the Jade Throne and squinted at the doors.

With Doctor Wu and Weiyong at her side, handmaiden and body-double Han Meiling bowed as much as her enlarged belly would allow. Sacrificed so that Kaiya could escape a doomed city, Meiling was yet another one of Emperor Geros' rape victims. Kaiya's own womb twinged. Memories of his calloused hands sent a chill up her spine and squeezed her chest. The fear disappeared as quickly as it appeared, the emotional armor of the *Tiger's Eye* forming up.

Hands supporting her stomach, Meiling tottered to the front of the room and started to kneel.

Kaiya held up a commanding hand. "As you are, Meiling." She stood and bowed at the waist. "I am so sorry for what you endured in my defense."

Meiling shook her head. "It is my honor."

More like a dishonor, at least in the eyes of a man looking for a virgin bride. Meiling had probably hoped to improve her marriage prospects by serving as an imperial princess' handmaiden. Kaiya forced a regal smile. "If you wish it, after you give birth, I will adopt your son and arrange a suitable husband for you."

Meiling blew out a sigh and bowed. "As you command, *Dian... Jie-xia.*"

"Please take care of yourself in the meantime." Kaiya gestured toward Weiyong and Doctor Wu. "My doctors are at your disposal."

Weiyong's face flushed. It was cute in its own way. He supported Meiling as she shuffled backward toward the exit.

As if Kaiya's own twins weren't enough responsibility, she was volunteering to take on a third child. She watched as Meiling departed and passed by three new petitioners. Behind the palace chamberlain stood a short human male with a rough, sun-drenched complexion and long brown hair. He supported a woman with a lighter bronze skin tone and unruly red hair. A free hand cradled the swell of her belly.

The chamberlain stepped over the threshold and bowed low. "I present—"

Kaiya bowed. "Prince Aelward of Tarkoth and Princess Alaena of Serikoth. I owe you both a great debt of gratitude."

"That ye do, lass." Prince Aelward chuckled. "Little did I expect to see ye in the big chair."

Kaiya bowed to the Jade Throne and shook her head. "No, my baby cousin sits here. Until he comes of age, I will act as regent."

"Then perhaps you can repay those debts of gratitude." Princess Alaena gritted her teeth. There had been no sign of a pregnancy four months before, when her rangers and Tian had rescued Kaiya from ogres, but now she looked even more pregnant than Meiling. Which meant Tian was not the father. Maybe the elf Thielas. The two had seemed close.

Prince Aelward nodded. "Princess Alaena's baby is due in a month, and I had hoped to have her resting in Vyara City by then. However—"

"He is coming sooner," Alaena said. "I am sure of it. I want a good midwife."

Always so blunt. Kaiya nodded toward Doctor Wu. "My personal doctor will see to your needs. However, Cathay might not be the safest place. A Teleri army with Emperor Geros at the head is just a day away."

Aelward and Alaena exchanged glances as Doctor Wu approached and placed her wizened fingers over the princess' wrist.

The doctor looked up and nodded. "Yes, your boy will come in three days."

Kaiya gestured toward the doors. "I suggest that you return to the Invincible in Jiangkou so that you might make a quick escape if need be. Doctor Wu will accompany you."

"Thank you," Prince Aelward said. "I also have bad news. Ayana Strongbow died peacefully in her sleep."

"My condolences." Kaiya bowed her head. The old elf wizard had guided her in magic and helped during the confrontation with Avarax. A loss, to be sure, even if the *Tiger's Eye* prevented Kaiya from feeling it.

The Eldaeri prince and princess turned and departed with Doctor Wu, passing yet more familiar faces waiting outside.

Iskuvi's refugee Queen Ausra stepped over the ghost-tripping threshold, with her husband's two teenage sisters at her side. A wet nurse bounced a toddler on her hip—the queen's nephew and heir to Iksuvi, except... the queen herself cradled yet another baby.

Which meant, if he were hers, she had been pregnant when they fled Iksuvius; and she now held the new heir in her arms. He appeared especially robust, even for a baby of Nothori stock.

All of the newborns and babies and pregnant women. A fluttering erupted in Kaiya's heart. To think she would be joining these women in motherhood before long, glowing... no, the supposed radiance was no more than an illusion conjured by poets to assuage fatigued, sleep-deprived mothers.

"Princess Kaiya, I was surprised to hear of your sudden return." Queen Ausra curtseyed in the fashion of the North, at least as well as she could while holding her treasure. "We heard only rumors of your escape from my homeland. I did not know what became of you until I received your summons just now."

Kaiya nodded. "The last time we met, I sent you into exile on a Cathayi ship. I am afraid I must do the same now. A Teleri Army of fifty thousand, with Emperor Geros at its head, is only a day away."

The queen sucked in a breath. "So the rumors are true. Fifty thousand. No one is safe."

"No. Least of all your son, the heir to an occupied nation, a symbol of its hope."

Queen Ausra nodded. "Born in safety because of your generosity."

So the child was King Evydas' son. Kaiya pointed to a captain at the doors. "His men will escort you to Jiangkou, where you will board a trade ship bound for Ayudra Island. I will make arrangements for you to stay at our embassy in Vyara City."

"Vyara City." The queen sighed. "When we spoke of Vyara City at the banquet, it had been about nostalgic memories." She rocked the baby. "To think Iskuvi's heir will be nothing more than a pauper there."

A pauper, like the Ankirans whom Kaiya had met, forced into exile by the same Madurans who now invaded Cathay from the South. In selling muskets and gunpowder to Madura, Cathay had invited a future enemy to its doorstep. As regent, she would have to consider recent history in order to formulate future policy. If the realm survived the current crisis...

Boots clopping across the Hall of Supreme Harmony drew Kaiya's gaze up from the queen. Minister Song shuffled behind three generals, who strode down the center of the room. Helmets were tucked under their arms, and capes flowed behind them.

All three dropped to a knee, fist to the ground. Minister Song bowed low. "*Jie-xia*," they all shouted.

The title of regent still sounded strange in her ears. She nodded at them. "Generals, I would hear your plans for the defense of the capital."

"As you command, *Jie-xia*." General Tang unfurled a huge map, the length and width of two men, with the help of the others. "Fifty thousand Teleri heavy infantry march on the highway, a day away from the city. We have eight thousand imperial infantrymen and a thousand cavalry, as well as a smaller number of provincial soldiers, at our disposal."

Kaiya kept her face impassive, just as her father would have. Still, even with her lack of military acumen, the odds did not sound promising. "How about the bulk of our soldiers in the South? They must have seen the light towers' signals. They could help bolster the city's defenses."

"No, *Jie-xia*." General Shan shook his head. "Our armies in the South are holding off an onslaught from the rebel Peng and his Maduran allies."

Kaiya buried a snort. Somehow, a treacherous cousin who wanted her dead had managed to ally with a lecherous prince who wanted her in bed. "What if they retreated to the city?"

General Shan pointed to the map. "We would cede control of the central valley and the food supplies it provides to Peng."

Looking at the map, it made sense, but— "If the capital falls, there will be no need for those supplies. We are overwhelmingly outnumbered."

General Tang cleared his throat. "If I may, *Jie-xia*. The Jade River and city walls negate the Teleri's numerical advantage. If they assault the north gate over the bridge, our guns would decimate them."

The bridge was wide enough for thirty men to walk abreast. Kaiya frowned. The stakes were too high.

"Before they could even form up on the other side of the river," General Shan added, "they would be in range of our cannon."

"Are there any places where they could ford?" Kaiya pointed and traced a line along the Jade River and Sun-Moon Lake.

"No, *Jie-xia*," the third general said. "The heavy winter snows have led to higher water levels. The only place any army could cross would be east, in Dongmen Province. Even then, they would have to conquer Linshan Province to reach the capital."

For whatever reason, the *Tiger's Eye* faltered. Her chest tightened. Heavy winter snows had stranded her in the Wilds, yet now helped defend her against Geros. It would be welcome news if the Teleri fell back to Dongmen Province, where she had sequestered herself for two weeks waiting for Zheng Ming.

Still, that left all the people in the towns and villages north of the river undefended, with no way of escaping. The women, falling prey to the depravations of the Bovyan scourge... her stomach clenched.

Again, the emotions disappeared just as quickly as they had surfaced. They *were* safe. Unless... "Are there any towns where they could commandeer boats?"

General Shan shook his head. "Not enough to ferry over a credible threat before we discovered them. I will assign the cavalry to patrol the river to ensure that."

She turned to Minister Song. "Minister, you will manage the non-military aspects of the crisis. Generals, I entrust the defense of the city to you."

A river and city walls stood between them and the invaders. It should have been reassuring. Still, Emperor Geros had proven resourceful and unpredictable.

Astride his horse, Emperor Geros led his army through a village on the highway. Cathayi peasants lined the road, holding low bows.

An industrious yet docile folk. No wonder Cathay's founder had unified the lands with so little effort, and then prospered. The grains in the North and rice in the South would all feed the Teleri's righteous cause in the future.

A runner pounded a fist on his chest. "Your Eminence, a message from your spy inside the capital." He proffered a tightly wound piece of paper.

Rice paper, from Leina. Geros unrolled it and read.

City in upheaval. Only 10,000 defenders. Camp outside the city. Approach under flag of parley. Await my signal.

It would be some signal. Geros grinned. Whereas the Teleri used Eldaeri messenger birds, stolen from Tarkoth a century before, Cathayi news travelled at the speed of ships and horse relays. It only took the right bribe at the right time and place to paralyze their communications systems. How surprised Princess Kaiya would be to find fifty thousand Bovyans at the city walls.

Geros looked south. They could be no more than a day away at their pace. If he took off on his horse, he could be at the city and closer to his love by early afternoon.

He snorted. A fool's errand, obviously, one which only a besotted rube like Prince Dhananad would take up.

That proved the Altivorc King wrong about Geros eschewing strategy. He turned and beckoned the only non-Bovyan in his army forward.

Feiying jogged up and pounded his fist to his chest. "Yes, Your Eminence?"

"Take a horse and set off for Huajing. You will find Leina in the Floating World, at the Jade Teahouse. You are to assist her in weakening the city's defenses, but your first priority is to steal the imperial regalia from the Temple of Heaven."

Master Feiying gawked for a split second before his expression blanked. "Yes, Your Eminence."

Chapter 28:
Home is Where the Heart Is

The last time Ming had looked at the Great East Gate, Emperor Geros had paraded him as a prisoner of war. Now, with Guanyin's Eye almost completely open, and Renyue less than a half-crescent to new, he stared through the darkness at the gatehouse parapet. A single Teleri soldier paced, bauble lamp in hand. Just enough to illuminate himself, leaving Ma Jun and Jie shrouded in darkness on the ground just outside the gate.

Unable to accompany his cuckold of a little brother up the Wall, the irritable half-elf grew even more sour. Maybe a fight would be good for her, or at least put her out of her misery.

Yuha tapped him on the shoulder and pantomimed something. It was either a buxom maiden or torrential rain.

With the only female around being a flat-chested spy, and not a cloud in the sky, Ming grumbled to himself. If only the shaman could speak Cathay. Though it wasn't like they could even hear each over the roar of the waterfall in the distance.

Yuha jerked a finger three times at the gate.

Rising, Jie and Ma Jun rushed toward it.

Drawing his bowstring, Ming aimed and shot. The arrow arced and lodged in the sentry's face. The bauble lamp floated off the Wall and shattered on the ground. Its light blinked out.

Now, Yuha scampered across the yard between the tree line and the gate. Arrow nocked, Ming ran after him.

Back against a wall, Jie held position just inside the gate. Light bauble lamps stood mostly shuttered, allowing for only a dim light. Ma Jun and Tian were nowhere to be seen. Ming met her gaze and raised an eyebrow. Her pointed ears twitched. She pointed toward the other side of the gatehouse, then up.

A muffled grunt emanated from somewhere nearby, and Ming raised his bow. Footsteps approached, followed by a sword-wielding silhouette.

"Hold, Ming," Jie said. "It's Ma Jun." How she could tell, he could only guess. He certainly wasn't going to ask and let it go to her head.

Ma Jun neared and sheathed his weapon. "I took care of two soldiers, but there don't seem to be any others on this level."

With a nod, Ming pointed up. "Only one on top of the gate." With one of his elf arrows stuck in his skull. He'd have to retrieve it, even if it was the one the little halfling had put his grimy paws on.

"Only three others on the second level," said Tian from somewhere in the dark, "as well as our own winch operators."

It was still hard to believe his little brother was such a skilled killer. Ming scanned the darkness. "Why would the Teleri leave such a small garrison?"

Tian's voice spoke again, this time just a few feet away. "In their minds, they control everything. Between their heartland and here. They need only hold strategic points."

"Once your father swore fealty to the emperor," Jie said, "the Dongmen provincial army became the Teleri rear guard. The soldiers serve the *Tai-Ming* lord without question, and now he serves the Bovyans."

Ming gritted his teeth at memories of Geros' condescending attitude. It made Father's capitulation, after having sworn fealty to the *Tianzi*, all the more unbelievable. Where was the sense of loyalty he'd always instilled?

"What about the imperial garrison?" Ma Jun counted on his fingers. "There must be at least five thousand national soldiers here. They would have resisted the invasion."

Ming shook his head. "Against fifty thousand Teleri and ten thousand provincial soldiers, they would've been slaughtered. I don't blame them if they surrendered."

"There must be someone loyal to the Jade Throne here," Ma Jun said.

"Count Du in Pujin." Ming pointed south toward the great falls.

Jie waved in another direction. "That way."

"Watchdog *and* compass," Ming muttered under his breath.

"It doesn't matter," Ma Jun said. "We got past the Wall; now we can go to the capital and find the princess."

Ming shook his head. "No, from here we have a chance to attack the Teleri rear."

"But we've already cut off their supplies." Jie drew a hand across her throat.

"The invaders will just live off the land," Tian said, "and as long as our father serves the emperor, the province will provision them."

Ma Jun held up a hand. "You will need an army."

Ming grinned.

Tian's city of birth seemed just as foreign as the wild elf village and every other place he'd visited since coming out of the *Viper's Rest*.

Yet one thing felt out of place as he walked at Ming's side: the people who ventured out of tidy wooden stores and into the stone-paved streets looked downtrodden.

There were very few, as well. In the six and a half *li* from the city gates to the castle walls, only forty-two citizens had passed by. Not enough to make just one of the three market squares he passed seem busy. If Tian didn't know any better, he'd think a plague had settled over the town.

He turned to Ming. "How many people live here?"

Ming kept his focus on the castle, as he had the entire walk. "Seventy thousand, maybe?"

Too round a number, but it would suffice. With the lack of patrols, without even the Metal Men around, it was a wonder the populace wasn't rioting. "It's too quiet."

"Huh?" Ming tore his gaze away from the castle. "Oh. Right. Yes. That's the sound of a subjugated people. *Our* people."

Tian met a lone commoner's eyes, and the man immediately stared down. Perhaps all of the lands Beyond the Wall would end up like this if the Metal Men succeeded.

A woman's scream rang out from down a side street they had passed twenty-six feet back. Ming froze in place and whirled around. Tian followed his line of sight.

Sounds of struggle arose. Men laughed. One of the four said, "Come on now, the fun is just starting."

Tian hesitated. They had to get to the castle… but they couldn't just let four men take advantage of a woman. He looked at Ming.

His brother's face flushed red. He unslung his bow and marched back toward the unseen commotion. Loosening the heavy Metal Man sword from its sheath, Tian hurried to keep pace. They turned the corner, and Ming already had an arrow nocked and ready to fly.

He lowered the bow and gawked.

Tian too, hesitated. It wasn't Metal Men pinning a young woman's hands to the wall. Soldiers from Beyond the Wall, wearing light green tunics with a twin mountain symbol stitched into the left breast, touched her in inappropriate places.

"Stand down." Ming's voice carried a tone of authority, though certainly his raised weapon punctuated the command.

The men backed away, hands raised. The young woman gathered her tattered clothes around her and scampered away.

Poor girl. Tian started to follow.

Ming raised a hand. "Soldiers of Dongmen are supposed to uphold propriety and honor, shining above mountains like the symbol emblazoned over your heart. Has becoming vassals of the Teleri wolves turned us into rapists? No, even the Teleri don't rampage in the streets, taking lone girls at will. You aren't even wolves, you are pigs."

One of the men opened his mouth, then closed it as his eyes widened. He dropped to his knee and bowed his head. "Young Lord Zheng! Please forgive us."

Gawking, the other men followed his lead. Tian tightened the grip on his sword. Unless they did something to silence these rogues, news of their arrival would be on every mouth.

Shutters from second-floor windows opened and faced peeked out.

"It's Young Lord Zheng!"

"He is alive!"

"He's returned!"

Voices rose not just in loudness, but in hope. They *adored* Ming. How could they not? In the forest, he looked lost and childish; now, his aura commanded respect. Even in ragged clothes.

Bowing, the lead soldier pulled a sheathed broadsword from his sash and held it up in two hands. "My Lord, I have dishonored Dongmen with my actions. You may take my head if that will allow me atone for my men's actions."

Ming received the weapon and unsheathed it. He was really going to execute the soldier. Without hesitation, the man brushed his hair to the side and exposed his neck. His comrades rushed up to his side and bowed.

One of them sank to both knees. "Please, Young Lord—"

"Silence." Ming's tone carried a lethal authority in it. "The condemned will announce his name and rank."

"Ku Wenshen, Lieutenant of Dongmen's Third Infantry Division."

Ming raised the sword. "Ku Wenshen, I presume the Wen in your name means cultured. You have tarnished not only your province and unit, but your own name." The blade swooped down.

Tian turned. Certainly not because of gore, when he'd seen so much. So why? Despite the heinous crime, public beheading was too cruel a punishment. He looked back.

Ming's blade rested a hair's width from Ku's neck. "Soldier of Dongmen," he said, "I have come to cut away the blight left by the Teleri. Rise now. Your honor will be restored when you find the girl and give her family three months of your pay."

Hair stood on the back of Tian's neck. His brother had such indomitable strength of spirit. A tear gathered in his eyes.

Likewise, tears plopped from Ku's face onto the pavestones. "Thank you, Young Lord. I will commit to becoming a better man."

"Good," Ming said. "Now, tell me where the imperial soldiers are."

"Disarmed and confined to barracks, Young Lord." Where they couldn't pose a threat to their father.

Ming patted him on the shoulder. "Take your patrol and go to the barracks and tell the guards to release the imperials into my custody. Have them brought to the castle."

"That is treason against the lord!" One of the soldiers whipped out his broadsword and swung.

Tian had a dagger in hand, but Ming was in the way. Yet Ming held his own, deflecting the swing with a loud clang before reversing the cut and hacking across the dissenter's arm. Blood sprayed, and he man staggered back several steps, holding the wound. The sword slipped from his fingers and clattered to the ground.

Ming pointed the tip of the weapon at him. "The lord committed treason against the *Tianzi*, who holds the Mandate of Heaven. Drop to your knee and swear allegiance to the Jade Throne."

The soldier looked to his comrades, who forcefully nodded. Still holding his arm, he submitted as commanded. "I swear my life to the *Tianzi.*"

Ming turned to Lieutenant Ku. "If he shows any sign of violating his oath, execute him. I *will* see that all of Dongmen Province recognizes the *Tianzi's* authority. "

Ku bowed. "As you command, Young Lord."

"And so begins our army." Ming grinned at Tian.

Only if these soldiers succeeded in convincing their superiors. Tian forced a smile.

Ming could never imagine his province's soldiers behaving so barbarically. Father had always chosen quality men, those of martial skill and high caliber. Now, he had let them become roving bandits, shirking the rule of law in favor of the rule of might.

He glared past the bridge over the moat, to the castle gate, and growled. No. Not in his province. Not in his hometown.

The double doors swung open, revealing the gasping chamberlain. "Young Lord Zheng! I did not believe that you had survived in the wilderness, and... Young Lord Tian." The man paled, looking as if he would faint. "I... I... will summon the lord and lady. Come in, come in."

Holding a low bow, a page shuffled forward and extended his arms to receive their cloaks and weapons. Ming placed his cloak and sword in the boy's hands, but kept his bow strapped to his back. Tian just stared while the page waited. With Ming's prodding, Tian proffered his blade.

Advisors and servants bowed as they passed. Ming afforded them nonchalant nods, yet kept gazing at the walls.

So many memories in these halls, of Father teaching them the virtue of service to the *Tianzi*. The responsibilities of ruling a province. How could he have made a deal with the Teleri?

In the corner of his eye, Tian might have been dancing, the way he startled at the nightingale floor's chirp. An efficient killer or not, heart thief or not, he was still a little brother.

The double doors to the audience chamber slid open. Soldiers dressed in light green Dongmen livery lined the walls. Directly ahead, his father, the *Tai-Ming* lord, sat cross-legged on the central dais.

From where she knelt to the left, Mother stumbled to her feet. Among several officers on the floor to either side of the dais slouched his second brother Lun, arm in a sling. He had survived the gruesome wounds, but looked too pale. Ming's own fault for his defeat at Emperor Geros' hands.

His third brother Shu was nowhere to be seen. His gentlest of brothers—now that Tian had turned out to be as deadly as the half-elf demoness—hadn't been injured at all, so where was he now?

Almost as disconcerting as Shu's absence was the Teleri presence. A Bovyan of Kanin stock, dressed in a high-collared uniform, sat on a chair behind and to the right. Several fair-skinned Bovyans formed a semicircle around his parents on the dais.

"Ming! Tian!" Mother staggered forward off the dais, her eyes glistening. "You're alive."

She wrapped Tian in a tight embrace, though his expression betrayed no emotion. He tentatively hugged her back. Of course he wouldn't remember that she loved him most of all.

"Is it true, that you married the princess?" she asked.

Tian cast him a sidelong glance at Ming before turning back to their mother. "I think… yes."

She squeezed him tighter. "So the children are yours." She released him, and turned to clasp Ming's hands. Warmth radiated between them. "Oh Ming, I was so worried those ghastly Bovyans had killed you. I didn't believe what their lying brute of an emperor said was true, that you had escaped."

"Yes, Mother. We are home now. I am happy to see you." Ming guided her toward the dais. While she returned to her kneel at their father's side, Ming sank to his knees and placed the elf bow on the floor in front of him.

Tian knelt as well, though the look on his face bordered between confusion and scheming. Was he assessing the threats? Devising an escape?

Father cast a rare smile, perhaps the first one in years. "Welcome home, Ming, Tian. I am overjoyed to see you both alive. And safe."

"We cannot be but so safe." Ming pointed his chin at the Bovyan leader, who listened to another whispering in his ear. A translator, perhaps. It didn't matter if they understood or not. "Father, I had hoped rumors of your collaboration with the Teleri were just that."

His father looked at the leader before turning back. "Son, I had no choice. The realm is falling into chaos. The *Tianzi* has lost the Mandate of Heaven. Emperor Geros appointed me Viceroy of Cathay."

Ming harrumphed. "So he gave you the highest seat in Cathay. As long as the Bovyans rule, that will be no better than a chamber pot. Besides the honor of becoming a puppet, what else did they offer you?"

"You." His father might have shown no emotion, but his tenor cut through the air like an arrow. A magical elf arrow, maybe. He gestured at Lun. "And your brothers."

Ming pointed at his father. Impudent, to be sure, but warranted given the severity of treason. "We all swore allegiance to the *Tianzi*. We are all ready to sacrifice ourselves to keep the realm free and prosperous. All you had to do was hold the gate. Our lives, your new position, aren't worth tarnishing your name in history."

His father scowled. *Actually* scowled, sending a chill down Ming's spine. "Do not take that tone with me, boy. History is written by the victors."

The Bovyan smirked and cleared his throat. "Now that have you exchanged pleasantries, you must speak in Arkothi, the official language of the Teleri Empire."

The gall. Whatever the puppet master thought, this was still Cathay. Ming continued in his native tongue. "Father, will you not reconsider?"

Father shook his head. "Never. The Emperor has kept Shu to ensure our loyalty."

"My father taught me that the only thing more important than family was honor."

Father snorted. "He also taught you to be practical. Cathay's imperial armies are busy fighting Lord Peng's rebellion in the South, and the Teleri will overwhelm whoever is left. Our province will remain de facto independent, and you will inherit the title of Viceroy."

As if a pretty title meant anything. "The Teleri Directori will rule over Cathay and harness our resources toward their war machine."

"An oath is an oath."

"Yes, it is." Ming grabbed his bow, nocked an arrow, and shot.

The arrow drove through Father's right breast. He sucked in a labored breath and coughed up blood. Around them, everyone stared for a full second of absolute silence. Ming's heart fluttered. Had he done the right thing?

Tian jumped to his feet, dagger in hand, and lunged toward their mother. The Cathay soldiers all took several steps forward, though Ming now realized they were unarmed. The Teleri all drew swords. One stabbed at Mother, but Tian pulled her out of the way.

Ming shot again and downed the attacker, then nocked and loosed, felling the leader. Nine remained. He leveled the bow at the closest. "Surrender."

The Teleri formed up into a tight square, weapons facing out. Cathay soldiers approached, but stayed out of range of the blades.

Ming loosed another arrow. It lodged into another Teleri, who dropped with a choke and a clatter of a sword. "I have more than enough arrows to kill the rest of you twice over."

The Bovyans grunted and mumbled among themselves until their highest-ranking officer ordered a surrender. Some Cathay soldiers collected weapons and herded the prisoners into a corner. Other soldiers surrounded Ming, giving no indication who they sided with. Tears filled Mother's face.

"Eldest Brother," Lun said, voice weak. "What have you done?"

Tian cast him a scathing glance. "That wasn't part of the plan. At least you could've given me some warning that you were about to commit patricide."

Stomach clenching, Ming sighed. It hadn't been his initial intention. Father, if anything, was steadfast once he made a decision. Now the one who had instilled in his children a sense of leadership and honor was dying, because he had forsaken those lessons himself.

Father gasped another breath, his shaking hand beckoning. Still alive.

Mother stumbled to his side and propped his head on her lap. Lun, too, huddled in. A lump formed in Ming's throat. He leaned over.

A trembling hand clawed at Ming's tunic. Barely audible, Father's voice rasped. "Fool. Your future was… secure. Now… you must… make your own… name. Make me… proud." His hand slipped away. His eyes stared blankly at the ceiling.

Tears blurred Ming's vision. Maybe he'd made the wrong choice. Maybe with enough convincing, Father would've changed his mind.

No. If Father was anything, it was decisive. No argument in the world would have changed his mind once it was made.

Standing, Ming made eye contact with each of his fellow countrymen before locking on Lun's. "When our children's children read the histories of these trying times, they will learn how we took decisive action in defense of the nation. All of you here today, swear to me that when asked, you will say that Lord Zheng Han of Dongmen Province realized the error of his ways and took his own life as atonement."

The soldiers dropped to a knee. "Yes, *Jue-ye*."

Jue-ye.

He was now *Tai-Ming* Lord of Dongmen Province. How would history judge him?

Ming turned to Father's military advisor. "Mobilize our provincial soldiers and have the commander of the imperial garrison present himself before me." He then nodded at the chamberlain. "Prepare a message for Emperor Geros."

Chapter 29:
Explosive

Peng Kai-Long squinted through a spyglass at the imperial army defending the mountain pass between his province and Fenggu. Smoke rose after each volley into the Maduran lines, now whittled down to fifteen thousand as they tried to slam through the bottleneck.

He snapped the glass closed. Prince Dhananad was a fool, convinced by Madura's past victories over pathetic neighbors that a sledgehammer could pick a lock. The Madurans hadn't weakened the imperials as much as he'd hoped, though they had spared Kai-Long's own men from the brunt of the hostilities.

Passing the spyglass to one of his advisors, he grinned to himself. Not only had he minimized losses, his numbers had doubled. Local *Yu-Ming* lords, ostensibly loyal to the *Tianzi,* had come crawling back to him, bolstering the Nanling provincial army to twenty thousand. The ten thousand men under minor lords in occupied Ximen also flocked to his banner, while his ally in Yutou kept the Ximen loyalists pinned down on the coastal road. His chest puffed. Everything worked as he planned.

Kai-Long turned and gazed at his well-rested armies. Only he was fit to rule, the sole descendant of the Wang

Dynasty Founder with enough political and military acumen to bring greater prosperity to Cathay.

Once he left no doubt who held the Mandate of Heaven, the provincial and imperial holdouts would surely choose him over a baby too small to sit on the Jade Throne.

A soldier raced up to the command post and dropped to a knee. "*Jue-ye*, we have intercepted a message bound to Madura from Prince Dhananad."

"Report," Kai-Long said.

"He has asked his father for an additional ten thousand men."

Kai-Long laughed. The Maduran fool had already received ten thousand reinforcements and lost them in several ill-advised charges into the imperial center. In the future, after losing forty thousand of their men in a foreign land, Madura's own capital would be too weak to repel an attack.

For now, however, Kai-Long's campaign to liberate the Madurans would have to wait until he consolidated his hold over Cathay. "The Madurans have outlived their use. We don't want them depleting our supplies."

"*Jue-ye*, we cannot possibly take the pass without help," General Zhang said. Others nodded in assent.

Kai-Long favored them with a mirthless smile. He had not shared all his plans: the Aksumi Mystic he'd hired to summon the Guardian Dragon of Cathay, nor the Black Fist spies who carried correspondence with the former empress Wu Yanli's father in Zhenjing Province. The first would remain secret. "*Tai-Ming* Lord Wu's army holds the western pass into Fenggu, behind the imperial lines. He is amenable to switching sides. When he does, we will attack."

Or rather, once everyone saw the Guardian Dragon of Cathay answer Kai-Long's call, perhaps not a single musket need be fired.

In the meantime, he needed to cut off the Madurans. He turned to the messenger. "Send word back home. Detonate the firepowder at the South Gate to seal it off."

A clap of thunder followed a flash of light at the open doors to the Hall of Supreme Harmony. The roar rumbled in from the north, rattling Kaiya in the regent's chair beside the Jade Throne. The military advisors and ministers all looked up, their murmurs mingling with the sound.

"What was that?" she asked.

Chief Minister Song bowed. "I would guess lighting struck somewhere to the east."

It certainly didn't sound like thunder to her trained ears. She gestured with an open hand toward the main entrance, which opened up onto the cityscape. The thunderstorm from the night before had given way to morning sun. It now burned off the fog, leaving the sky a pale blue. "There are no storm clouds."

More chatter among the assembled men.

She sighed. If there *were* a lightning strike, then fires would follow. Alarm bells would be ringing any moment now. "General Shan, send a messenger to find out—"

A low drone bellowed out from a bell in the east. Several others followed. Fires? Certainly the Teleri, entrenched beyond cannon range outside the north gate for three days, had no way of striking inside the city, certainly not in the east.

Could they? Kaiya scanned her advisors, searching for any sign of treachery. Geros had sent a demand to parley. Her sharpshooters had used warning shots to rebuff him. In the ensuing three days of tortuous waiting, the remaining handful of Black Lotus Fists hadn't reported any incursions across the river.

A page raced through the door and down the center of the hall between the rows of men. He dropped to a knee, fist to the ground. "*Jie-xia*, our firepowder magazine in the east exploded."

Kaiya's brow furrowed. That magazine wasn't far from the walls, but it couldn't be coincidental, not with a Teleri army at their doorstep. Though why the east? She turned to Chief Minister Song. "Find out about fires and damage to the walls. I entrust all civilian response to you."

She then faced the military officers. "How would the enemy strike within the city? And why in the east?"

"Perhaps the insurgents are in league with the Teleri," a general said. "Sowing chaos before they strike."

"The magazine is well guarded." General Shan pointed to a map of the city. "We have eliminated most of Peng's rebels inside the city."

Kaiya wondered. She found Weiyong in the crowd, and he looked down. Unbeknownst to her other advisors, Golden Fu manipulated the remaining insurgents, who wouldn't help the Teleri. From what Weiyong had said, Fu was willing to support her, and even take on covert tasks. Then again, despite his proclaimed patriotism, he had an unpredictable streak. "General Shan," she said, "where are the firepowder stores?"

He pointed to eight locations on the map—one in each cardinal directions. His eyes rounded. "They might be trying to neutralize the advantage our guns provide."

Kaiya sighed. With so few troops, the capital's defense relied on their ability to concentrate musket and cannon barrage on the last remaining bridge over the river. It, too, was laden with enough firepowder kegs to destroy it. "Move some of our firepowder reserves to different locations."

Another flash flared at the entrance. Kaiya gripped her chair's armrests, just as another rumble erupted from the northwest. Significantly louder than the previous explosion, the aftershock shook the hall.

She looked to General Shan. "Another magazine?"

"I will find out." The general stood and marched to the doors with several aides in tow.

Kaiya frowned. The northwest magazine was very close to the north gate. If the blast had damaged the walls, they would have to blow the bridge, cutting the northern fifth of the country off from the rest.

Deep horns blared in the distance. A series of poofs burst somewhere to the northwest. Cannons.

Another page appeared at the entrance and bowed low. "The northwest firepowder magazine exploded."

Kaiya rose. "Did it damage the walls?"

"Not that we know of yet, *Jie-xia*."

She pointed. "Those are our cannons firing."

As if to contradict her, the deep bursts stopped, followed by the staccato of a thousand rasping pops. Musket fire?

Another series answered, and then another. Twice as fast as the typical Cathay volleys. That couldn't be humanly possible. She rose to her feet.

A panting soldier arrived next, dropping to his knee at the threshold. "*Jie-xia*, General Shan sent me to report. The Teleri are attacking."

She held a finger up. "Listen." The volleys prattled on in the distance, the initial frequency falling into perpetual shooting. "We do not fire so fast, do we?"

The soldier met her gaze and shook his head.

Kaiya gritted her teeth. "Then they have guns." But how? Likely taken from the embassy in Iksuvius, and Ming's defeated soldiers. "*Our* guns."

The military men set their jaws and exchanged glances. Many of the ministers moaned and wailed. So pathetic. Even without the *Tiger's Eye*, she wouldn't have devolved into such blubbering. She'd survived assassination attempts, stared down a dragon, been chased by orcs and ogres. No matter how afraid or hopeless, she'd always put on a brave face.

Except when Geros had raped her.

Kaiya's heart pounded in her chest. Images of him marching into the capital roiled her stomach. Or perhaps that was just the morning sickness. The *Tiger's Eye* certainly found inopportune times to weaken. She bit her lip and composed her expression into regal aloofness. "Send word to the gate. They must blow the bridge *now*."

"Yes, *Jie-xia*." Bowing, the soldier stood and ran off.

She sighed. Rebellion and invasion whittled away at the realm. Now, her own decision would cut away the North from the rest.

Geros watched as his men in the trenches fumbled with the Cathayi muskets. They had gotten better with practice, especially after his ingenious idea of specialization. Unlike the locals, who loaded, fired, and backed off to reload, he had several men reload and pass the guns to shooters.

Thanks to the Eye of Geros, their shots traced yellow lines across his vision.

Once they conquered Cathay and learned the secret of firepowder, the musket might be worth integrating into their own armies.

For now, he just needed the enemy to waste their own firepowder as they shot blindly into the fog. A cannonball pounded harmlessly into the earthworks not far away, sending dirt flying. The three days of preparation and the wait for the right weather had been worth it.

Leina's first explosion in the east had been the signal to deploy, the second in the north to start shooting. Now, a third explosion roared from the gatehouse, followed by screams and shouts.

Enemy cannon and musket fire stuttered to a trickle. Feiying had worked hard in the rain and dark, cutting the defenders' firepowder barrels from the bottom of the bridge so that his men could collect them downstream. He also jury-rigged some explosive device connected to the Cathayi's fuses. They apparently assumed the Teleri didn't know much about firepowder, since as expected, they had just destroyed their own gates instead of the bridge.

"The gates are open!" one of his men yelled.

Geros straightened out his uniform and turned to his signaler. "Order the assault."

The man blew the sequence on his horn. His riflemen continued shooting as they cleared a space for his heavy infantry to pass through. With shields angled up at the walls, the staggered column marched quadruple-time in perfect precision, as only trained Bovyans could.

A runner approached and thumped a fist on his chest. "Your Eminence, a message from Viceroy Zheng in Dongmen Province."

Geros hazarded a glance at the bridge. The enemy had resumed its volley fire, albeit at a slower pace. Lines of yellow streaked across his visual field. He needed to join his men *now*. "Report."

"An army of two thousand soldiers from Linshan Province have crossed the Jade River and plan to sabotage our supply lines." He pointed to a map on the table. "The Viceroy has mobilized ten thousand of his provincial soldiers to combat this threat."

Geros frowned. With that blank expression, Viceroy Zheng Han could bluff Fortuna herself in a game of mahjong. All reports spoke of his staunch sense of honor and loyalty; but then again, he had betrayed the *Tianzi*.

Geros motioned for one of his aides. "Leave five hundred men at the north gate once we take it. Make sure that the Viceroy's son *leads* them." His hostage, ready to take the first arrow.

"Yes, Your Eminence." The aide thumped his chest.

Geros' heart soared. Grabbing a Teleri flag, he jogged toward the bridge. The head of his column had already entered. "To me, men. The capital of Cathay is ours!"

Soon, very soon, he would be reunited with Kaiya, who according to his spies now ruled as regent of her crumbling homeland. This time, he would prove his love by bringing peace and stability to her nation.

After the third explosion, Kaiya shuffled in the regent's chair. The sound of cannon fire trailed off to intermittent bursts, though musket volleys continued in diminishing numbers and frequency. Perhaps Geros had withdrawn out of range.

The military officers all met her eyes, many smiling and nodding. Of course, with the bridge destroyed, the threat on the capital had ended for now. The Teleri would have to build bridges, and they were no engineers. Their only other choice was to head far upstream and wait for the spring melt to end, before fording the Jade River and fighting through forested Linshan Province.

A victory, for now.

At what cost? The great bridge, a marvel designed by the Founder's consort herself, perhaps irreparably damaged. Her people in the north, now under Geros' boot. Her stomach roiled again, the pent-up emotions pushing up against the *Tiger's Eye* dam. It might burst any time now, reducing her into a quivering sack of feelings and doubts.

She leaned back in her chair. No, she had made the logical decision. Leave the bridge in place, and the Teleri would soon occupy the North *and* the capital. "General Tang," she said, "send someone to check on our firepowder stores. We must maintain vigilant watch along the banks to make sure the Teleri do not find some other way to cross."

"Yes, *Jie-xia*." General Tang bowed and started to stand.

A pale, sweating foot soldier rushed into the hall and dropped to a knee. "*Jie-xia*, the enemy has breached the gates. General Shan—"

Kaiya leaped to her feet and raised a hand. "The bridge?"

"Intact. When we went to blow it, the gates exploded instead. General Shan holds the gate tower, while General Sun defends the northwest quadrant."

Chest tightening, Kaiya sunk into the chair and gripped the armrests with sweaty palms. Because the Founder mandated that nothing above one story could be built north of the palace, much of that area was parks and temples. Very little defensible terrain. Outnumbered and apparently outgunned, they didn't stand a chance. Emperor Geros would be there soon, ready to take her again.

Several times a day, for the rest of his curse-shortened life. Those hands, the anger…

Kaiya took a deep breath. Hold it together, she had to hold it together. This wasn't about her, but the nation. Twenty million young women alive today, and untold girls yet to be born, would share her fate. Reduced to playthings and breeders for a depraved race of rapists.

She loosened her fists and stood. "General Tang, what is our contingency plan now that the Teleri have gained a foothold in the city?"

From where he knelt, General Tang bowed. "We will fall back and defend the palace. We have enough munitions and food stores here to last a year."

Kaiya clenched her jaw again. Such a strategy would mean leaving a million souls in the city to predation by the Bovyans. After a year, the Teleri would be thoroughly ensconced, with more and more reinforcements streaming through the Wilds.

With a shaking voice, the chamberlain announced a visitor at the door. How strange that anyone would come at such a desperate time. "Lady Lin Ziqiu brings a message from her father, *Tai-Ming* Lord Lin of Linshan."

Kaiya lifted her gaze from the generals to the seventeen-year-old who had deceived her for so long. She walked with a purposeful stride between the rows of men, her serious expression so different from the carefree flightiness that had defined her for years.

"*Jie-xia.*" Brushing her brown travelling skirts to her knees in typical court fashion, she pressed her forehead to the ground. She looked up and grinned, her capricious mask showing for a split second before returning to dignified serenity. "My father sends his greetings. He is mobilizing twenty thousand of his men to help repel the invaders."

"Thank you for coming," Kaiya said, though Linshan was five days away. By the time they arrived, Geros would occupy the city and could repel them at the east gate. In front of her, the military officers' dire expressions confirmed her worries. There had to be some way to spare the capital from the ravages of Bovyan indiscretion.

What would Father have done? Nothing, perhaps—he had never gone to war. No *Tianzi* from her bloodline had, except the Founder himself. What would *he* have done? She had no way knowing, but... She turned to the military advisors. "What did the Founder say about facing more powerful enemies?"

An officer bowed. "Create the illusion of weakness where you are strong, enticing the enemy to attack."

Kaiya nodded. But still, with nothing save for weakness, there was little need to create any illusion of it. She beckoned another general to speak.

"If the enemy is on the march, dangle out bait and keep him moving. He will tire."

Not likely for Bovyans, but…

Kaiya rose. The imperial armies remained strong in the central valley. There was one piece of bait which Geros had thrown caution to the wind in order to pursue, but it would mean the regent fleeing the capital. "Emperor Geros will pursue me to the Eldaeri Isles and back. I would be the bait to lure him into Fenggu, where our main army can crush him."

A soldier cleared his throat. "Or be crushed by him. Our army would be caught between the Teleri and the traitor, Peng."

Kaiya sighed. Chief Minister Hong's machinations had drawn so many men away from the capital. It was so clear. Maybe even now, he was responsible for the sabotage of the armories. He would need to be tracked down and—

"And, forgive me, *Jie-xia*." Chief Minister Song pressed his forehead to the floor. "The regent should not abandon the capital."

"Shed your skin like a cicada," General Tang said, "and while the enemy is distracted, you can escape in secret."

Kaiya shook her head. "The point is to make him chase me. There can be no secrecy."

"If I may, *Jie-xia*." General Tang bowed. "It works the other way, too. You have a double."

A very pregnant double who would have difficulty travelling. However, it appeared they had exhausted all other options, and even this plan carried significant risks. Kaiya nodded to the assembled ministers. "Chief Minister Song, inform Meiling of this task. General

Tang, prepare an escort. What else needs to be done to create the illusion?"

"Spread disinformation among the populace," an officer said, "that the regent has fled Huajing to join up with the remnants of the imperial army in Fenggu. Enough men to get the Teleri to commit the bulk of their own solders to pursuit."

Lin Ziqiu cleared her throat. "Blow holes in the city's eastern walls so that my father's army can reinforce your men here when they arrive."

Kaiya nodded. It was the logical choice to protect as many people as possible. Even if it meant putting Meiling through more hardship, and risked the utter obliteration of the imperial armies caught between Cousin Peng and the Teleri. Maybe even Peng would put his ambitions aside to save Cathay from a foreign invader.

"*Jie-xia*," a voice called from the entrance.

Kaiya looked.

Doctor Wu held up a familiar mirror. "Lord Xu wishes to speak."

Lord Xu! Kaiya's heart leaped through the *Tiger's Eye*. With his formidable magic, perhaps he could find a solution to this problem. She searched the room. "Where is the councilor?"

His image materialized above the mirror, much larger than life, perhaps as large as his ego. He didn't bother to bow. "*Jie-xia*, it is you who must personally go to Fenggu and rally the imperial armies. Only you can do it."

Kaiya snapped her gawking mouth shut. "The regent cannot—"

"—do anything of consequence hiding behind the palace walls." Xu flashed that annoying smirk, the one she hadn't seen in a year.

"Can't you do something to destroy the Teleri?"

He shook his head. "My attention is divided by conflicts around the world. It is your time. In twenty days, a rare conjunction of the three moons and the energy of Teardrop Lake will allow you to draw on far more power than when you confronted Avarax. Enough to defeat the Teleri yourself."

The famed Godseye Conjunction. It had heralded the start of the Founder's dynasty. Still… Kaiya stared at the floor. "I have lost my magic."

"You will find it again. I have foreseen it."

Her heart pounded in her chest. She would regain her power. More importantly, the realm would be safe. She nodded. "Very well."

"I will meet you there," the elf said. "Bring the fallen star from the Temple of Heaven."

Kaiya looked down at the city map. The Temple of Heaven would soon be behind enemy lines, and even if the Teleri didn't know its significance, she had no way of getting there.

In any case, an attempt to remove the artifact, even on order of the *Tianzi* himself, would be met with firm resistance from the priests and monks. She met Lin Ziqiu's gaze. "Find your master. I have a mission that only he can do."

Chapter 30:
I Spy

Jie flexed her fingers, but try as she might, her arm wouldn't budge. Sighing, she looked up from her horse, to where Ming rode at the head of six thousand men under fluttering green banners. Tian and Ma Jun rode beside him, with Yuha clutching Tian tightly enough to make her jealous. They discussed what could only be described as a monumental logistical risk.

Ming had sent horse couriers out to the *Yu-Ming* lords, announcing his ascension as *Tai-Ming* and ordering them to join the main provincial army as it marched down the highway. Supply lines would come later. In all, they hoped to muster fifteen thousand men.

Still, they would be lucky to acquire a thousand muskets, since the Teleri had plundered the provincial capital's armory. The firearms Ming's army had salvaged were left in the hands of a castle garrison, to fend off any minor lord whose loyalty went only as far as the range of the weapons pointed at him.

Horse hooves rapidly clopped in the distance, making Jie's ears twitch. She spurred her own mount to meet up with the brothers. "A horse approaches." She pointed down the highway.

Unslinging his bow, Ming nocked an arrow. How gallant he looked in his armor and green surcoat, like a member of the Founder's cavalry. Despite his many shortcomings, he would make a fine lord.

If he survived.

She squinted at the cloud of dust up ahead. A green pennant fluttered above the rider. "One of ours," she said.

Once he got closer, the rider leaped from his saddle and sank to a knee. "*Jue-ye*, news from the capital."

"Speak." Ming beckoned the man up.

"Emperor Geros received your message and welcomes your arrival. Also, there were explosions inside the city, and the Teleri breached the walls."

Explosions. Potentially from lightning strikes, but more likely an act of sabotage, given the timing. Jie sucked on her lower lip. As much as they hated the Jade Throne, the insurgents wouldn't work for a foreign invader. Perhaps Teleri Nightblades had infiltrated.

Surely the Black Lotus would be able to root them out. The Nightblades were such amateurs by comparison. Unless the clan was e otherwise indisposed. She turned to Tian. "There are enemy spies inside Huajing, I'm sure of it. Our own army is still seven days away at this marching pace. You and I must go ahead."

And hasten their reunion with the princess.

As distasteful as that would be, the fate of the nation relied on them. How much easier life would be if she hadn't been left at the Black Lotus Temple as a baby. If her good-for-nothing elf father had never abandoned her. She would've never ended up a spy, never met Tian or the princess. Never had to feel as empty as she did now. She ran a hand through her hair.

The hand attached to her bad arm.

Heart pounding, eyes wide, she stared at the arm and willed it to move again.

Nothing.

From his hiding place in the abandoned streets, Liang Yu gazed at the eight-tiered stupa. Sparkling in the midday sun, its blue gables stood high above the white marble walls surrounding it.

As always, a complement of twenty-four honor guards dressed in ceremonial robes circled the walls. Thirty-two priests now defended the steel gates.

Perhaps Princess Kaiya was sending him into a trap. It certainly wouldn't be the first time she'd tricked him, and all these leader types sacrificed their loyal servants on a whim. The extra protection around the temple might not faze armored Bovyans, but it posed more of a challenge for a middle-aged man.

Maybe not for a pretty young woman.

Challenge accepted. Per his command, Lin Ziqiu intercepted the guard approaching the insertion point close to the rear of the complex. She leaned against the wall, feigning exhaustion. His usual fifteen steps a minute sped up to meet her.

She looked up. "Sir, the Bovyans are rounding up women. Please, help me hide."

The guard's eyes shifted left and right, passing right over Liang Yu's hiding position before settling back on Lin Ziqiu. He beckoned her back in the other direction, toward the main gate, and turned around.

With speed enough to impress a man half his age, Liang Yu darted across the street. Jabbing the walking staff into the ground, he flipped over and drove the climbing claws on his feet into the mortar between the marble blocks, about three-quarters of the way up near the top of the wall. From this inverted position, he curled up, dug the hand claws into the mortar, and pushed himself to the top.

Now at the height of two men above the ground, he crouched and peered down the streets. All empty. Sporadic gunfire popped in the distance. He turned to survey the elliptical temple grounds, which no commoner had seen since its completion three hundred years before.

The stupa stood at one end, on a circular, three-tiered marble base. Just like the hand-drawn diagram Regent Kaiya had sent with Lin Ziqiu.

Or maybe she knew more, but just hadn't told him. No guards prowled the grounds, just a single priest sweeping the marble dais across from the stupa. Still, that priest held the broom like a weapon, and seemed unperturbed by the Teleri invasion.

In fact, he moved with an unsettling familiarity as he looked up and south toward the Iridescent Moon.

Liang Yu followed his gaze. The moon waned to new, disappearing for a few seconds at noon. Below, eight honor guards entered the compound from the gates, one carrying Lin Ziqiu in his arms. She must have put on a convincing show for them to let her in. He was taking her toward a long rectangular building close to the entrance—the priests' quarters, according to the princess' sketch. The temple administrators would probably have something to say about that. The priest—

The monk had worked himself closer to the stupa, not far from where eight more honor guards emerged.

Too many unknowns! Intentional or not, the princess had given him so little information about the temple:

Whether the stupa was one large room or several. How many men defended it. Even the size of the fallen star.

Liang Yu snorted. He was a planner, not an operative. In his day, this would be just the sort of mission The Surgeon Feiying and The Beauty Meiyun would have savored. Always rushing in, trusting their abilities and instincts over the proven benefits of methodical planning. It had gotten Meiyun impregnated by an elf, and Feiying killed.

With so little time before the regent retreated south, there was no choice but to improvise now. Liang Yu slunk along the top of the wall toward the rear of the stupa. Sliding down, he landed like a cat on the marble ground and ran to the base. After a quick glance to assess the position of the approaching honor guards, he ducked under the railing of the first tier and made it to the second, and then to the curved stupa wall. Inching around, he slipped into each of the towering doorways along the way toward the front. Not a single door; all just façades. He continued, stopping where he could just see the approaching guards. A dozen more steps in their agonizingly slow march and they would pass through the doors.

The sweeper… where had that priest disappeared to? Already inside, perhaps. Yet another unknown element, especially with the familiarity of the gait.

Who was he? With an ability to make connections equal to his own, and an uncanny memory, Meiyun would have figured out this conundrum already. Yes, with their complementing skillsets, the three of them had made an unparalleled team.

With her observational skills, perhaps Lin Ziqiu could be the new Beauty. If he recruited a new, more pliable

Surgeon, he could establish a *Black Fist* clan to rival the Black Lotus, to serve the most worthy leaders.

One day.

For now, there was an unenviable task at hand. The arriving honor guard passed through the entrance, and Liang Yu darted after them. Inside, shuttered light baubles cast the gallery in a dim light. He pressed himself in a column's shadow when the guards came to a halt. One by one, they turned left, marching down a single corridor that appeared to wrap around the stupa's interior. The space between each man allowed the next to always maintain line-of-sight around the bend of the hall.

Unless he went to the left, counterclockwise.

A clear shortsightedness on the part of whoever came up with the pattern. Or perhaps part of the princess' trap. Liang Yu dashed as quickly and quietly as his age-inhibited body allowed. Not six paces later, he ran into a priest. The man's eyes widened as he opened his mouth.

Forsaking all stealth, Liang Yu reached him in three long strides and jabbed his walking staff in the priest's solar plexus. His shout died with the blow, and Liang Yu spun around to his rear and seized him in an unremitting chokehold.

One second, two seconds. Only about half a minute remained before the first guard made it around to their position. Three seconds, four seconds. The priest crumpled, his struggles ceased. He would come to a few minutes later with an awful headache.

So much for quiet. Liang Yu raced down the hall, smashing another priest on the side of the head. The princess either knew nothing of the security protocols, or had deliberately set a trap.

A little farther, and at last he came to a set of double doors, flanked by two more priests. Before they could unsheathe their swords, Liang Yu knocked them out with two quick thrusts of his staff. None so far, at least to his age-weathered vision, looked to be the sweeper.

The heavy eldarwood doors creaked open with a hard push. A quiet rhythmic whirr pulsed outward, along with a musty smell.

Liang Yu stepped into the central hall, scuffing through a year of accumulated dust. Of course, the *Tianzi* had missed New Year's prayers this year, the only time when anyone ever entered the inner sanctum.

Sunlight poured in through eight windows on each of the eight levels. Eight red columns with golden scrollwork reached to a green-and-blue tiled dome. In a niche above, the shard from a fallen star pulsed with a light blue glow. It was all stunningly beautiful, a view only several *Tianzi* and High Priests had beheld for the last three centuries.

Liang Yu squinted. At the height of eighty-eight feet, the chunk's spherical shape blurred in his old eyes. How could he possibly reach it, let alone escape?

A disembodied voice echoed around him. "Surely the Architect has come up with a flawless plan to reach the fallen star."

That voice.

So familiar. Liang Yu spun around. A shape dropped down directly in front of him, just outside the entrance. He must have been hiding on the ceiling outside the doors.

The sweeper pointed at the two unconscious priests. "You always had others do most of the dirty work. I was surprised."

No. It couldn't be.

The face was too gaunt, yet the thinness almost emphasized Feiying's hard features.

Liang Yu's eyes must be opened wide enough to fall out. "You… you are dead."

Feiying grinned. "I thought the same about you. I saw the elf knock you into Vyara City's harbor with a blow that would kill the stoutest warrior. Meiyun and I never found your body."

Liang Yu shrugged. "The *Viper's Rest*. And a peasant girl."

"I never considered it," Feiying said, nodding slowly. Of course, the Surgeon was not so much a thinker as a near-infallible tool for executing complex plans. "To think we are reunited after thirty years in engineering the downfall of the motherland that forgot us."

Engineering the downfall? Liang Yu nodded, but wondered. Betrayal had only strengthened his own resolve to root out corruption and favoritism in the realm. Apparently, it had pushed Feiying to treason.

It must've been him working for the Teleri, which could account for his disappearance long ago. He was likely the one behind the Bovyans with Black Fist skills, the one the Black Lotus Clan had sent Princess Kaiya's half-elf to Arkothi lands to root out so many years before. Now, his reemergence could explain how the enemy had struck within the city. Though with Feiying's particular skillset, he must have a contact working on the inside to guide him.

Time to find out who. Liang Yu said, "I was never told about you. I thought I was the only asset inside the city."

"I've only been here for a week, and then it took time for me to contact her. The Floating World is infested by the Black Lotus."

So the contact worked out of the Floating World. Female. Liang Yu looked back up at the shard. "What could the Teleri possibly want with it? She never told me."

Feiying followed his gaze. "Me, either. Legitimacy perhaps. A symbol of imperial rule."

Muffled shouts broke out in the outer hall. The honor guards would've seen the unconscious priests by now. Liang Yu pointed at the doors. "Close them."

"So here we are, together again," Feiying said, starting to shut the doors. "What's your plan?"

"Wait, Master!" Lin Ziqiu slipped through the closing crack, breathless.

Feiying sheathed the sword he'd pointed at her. "Master?"

"Feiying, this is my disciple, Ziqiu." Liang Yu chuckled. "It looks like we have a new Beauty."

Ziqiu cocked her head, but Feiying pursed his lips. Of course. She had no idea who the Beauty was, and he'd always been smitten by Meiyun.

Bad idea to bring up those old scars. Liang Yu looked back up. "I didn't have time to plan. Maybe you could just improvise, like always."

A smirk replaced Feiying's sour expression. He placed a hand on one of the columns. "Spider-climb up between this and the walls?"

"We're old men." Liang Yu nodded to Lin Ziqiu. It would be better for the relic to be in *her* hands instead of the Teleri's.

Eyes scanning the columns, she shook her head. "It is narrow enough on this level with the hallway wall, but it flares out from the second level."

Curse his poor eyesight. He squinted at the upper levels, which tapered toward the dome. He nodded to Feiying. "Can you do it?"

"With help." He laughed. "I'm old, but I have kept my body prepared for tasks like this. Ziqiu, meet me on the second level."

Both spider-climbed between the column and the wall to the second-level ledge. Twiddling his index and middle fingers, he described an old *Black Fist* trick. She pressed her back against the outer wall while he set his against the column. Foot to foot, they ascended. Easy work for *Black Fist* in their prime, but Feiying was no longer young, and Ziqiu was a mere trainee. Outside, the guards pounded on the barred doors. Luckily they didn't have a battering ram, nor the space to use one if they had.

At the top, Ziqiu reached over and grasped Feiying's ankles, and both lunged upward toward the lip beneath the dome. Feiying caught it, and then swung her up on the other side.

They worked so well together, like he had with Meiyun before. They'd been a great match, really, and it was a shame she never loved Feiying like he did her. Maybe their Vyara City mission would've ended differently.

Feiying examined the dome's interior, then donned his cat-claws. The scraping of the spikes into the mortar between the tiles sent dust dropping. It was excruciatingly slow. The pounding at the door got louder, and the bar buckled.

At last, he made it to the niche. With one hand, he scooped the fallen star out and tossed it to Meiyun... Ziqiu.

How uncanny, the way these two worked together, just like the Surgeon and the Beauty.

"Now how do we get down?" she asked.

"Watch." Feiying swung again and landed on the ledge. He scooted over to a column, and then lowered himself down. Wrapping his arms around the column, he made it look easy as he slid down.

Ziqiu stalled on the ledge. "My arms aren't long enough to do that!"

Liang Yu sighed. Now she was stuck, with the imperial regalia.

Another hard smash into the door. They were running out of time.

"Don't worry about me," she said. "You divert the guards, and I'll find a way to escape and get this to Princess Kaiya."

"What?" Looking first to Ziqiu and then to Liang Yu, Feiying drew his curved sword. "Who are you working for?"

Heart racing, Liang Yu separated his staff into a sword and spear. He sank into a defensive position and angled himself away from Feiying's strong right.

"You still work for *them*, even after they left you for dead." Feiying snorted. "Join the winning side. We'll hunt down the Black Lotus, and establish our own clan."

Liang Yu shook his head. "Cathay comes first."

"Still a slave. I'd hate to kill you. You know I've always been the better fighter."

It was too true. Liang Yu shifted his stance. The only way he would survive this encounter is if the honor guard broke through the doors and created a distraction.

Unless he came up with a good plan.

Like showing weakness where there was strength. Simultaneously attacking and defending. Liang Yu turned to expose his ribs.

Feiying lunged forward, blade sweeping. Liang Yu lifted his sword to defend while thrusting with his spear.

An elementary move, one which Feiying easily avoided. Liang Yu followed up with a sword chop and another spear stab.

After an initial parry of the sword, Feiying followed with a downward slash, cutting into the spear haft. He might as well have yawned. "Come now, Liang Yu, I know all your moves. You follow such a predictable script."

Liang Yu disengaged and flipped the spear back. The precise cut went at least halfway through the shaft, two hand lengths from the blade, rendering it useless.

As a spear, at least.

Smashing the ruined weapon across his knee, he finished the break and transformed the spear into a knife.

"Not bad," Feiying said. "You've finally learned to improvise. Though now you've lost your reach advantage." He surged in with several quick moves, one which cut across Liang Yu's bicep and another that sliced across his abdomen.

All intentional distractions, surgical strikes meant to weaken first. The pain burned. He staggered back.

Feiying leaped forward again, but yelped and disengaged. A throwing pin lodged high in his right breast.

Liang Yu looked up, from where the pin had flown. "Ziqiu, I will not survive this. You must escape and warn the regent: the Teleri's agent is a woman in the Floating World."

"Fool." Blood flecked Feiying's lips. The pin must've penetrated his lung. Maybe there was a chance.

The doors burst open with a crack of the bar. Soldiers rushed in.

Feiying swung his sword, the first blow knocking the knife from Liang Yu's hand and the second cutting deep into his right flank.

Such a perfect attack. Pain flared and only grew worse. A ruptured liver, with a precise insertion as only the Surgeon could perform.

There was no surviving the wound, but the right plan could eliminate the threat to the regent. He just had to get close enough. Liang Yu thrust with a feeble stab to the right, one which would invite a counter-attack to the left.

Feiying twisted toward the left, as planned. Liang Yu dropped the sword and tackled Feiying, using a hand to drive Ziqiu's pin deeper.

With a moan, Feiying staggered back and fell. The honor guards surrounded them, not that it mattered. Neither of them would live through the wounds. Liang Yu rolled off of him.

Feiying let out a labored chuckle. "I wonder what the Black Lotus will make of this. The Surgeon and the Architect came out of hiding to kill each other. Master Yan will be shaking his head."

"Goodbye, old friend," Liang Yu said. "Even though it ended this way, I'm glad to have met you again."

Feiying nodded. "Now, the Three Young Masters are truly dead, with only a half-elf to show for it."

Half-elf... Princess Kaiya's half-elf, raised by the Black Lotus, was Meiyun's. Liang Yu laughed, even though each chuckle sent pain surging through his body. So obvious, and yet even he had missed it. "She doesn't even know, does she?

Feiying's voice was barely audible. "I told her, but only while she was drugged with musk and *Yinghua* flowers."

Maybe she remembered, maybe she didn't. Liang Yu's vision dimmed.

High above, Ziqiu slipped out of the closest window. How had the Architect not thought of such a simple solution?

Chapter 31:
City Under Siege

The carriage wheels purred over the city's pavestones. It was a mere whisper in Kaiya's ears compared to the clopping of the three hundred imperial cavalry and the sporadic musket fire. Outside, frightened citizens ran by clutching possessions, oftentimes stopping to bow toward her carriage. An occasional patrol of soldiers passed, the men affording her quick nods before continuing on their way.

In the distance, several crooked columns of smoke filled the air with the smell of burning wood. Thank the Heavens for the *Tiger's Eye*.

Her hometown under siege conjured memories of her escape from Iksuvius, the start of the mad flight from Geros. Then, Iksuvi's King Evydas had fought and died in the futile defense of his city. Now, she, the regent, was fleeing hers.

The carriage slowed to a stop, and she looked out the window. They'd reached the southern market square, now abandoned. Vendor stalls sprawled across the flagstones, their remaining valuables strewn about.

It was all similar to her dream with Jie, Tian, and the Teleri army; though they were now far from the river docks and not a cloud blotted the blue sky. A stream *did,* however, rustle nearby. Once upon a time, before an earthquake changed its path, it emptied into nearby

Qingjinghu Amphitheater, where she'd witnessed an attack on Tarkoth's Prince Aelward over a year ago. Now, White Duck Stream drained into Sun-Moon Lake.

The cavalry commander, Zhuang, rode up. "*Jie-xia*, we do not have much time. The Teleri already control the northwest quadrant. Our scouts say they are marching toward the palace. When they find out you are not there…"

Yes, they needed to have enough of a lead to avoid capture, but not so much that Geros would give up the chase. Which wasn't likely anyway.

"Wait," she said. Liang Yu was supposed to meet her here after he completed his mission. The minutes raced by as she repeatedly checked the Iridescent Moon. They had to stay ahead of Teleri pursuit, and needed to reach Fenggu in two weeks.

Maybe Liang Yu had failed. Maybe he'd betrayed her. *Tiger's Eye* or not, her heart began to skip.

"Easy, *Jie-xia*." Sitting across from her, up to now forgotten, Doctor Wu placed a cool hand on her knee. Since Princess Alaena had given birth to her baby boy and the elf Thielas had returned to protect the Tarkothi ship, Doctor Wu had not left Kaiya's side. "Xu's predictions are rarely wrong."

From her side, Fang Weiyong, his head still unshaved, nodded. Not that he would know much about the enigmatic elf.

Kaiya lowered her hand from where she'd been fiddling with her hair. A girlish habit she'd abandoned… right about the time Tian shaved her bald. She pressed Tian's lockpick pouch, always concealed in her sash as a memento, even if the *Tiger's Eye* blocked any feeling toward it. "But Lord Xu *has* been wrong, hasn't he?"

The doctor pursed her lips. So much for reassurance. Perhaps abandoning the capital was a mistake. Maybe it would be better to stay and give the people hope.

Kaiya harrumphed to herself. What hope could one woman hiding safe behind palace walls give to a beleaguered citizenry? No, serving as bait, drawing Geros' army out of Huajing, was the most effective way to serve her people.

Light feet pattered across the market. Kaiya looked out.

Dressed in loose-fitting clothes, not too unlike Jie's, Lin Ziqiu stopped several feet away as guards interposed themselves.

"Allow her through." Her voice came out weary. As much as the *Tiger's Eye* stifled her emotions, it did nothing to ease physical fatigue.

Ziqiu appeared at the window and bowed. She reached into the fold of her shirt and withdrew a glowing blue sphere the size of a cannonball.

A perfect sphere, like all the other stars still dancing in the night sky. Up close, it was so bright it almost shone through Ziqiu's outstretched fingers.

Kaiya took the fallen star in two hands. And nearly dropped it. It was deceptively heavy, dense like gold or lead. Cool and perfectly smooth and round, the globe reflected in the doctor's eyes. A low pulse emanated from within, sending a shiver through her spine.

The tone! It was always present in Huajing, a barely audible throb every few minutes, magnified by the geomantic perfection of the Temple of Heaven. It was the power she'd drawn on when she healed her brother and father. It resonated so closely now, yet the energy seemed so distant, beyond her reach.

She looked up and met Doctor Wu's smile.

"Soon," the doctor said.

Soon? Would she regain her power soon? Kaiya turned back to Ziqiu. "Where is Liang Yu?"

A tear formed in the girl's eye. "Dead. Killed by an old comrade in our attempt to secure the star."

With a sigh, Kaiya nodded. Though misguided, Liang Yu had the nation's best interests at heart. In the end, he proved his worth. "If we make it through this crisis, I will ensure his name is enshrined in the *Jianguo* shrine with the realm's other patriots and martyrs."

"Just before he died," Ziqiu said, "he mentioned that a Teleri agent worked in the Floating World."

The Floating World. Kaiya nodded again. Ming had spent some time there, and supposedly Hong owned a house... She jerked her head toward Ziqiu. "Chief Minister Hong. Many of his policies led to the realm's state of disarray."

Ziqiu's eyes widened. "No, the agent is a woman. But Hong keeps a half-Ayuri concubine there."

A woman, working for the enemy, to manipulate an old man who just three years ago was a minor official. Kaiya shook her head. What kind of person could engineer so many improbabilities to fruition, and deceive even the paranoid Liang Yu the whole time? Not even Tian, with his ability to see connections, could rival this adversary.

"We must set off now if we are to stay ahead of Emperor Geros." She pointed in the direction of the Floating World, which might as well have been its own city. "I want you to find out as much as you can about this concubine."

Riding at the head of his army through the conquered city, Geros scoffed at Cathayi wastefulness. So much stone used to pave city streets. Garish banners of red and bright yellow hanging from storefronts. Ostentatious ceramics and furniture. No wonder they were such a weak people. He would teach them the value of frugality.

He'd put Cathay's abundant resources, and its industrious but docile tradesmen, to good use. The First Geros' Last Testament bade the Bovyans to bring peace and order to the lands of the old Arkothi Empire. Why not all of Tivaralan?

An aide rode up and thumped his chest with a fist. "Your Eminence. Most of the enemy has withdrawn to the palace. All other resistance is disorganized."

All too easy. "Our casualties?"

"Sixty-four men killed, eight hundred seventy-seven with varying degrees of injury."

Leaving more than enough able-bodied Bovyans to maintain peace. Still, a visit to the wounded would raise morale. "Where are the injured soldiers?"

The aide pointed. "We have set up two field hospitals, one in the central square and one in the northwest park."

A park. An entire stretch of land, wasted by the vanity of the Founder's consort. "Is there any word from Master Feiying?"

"No, Your Eminence."

Geros clenched his jaw. He should have returned from the Temple of Heaven by now. Exchanging the fallen star with the Orc King would ensure a longer life, one where he could see the results of all the plans he'd set in motion.

Soon enough. Though not a Bovyan, Feiying was unfailingly reliable. "Find him at the national temple. What about the firepowder stores?"

"I am waiting to hear from the field commanders."

Geros nodded. "Under a flag of parley, demand an audience with the regent." And in the city's southeast… "Find Leina in the prostitute's district and command her to meet me at the palace." Rewards were due.

The aide pounded his chest again and rode off to convey the orders to underlings. The army marched in perfect unison behind him. Smoke plumes rose in the distance, yet the city remained otherwise quiet. No panic. Citizens lined the streets and held low bows. How easily they submitted. The Nothori and Arkothi peoples were far less compliant at first. Perhaps a sizeable garrison wasn't needed.

With a white flag of parley in hand, one of his officers waited by the moat around the palace. On the other side of the bridge stretched a broad courtyard with no cover. A high wall of white marble rose above, lined with Cathayi musketmen.

Geros dismounted. Squaring his shoulders and drawing himself to his full height, he crossed the bridge with two generals three paces behind him. Muskets followed his every step. Scanning the officials atop the gatehouse, he came to a halt halfway into the courtyard. She wasn't there.

"Where is my wife, the regent?" he demanded.

An official in blue robes stepped forward from the crowd. "She has fled the city."

Fled! Geros jerked a head toward his aide. "You said she was here."

Brows furrowed, the aide nodded.

Geros snorted. Kaiya was smarter than that. She could hole up behind the palace walls indefinitely, but instead risked being caught in the open. He looked back at the minister. "Open the gates and surrender."

The minister laughed. "The palace is a city in itself, provisioned for ten years."

Geros snorted. The gall. "I can wait." Turning on his heel, he headed back over the bridge. He leaned toward the aide. "Deploy five thousand men to maintain order, crush whatever resistance remains, and blockade the palace. "

On the other side of the moat, Leina pressed her palms together in the Ayuri manner. She had certainly aged in the last five years, but still maintained a unique beauty.

And a sharp mind. Both were formidable weapons when some men were foolish enough to abandon all sense of logic and reason for a pretty face and charm. She met his eyes. "Your Eminence."

"Leina," he said. "You have done well. I have already sent orders to our garrison in Ankira to have your mother brought here, to be released into your custody."

Leina's lip quivered. Tears welled into her eyes. She sank to her knees and pressed her forehead to the ground.

Cathay's weak customs were rubbing off on her. Still, she proved to be a valuable asset. Motivated by dislike of the Cathayi, she might prove an unparalleled advisor in the new regime.

A soldier ran up and thumped his chest. "Your Eminence, Master Feiying is unaccounted for."

Geros stiffened. He needed that artifact. He turned to Leina. "Did he bring anything to you?"

"No, Your Eminence." Leina shook her head. "After he helped sabotage the firepowder stores, he disappeared."

"Return to your home and await further orders. In the meantime, see if you can find out anything about him. You will coordinate our Nightblades."

Leina nodded. "Yes, Your Eminence. But I fear that a man of his particular abilities will not be found if he chooses to remain hidden."

Only too true. However, the straightforward Feiying did not play games. Nor did he have any reason to betray the Teleri. Geros' jaw clenched.

Another soldier approached and pounded a fist to his chest. "Your Eminence, we have news of the regent. She fled south four hours ago in a carriage, escorted by Cathayi cavalry."

Geros slammed his fist into his hand. Without horses, they had little chance of catching her. The stunning victory meant nothing without her or the fallen star. Still, she had nowhere to flee with the Madurans blocking her way out of Cathay's central valley.

"General, prepare the army for a march. I will chase her across Cathay if need be, and crush whatever army she summons in her defense."

Chapter 32:
Occupied Lands

Tian crouched among the shrubs, high on a hill overlooking farmland. The capital's north walls rose through the light morning fog, barely visible. In front of them, a river flowed out of the enormous Sun-Moon Lake.

At his side, Jie pointed at the bridge and the gatehouse, its doors gaping open at strange angles. Black banners emblazoned with the nine-pointed Teleri gold sun declared new ownership. "Does it look familiar?"

Apparently, before his banishment by the *Tianzi* himself, he had passed through these gates dozens of times in his youth on the journeys between Dongmen and Huajing. Still, they felt just as foreign as his hometown. He shrugged.

On his other side, Yuha peered through Jie's spyglass. The poor man had probably never thought he'd see the Great Wall in his lifetime, let alone go a couple of hundred *li* into the strange land beyond.

He passed the scope over. "So many Metal Men, but a Man from Beyond the Wall leads them."

Tian stared through it. Twenty-seven dark shapes prowled the battlements, though one stood a head shorter and much thinner than the others. Another collaborator. Yet more disconcerting was the heavily-guarded bottleneck. "We could pose as farmers or merchants."

Jie rolled her eyes. "Because Kanin Shaman come to the city so often, and it's not like every last Bovyan knows about the princess' half-elf. In any case, I doubt any citizens will approach the city while it's occupied."

Such a sharp tongue. He chuckled. "There has to be another way in."

"*You* can make it in." Jie pulled out hand straps with metal spikes… *cat-claws*. "All you have to do is climb along the underside of the bridge, creep along the waterline, and then scale the walls in a less guarded section. Then come around and kill them all."

Tian gawked at the bridge, which looked a *li* long. It would take extraordinary stamina to accomplish such a feat, and then to climb the walls, and then fight. Even though his body had already done amazing things, "This task is impossible."

Jie searched his gaze. "At the very least, you have to go in alone. Along the northeast wall, you will find a locked grate where White Duck Stream feeds into the lake." She pointed back toward the lake, past the castle where the blue flag of Cathay still flew, to a spot on the walls. "Yuha and I will commandeer a boat in one of the villages we passed and meet you there."

Tian snorted. They'd followed the highway along the lake's edge for dozens of *li*, not finding a single undamaged boat in the several towns they'd ridden through. Then, there was the locked grate. "Do you have a key?"

Sucking on her lip, Jie squinted at him. Then, she sighed. She reached into a pouch and gave him a smaller bag. "Take my lockpicks."

Tian hefted the tool bag. There was a comforting familiarity to it. "Are these mine?"

"No, yours are..." She frowned. "No. But everyone in our clan has a similar set."

He withdrew one of the long metal wires. It felt right in his hand, just like the weapons had before.

"It will come back to you." Jie grinned. She offered the cat-claws again.

He took them and stared through the thinning fog.

Yuha prodded him. "What's our plan?"

"You and Jie will find a boat and meet me across the lake." Tian pointed toward the spot Jie had indicated. Hopefully, Yuha's limited Arkothi would be enough for the two of them to communicate. He patted the shaman on the shoulder.

"Remember," Jie said. "We have to hurry. The princess will be at the palace, along with whoever is left to defend it. Enemy agents will be trying to penetrate it."

Tian squeezed her hand, regardless of Yuha's reproachful glare. With a nod, he scrambled down the hill. He covered himself in yellow brush and crept among the low rows of greening winter wheat, well to the east of the bridge.

The fertile smell of spring piqued memories of a little girl with doe eyes, which merged with a half-elf girl with larger eyes.

After a *li*, the fields ended at a stretch of rocky flatland about twenty paces wide. Beyond that, a stone retaining wall ran along the river bank. All designed so that a defender on the walls could see an approaching enemy. In his forest-green long coat and black pants, he'd stand out to anyone whose gaze happened to pass over him.

He scanned the battlements. Though the Metal Men paced the gatehouse in the distance, none actually ventured onto the walls. Perhaps swimming across here would be safer than trying to climb under the bridge. Then again, the *li*-wide river coursed with spring melt. He'd never make it across without either getting washed away or freezing to death.

Working his way through the wheat toward the bridge, he came to hastily constructed earthworks near the highway. From the scars in the ramparts and the sprayed clumps of dirt, the position must've faced a light bombardment from the city.

The piquant scent of burnt firepowder lingered in the air. Paper cartridge remains littered the trenches. The attackers must've fired back, despite the impossibly long range from here to the walls. A lot of firepowder and musket balls must've been wasted by both sides. A deliberate strategy, no doubt.

This Emperor Geros must be a formidable adversary. Images of a hulking man with a scar on his cheek blinked in and out of Tian's memory.

He peeked up from a trench. Covering the distance from here to the bridge would take ten seconds. A risk, unless there were some distraction. Wait for someone to approach the city? Unlikely, since as Jie had said, no one in their right mind would walk into an occupied city.

Or would they? Wagon wheels creaked and horse hooves clopped to the east. Up the highway, which continued to northwest, a caravan approached with a Metal Man on horseback at the head. Sixty-four more flanked the sides as commoners pulled twenty-seven carts of foodstuffs and firepowder. Counting, always counting; numbers brought order to his thoughts.

Heart pumping, Tian edged toward the end of the trench closest to the highway. Little chance he could blend in with the porters with his uniform, but he could use them as cover. He took a deep breath, and his pulse settled. Toward the back of the line, he waited for the second-to-last Metal Man to pass. Tian tossed a rock onto the highway behind him.

The soldier turned.

Tian zipped under the nearest wagon and clung to the bottom. He held his breath. Maybe he hadn't gone fast enough. He didn't stand a chance against so many enemies.

The Metal Man's booted feet jogged up to just beside the wagon…

And resumed their march. The wagon continued, the wheels thumping into the edges between the pavestones. The porters whispered among themselves, lamenting the death of the old *Tianzi*. The head of the bridge came closer. With a little speed and luck, he could slip out without being seen and then duck under the bridge.

And hold on to what? Maybe Jie knew something about the underside of the bridge, or assumed he did. Too much of a risk. In any case, as long as the Metal Men didn't check underneath the wagon, this was an easy ride into city.

The bridge rose up in a gentle arch before descending again. The gate guards didn't even stop the caravan as it rolled through the darkness of the gatehouse and into the city. It continued straight down a tree-lined road.

Tian's hands, arms, abdomen, and legs all ached from the effort. All the feet visible from his spot wore heavy boots, which clopped on the white stones.

If his muscles gave out, the enemy would see him. Maybe climbing under the bridge would've worked better; at least he could have worked at his own pace.

No. No point in regrets. He drew in a slow breath and contemplated the sound of one hand clapping, distracting his mind from the burn.

The caravan turned onto a winding path of packed gravel. The white canvas and poles of tents were pitched among the grass and trees. A campsite, or rather an urban park used as such.

Men groaned all around. At last, the wagon came to a stop. The straw-sandaled feet of Cathay porters pattered away, followed by the Metal Men's boots.

Tian's limbs protested as he lowered himself to the ground and blew out a long breath. The new angle provided a slightly better view. Bandaged and splinted Metal Men, some on crutches, queued outside of several tents. This was more than a campsite; it was a field hospital. Sabotaging the medical supplies, poisoning the food, and assassinating the doctors would slow the enemy down.

His stomach clenched. What kind of man thought of such things? He rolled out on the side of the wagon away from the tents and stood. Manicured trees with budding limbs stood at regular intervals. Each could provide cover as he worked his way into the city and found clothes that would make him look more like a citizen, less like a military officer.

"You!" a voice called from the tents. "Stop!"

With his back to a tree, Tian cast a glance at the supply wagon and the medical tents beyond. A boy, not yet a teen, froze with his hand on a loaf of bread. Dozens of the Metal Men started toward him, pointing.

Tian suppressed a sigh of relief. They hadn't seen him, but... Two able-bodied Teleri loped toward the would-be thief.

The porters—the only other Cathay people around besides the boy—stepped to the side. Tucking the bread into his shirt, the thief dashed off, running right by Tian. The two Metal Men gave chase, also passing him without any sign they'd seen him. No telling what they would do if they caught the boy.

Tian bolted after them, darting from tree to tree, occasionally checking back to see if any other Bovyans followed him. Reaching the edge of the park, where it bordered a paved avenue, he stopped. Buildings of wood and stone stood in a row across the street, many with colorful signs he could read.

Shoes. Tanner. Butcher. Vegetables.

Still, the shutters on the sixteen storefronts remained closed, as were the residences above. No one so much as poked a head out of the windows.

The boy sprinted across the street, then ran down the deserted road, the pursuers only a dozen paces behind. That they hadn't caught up with their longer legs was a testament to the boy's speed and guile. He'd be fine on his own.

Maybe he wouldn't. Gritting his teeth, Tian followed.

The boy turned down a side street. When Tian reached the corner, he looked around just in time to see the Metal Men turn into an alley. Tian made a quick scan of the surrounding area. In the windows above stores, people now peeked out from cracked shutters.

He took a deep breath and ran to the alley, stopping at the edge of a building for cover. He craned around the corner.

In the morning shadows, the boy stood with his back to a dead end, his hands pressed against the wall.

One of the Metal Men put his hands on his hips. "Return the bread now, cretin, and your punishment will be light."

Tian eased the grip on his dagger. If the punishment was light, then he didn't need to risk exposing himself.

Dark shapes dropped down from the balconies overhead, enveloping the two Metal Men. They collapsed to their knees with muffled grunts.

Tian started to back away from the ambush. A hand clamped down on his shoulder. He raised his hand and stopped a knife from pressing into his throat. Securing his assailant's hand on his shoulder with his own, he spun and swept his leg out. A twist of the wrist, and the knife clattered to the ground. He straddled his attacker…

A teenaged girl.

Her eyes widened. "Zheng Tian! You're supposed to be dead."

Black Fist. The ambush was so elementary, only a child would fall for it. Or a Metal Man. And him, apparently. This girl must've been the rear lookout. Not only that, she knew his name. He raised an eyebrow. "Who are you?"

She pouted. "Feng Mi. You rescued me from the Trench when I could barely walk. You taught me the *Ghost Echo*. We attacked Wailian Castle together. Don't you remember?"

Had she? *Honey?* She was cute enough. Yet with his memory, she could've been the once-in-three-generations Doe-Eyed Girl and he wouldn't recognize her. Composing his best apologetic expression, he shook his head.

Behind him, a male said, "Who…"

Tian turned and met a young teen's eyes, which widened. Beside him the first boy stared as well.

"Zheng Tian," he droned. "I'd never believe it was *you* following me. I thought it was a Teleri Nightblade. Come on, back into the shadows." He beckoned them back into the alley.

Tian helped Feng Mi to her feet. She gazed at him with adoring eyes. Heat rose to his cheeks, and he quickly turned into the alley.

Two other young male *Black Fist* worked at stripping the Metal Men of their armor. They all looked up from their work and gawked. He might as well have been the village shaman, given the attention.

Feng Mi skipped over. "You really don't remember me? You taught me the *Ghost Echo* at the temple."

"I lost my memories to the *Viper's Rest*."

Her mouth formed a circle and the others nodded. Such bright faces, so young. The Black Lotus Clan must have been severely depleted to depend on youth.

"Who is leading?" he asked.

Feng Mi stared at the ground for a few seconds before meeting his gaze. "Me."

Her? He sized her up with a discerning eye. "If I taught you a technique at the temple, you can't be that old."

One of the boys nodded. "Most of the clan is defending the inner castle. Feng Mi was the most senior on the outside."

Tian looked from him back to girl. Princess Kaiya must've been in the inner castle. "How many adepts do you have? Who's giving you orders?"

"There are seven of us. We take turns going to Cold Sun Bell Foundry, getting orders from Master Yan."

"What's your mission?"

"For now, harass the occupying army."

"Two at a time." Tian snorted.

The first boy crossed his arms. "We were sabotaging their supplies. I was just a diversion so our last two could do the sabotaging."

The others nodded.

It was almost cute. Though it made sense: as long as the senior clan members defended the princess in the castle, the younger ones could operate on the outside. Tian scratched his chin. "How many enemy soldiers are there?"

"About five thousand," Feng Mi said.

Only five thousand, out of an expeditionary force of fifty thousand. They must've sustained significant casualties breaching the north gate. Still, five thousand was more than seven—now eight—Black Fist could defeat. Tian scratched his chin. "Where are they concentrated?"

Feng Mi used a finger to sketch the city in the air. "Mostly in the northwest quadrant and around the palace. Smaller units stationed at the north and west gates, and around the holes left in the east walls."

Leaving the south gate undefended. A trap perhaps, to entice an attack there, or maybe allow an escape route. If only he could remember the city layout. "What does that tell us about their objectives?"

The youngsters glanced among themselves.

The first boy said, "They're keeping our soldiers bottled up in the palace."

Tian cocked his head. That wasn't what he would've thought. More like preparing an assault. "How many soldiers are in the palace?

"Eight thousand."

Tian scratched his chin again. None of it made sense. Outnumbered, cut off from their homeland, the Teleri had still managed to control the entire city and its resources. "Why hasn't the regent ordered a counteroffensive?"

Feng Mi shook her head. "The regent fled the city to draw the main Teleri army away."

Fled? Main Teleri army? Tian looked from spy to spy. "How many soldiers?"

"Forty-five thousand," one of the older boys said.

They'd hardly suffered any casualties, then. "Who's protecting the regent?"

"Three hundred of the Huayuan provincial cavalry," said another boy.

Tian glared at them. This was the woman that he supposedly loved. "What about a Black Lotus Fist? Aren't we supposed to protect the Imperial Family?"

Feng Mi popped her lips. "I was guarding her, but she ordered me to stay in the city."

"And you obeyed?"

She shrugged. "Our orders to guard her were given by the late *Tianzi*. As regent, she is head of the Wang Family. I could not disobey."

Tian snorted. If anyone was more stubborn than the Black Fist, it had to be this Doe-Eyed Girl. With Yuha or not, he had to go after his *wife*.

Even if he didn't love her.

She needed his protection. "I'm going after the regent."

The others gaped. As he turned to leave, Feng Mi grabbed his sleeves. "How can you leave at a time like this?"

Tian met her gaze. It wasn't as though he had much to contribute. "This evening, Yan Jie will come in through the sluice gate where the White Duck Stream empties into the lake."

Glancing around the square, Jie didn't think the town looked occupied. They were about six *li* from where they'd parted with Tian, whose lack of confidence in his own abilities had proved troublesome. Here, people went about their everyday lives, though most stared at Yuha as they passed. Not a single Teleri prowled the streets. They must've just marched through without leaving a garrison.

They'd apparently procured supplies, though. People crowded around carts and stalls, bidding outrageous prices for common vegetables. Spring greens, carrots, radishes, and winter squashes—usually in abundance this time of year—barely filled one farmer's cart. No meat hung in the butcher's stall, and indeed, from the smells, there were too few pigs and cattle around. A decent amount of fresh crustaceans sold for high prices, but there were hardly any salted fish.

Down toward the docks, men, and children cast lines. No boats bobbed in the lake beyond. Jie beckoned Yuha to follow. Many of the fishermen gawked as they approached. Give a shaman and a half-elf a fish… there had to be a good punchline for the oddity of it.

She bowed to a middle-aged man with a weathered complexion. "Where might I find a boat?"

"If we knew, do you think we we'd all be fishing from the banks and docks?" He swept a hand across the riverfront, at all the other fishers. "You won't find a boat anywhere on the north shore of the river or lake. If you want one, go ask the regent in Huajing."

Another man, carrying a rod, walked up. "First, the regent impounds the boats across the lake, for *fair* compensation. Then the Teleri come and force us to sell over half our food stores. What good is the money if a turnip costs five times the regular price, and neighbors turn on neighbors in the struggle to feed themselves?"

The first man spat into the water. "And then, the Teleri captured the city anyway. Incompetence, I tell you."

"Would've never happened under the late *Tianzi*." The second harrumphed.

Jie nodded, but had her doubts. The *Tianzi* might've had a good mind for trade and economics, but Cathay was ill-prepared to defend itself on this side of the Wall. Meanwhile, invasion might as well have been the Teleri's national religion.

She turned to Yuha, cupped her hands to pantomime a boat, and shook her head. "No boat."

He pointed up shore, where dozens of eldarwood trunks bobbed in a holding pen on their trip to the shipyards. He wound his hands around in a circle, while the fishermen gaped at him. He grabbed her hand and pulled her toward the logs. Several of the fishermen followed.

Yuha repeated the motion. Lashing the logs together? Was he suggesting building a bridge? They had neither the carpentry skills, nor the time. Not to mention Sun-Moon Lake was several *li* wide. He threw his arms up and dragged her to a vegetable garden just twenty paces from the riverbank.

He looked up and down the rows before locking on some vines. He marched to the thatched hut and called inside, using heavily accented Cathay. "Helllloooo?"

A young woman poked her head out, her eyes widening before shifting to the small crowd that gathered.

Beaming, Yuha placed a hand on his chest, then swept it outwards. He then pointed at the garden. "Want."

The woman's gaze shifted to Jie. "What does he want?"

Jie flashed a sheepish grin. As if she knew.

Yuha beckoned them to the garden, and the woman followed, revealing a baby swaddled in her arms. Yuha smiled and nodded at the child, then came to the vines. "Want."

The mother cocked her head. "Whatever for? There aren't enough tender leaves for even one meal."

"I give you." Still smiling, Yuha removed a necklace with feathers and polished river stones and proffered it. A trade? Around them, the fishermen chuckled.

"A pretty necklace won't feed my family."

Whatever Yuha wanted, it seemed urgent. Jie produced a silver *jiao*.

She held up a finger. "One plant."

"One?" Jie threw up her hands. "That's enough to buy a field of vines."

"We can't eat silver."

Yuha put a hand on Jie's shoulder and nodded. He held up one finger.

Just one? He must be insane.

The look the young mother afforded them left no doubt she felt the same, but she nodded, nonetheless.

Yuha took the woman's free arm and clasped her wrist. He closed her hand around his own wrist and nodded again. Freeing his hands, he enunciated a few melodic words.

The ground trembled. Before everyone's rounded eyes, the vines lengthened and fattened. Side tendrils unfolded, and small white flowers opened.

"Heavens," the woman gasped.

Some of the men ran among the vines, now crawling over the land and toward the riverbank and logs, and dabbed their fingers from flower to flower. Snow peas grew out from where they touched. Other men ran back into the town.

Yuha, and Jie behind him, followed the snow peas. He wound his hands in circles again, and the vines wrapped around several of the logs. He busied himself with snapping off the side tendrils.

Jie stared. He was making a raft.

Around them, the excited townsfolk harvested peas and pea leaves. Within an hour, Yuha had bartered his services for oars and a long pole, with yet more people begging to trade. By the time they set off, his shoulders hunched and he walked with a trudge.

Nonetheless, he pushed off with the pole and guided the raft across the lake to the city walls. Once they reached a deep point, he knelt and paddled. Slow going, for sure, and Jie was useless because of her arm. All she could do was point toward their destination.

When they reached the city wall, Yuha poled again. Past the palace, past the castle and the *Tianzi's* personal residence. At last they floated to the grate where White Duck Stream emptied into the lake. She looked up to the Iridescent Moon, now waxing to half-crescent in the fading sunlight.

Jie pressed up to the grate. With a rattle, it opened. "Tian?"

No answer. It'd been thirteen hours since they'd parted. He should've arrived long before. Had he unlocked it and left? No, he wouldn't be dumb enough to do that, not even in his amnesiac state. So who'd unlocked it?

Chapter 33:
Threshold of Greatness

Standing alone outside his tent, Peng Kai-Long stared at the imperial army's flickering torches in the mountain pass above. They lit the night like fireflies, stretching out in orderly lines as the night progressed. Without a doubt, the imperials were preparing for the total annihilation of the dwindling Maduran army camped out below.

His plans could not be working any better. *Tai-Ming* Lord Wu, in exchange for Kai-Long's marriage to his pretty second daughter, now marched on the imperial army's rear. Just two weeks away, Zhenjing's provincial armies would swell Kai-Long's numbers to three-quarters the size of the imperials.

"*Jue-ye*, urgent news," a voice called from inside his tent.

Inside his tent! Only the Water Snake Clan operative, who had saved him before, could've crept behind his back and through the guards. Kai-Long slipped past the flap.

In the darkness, a voice spoke in a low whisper. "The imperial army is retreating north to Fenggu."

Retreating? Kai-Long opened the flap and pointed at the sea of torches winking in the distance. "They are fanning out. I would wager they will launch an attack on the Madurans at first light."

"You'd lose that wager." The Black Fist's words held a hint of laughter. "They are setting out torches to cover their march."

Clever. General Lu, the imperials' commander and self-proclaimed *Guardian Dragon of Cathay,* had learned the Founder's rules of warfare well. "The imperials must have heard of Lord Wu's betrayal." Their rear guard could hold this pass while the rest overwhelmed Wu. Kai-Long's stomach clenched.

"No, *Jue-ye,*" the spy said. "A Teleri legion has captured Huajing and now heads this way."

The Teleri? Kai-Long's jaw clenched. They couldn't have possibly breached the Wall… unless Lord Zheng in Dongmen and perhaps Lord Lin in Linshan had joined them. This situation had devolved into an unmitigated disaster, thanks to the accursed court sycophants and ambitious lords. "Why are we just now learning about the Teleri invasion?"

"The Water Snake network is weaker in the South. A situation that will be remedied once you rule and root out the Black Lotus. We should attack the imperial rear."

Kai-Long snorted. These spy clans were just as backstabbing and ruthless as the ambitious lords. "I might not rule if the Teleri occupy the capital."

"If I may, *Jue-ye*, find opportunity in disaster," the man said. "If *you* are the one to defeat the Teleri, you solidify your claim to the Dragon Throne."

"I need to know how many men the Teleri have."

"Initial estimates are thirty thousand, with Emperor Geros in command."

So few. A fifth of the imperial army; a fourth of his own. Kai-Long cocked his head. Emperor Geros was no fool, and yet his army did not stand a chance against either the imperials or Kai-Long, let alone their combined forces.

Unless the Bovyan didn't plan to engage in battle.

Kai-Long stepped back out into the night. "Deploy the troops," he yelled. "Be prepared to attack the Madurans at dawn." If anyone was to defeat foreign invaders, even those he had invited himself, he would be the one.

"Wouldn't it be wiser to ally with the Madurans and attack the imperial army?"

Kai-Long shook his head. "No. We will take care of the Madurans first."

Timing was everything, according to the Founder. Kai-Long cast a quick glance to the south, where the Iridescent Moon, Guanyin's Eye, and the White Moon came closer together. In a few days, they would meet in the Godseye Conjunction, an omen of great change.

As the camp roused to life, Kai-Long made his way to a private tent not far from his own. The grunts and moans of wanton sex emanated from within. It was a wonder the camp wasn't already awake from the noise. The guard outside stepped aside, and Kai-Long pushed open the tent flap and entered.

A Cathay soldier, a specimen of masculinity with chiseled features and square shoulders, looked up from where he mounted a panting girl. Unlike the Night Blossoms of the Floating World, she was a homely prostitute, her tanned complexion suggesting she had followed the army up from the south.

The man grinned. "It couldn't wait?" Despite his decidedly Cathay features, his accent stank of the Aksumi South.

Kai-Long snorted. "Get out, girl."

Wrapping a blanket around her—though most of the men had probably seen her naked anyway—she collected her clothes and ducked out of the tent.

Kai-Long watched her leave and turned back. He spoke in Ayuri. "We will attack the Madurans in the morning. I will be in need of your services earlier than planned."

"So your interruption *could* wait." The soldier stretched his arms and yawned. His form shimmered, the honey tone darkening to chocolate, his long black hair shortening into coarse, white-flecked curls.

Gone was the handsome face, replaced by middle-aged, blunt features. An amazing illusion, indicative of Master Melas' power. He had been the one to infuse glass baubles with the image of young Kaiya, which had been used to sneak a Black Lotus operative into Wailian Castle three years before.

"I leave nothing to chance," Kai-Long said. "It has to be perfect. Show me."

"I have to conserve my energy." Melas laughed. "Fear not, I understand how to find and summon your Guardian Dragon."

Such confidence, especially since Kai-Long didn't even believe in such tales. Still, the rest of Cathay did, and history claimed the Guardian Dragon had appeared after the Hellstorm to anoint the Founder. "Surely someone of such great power can show me what is possible without depleting himself."

The Mystic harrumphed. He uttered several foul words and opened his hand. In his palm danced a flaming pearl. A dragon pearl, just like all in all the paintings.

The air shook and shimmered. A black space opened in midair, as if someone had torn a gash there.

Kai-Long stared at it, mouth agape. "Beautiful. Will the Guardian Dragon come for it?"

Melas closed his hand, snuffing the illusion out. The gash in the air closed. "Of course. I've summoned him more than once with the pearl. Had I not dispelled the pearl image now, he would've emerged from the rift."

"Rest well. I need the dragon to appear for at least a few minutes once we engage the Madurans, and again on the night of the Godseye Conjunction." Kai-Long grinned. General Lu fancied himself as the Guardian Dragon of Cathay. Wait until the vain man saw the real one.

Gazing at the mirror, Prince Dhananad fiddled with the sole remaining gold button of his high-collared uniform. The other six had long since snapped free, and his tailor had tucked tail and ran over a month before. The once-magnificent fabric had faded, with threadbare patches on his knees and shoulders.

At least his handsome looks made up for it.

His assistant stepped back with the foundation brush, and Dhananad patted his smooth complexion. It covered that horrid scar on his neck, while the eyeliner brought out the mysteriousness in his gaze.

The tent flap opened. In the mirror, his last surviving Golden Scorpion pressed her hands together. Her voice betrayed about as much emotion as her featureless metal mask. "Your Highness, you must hurry."

He snorted. What was the rush? If today was the day he'd die, he would look good doing it. Curse Princess Kaiya for leading him on. Curse Lord Peng for tricking him. Curse Father for his abandonment. Would that Yama drag them all down to Hell with his infinite arms.

With deliberate grace, he lifted his chin and sauntered out of the tent. Around him, men screamed and ran like rats from a disturbed nest. Cowards. More musket shots rang out.

"Order the surrender!" The Scorpion pulled him to the side. A musket ball buzzed by his ear.

Wait. The attack, which had started half an hour before, had come not from the Cathayi imperials, but from Peng's ragtag rebels. Dhananad stared back to see the lines of Peng's musketmen, shooting even the soldiers who'd thrown down their arms. Butchers!

His stomach twisted into knots. He cast a glance toward the imperial army, whose flags had not moved from the mountain pass.

That bastard Peng. It had gone past dereliction and abandonment and had escalated into downright betrayal. Well, if the imperials weren't attacking, the Madurans could at least punish that traitor. He grabbed a Maduran banner and waved it. "Soldiers of Madura, to me! Show the Cathayi we will not die like pigs!"

A smattering of cheers rose up among his men, gradually at first, then building to crescendo. It sounded nothing like their half-hearted chants in previous battles, when he'd motivated them with the threat of punishment back home. The archers and spearmen formed up, even as their comrades fell around them.

He drew his *talwar* and raised it high. "Let history remember our brave expedition by this last glorious fight, when we punished the betrayer who had begged us for help. Charge!"

His men roared in approval and surged toward the musket volleys.

A firework exploded above. High in the dawn skies, a snaking form of golden scales materialized. Eyes glowed red, boring into his heart. Guns stuttered to a stop. The besieged camp fell silent, all gazes transfixed on the dreadful sight.

A dragon.

A real dragon.

The bastard Peng's voice rose up above the eerie quiet, speaking words in the hideous Cathayi tongue. His men cheered. In the mountains, horns blared.

The Scorpion tugged at him. "Your Highness, the imperials are descending. We will be crushed between them."

Peng spoke again from behind his lines, his diction reminiscent of a peasant Ayuri with a horrid accent. Hard to believe he was related to Princess Kaiya. "Prince Dhananad, surrender and you will be spared."

Spared. Dhananad rubbed the scar on his neck, a souvenir from previous Cathayi treachery. No, he was just a child then, and the nick had been an accident. He was more valuable alive. He started to sheath his *talwar*.

The Scorpion's hand stayed his arm. "No, Your Highness. They will use you to conquer Madura. It would be more honorable to die."

Die? No—while there was life, there was hope. If his men held out a little longer... He shook his head. "No, we shall retreat and surrender to the imperials instead of that snake Peng." Princess Kaiya would certainly spare him.

"Peng will catch you first." The featureless mask mocked him.

"No!" He grabbed the damned Scorpion's neck.

Pain seared through his neck, and the dark blue sky filled his vision for a split second before spinning to the mountains and then trees. His ear smashed into the ground. He started to turn his head… it wouldn't move. He tried to move his arm… where was his arm? It hurt, his entire body hurt. Such excruciating pain was unimaginable.

His vision dimmed into an ever-narrowing tunnel, focused on a headless body in a threadbare uniform. Above it, his Scorpion sheathed her glowing sting and started removing the corpse's jacket.

All faded to black, and the pain subsided.

Kai-Long walked among the tattered remains of the Maduran campsite. Bodies lay strewn at awkward angles, many unarmored, ungroomed. Moans and screams echoed in the early morning sky, several abruptly silenced by the slash of a sword. It had been more a slaughter than a battle.

Meeting the gaze of the few Maduran survivors, Kai-Long pursed his lips. "Has Prince Dhananad been accounted for?" The coward had likely fled into the nearby woods at first sign of the attack. No matter. Trapped by the mountain's roots, it would not be long before they caught him. "He should be easy to spot in that flamboyant uniform of his."

"No, *Jue-Ye*," an aide said. "We are searching among the Madurans, both dead and alive."

Alive, right—some of rodents had survived the order to kill them all in battle. The remnants were likely the most cowardly, the ones who had surrendered before the first shots were fired. Now they were mouths to feed, chained feet to slow him down. Kai-Long scanned the vermin. "Kill them all."

The aide's eyes widened. "*Jue-ye*, they surrendered."

"They were foreign invaders who sought to rape and pillage our glorious nation." At his invitation. When he sat on the Jade Throne, future histories would write otherwise. Kai-Long glared back.

The man bowed. "Yes, *Jue-Ye*. What about the servants and whores?" He pointed to a gaunt older woman, not worth the air she breathed. She scowled at Kai-Long with unbridled disdain.

A pair of prostitutes, dressed in faded *sari*, passed by with heads bowed. One cast a fearful glance at him as she trudged. Without make-up, her skin looked rough and blemished, though still pretty by Ayuri standards.

The other, however, had a wondrous complexion when she met his eyes. How this woman, who might have been a noble, fallen in with this lot?

Lest anyone think him as cruel as the Founder, Kai-Long smiled. Hardness must be tempered by softness, severe punishment must sometimes be moderated by lenience. "Spare any servant who is willing and able to work for us. If they wish to stay, the prostitutes can join our own as an exotic treat for the men."

An imperial soldier bearing a flag of parley ran up and dropped to a knee. "Lord Peng, General Lu believes you have won the Mandate of Heaven. He wishes to declare his loyalty to you."

Kai-Long hid a grin. The famous, self-styled Guardian Dragon would lend legitimacy to his cause once they confronted the bulk of the imperial army. "Where is he?"

"Our army awaits your orders in the pass." The messenger pointed back toward the pass.

"There is a town on the other side of the pass," Kai-Long said. "The Valley View Pavilion there serves a unique tea. Extend my invitation for lunch to the general."

Bowing, the man rose and hurried off. Soon, they would confront the main imperial army. With the Guardian Dragon of Cathay on his side, he'd win them over without a shot fired.

The Water Snake agent, dressed as a soldier, watched the messenger leave, then leaned in and whispered, "Regent Kaiya is on her way south in a carriage with an escort of imperial cavalry. They are half a day out of the capital."

Kai-Long turned to the Black Fist. "I thought she would hunker down in the palace. But no, it seems she comes to rally the troops." Against him, or... "To fight the Teleri. They are not coming to engage the army, but to capture her."

A possible snag in the plan. If she got to the imperial army first, she might vanquish the Guardian Dragon as she had Avarax. Kai-Long had to reach the army before her.

He beckoned another aide over and whispered, "Send word to General Lu to move up our meeting by two hours, and in the meantime, have him prepare his troops to march. And bring me a brush and paper."

He'd write a message to his secret allies, *Yu-Ming* Lords Fen and Mu in Jiangzhou Province. They might not risk open rebellion by detaining his meddlesome cousin, but they could certainly slow her down with hospitality.

Or sabotage.

The rattle of the imperial carriage's wheels over pavestones pounded in Kaiya's ears. It mingled with the clopping of the imperial cavalry and set the rhythm for the melodies in her mind. The fallen star played a steady refrain, pulsing to the beat of her heart.

Or perhaps her heart answered the star. She cradled Lord Xu's magic mirror for the first time since her confrontation with Avarax a year ago, studying songs of power. Chants to stir troops into a frenzy. An aria designed to curb aggression.

And music to make the bravest armies cower. That would be the one to force the Teleri to surrender.

The acoustic theories made sense, and she'd used them in the past on a smaller scale. But even if… no, *when* she regained the power of her voice, Heaven knew if it would work. She sighed.

"Sighing is a sign of shallow breaths," Doctor Wu said from the seat across from her. "Your liver energies congest and lock your *Qi* inside. Perhaps the regent should call for a break and take some time to get out and breathe deeply."

Kaiya met the doctor's gaze and smiled. Six days out of the capital, hitching new horses at the courier stations along the way, they approached the border of Jiangzhou and Fenggu Provinces. At this rate they'd make it to the pyramid in a day, a good week before the conjunction. If time were the only constraint, they could afford to take a break. She waved a hand outside the carriage window.

Zhuang, the cavalry commander who had taken her into custody at the way station, rode up. "Yes, *Jie-xia*?"

"What is the news on the Teleri army?"

He pointed back the way they'd come. "The courier system reports that the Teleri have fallen well behind."

"How far to the next way station?"

His forehead furrowed. "I would guess eighty *li*."

A ways away, though it made sense: they had departed the previous relay point not long before. "Inform the troops that we will rest there."

"As the regent commands." He bowed, and then spurred his horse forward.

Outside the windows, eldarwood trunks ambled by. What had Tian said? That the Mandate of Heaven was just an illusion, that Cathay's greatest asset was its eldarwood ships? That as long as the ships brought luxuries from abroad, the people would be content and the nation would be stable?

Kaiya sighed again. Cathay had reached the pinnacle of its prosperity under Father's rule, and the realm now teetered on the edge of fragmentation and occupation.

A loud crack burst from below. The carriage lurched, the rear rising and slamming back down again. The jolt threw Kaiya into Doctor Wu's lap. The doctor helped her back into her seat, and she slid over to the window. Outside, the orderly ranks of mounted soldiers staggered to a halt.

Commander Zhuang rode up and opened the door. "*Jie-xia*, are you all right?"

Kaiya composed her expression and stepped out of the carriage. "Yes, Commander. What happened?"

Soldiers milled around the carriage, several forming up a defensive line around her. Face pallid, rubbing his arm, the driver bent over and looked under the chassis. "The front axle snapped near the right wheel. Had we been travelling at normal speed, the carriage might have flipped."

Kaiya pursed her lips. "Can it be repaired?"

The driver bowed. "I cannot say. Only a wheelwright could tell."

Commander Zhuang pointed. "The maps indicate the town of Hualian not seven li away. Shall I send a patrol ahead?"

Kaiya nodded. "If you cannot find a wheelwright, then go to the castle and ask Lord Fen to provide a palanquin." She'd met the *Yu-ming*'s son years before, under the pretense of visiting the scenic gorge nearby. Hopefully, the young man didn't hold a grudge.

Commander Zhuang bowed. "We will never make it to Fenggu in time if you ride a palanquin."

"Then bring me a horse. We will all ride to Hualian. If it turns out the carriage is beyond a quick repair, then we will be seven *li* closer to our destination."

Doctor Wu placed a weathered hand on her shoulder. "No, *Dian-xia*. Not in your condition."

Kaiya suppressed a scowl. Only a handful of people knew of her pregnancy. "Doctor, we have no choice."

The doctor's severe gaze almost cowed Kaiya into acquiescence, but the *Tiger's Eye* held strong. A soldier swung down from his horse and knelt on all fours beside the saddle.

Using him as footstool, Kaiya mounted. She turned to the doctor. "Don't worry, we won't be riding at a full gallop."

Doctor Wu shook her head, but then beckoned a horse over. Without a word, the soldier dismounted.

With a spryness of a woman a quarter of her age, the doctor swung into the saddle. "I am coming with you, stubborn girl."

They set off at a trot. By the time they reached the castle in Hualian, Kaiya wished she had listened. Cramps gripped her womb, and a wet hotness pooled between her legs.

A few weeks into the pregnancy, this shouldn't be happening! Her chest squeezed.

The visit to Lord Fen's castle looked to be a request for a bed instead of a palanquin.

Chapter 34:
You, Spy

In his dark green and black uniform, Tian might as well have had a target on his back. All the Metal Men lurking the streets would see him as an enemy soldier.

Thank the spirts, they made plenty of noise, affording him time to duck into alleys before they spotted him, but still, it made for a slow traipse through the enormous city. At this rate, the Teleri might very well catch up to Princess Kaiya before he even made it to the city's south gate.

Waiting in an alley for a patrol to pass, he caught sight of a laundry line on a second floor balcony. He pop-vaulted up and took a closer look.

Plain beige robes and pants hung among socks, shirts, and undergarments. He swapped out his tunic for simple but loose-fitting clothes that would make it easier to dissemble if a Metal Man stopped him. He folded his own garments and left them on the balcony with a silver *jiao*.

Tian jumped down and landed lightly in a crouch. Not letting his guard down despite the disguise, he continued on his trek to the south gate. A handful of people ventured out—twenty-seven males, no females for the first *li*. Those that stopped and talked all repeated the same thing: the *Tianzi* had been murdered by his sister, the regent, who now refused to repel the occupying army.

Impossible.

According to his Black Lotus brothers' and sisters' earlier report, Princess Kaiya had fled the city.

Others huddled near street vendors, chatting. Apparently, collaborators had started going door-to-door, taking a census for the Teleri and issuing identity papers.

One citizen held up his own, a sheet of rice paper with a wax seal. "They say that as long as you carry one, they won't bother you in the streets."

Nodding, his larger companion showed off his own. "It'll be safe again, like before the insurgents started attacking the nobles."

Tian wondered. If the Metal Men treated the people from Beyond the Wall like they had the Kanin peoples, safety would be purchased at the cost of dignity. Men forced to work. Women forced to procreate.

In any case, if he could procure such an identity paper, he could make it through the city unmolested. He skidded to a halt at a pile of charred stone and splinters. Soot covered the pavestones, blackened nearby buildings. A fire had struck here.

No, more than a fire. A blast, from the way the debris field spread out. Curious, Tian worked his way toward the epicenter. The scorched frame of stone and wood was all that remained of what must've been a fairly large building. The stench of spent firepowder hung in the air. A significant amount of it had been stored here. Perhaps an armory.

Princess Kaiya had probably had it destroyed to prevent weapons from falling into enemy hands. Or perhaps the enemy had ignited it later. He continued on his way, avoiding patrols until he could borrow identity papers.

Up the street, a queue of chatting young men looped around a corner building. A promising place to glean information. Tian approached and cleared his throat. "What is this for?"

Several in line turned around. An exceptionally burly man, almost large enough to be Bovyan, said, "The Teleri are offering work."

Tian craned around to see the line entering the stone building. The sign above the door indicated a stonemason's workshop. He turned back. "What kind of work?"

"Repairing the east walls."

"What happened?"

"Where have *you* been?" Another fellow cocked his head. "The regent left two gaping holes."

Tian offered him a sheepish smile.

"Right," the big man said. "The regent is busy destroying things, and at least the Teleri are trying to fix it."

"Is that what happened to the armory?" Tian pointed northeast.

"Two of them." Another man waved toward the east. "Before the Teleri even breached the north gate."

Before. Why would Princess Kaiya do such a thing? Unless it hadn't been her. Jie had mentioned something about Teleri Black Fist operatives in the city. If they'd destroyed two armories, they must've been well-informed and well-organized.

The larger man's eyes locked on Tian's. Insistent. Not unlike the earlier man showing off his identification papers. Could they be Metal Men? Though big, neither was as enormous as the brutes he'd fought in the Wilds.

Also, all of those had been fair-skinned, except for one who looked Kanin, in Father's castle.

Tian pointed at the man's identification, clutched in his hands. "Where do I get my papers?"

"The scribes didn't come to your home?" The man raised an eyebrow. "What part of town do you live in?"

Where, indeed? More people had been out north of here, so they had likely already registered with the city's new owners. Tian jutted his chin in that direction.

The man nodded, but his gaze shifted past Tian, up, and then back. "Perhaps they haven't come to your neighborhood yet. You are brave to come out without them."

Tian shrugged. "It seems safe enough."

"Well, you'd better get your papers." The man pointed toward the front of the line. "They won't let you work without it."

"Right." Tian backed up and bowed, then walked east. Once the stonemason's and the line fell out of sight, he picked up his pace. That large man, and likely the first one with identification papers, were both smaller Metal Men of Cathayi stock.

Of course. With only five thousand soldiers to maintain order, the Teleri were now engaging in an organized campaign of disinformation. Seeding rumors and subjugating the city with propaganda alone.

Hair prickled on the back of his neck. Something wasn't right. Somewhere out there, eyes watched. He glanced at the windows in the buildings around him.

Nothing.

No shutters closed, no faces withdrew. Beyond the distant marching boots, there was no indication of anyone else around.

Except for that unsettling feeling.

Another look around. Nothing. Still, the last man must've sent a signal to his friends. Now, they followed him. It would only take time to expose them. Tian continued on his way.

In the city's vast central square, fourteen merchants stood by their carts while seventy-three citizens shopped. A patrol of twelve Bovyans prowled from cart to cart, but didn't interfere with trade.

Ducking low, Tian worked his way through the people. Very few dared make eye contact with each other, let alone the Metal Men.

Then, a large Cathayi man's gaze fell on Tian for a split second. A bodyguard, maybe? He might not compare to a Bovyan in size, but he was easily the largest Cathayi around. Like the other two. No weapons to speak of. The weight of his stare…

Tian stopped at a vendor selling pork buns. He held up a polished silver coin and found the large man's reflection. Definitely watching him. Likely the source of his disconcertion.

Chewing on the pork bun as he continued his walk, Tian kept track of the man in reflective surfaces. He continued south along the nearly-deserted main boulevard. For the first two *li*, he encountered only two citizens heading north, and no Metal Men at all. Only this one shadow, pretending to mind his own business, walking just far enough away to stay in sight.

Capture him, and chances were he wouldn't talk. Lose him, and he would stick around to cause more trouble for the young Black Lotus Clan members.

A quick glance around revealed no sign of anyone watching from alleys or windows. It was time to act.

Jie listened at the sluice gate for a few minutes, differentiating the various sounds above the lazy flow of the stream. Fish swam, plopping in and out of the water. Crustaceans clawed their way over the paved streambed, undoubtedly enjoying the feast of garbage. No signs of human activity, besides the missing lock on the grate.

She motioned Yuha to help her open it. With her good arm, she pulled herself into the rectangular tunnel. Though wide enough for eight men to march abreast, the passage was just tall enough for her to stand upright. The water came up to her waist.

Meanwhile, a hunched-over Yuha grimaced. He stared at the refuse with unbridled disdain. White Duck Stream must've looked and smelled nothing like the pristine streams and rivers meandering through his homeland. His doeskin pants would stink for days.

With a snort, Jie waded toward the other end of the tunnel, where the stream passed under the city walls. Like all the waterways in Huajing, the streambed was paved. At the mouth of the channel, she paused and peeked out.

Noble's villas and pavilions, along with the occasional temple, formed a dark silhouette against the dusk sky. A stone bridge arched over the stream not far away. In the aristocrats' section of the city, on such a beautiful evening, there would usually be poetry parties and receptions. Yet tonight, only birds chattered. No sign of any human activity—

A person moved, ever so slightly, in the shadows of a pagoda.

Jie ducked back into the tunnel and palmed a throwing star. Whoever was out there didn't want to be seen. If not for her elf vision, she might've missed him.

"Master Jie," a voice called. A male voice. Familiar. But not coming from the movement near the pagoda.

A Ghost Echo, perhaps? But why? She glanced out again, zeroing in on the source of the voice. A person, not quite grown, crouched by a stone lion. He must've been expecting her. The person by the pagoda, however—

Something whizzed through the air at her.

Jie stepped back and nearly bumped into Yuha.

A dart. Coming from the pagoda. She sprung out and whipped her throwing star at the large man as he dashed toward the cover of manicured bushes.

The star zipped past him. Curse the bad arm, throwing her balance off!

The boy at the stone lion came out from his hiding place and hurled his own star. The bushes quivered, and the man, still hunching low, grunted and yanked the star from his calf and hobbled toward a nearby wall.

With deliberate aim, taking into account her new throwing mechanics, Jie flung a spike at him. It flew true, lodging into his right upper back. He tumbled and crashed face-first against the wall.

Both she and the boy raced forward, converging on the Teleri at the same time. He turned and reached for a shortsword.

The Black Fist boy slashed with a knife, severing the man's wrist tendons before he could draw his own weapon. A dagger in hand, Jie hooked his ankle with her foot and swept it up, then kicked out the other knee.

The Nightblade collapsed onto his back. His chest heaved with labored breaths, while blood pooled around his lips.

"Roll him over," Jie said. "He's less of a threat."

The boy met her gaze, revealing a teenager with thin lips and narrow eyes. Huang Zhen. They'd served in the same cell in Jiangkou during Lord Tong's rebellion. He bowed and pushed the Bovyan over.

The Teleri flopped like a sea cucumber. Her throwing spike was now buried deep into him, undoubtedly puncturing a lung. Even if he could talk, he wouldn't last long.

Huang riffled through his possessions. "Master Tian told us to be on the lookout for the Nightblades and to triangulate the source of their orders. This one started trailing me at the *Jianguo* Temple on my way over to meet you."

Jie snorted. "You could've found a way to warn me. He almost hit me with his dart."

"Hit *you*?" Huang's eyes widened.

She used her good hand to hold the other arm up. "I'm not what I used to be." She beckoned Yuha over.

Gawking, his head turned left and right, and then down at the stone road, which he stamped on a few times. He mumbled several foreign words which nonetheless conveyed the universal message of awe. The poor man had probably never seen a city before.

"Where's Tian?" she asked.

Huang's lip quivered. "He went after Princess Kaiya."

Jie sighed. Yet again, he chose the princess first. "Where is she now? The palace?"

"No, she fled south to Fenggu Province just yesterday."

Jie shook her head in disbelief. The *Tiger's Eye* must've worn off in order for the princess to do something so emotional and stupid. She'd be safer behind the castle walls, where they could hold out for years. Tian, too, had gone. Had the princess not fled, perhaps they'd be reunited by now.

Jie's stomach knotted. "She has put herself in danger, for no reason."

"No, no." Huang held up a hand as he tried to pry the star out of the Nightblade. "The regent wanted to draw the Teleri army south, away from the capital."

"And?"

"It worked. Only five thousand enemy soldiers remain in the city, mostly surrounding the palace."

Jie sucked on her lower lip. "How many men do we have?"

"Maybe eight thousand? But they're holed up in the palace."

Choking breaths coming to a stop, the Nightblade stilled.

Jie tapped him with her foot. No response. Even if he *were* playing dead, they would likely not get any information out of him.

Kneeling over him, Yuha placed fingers along the man's carotid pulse. "Dead," he said in Arkothi. He bowed and chanted several words.

She sniffed. "He has a faint flowery smell."

"I didn't notice." Huang gaped at her. Of course, her elf senses surpassed a human's.

She pointed at the shoulder of the man's black stealth suit. "Gold and silver cosmetic dust."

Huang's brows furrowed, his eyes shifting back and forth. "The Floating World."

Jie nodded. Perhaps this operative had already partaken of the Floating World's pleasures. Or he'd been there for other reasons. "Are there any available Fists who gathered information there?"

"Feng Mi. During Minister Hong's entrapment of Chief Minister Tan, she was the one who choked him out."

Jie sucked on her lower lip. In retrospect, Minister Hong never showed any knack for conspiracy, yet had somehow cornered a master conspirator. "Where's Chief Minister Hong now?"

"The regent dismissed him and he's now unaccounted for."

A man's muffled yell trickled through the air, so quiet Huang Zhen didn't notice.

With her elf ears, Jie tracked the source. A villa, not far upstream. She gestured in clan code. *Over there. A sound.*

It might have come out unintelligible with only one hand, but Huang nodded and padded lightly in the direction she'd indicated.

"Dump it," Jie whispered to Yuha, pointing at the corpse before running after Huang.

"Spirits not approve," Yuha grumbled.

Kneeling by a wall, Huang motioned for Jie to halt. He pointed.

With barely a sound, a dark human shape in the shadows of a nearby villa wall dragged a body toward an evergreen hedge. Undetectable without elf vision.

Investigate, Jie signaled.

Huang nodded, and then crept up on the interloper. He reached in.

The stranger let go of the body and grabbed Huang's arm. With a graceful spin, he dumped Huang on his back, mounted him, and placed a short blade to his throat. He was good. Nightblade good.

Jie whipped a throwing star at the Nightblade's back, but he twisted out of its path.

"Stop." He stood and held his hands up. "It's me. Tian."

Jie's heart skipped a beat. It was Tian's voice, though perhaps the Nightblade had learned the *Mockingbird's Deception*. Still, whoever it was helped Huang to his feet. She dashed over.

Up close, it was clearly Tian. She careened into him, wrapping her good arm around his back. "I thought you'd run after the princess again."

"I'd planned to. But something puzzled me." He pointed at the body. "This Teleri tried to trail me. I evaded him. And stalked him instead. He came here. He started making notes. About the mansions in this district."

"The nobles' quarter," Huang said.

Jie shuddered. "Standard operating procedure for the Teleri as they subjugate a land. They will kill all male royalty and take all women of childbearing age to breed the new ruling class. No doubt they'll be sending troops here once they've accomplished more pressing objectives."

"They already know so much," Tian said. "About the city and its defenses. They were able to capture a well-defended city. While taking minimal losses. They must have had someone in the city. For quite a while."

Leina stared at the *Weiqi* board, continuing the game with her only worthy opponent. She placed a black piece down right next to where she had set the white, closing off an escape route. Cathay was doomed, and if they saw the board as she did, they would just surrender and spare their soldiers brutal deaths.

A tear formed in her eye. News out of the far south had come to a sudden halt once Emperor Geros had captured Huajing and proceeded on his mad pursuit of Princess Kaiya. He had promised the release of Leina's mother from the Madurans, but... Practically speaking, an old woman with a small escort would have little means of making it first through Peng's rebellion and then Cathay's imperial army.

If her mother made it to the capital, at least, she would find it pacified. Leina was seeing to that, even with her limited resources. Five thousand heavy infantry, with nearly six hundred injured and unable to fight. Thirteen Nightblades, though their leader Feiying had disappeared and two had not reported back. The enemy might outnumber them two to one, they might have a handful of the mysterious Black Fist at their disposal— but she kept them plugged up in Sun-Moon Palace and tricked the populace with rumors.

Leina stood and stretched out her tired legs. The stress of strategizing weighed heavily in her neck and shoulders. How ironic that a nation of rapists, who saw women as a vagina and womb, now relied on a female to spearhead their occupation. How ironic that she did so. Cathay might be a hateful nation of greedy, immoral merchants, but they probably didn't deserve absorption into the Teleri Empire.

Regardless, as long as there was hope for her mother, she would do Geros' bidding. Her home would serve as the brain center for the occupation, with the Nightblades coming and going in secret, relaying her orders to the Teleri officers.

She walked through the sitting room, avoiding the spot where Old Hong had died. Even though the Nightblades had disposed of the body, it seemed like his spirit still lingered there, gazing at her through those sad eyes. Shuddering, she came to the pantry and released the dwarf-made trigger to the secret door into the Jade Teahouse.

The common room was empty, save for pretty little Purple Autumn sipping tea at a bloodwood table with the proprietress. The silence felt so different from the Floating World's heyday, when Night Blossoms entertained rich patrons at this late hour. The teahouse's high-class clientele had fled the city, and the Bovyans were not allowed to partake of women until they set up the mating compounds. Leina shuddered again at her own experiences in a rape camp in Madura.

With a sway in her hips, she sauntered over to the table. "May I?"

"Please." Purple Autumn nodded and extended her hand to an open seat. The poor girl had spent so many days here, wearing a simple dress instead of one of her extravagant gowns.

The proprietress stood. "I'll get another tea cup."

Leina settled into the bloodwood chair. "I've seen you here a lot recently."

"The Teleri prowl the streets, and I have nowhere else to go." Purple Autumn dabbed her eyes.

With a pat on the girl's arm, Leina cast a sympathetic smile. Always women suffered the most in war, through loss of children or their dignity. The poor girl's mysterious patron must've been one of those who had fled, deserting her. Leina's own surviving patron, Liu

Dezhen, hid behind the palace walls with his infant son, the *Tianzi*. He had probably forgotten all about her in an attempt to save himself.

"Where are you staying now?"

"Here, until my money runs out." Tears gathered in Purple Autumn's lashes.

If not for the Nightblades' constant coming and going, Leina would offer Purple Autumn a place to stay. Maybe she still could. The girl was just a sixteen-year-old pampered prostitute who wouldn't notice the frequent backdoor visitors. Even if she did, she had always proven smart and witty. Perhaps given the chance to avoid gang rape at the hands of the Bovyans, she might make a capable lieutenant.

Chapter 35:
Allies

A *guzheng* twanged somewhere nearby, each note strummed to the beat of Kaiya's heart. Cool silken sheets caressed her body while the residual shiver of lovemaking receded in her core. Limbs languid, she shifted to her side.

Tian. He lay there beside her, the smooth tone of his bare body sending her pulse pounding again. He flashed his crooked smile, and her belly erupted into a swarm of butterflies.

He rolled onto her, pressing his chiseled abdomen and chest against hers. Heat flared inside of her. He propped himself on his elbows and met her gaze.

His dark eyes saw past the regal princess, saw *her*. "Don't tell her. The babies are safe for now, but she couldn't handle the news."

News? Her? Who did he mean? And why was he speaking in Levanthi-accented Ayuri?

She blinked and looked again.

Tian was gone.

Replaced by Geros.

Pressed against her, he grinned. When he spoke, it was in Ayuri as well. "We'll keep it to ourselves."

Jolted from sleep, heart racing, Kaiya jerked up to find herself on a soft bed, covered by a cool silk sheet.

Neither Tian nor Geros were to be found. The *Tiger's Eye* rose up around her, squelching the conflicting tidal wave of emotions.

Where was she? The Paladin Citadel in Vyara City? That would explain the sing-song intonation of Ayuri spoken among the dark, human-shaped forms around her. Somewhere nearby, a *guzheng* played. She blinked, clearing her vision.

The elegant bloodwood furniture, fine porcelain vases, and hanging scrolls could only belong in a Cathay noble's villa.

"She's awake!" a deep voice said in Arkothi.

Kaiya tracked the voice to its source, a man with a curly mop of brown hair. He stood beside Doctor Wu, but only came up to her chest. Fleet! And next to him, the chocolate-skinned Mystic Brehane.

"Athran smiles upon you," said someone on the other side of the bed, in halting Arkothi.

She turned to see Cyrus Estazadeh, one of the few remaining true Akolytes, bowing his head.

By his religion's moral standards, her sleeping robe exposed too much of her bust. Kaiya pulled the sheets up to her chest, and Fleet's lower lip jutted out.

At Cyrus' side, Sameer pressed his palms together in Ayuri greeting. "Princess Kaiya, I am glad to see you awake."

"How long have I been asleep? Where are we?"

"Foolish girl," Doctor Wu said. "We are in Lord Fen's castle in Hualian. It has been three days since you fainted from blood loss. You are fortunate the Akolyte's divine magic could heal you."

Three days. Only four days left to reach the pyramid. Kaiya looked from her to Cyrus and placed her fingers and thumb in a circle over her heart, in the fashion of the Levanthi. "Thank you, Cyrus. How did you find us?"

Cyrus started to speak when Fleet cut in front of him with a wide smile. "We were paddling up river when we saw your men on the highway, just outside the city. We thought they were going to join up with the Cathayi army until we saw you with them, hunched over your horse."

Doctor Wu wagged a finger at her. "If not for the Akolyte thrashing through the water to get to us, you might have bled out."

Cyrus bowed. "Your baby is safe."

Kaiya met each of their gazes. Their expressions said it all; they knew. No point in hiding it, anyway. "Babies."

Fleet leaned in. "Whose—ow!"

Sameer let go of the madaeri's ear and pressed his hands together. Brehane sidled over and clasped her hand. The warmth was as reassuring as it had been during their escape from Iksuvius, when the altivorcs were chasing them.

Kaiya turned to Doctor Wu. "How far away are the Teleri?"

"They have gained ground on us. The latest scouting report puts them in Long-An."

Closing her eyes, Kaiya summoned a map in her mind. Now if only she had a better sense of geography. Long-An lay north, but the distance... Well, they had passed through the town the day the carriage axle snapped. Which meant... She opened her eyes. "Summon Commander Zhuang."

Doctor Wu frowned. "You are in no condition to ride a horse."

"What about the carriage?"

The doctor shook her head. "Lord Fen's men say it could take them several days to repair."

Several days seemed too long to repair an axle. With the Teleri in pursuit and the conjunction just four days away, they didn't have several days to wait. She sighed. "How can I travel while keeping my unborn children safe?"

"A palanquin," Doctor Wu said.

Kaiya shook her head. "The palanquin won't outrun the Teleri, nor will it make it to the pyramid in time."

"Pyramid?" Fleet stood on his tiptoes. "There *is* another way. On the other end of Hualian's famous gorge lies a town on Teardrop Lake. Yanhu. You can take a boat to the pyramid."

Kaiya gawked at the madaeri. How did he know so much more about *her* country? "Will there be enough time?"

Nodding, Fleet pointed out the window. "That's the way we planned to go."

"You are going to the pyramid, too?"

Sameer chuckled. "In Iksuvius, you offered us a tour of the Cathayi pyramid."

She had. Though not under such unforeseen circumstances.

"How serendipitous." Doctor Wu pursed her lips.

With a glance around the room, Kaiya found clean travelling clothes on a bloodwood chair. "I will dress now. Have Commander Zhuang meet me here in ten minutes."

When everyone had filed out, Kaiya threw off the covers. Her bare feet found the hardwood floors, though her legs wobbled as she stood. Staggering over to the chair, she shrugged off the robe and slipped on the dress. Tian's lockpick pouch tumbled out of her folded sash as she picked it up. After winding the sash around her waist, she retrieved the pouch.

As always, it felt heavy in her hand, like her heart whenever the *Tiger's Eye* faltered. Always at the most inopportune times, and a now with increasing frequency. If—no, *when*—it finally gave way for good, she might be left a quivering tangle of emotions, unable to mother her fatherless twins, let alone rule a crumbling nation.

A knock at the door startled her. "*Jie-xia*," Commander Zhuang called.

Kaiya straightened. "Enter."

The doors slid open and Commander Zhuang marched in with two aides. They all dropped to a knee.

"*Jie-xia*," the commander said, "messengers report that Lord Wu leads the Zhenjing provincial army through the western pass into Fenggu. The main imperial army is also marching north."

Both converging near the pyramid. Kaiya nodded. As long as they stayed just ahead of the Teleri, Emperor Geros would be walking into the imperial army's waiting guns. There would be no need to rely on magic that she might not be able to conjure.

She said, "Send word to Lord Wu to hold his position and fall upon the Teleri rear when they pass him on the central highway."

With his officers nodding in agreement, Commander Zhuang's lips twitched before finally smiling. "Very good, *Jie-xia*. I will send one of our men immediately. We are ready to ride on your order."

She shook her head. "I cannot ride a horse in my condition. I will have to ride in a palanquin."

His eyes widened. "The Teleri will overtake us before we meet with the imperial army."

"Which is why you will continue on the highway with a decoy while I go through the gorge." Similar plans had ostensibly worked twice before, first in the escape from Iksuvius and again when fleeing from Dongmen.

Commander Zhuang rose to his feet. "*Jie-xia*, we cannot leave you unprotected."

"I have travelled with far less protection." She beckoned to the door, where her friends waited. "They will be with me, and while I do not doubt your men's abilities, you serve the realm better with my plan."

He exchanged looks with the two officers, who shook their heads. He opened his mouth in protest.

"That is my command."

"As the Regent commands." He bowed. "I will have Lord Fen prepare palanquins for you. We will procure some of his uniforms and banners to disguise thirty of us as his soldiers, to make it appear as if it is his family fleeing ahead of the Teleri invasion."

A sound idea. Kaiya nodded. The Southerners and thirty imperial cavalry would be more than enough protection against enemy patrols.

Peng Kai-Long rode at the head of one hundred thousand soldiers, the imperial and provincial banners mingled amongst them. In every town they passed, the people all kowtowed to him. One day, soon, they would be rewarded. The nation would prosper again, growing as other civilizations bowed before Cathay's superior culture.

From his place right behind, General Lu spurred his horse forward and bowed. *"Huang-Shang."*

Kai-Long lifted his chin. The formal address for *Tianzi* might be a little premature. There was still the rest of the imperial army to convince, and then coronation rites to be held. "Speak."

"The rest of the imperial army is encamped near the Luzhou, about five days away at our current march. If it is your will, I shall send word to have the commanders meet us first, to ensure their loyalty."

"You did not think the Guardian Dragon answering my call on the battlefield was reassuring enough?" Kai-Long straightened on his horse and stared back.

The general cast his gaze down. "Of course not, *Huang-Shang.* The Mandate of Heaven is clearly with you."

As long as the Aksumi Mystic stayed pleased. Kai-Long snorted. The illusionist's sexual appetite was becoming quite the tale around camp. He had already partaken of several of the new Maduran prostitutes they'd rescued from Prince Dhananad's defeated army.

Except the noble-looking one. If rumors were to be believed, she had yet to take any clients. How she fended off drunken soldiers, or even fed herself…

The Water Snake spy, disguised as a messenger, ran up. He dropped to his knee and held up a missive. *"Huang-Shang,* the latest dispatch from the North."

"Rise."

With his head still bowed, the man stood and proffered the message. Taking it with a hand, Kai-Long snapped it open and glanced over the news. Nothing they didn't know already. The Teleri army and Lord Wu's men were all five days away from the Luzhou. He squinted, trying to decipher the coded language embedded within.

From Fen. Regent left. In gorge.

Kai-Long gritted his teeth. Lord Fen was supposed to have kept the princess until the Teleri arrived. Through the gorge would take her to Yanhu, on the lake, off-course from Luzhou… unless she found a boat. Damn her!

The spy cleared his throat. "We have several friends who can solve this problem."

Friends, as in Water Snake Black Fist, most likely. Kai-Long nodded. "Yes, take care of her."

Water bubbled over rocks outside of the palanquin, setting a soothing rhythm for Kaiya to practice a magical song in her mind. If not for the urgency and secrecy, it might've been worth walking through the gorge, where smooth white rocks towered high above a stream.

The path, carved in the cliff face some thirty feet above the brook, was just wide enough for the porters to carry her palanquin. Interspersed rock columns supported an overhanging path. To think that, if not for the *Tiger's Eye*, she would be frozen in fear from the tight confines *and* the thought of the height.

The procession came to a halt, and the porters lowered the palanquin to the ground. Kaiya slid open the window and looked out. "Why are we stopping?" With the narrowness of the path, they had to exit the gorge by sundown.

"*Jie-xia*," Doctor Wu said, "The porters need rest. You should stretch your legs, as well."

Kaiya squirmed around, readjusting her seat. Yes, her legs would benefit from a walk. "Very well."

The door slid open, allowing in the afternoon sun. She climbed out and found herself on a broad ledge that jutted out from the path, uncovered by the overhang. Her feet tingled as she shook them out. Around her, guards dismounted. The three Southerners sat. They had abandoned their own palanquins at the mouth of the gorge in favor of walking.

Fleet balanced on the lip of rocks that lined the ledge. "Kind of reminds me of when we fled through that ravine in Iksuvi, escaping the altivorcs."

Kaiya sighed. That misadventure had taken days and claimed her loyal imperial guards Zhao Yue and Li Wei. Tian had been so sure Fleet was leading them into a trap, and yet, the madaeri saved them time and time again.

Now, he froze in place, ears perked. Just like when the altivorcs ambushed them.

Kaiya closed her eyes and listened. From above, something clicked and twanged. Air displaced, coming toward her. She dropped to the ground. A bolt thwacked into the palanquin. She dared a glance up. It would've hit her in the head.

A cocking clack betrayed the weapon as a repeating crossbow. The trigger clicked. The string twanged. Another bolt whizzed at her. She rolled to the side, and a cramp gripped her womb. The bolt struck the ground right where she'd been.

Then Sameer was there. His *naga* swirled so fast it seemed like a parasol of glowing blue. *Clack. Click. Twang. Woosh. Thunk,* the *naga* cut through another incoming bolt, this time from another direction.

"Protect the regent!" Commander Zhuang mounted up, withdrew his bow, set an arrow to the string, and loosed.

Around him, other cavalrymen jumped into their saddles. Yet with the limited space, the horses lost the advantage of mobility. Instead, they formed a protective ring. Several horses reared as bolts struck them.

"Get back," Cyrus said. "Back onto the covered path."

Fleet zigzagged between falling bolts and came to her side. Helping her to her feet, he pulled her back behind a column of rock. Sameer backed up with them, swinging his *naga*. Brehane already waited behind cover.

"Thirty men on the other side of the gorge," Fleet said, pointing. "Armed with repeating crossbows."

It was too similar to the altivorc ambush from before. Another cramp squeezed her belly. Kaiya grimaced, and then peeked around the column.

Hand on the golden circlet of Athran around his neck, Cyrus braved the storm of bolts, helping wounded men back. Blood stained his robes—whether his or one of the guards, it was impossible tell.

Someone, or a few someones, shuffled around the rock columns, too far away to be one of imperial soldiers. Fleet's eyes darted in that direction even before Kaiya pointed.

A dark shape leaped at her, the flash of the sun reflecting off his sword blinding her. A blade whistled through the air and cut into flesh. A man screamed.

"Black Fists," Fleet yelled. "They're cornering us on the path while the crossbowmen keep us pinned down."

No wonder. They were certainly too well coordinated to be random bandits. Vision brightening and coming into focus, Kaiya took stock of the situation. The guards fought and loosed arrows while enemy Black Fist darted back and forth, engaging and disengaging. Men clutched wounds and yelled; others just fell to the ground, silent. Bolts continued to fly in from a sharp angle above.

"Protect me," Brehane shouted. She turned out from behind the cover of a column and started chanting in the guttural language of Shallow Magic. Sameer stood beside her, nonchalantly knocking away incoming bolts. At the end of her spell, a fireball exploded across the gorge, louder and brighter than any firework. Brehane collapsed into Sameer's arms.

Kaiya blinked away the orange afterimage. Brehane had become so powerful.

The barrage of bolts dwindled, and the imperial soldiers now renewed their own shots with increased speed. Soon, incoming attacks trickled to a halt.

Commander Zhuang dropped to a knee in front of her. "*Jie-xia*, we have repelled the insurgents."

At what cost? Kaiya looked around again. Several black-clad Black Fist lay on the ground, their blood painted across the stone path. Her men, too, had taken significant casualties. It also meant that the Black Lotus had turned against her, and that they knew she was coming through the gorge.

Fleet appeared around a column, clasping a torn swath of cloth with a *wen* emblem. A link of wisteria blossoms, the symbol of the Lord of Yanhu.

Right where they were heading. Now that the wounded needed tending, there was no way they could exit the gorge by nightfall.

Chapter 36:
Spider in the Web

Jie paused outside the doors of *Tiantai* Shrine's main building, confirming that she hadn't been followed in the predawn hours. Even with a useless arm, stealth still came naturally, and elf senses prevented anyone from sneaking up on her.

It was deserted and dark, the surrounding derelict compound and overgrown gardens lit only by the Iridescent Moon as it waned to its fifth gibbous. Satisfied, she pushed the door open just wide enough for her to slip through.

The interior hadn't changed from a year before: just a plain stone floor and a large chest on a raised dais.

Everyone in Huajing believed the chest had once housed some jade relic from the previous dynasty. However, she had learned its true purpose during the princess' clandestine departure for Vyara City a year before. She depressed a button on a rear hinge, which led to a whispering swish inside the chest. Opening the lid now revealed a set of steps leading down into the secret passages beneath the palace and castle. Maybe her clan brethren could surreptitiously scale the palace walls in designated areas, but now her handicap relegated her to easier ways.

The musty stone corridors appeared completely undisturbed. Only the senior-most imperial guards knew of the passages, and from the layer of dust on the pavestones, none had come through here since the princess' journey.

The tunnel leading into the inner castle had been walled off as if it had never existed, suggesting that the castle defenders had come at least this far. However, the steps leading up to the outer palace grounds remained unblocked. At the top, she released the dwarf-made trigger and the wall slid open without a sound.

The manicured garden from a year ago now looked like a supply depot. Crates crushed new spring grass while kegs of firepowder crowded shrubs under the eaves of adjacent buildings. With a sigh, Jie made her way toward the Hall of Supreme Harmony, where her clansmen said the leadership gathered.

Walking among the many buildings, she stumbled upon a city of tents in the vast central courtyard. Some armed men moved about, but for the most part, everyone seemed asleep. Unwilling and possibly unable to castrate any belligerent soldier who might decide to take advantage of a palace maid, she avoided contact and instead crept up the steps to the hall.

She passed through open doors and into the vast, dark chamber. With no one inside, the light baubles remained mostly shuttered, filling the room with a dim illumination. Two maps lay on the floor, with black and white pebbles on them like a *weiqi* game. One map depicted the nation, with the white stones representing the imperial forces and their provincial allies, and the black stones a mess of Peng's rebellion, Madurans, and Teleri.

The other map was the capital. The position of black stones showed just how little the army crowded into the palace knew of the occupation. Black Fist secrecy likely accounted for much of the ignorance. The lack of communication that checked and balanced loyalties in times of peace now proved a weakness in times of war.

Jie began rearranging the enemy positions. Several thousand outside the palace gates. A central command center in the northern marketplace, not far away. Four hundred, mostly wounded, in the northwest quadrant. Two hundred at the north gate, five hundred at the west gate, and eight hundred along the holes in the east walls. Patrols fanning out and back.

With the eight thousand Cathay soldiers on hand, a surprise attack coordinated from the rear and flank could defeat the Teleri. Though, as Tian said, they had to first root out and eliminate the brains behind the occupation. If the foolhardy commanders here behind the palace walls knew about the secret tunnels, they'd rush out at the first opportunity.

Servants opened the double doors and filtered in, opening the shutters as they went. Many paused when their gazes fell on her. One rushed out, yelling, "Intruder!"

Jie harrumphed. Certainly someone would recognize her as Princess Kaiya's handmaiden.

Soon enough, imperial guards burst in with flashing *dao*. Not that she could fight them all even if she had the use of both her arms. She ignored them, continuing with her work of organizing the stones on the city map. Though they kept their weapons bared, they didn't try to stop her.

Presently, Minister Song and two generals stepped over the threshold.

The minister jabbed a finger at her. "Who are you? How did you get in here?"

"And why are you rearranging our maps?" General Tang, whom she recognized from the past, glared at her. The soldiers would be better served if General Shan were in command.

Jie stopped and bowed. "I was Princess Kaiya's bodyguard, though I masqueraded as her handmaiden. The acting *Tianzi's* mother Wang Kai-Hua can vouch for the handmaiden part. You have heard of the *Tianzi's* agents—that is my clan."

Minister Song gawked, and then nodded.

"And the maps?" General Tang pointed.

She waved a hand across the rearranged stones. "Our clan has observed enemy positions and I have made changes based on what we know now. We have harassed their supply lines. You have enough men to defeat them."

The other general—Sun?— furrowed his brows. "We knew that. However, we are stuck behind the walls while they concentrate *our* muskets and *our* firepowder on the only way out."

"There is another route. The same way I came in."

General Tang harrumphed. "The soldiers can't climb walls like the *Tianzi's* agents."

"Neither can I." As much as she hated her handicap, Jie used her good arm to hold up her useless one.

"The escape tunnels." The imperial guard commander's voice sounded awestruck.

She nodded.

"Only the senior-most imperial guards know how to get in," he said. "And they are all behind the inner castle walls. How do *you* know?"

"I watched the late Chen Xin engage the trigger."

The imperial guard general bowed.

General Sun stomped on the floor. "Then we will mount a counter-attack."

"No," Jie said. "Not yet. We don't know if there are any spies among us, and there is a mastermind behind the occupation. Once my clansmen find him, I will let you know how to get out. In the meantime, plan that counter-attack."

Tian stared at the lines of thread weaving across the abandoned Floating World theater stage, each sagging with clues and evidence. With the Bovyans' lack of high culture and their mating habits highly regulated, the entertainment district would be a safe place for his attempts to uncover the brains behind the Teleri occupation. The threads came up organically as he categorized the Nightblade sightings, Teleri patrol patterns, and citizen arrests.

The origins and impact of the myriad rumors regarding the *Tianzi* held a particular interest. He had gone mad. He had died. He had fled the city. The Metal Men were clearly working hard to undermine the people's confidence.

With the rest of his gang of young Black Fists out on missions, Feng Mi and Huang Zhen watched him from the audience seating.

Despite what they thought, the Teleri didn't have any interest in the palace and castle, except to make it seem like they did. His people had already countered half-hearted insertions by Nightblades, and they'd proven adept at avoiding capture and tailing. No, those attempts were merely a distraction, to prevent organized resistance to a small occupying army.

"Do you remember your first days in the clan?" Jie said from the entrance.

All heads turned her way.

Of course Tian didn't. He shook his head.

"It was here, in the Floating World," Jie said. "Even then, at ten years old, you used the strings to connect evidence. How you see anything in these cobwebs you construct…"

He shrugged. Even if he had no memories of those first days, using the strings made perfect sense. There was an order to it, one which only he seemed to see.

He pointed to three pieces of evidence, one at a time. "The timing between these events suggests at least seven Nightblades and no more than twelve. If we know their number, I can triangulate the source of their orders. A spider lurks somewhere in this web."

Jie laughed. A cute laugh which stirred a sense of nostalgia, even if no concrete memories surfaced. "In *that* web, *you* are the only spider I am seeing."

The two younger ones chuckled. With a snort, he contorted between several strands… and paused. "What do you mean?"

She tilted her head. "Just that you look like a spider in your web."

He turned around, a full rotation in place, as he scanned his notes. A Nightblade sighting at the palace. Another in the noble's district. One by the east wall. No activity in the far west of the city. Now, he had an excellent vantage point to see it. "Here. In the Floating World."

"What?" Jie worked her way down the aisles.

Tian tapped a foot on the stage's hardboards. "The spider is here. In the Floating World."

Jie came to the edge of the stage and pointed with her good arm at the note about the Nightblade she and Huang Zhen had killed in the noble's quarter. "That one had a smudge of prostitute's make-up on his suit."

Huang Zhen nodded emphatically. "And smelled of perfume."

"Right." Tian traced a line connecting Chief Minister Hong to the center of the web. "You also believe our proverbial spider might be hiding out here?"

"Hong is connected to the insurgency through Chief Minister Tan, and then the decisions to move soldiers away from the capital." Jie pointed at the same thread, then another branching off of it. "He had access to couriers and could've ordered the assassination on the princess at your father's castle. He was present when the *Tianzi* sealed off the inner castle, yet somehow ended up on the outside, in the palace grounds."

Feng Mi stood. "I've turned the Floating World upside-down, inside-out, and there's no sign of him."

Tian tapped his chin. Stubble prickled his fingers. "I'm certain the mastermind is here. What did Hong have to gain? What did he want?"

Jie sucked on her lower lip. "From my observations, he was obsessed with the princess. Maybe for power, maybe just because she was unattainable to someone of his station."

She shouldn't have been attainable to Tian, either. He pointed to the thread which included the assassination attempt on her. "Then he wouldn't want her killed. He was either very skilled at manipulating all these improbabilities into reality…"

"Or he is an unwitting puppet," Jie said.

"If that is the case, who pulls his strings?" Tian scratched his chin again. Having been posted abroad during the insurgency, he didn't know all of the minister's associations firsthand.

"Peng Kai-Long," Jie said. "I saw them together several times."

The one behind the rebellion in the South. Tian closed his eyes and tried to conjure a memory of what this Peng looked like. "Why would he want the nation invaded?"

"To divert the imperial armies?" Feng Mi said.

Huang Zhen nodded. "To defeat the Teleri and win the admiration of the people."

"He would need to take command of the imperial army first." Tian snorted. Not very likely. "And he would have no means of communicating with Hong now. His past actions make him appear very hands-on. Even if he lets others get their hands dirty."

Jie sucked on her lower lip. "Emperor Geros delegates efficiently."

"But the clan would be aware of Hong communicating with someone out of the country."

"What if Geros used an intermediary?" Jie pointed back at the web. "You believe the occupation is coordinated from here, in the Floating World, and Hong is not here."

Feng Mi jumped up and down, expression bright. "Hong's concubine."

A concubine. Tian swept his gaze over his notes. Nowhere was there any mention of a concubine. "What do we know of her?"

"Half-Ayuri from Ankira," Feng Mi said. "She arrived in Cathay about three years ago, searching for her father."

Tian furiously scribbled notes and clipped them to a new thread intersecting Hong's. "What was Hong doing three years ago?"

Jie sucked on her lower lip again. "That was during Lord Tong's insurgency. He was promoted to Minister of the Imperial Household after serving as a palace valet."

"...And would've arranged many of the matchmaking meetings," Tian said. "For Princess Kaiya."

Not that it mattered to the Teleri's spider. Still, it showed a pattern of ambition, making Hong attractive to someone looking for influence inside the court. "He made sure she didn't marry. All so he could one day claim her for his own." His stomach twisted. Jealousy? Over a woman he didn't remember?

"He visited his concubine often," Feng Mi said, "especially after he became Chief Minister and bought a house. We deemed it typical male behavior."

Or plotting? Tian maneuvered the concubine's thread over several others. "We are going to pay a visit to Hong's house. If she is still there and coordinating the Teleri occupation, we will eliminate her and launch Jie's counter-attack." He turned to Jie. "Go back to the palace to help them prepare, and await my message."

Back to the palace. Jie snorted to herself as she crept through the darkened streets. Tian might not have run after the princess, but it wasn't as if the time they had together now brought them any closer. In fact, with her handicap, they seemed to be growing further apart. At least before, he had respected her as a comrade. Now she was nothing more than a messenger girl.

A messenger girl with superb senses. She froze in place. Somewhere, someone watched her. How far she'd fallen. Her skills must have deteriorated for even a Nightblade to best her in routine stealth techniques.

Well, her stalker probably hadn't counted on her elf vision. She scanned the surroundings, focusing on the shadows cast by the moons. Two-story row houses lined the road. Trees stood every—there, behind one of the trunks. A stout man. Too short for a Bovyan, though with her bad arm, he could probably overpower her.

Now who would be out so late? Certainly not a rapist in an occupied city. No women came out, and Teleri patrols roamed the streets. Better not to find out. Jie darted to the closest tree and prepared to evade.

"Wait," the man called out in heavily accented Arkothi. He stepped out from behind the tree and raised his hands. His cloak flared open, revealing a broadsword at his waist. "I have a proposition for you, half-elf."

The dark olives of his complexion in her night vision suggested someone from the South, yet his accent didn't sound familiar. The features—heavy, with fangs.

An altivorc, and a prince, no less, given his good looks. Her experiences with altivorcs over the years had never been friendly.

She reached for a throwing star. "What do you want?"

He scanned up and down the street, then up into the windows. He lowered his voice. "I have been searching for you. My king has a proposition. And as a reward, he will heal your arm."

Chapter 37:
Lights and Magic

A light breeze whistled through the boughs of flowering plum trees, sending their petals tumbling down like fragrant snow around Kaiya. Her younger self would've fought the urge to spin in a circle at the beauty, but the *Tiger's Eye* made maintaining imperial propriety easy.

Just as well, since Doctor Wu would undoubtedly reprimand any spring frolicking as dangerous to the babies. At her insistence, they now rode horses slow enough for a tortoise to keep pace. The trail through the gorge descended, while the stream widened. Soon, the gulch would open up to the quaint town of Yanhu, where the *Yu-Ming* lord had aligned himself with either Peng's rebellion or the Teleri invasion.

Fleet walked ahead, at point. A small, dark silhouette as dusk approached, he would occasionally pause and signal for the rest of her entourage to stop.

Her honor guard had dwindled, with those too wounded to travel left behind with her palanquin and porters. It had been hard to convince Commander Zhuang to comply. The one thing she missed most about the power of her voice was not having to waste time with logical arguments.

They reached the mouth of the gorge as the Iridescent Moon waxed to its first gibbous. The White Moon

Renyue waxed to half, while Guanyin's Eye neared full-open. Only four days until the conjunction of the three. Their light now mixed together, casting the lake town of Yanhu in a curious hue.

Yet it was Teardrop Lake itself, glowing a faint blue, which lit up the sloped roofs, winding paths, docks and boats. It'd been years since she visited.

Fleet pointed. "Soldiers. At least sixty of them, two kilometers… three *li*… away."

Kaiya squinted along the stream, now about six or seven paces wide, but saw only indistinct shadows. Her ears couldn't pick out the men breathing from such a far distance. Still, they had twenty of the best cavalry soldiers with them. "Commander?"

"They won't dare stop imperial cavalry." Commander Zhuang rested a hand on his sword hilt.

Fleet chuckled. "Sometimes a surgeon's knife works better than a hacksaw."

The soldier glared at the madaeri, then turned to Kaiya with pleading eyes.

Kaiya stared out into gorge. "What do you suggest?"

Commander Zhuang bowed. "Wait until dawn. Then we ride in a defensive position around the regent. Even if that traitor of a lord wishes her ill, the general populace will bow down before her."

"If they are on their knees, the traitors will have a better shot with their crossbows." Fleet rolled his eyes. "Let me go first and borrow a boat."

"Borrow?" Kaiya raised an eyebrow.

He grinned. "Procure. Commandeer. I am sure commandeering a boat in an emergency is well within the regent's purview. I will row it as far as it will go upstream, flash a signal with my light bauble, and you sneak down in small groups to meet me."

Kaiya turned to the commander. "I appreciate your fervor and dedication. However, in this situation, perhaps something more subtle would be prudent."

Lips drawn in a tight line, Commander Zhuang shuffled in place before bowing. "As the regent commands."

Kaiya pointed back the way they'd come. "Whoever cannot fit in the boat shall return to the wounded and the porters in the gorge. As soon as you are able to travel, return to this town and await my command."

"Yes, *Jie-xia*." The commander bowed again, though his lips quivered.

Fleet skipped down the road without any obvious concern for his safety. Kaiya tracked him until he disappeared into the background.

"Sit and rest, *Jie-xia*." Doctor Wu appeared at her side. Though the old woman's hand on her shoulder felt light as silk, Kaiya sank to the ground. The imperial cavalry clopped forward, their hooves' rhythmic beat lulling. Her leaden eyelids weighed down on her brow.

"*Jie-xia*," Commander Zhuang's voice called. Someone shook her shoulder.

Kaiya's eyes flew open. She was lying on her side, a pack beneath her head and a cloak covering her from the night's chill. Sitting up, she looked around.

"The halfling has returned," Commander Zhuang said.

Returned… several hours must've passed, even if it seemed only a few minutes. Down near the town, perhaps a *li* away, a tiny light flashed three times. She stretched out her arms. "How long have I been asleep?"

Sameer strolled up and extended his hand. "Less than two hours."

Kaiya took the Paladin's hand. Around her, the imperial cavalry murmured, but bowed as she flashed an imperious glance.

"May I escort you to the boat?" Sameer pressed his hands together and bowed.

The commander gritted his teeth. "That is my responsibility."

Sameer bowed. "On horseback, you must be a formidable archer. However, I am accustomed to fighting on my feet. Please give me the honor of walking with the princess, while you follow behind with your deadly bow in hand."

As diplomatic as ever. Kaiya suppressed a smile that the *Tiger's Eye* couldn't contain.

Commander Zhuang grunted. Beckoning two of his men, he mounted up and drew his bow. "We will follow fifty paces behind you, *Jie-xia*."

"Thank you, Commander." Kaiya took Sameer's hand, and he helped her down the slope to the stream. Her feet squished into the rich soil. Just like the time Tian had helped her along a river bank in the Wilds. He'd been so sweet, for the first time since they were children. Now, she pressed his set of lockpicks in her sash. Her heart fluttered, and a tear formed in her eye. Heavens, the *Tiger's Eye* crumbled with disturbing frequency. It had to hold out, just a little longer.

Each footstep strengthened her resolve. On the other side of the stream, the first shoots of spring poked out of the farmland. After several dozen paces, they came to a broad weir. Beyond it churned a farm's waterwheel, silhouetted by the moons' light. The breaths of several men hid among the splashing water.

"Look out." Kaiya gripped Sameer's arm and pointed toward the waterwheel.

Hoe in hand, a man stepped out on the other side of the stream. "No trespassing on my farm!"

Kaiya squinted. He didn't seem to have any weapons other than the hoe, and he wore a simple robe. Sameer's body relaxed beneath her grip.

"Forgive us," she said. "My friend has never visited this area and wanted to see your waterwheel. We will be going on our way." She waved up toward the road, where three of her horsemen trotted.

"Too authoritative a tone," Sameer hissed. "I don't even understand your language and I can tell. Plus, your posture is too regal."

He was right. Slumping her shoulders, Kaiya cast her gaze down. Perhaps a commoner wouldn't notice.

"Princess Kaiya?" The farmer lowered the hoe and bowed.

So she looked and acted like an aristocrat. A farmer had even identified her by name despite the darkness.

He also happened to be out at a late hour.

She met his gaze. "How did you know?"

He started to kneel, then glanced back toward the town and stopped. He leaned in as far as the stream would allow and whispered, "Lord Zhi ordered us to keep an eye out for you. He has offered a reward of ten golden *yuan* for anyone who reports you."

"Why?"

The farmer shook his head. "These are uncertain times. Lord Peng marches this way, and rumor has it that a foreign army does as well. Talk in the village says our lord is trying to align himself with the one he thinks will win."

Apparently, Lord Zhi gave the imperial army even less of a chance than she did.

The man pointed back toward the town. "Many of our lord's men are watching the roads for you. Please be careful, *Dian-xia*. The people support the *Tianzi*."

Even if the *Tianzi* was an infant. Kaiya bowed her head. "Thank you. I have nothing to give you now, but when the imperial armies prove who has the Mandate of Heaven, I will make sure you are rewarded."

She turned to Sameer and gestured toward the town. "Potential enemies are watching the roads. We need to stay by the stream."

Sameer nodded and pulled her along. Not far behind, small footsteps squelched in the mud. Kaiya looked back. Two small shapes, likely Brehane and Doctor Wu. Well behind them slunk two more people. Up ahead, maybe a quarter-*li* away where the stream again widened to about ten paces, a boat waited. Not much farther now.

"Halt!" A voice called from a road running above the other side of the stream. Between her and the boat, six men leveled repeating crossbows at them while another ran back toward the town. "Identify yourself," the first man called.

Sameer drew his *naga*, glowing a brighter blue than she'd ever seen.

So much for peaceful negotiation.

Crossbow triggers clicked. Bolts zipped through the air. Sameer interposed himself between her and the attackers. His *naga* danced, deflecting the incoming barrage with superhuman speed. Wooden shafts snapped with staccato cracks.

From upstream, Brehane and the others' footsteps quickened.

"Loose!" Commander Zhuang yelled from the road above.

Bowstrings twanged and horse hooves clopped. Several more horses charged from the mouth of the gorge. Arrows found their targets, and the local soldiers fell back. The commander had gotten his wish, and it was apparently the better plan after all.

"Hurry," Sameer said, pulling her into a trot. He swung his sword on occasion, clipping errant bolts.

Kaiya's feet squished between mud and water. She nearly tripped a couple of times, but they made it unscathed to the boat.

Boat? It didn't look that much wider than the canoes the Maki used during her winter sojourn in the Wilds. It might hold six, maybe seven with the madaeri and the smaller women.

Despite the arrows and bolts, Fleet relaxed near the rear, his feet kicked back. He waved as they approached.

Sameer helped her in and pushed the boat with the current. Brehane and Doctor Wu tumbled in, and Cyrus joined Sameer, sloshing through stream as they splashed through knee-high water. The barrage of bolts dwindled to a stop, and the imperial cavalry kept pace on the road above.

"I don't know much about boats," Cyrus said, climbing in, "but how is this going to get us across the lake to the pyramid in four days?"

Fleet threw his hands up. "Not enough room for you to lie back, Your Majesty?"

"It *is* a little narrow." Sameer chuckled as he boarded, nearly capsizing the boat.

"Now you see the benefit of being small." Fleet grinned and pointed to the oars.

Kaiya gave the canoe a once-over. The Paladin was right; it would be a tight for four days, over open water, and... "Wait. We won't be near the shore, and we can't possibly paddle the whole time."

Fleet laughed. "We are going to steal—I mean, appropriate—the local lord's pleasure boat. I just used the canoe to get upstream."

"And where is this boat?" Brehane glared at the madaeri.

He pointed downstream. "Docked not far from the mouth."

Sameer sighed. "Guards?"

"Nothing we can't handle."

Kaiya stared at Fleet. He hadn't been so flippant in their escape from Iksuvius. "How about a crew?"

He puffed out his chest. "I'm quite the sailor." He then turned and scanned the banks. Where the madaeri found time to get good at everything was a mystery.

The waterway skirted away from Yanhu, and they reached the lake without further incident. The imperial cavalry had only kept up as far as a bridge that led into the town.

The lake's light blue waters reflected in Doctor Wu's eyes, bringing out their luminescence. Without the stream's current pushing them along, the men strained as they rowed along the lake's edge toward the town.

Lights shined in windows. Shouts carried across the water. Kaiya squirmed in her seat. It sounded like the imperial cavalry had drawn Lord Zhi's men away.

She looked toward the closest dock, where an elegant skiff was moored. The name *Wind Dancer* was emblazoned in red on the hull.

"See?" Fleet pointed at the dock. "Completely unprotected."

They rowed up and climbed aboard the larger vessel. Large enough for the lord to entertain eight guests while he showed off his sailing skills, it would be comfortable enough for the six of them. Fleet worked the rigging while Sameer and Cyrus untied it from the mooring.

The sail billowed out and the skiff lurched forward. Kaiya's stomach rebelled, either from morning sickness or seasickness. She fought it down. The waters shined brighter the further they sailed from the shore.

Brehane's expression danced with wonderment. "Why do the waters glow?"

Kaiya gestured toward Shenyue. "The Blue Moon is the Eye of Guanyin, Goddess of Mercy and Healing. When the Lord of the Sun, Yang-Di, created Tivara as a gift to her, she shed a tear. It landed here, giving birth to the Cathayi."

"Listen." Doctor Wu held up a finger. "Do you hear it? The energy of the world."

Closing her eyes, Kaiya listened. The vibration pulsed in her ears, slow but powerful. She opened her eyes.

At her side, Brehane nodded. "Yes, I feel it."

"Like around all the other pyramids we visited," Sameer said.

"Yes, yes." Fleet yawned. "Where the elves first built their cities. Where the Tivari erected the pyramids. Places in the world where energy is the strongest. I can't even count how many times I've repeated this story to you."

With a snort, Doctor Wu broke her glare from the madaeri. "Keep listening. It will only get louder."

It did. Over the next several days, the vibration resonated in Kaiya's core. At times, memories stirred her emotions, poking through the *Tiger's Eye*.

Lord Xu's vision must be true. For better or worse, she would regain her emotions and her power at the pyramid.

Kai-Long looked up at the sky, where the White Moon neared the Blue Moon. Tonight was the night, when the three moons would conjoin, just like they had three hundred years before to herald in the start of the Wang Dynasty.

A constellation of seven twinkling stars hovered above the moons, like a crown. Legends claimed the Golden Flock was frequently visible during the Age of Orcs, only to vanish after the War of Ancient Gods. It had appeared once since, during the Hellstorm, making it an omen of great change.

Tonight, it would herald his ascension to the Dragon Throne.

He shifted his gaze down from the hilltop to the imperial army camped not far from the pyramid. Soon, General Lu would return from his parley on Kai-Long's behalf.

Lord Wu's provincial army held the mountain slopes on the imperials' flank. At Kai-Long's signal, they would switch banners to declare their loyalty to him. The final touch would be the reappearance of the Guardian Dragon.

When they yielded to him, his army would number three hundred thousand. Cousin Kaiya might have escaped his trap in the gorge and Yanhu, but there was nothing she could do to prevent his victory now.

On the evening of the fourth day, the song of the world's energy sang loud in Kaiya's ears. Guanyin's Eye rose low as always on the eastern horizon, silhouetting the pyramid beyond the shore. Gigantic trees lined the side of a road to the pyramid. Light filtered through the buds, forming veins of webbed light that branched toward the heavens.

Kaiya gazed at the grove for the first time in years. The elf angel Aralas had planted the Trees of Light over a millennium before, prior to the War of Ancient Gods. One still stood near Wild Turkey Island, where Geros had first raped her. Her most recent dream resurfaced, and the *Tiger's Eye* faltered, sending a shudder down her spine.

Much farther up the shore, thousands of other lights flickered. Campfires and torches. Kaiya pointed at them. "Fleet, can you make out the sigils on the banners?"

Fleet craned forward. "A golden dragon on a blue field."

The imperial banners. The imperial army must be camped here, stretching from the shore to a nearby mountainside. No, that couldn't be right; the imperial army numbered close to a hundred and fifty thousand, and it looked like far more men than that. She gestured toward the mountain. "How about them? Can you see the banners?"

Fleet whipped out a spyglass and stared through. "A black wolf on a red field." He proffered the scope.

Peng's army, so close, and busy. Kaiya took the glass and scanned from mountain to plain. Men marched in orderly ranks. Preparing to engage? At dusk, no less. "We must hurry to the pyramid. How much farther?"

"Just a few minutes." Fleet pointed toward the Trees of Light, looming large above them.

Kaiya squinted. Beneath their canopies, two humanoid shapes moved. Lord Xu? Or scouts, perhaps. One was quite smaller than the other, and they were far from the two armies.

The skiff ran aground. Kaiya pitched forward in her seat. Clambering over the bulwarks, she splashed into the knee-high water and slogged to shore. Her companions followed, except for Fleet who sounded like he was fiddling with the rigging.

Doctor Wu waded after her. "Don't get too cold. It's bad for the babies."

Kaiya suppressed a laugh. The doctor was so persistent, but that wasn't important. Not now, when they were so close. So close to regaining her magic. So close to preventing the Cathay armies from fighting each other instead of the invading Teleri.

Her feet found solid ground and she strode into the grove. Light from the trees illuminated the path in gentle white. The omnipresent energy pulse went silent.

Up ahead, the two shapes from before came into focus. A black cape flowed behind the taller, merging in color with his long dark hair.

Certainly not a scout, looking so conspicuous.

The other wore tight black clothes, but stood no taller than a large child. He paused, then whirled around and met her gaze.

Pointed ears poked out from beneath short brown hair. Large, almond eyes.

Jie.

The other turned around, revealing a stout, handsome man with a turquoise complexion and a thin crown on his head. He resembled the altivorc prince Kaiya had seen in Iksuvius, but even more handsome.

The two exchanged words in a guttural language. Jie spoke it? Maybe, like Avarax pretending to be Hardeep, she'd deceived Kaiya all this time.

At Kaiya's side, Sameer and Cyrus both drew their weapons.

"I had a feeling I would find you here." The altivorc prince withdrew a magic wand and leveled it at them.

Chapter 38:
We All Spy

From his hiding place on the ground level of a recently abandoned brothel, Tian peered through the shutters at the small home connected to the Jade Teahouse. Though no one had used the front door since he'd arrived three hours earlier, his team flashed mirrors anytime someone came or left through the secret door in the roof. Three times so far.

This had to be the place. Right now at noon, at least four Nightblades congregated inside. No telling how many were there in total, so it was too risky to launch an attack with just him and four young Black Fists. They could ambush individual Nightblades as they left, but the concubine would likely grow suspicious if her eyes and ears began disappearing.

He was about to give the signal for his comrades to regroup at the theatre when the front door of the house opened. Tian reached into the fold of is robes for a throwing star.

A pretty Cathayi girl walked out. Probably no older than fifteen or sixteen, she wore a plain grey dress. Not the concubine, whom Feng Mi said was in her late twenties, and had mixed Ayuri blood. Nor a Teleri Nightblade, since they were all male. Maybe a collaborator.

Tian abandoned his post and slipped out the front. The girl had reached the teahouse and now opened the door.

A servant or prostitute, perhaps, though she might still be an enemy asset. No matter which, she'd recently been inside the concubine's house, which meant she knew more than him.

He flashed hand signals to inform the team of his decision. *I go in. All clear?*

Mirrors flashed twice, indicating a safe window of time. Tian made a quick check of the empty streets, dashed across the street, and opened the green door to the Jade Teahouse. Bells jingled as he entered.

Light bauble lamps with thin jade screens shed a dim light over the bloodwood tables and chairs in the common room. A curtain of stone beads dangled over a back corridor, likely where the Night Blossoms provided private entertainment.

Hovering over a chair in the far corner, the girl paused as her eyes met his. They flashed downward as she sat.

A door at the back slid open, revealing a middle-aged woman kneeling in a green silk gown. "Ziqiu, welcome back. What would you like?"

"Jasmine green tea," the girl answered with a bow. "I am expecting a client."

The proprietress covered her giggle. "The same one, I would wager."

"You would win that wager." The girl, Ziqiu, smiled and nodded.

"Maybe it is a sign that humming birds will return to the blossoms." The proprietress turned toward the kitchens, but paused when her eyes swept across Tian.

She looked to Ziqiu, who shook her head ever so slightly, then back to him.

Eyes wide, she bowed. "Welcome, my lord. The flowers do not bloom these days, but might I offer you some tea?"

Flowers not blooming. A reference to the sex trade. "I will have the same as her." He lifted his chin to Ziqiu, who studied the hardwood floors.

The older woman gestured with an open hand toward a table far from Ziqiu. "Please, make yourself comfortable and I will be back with the tea."

"Thank you." Ignoring the seat she indicated, Tian strode toward Ziqiu. The girl kept her head down, but her eyes still watched him. He placed a hand on the back of a chair at her table. "May I?"

Ziqiu bowed. "I am sorry, my lord. I am expecting company."

Tian sat anyway. "I have not seen another soul in days. At least share your ear until she joins you."

"He," she said, at last looking up at him.

A male. Another information relay, perhaps. Tian grinned. "Will I make him jealous?"

She studied his face, then shifted a hand from the table to her lap. "Have we met before?"

"I don't believe so. I haven't visited the capital in a while." For ten years, thanks to his banishment.

Her brow wrinkled. "Your accent... you are from the North."

Observant, this girl. No use in denying it. Tian nodded. "You, too. Linshan Province?"

She shyly tilted her head and covered a hand over her cheek. "Yes. Better opportunities here."

Tian searched her eyes, at least as best he could from the angle she presented. Something in her tone... she was telling half-truths and using body language to misdirect. Trying to present herself as a country girl who came to the big city as a prostitute. She was hiding something.

The front door opened, and the girl's expression lightened up. Relieved. She beckoned whoever it was, and then settled her gaze on Tian. "My… friend."

The innuendo sounded too forced. The stranger at the door was no buyer, at least not of flesh. The footsteps clunked across the floors, the sound and length of the stride suggesting an average-sized man in boots, certainly too small for even the Metal Man spies.

Bowing, Tian rose. "Thank you for the company."

Her eyes shifted from him to the stranger and back. Tian turned to evaluate him.

A thin man with soft features, smooth hands, and a light complexion. He was someone who had grown up in affluence, perhaps the son of a high official, from his body language. His plain cotton robe concealed a dagger. Tian offered him a smile.

Eyebrow raised, the man looked from Ziqiu to Tian.

In the corner of Tian's eye, Ziqiu shook her head, imperceptible to the untrained. These two were up to something, and if he gave them space, they'd likely reveal what it was. Either that, or he would be listening in on the primal screams of purchased sex. He walked over to the table where the proprietress had already set a white-and-blue porcelain tea set.

Sitting, he sipped the tea and stared into the cup. The pair stood and retreated behind the curtain of jade beads. That side of the teahouse shared a wall with Hong's concubine's house. Perhaps they were once part of the same building until partitioned.

Tian stole a quick glance toward the kitchens, where the proprietress' shadow moved about. He went to the front door, counting his steps along the way. Eleven. From here to the back corridor would take three seconds at a fast but quiet pace. The proprietress' shadow disappeared.

Pushing the door open, he yelled, "Thank you," then dashed to the back and slid under the jade beads and into the private hall.

One foot in front of the other, he tip-toed to each of the sliding doors and listened. Low whispers emanated from the third. Tian slipped into the second, crept across the firm reed mat floor and pressed an ear horn to the thin wall.

"Teleri spies are relaying Leina's orders," the girl said.

The man harrumphed. "I can't imagine the Teleri relying on a woman."

"She is very intelligent. And there is always at least one spy around. They are skilled, so you won't be able to get in."

"Then it's up to you," the man said. "Catch her off-guard." Something clunked on the floor.

The thud's sound indicated the dagger. These two must have some sort of training to have uncovered the spider in the web before the Black Lotus. Whoever they worked for, friend or foe, they had the same goal at this point.

Ziqiu gasped. "Song, I can't. I've never killed anyone."

Tian had and could. If they worked together—

A soft click emanated from the hallway, followed by the very soft padding of three people trained in stealth. The door to the next room slid open with a woosh and the thump of wood on wood. Ziqiu screamed. Metal clanged on metal.

Drawing his knife, Tian swept through the door and turned into the adjacent room. Three Nightblades held swords in an offensive formation. The man from the common room, Song, held the dagger in one hand, his other pressed against a bleeding slash across his abdomen. Ziqiu huddled behind him.

One of the Nightblades growled. "If you are going to plot against us, then at least be smart enough to do it somewhere we can't hear."

Apparently, neither the walls between the private rooms, nor the partition to the concubine's house, were particularly thick. The Nightblade leaped toward Song with a downward slash.

Song lifted the dagger. It stopped the sword cut, but jarred from his hands. The Nightblade kicked it out of Song's reach and took a step back. "Now, come with us."

Tian jumped toward the closest enemy. He drove his knife into the back of the Bovyan's neck and plucked his sword from his hands. The two others turned. Song tackled one and fought for the weapon.

Holding his sword two-handed, the third Nightblade edged toward the door.

Tian interposed himself between him and Ziqiu. "Go into the street. Yell *Tian Attack*."

Staring at him with wide eyes, the girl nodded and dashed out.

The Nightblade flung a star at her, but Tian knocked it out of the air. He swung the sword and stabbed with the knife.

Dodging, the Nightblade countered with a horizontal chop. Tian ducked under the blow and thrust his sword into his enemy's exposed armpit. As the Metal Man recoiled, Tian followed through with a stab and lodged the knife in his solar plexus. Yanking both weapons free, Tian turned to the struggle on the ground.

The Nightblade straddled Song and pressed the sword down. Song pushed back, while the blade bit into his hands.

Dashing over, Tian yanked the Nightblade's head back and slashed his throat, sending blood spraying across the mats.

Song coughed, flecking his lips with blood. "Who *are* you?"

Tian helped him into a seated position. "A friend, for now. Wait here." He peeked into the hall, where a secret door opened into the adjacent house.

The concubine's house. He ran over and paused at the entrance to listen. Inside, furniture crashed, doors opened and slammed shut, metal clanked against metal.

"Fall back, fall back," yelled an unfamiliar male voice.

"Protect Leina," another screamed.

The light footsteps of an untrained woman shuffled toward the secret door. Tian turned the corner.

An exotic beauty stopped in her tracks, large eyes rounded, shoulders hunched. Her blue gown accentuated cinnamon-toned skin.

Here cowered the mastermind behind the Teleri occupation, perhaps behind the entire splintering of Cathay.

The Spider in the Web.

Tian raised his sword. Behead the demon, and the body would surely fall.

Leina knelt and closed her eyes, too afraid to watch the implement of her impending doom.

It didn't matter, really. If the latest reports were true, Peng Kai-Long had slaughtered the Maduran army. Her mother wouldn't have survived. Peng had little use for an aging woman, not knowing her significance.

Leina fought back tears. All these years in Cathay, sacrificing her body to Old Hong, all for naught. A country, brought down by her in the slim hope of being reunited with her mother. The greedy men deserved their fate; but now, countless women would endure gang rape because of her choices.

She deserved death. She bowed her head and brushed her hair to the side to expose her neck. If this swordsman could defeat three Nightblades, hopefully he was skilled enough to kill her mercifully. If only she could have seen her mother one last time.

"No!" Purple Autumn screamed, sending a jolt through Leina's heart.

She had consigned herself to death already. She opened her eyes and straightened.

Purple Autumn's hand rested on the handsome young man's shoulder. He looked familiar, with large, intelligent eyes and a high-bridged nose.

Leina tilted her head. "You are one of Zheng Ming's brothers." Like the one the Teleri were holding at the north gate.

Lowering the sword, the man nodded.

Face flushing, Purple Autumn gasped. "That's why I thought I recognized you."

Leina let out a wistful sigh. Making love to Zheng Ming had been the best experience in her three and a half years in Cathay, even if the passion and ecstasy had lasted just one afternoon. Apparently, Purple Autumn knew him, too. How foolish Leina had been, letting the girl into her home.

"All clear," a young male's voice said from somewhere in her house.

"All clear," repeated a girl. Honey's voice. She was a Night Blossoms trainee who sometimes came to the Jade Teahouse… and apparently a Cathayi Black Fist.

"Your operatives are dead," Zheng said. "You are next. First, tell me. Why did you help the Teleri?"

"Emperor Geros held my mother hostage in Ankira."

His tone betrayed no emotion. "And now?"

"I don't know. Murdered by Lord Peng. Or lost on the road."

His expression softened. "Your life is forfeit. But tell me what you know. I will do everything in my power to ensure your mother's safety."

Leina bowed and motioned toward her parlor. "Come. Perhaps you can undo what I have done."

Zheng nodded again and followed her. Inside the parlor, three of the Nightblades lay dead. Five young spies, four boys, and Honey gathered around, watching her. Evaluating. Chairs lay strewn in splinters, the rug ruffled up. Only her *weiqi* game sat undisturbed.

Zheng gazed at the game board. "How many Nightblades do you have in the field?"

She held up five fingers. "Plus the three sent after you in the teahouse."

He shook his head. "Dead. When will the others report back?"

"In three hours."

With a nod toward one of the boys, he pointed to the front door. "Go to the palace. Tell Jie she can commence the attack. In three hours."

Leina's stomach knotted. They were revealing names, which meant she would not survive this afternoon.

She pointed at the board. "The Teleri Empire has been targeting Cathay for some time, using Madura and the Nothori nations to keep your armies distracted while they connected the roads through the Kanin Wilds. I was sent here three and a half years ago, while they were establishing the Water Snake Clan."

Purple Autumn's lips formed a pretty *O*. "During Prince Kai-Wu's wedding ceremony. I remember that. It was the first assassination attempt on Princess Kaiya."

Leina shook her head. "The timing is right, but that was purely coincidental. The Water Snake had nothing to do with it. I suspect Lord Peng was behind that."

The man's lips pursed, his knuckles white around the sword hilt. "How do you communicate with the Directori?"

"Through messenger birds. The birds are in the attic rookery. The codes are in my bedside table drawer." Leina pointed toward her room. "Then-First Consul Geros had estimated seven years to finish the roads and pacify the surrounding area. I had that much time to undermine Cathay. But when Princess Kaiya escaped home, carrying his son in her womb, he moved his timetable up."

Zheng's face betrayed nothing, but Purple Autumn gawked. Perhaps revealing the princess' secret would end up hurting yet another woman. Leina sighed.

"What about Hong?" Zheng's tone held monotone. "Did he have anything to do with the plot? Where is he now?"

Old Hong. Leina's chest constricted as she looked at the spot where he'd died. If her dalliance with Ming had been her only joy in her three years in Cathay, Hong's kind gestures had at least blunted the horror of the rest.

And she'd poisoned him. "He was an unwitting fool I manipulated. Him, and Young Lord Liu Dezhen. They undermined Cathay—Hong, because he didn't foresee the results of his actions. Young Lord Liu, because he wanted his son to become *Tianzi*."

"Where is Hong now?" Zheng asked.

She set her jaw rigidly, hoping to sound disinterested. "Hong is dead, by my hand."

Zheng nodded. "And you sabotaged the firepowder?"

She shook her head. "The leader of the Nightblades did that. A non-Bovyan, one of your own. He arrived just ahead of the invading army."

"Oh…" Honey nodded. "He must be the one Master Jie hunted in Eldaeri lands."

Leina shrugged. "I did not even know the Black Fists were real until several days ago when I met him."

"Where is he now?" Zheng asked.

"I don't know. He disappeared the day of the invasion."

Purple Autumn gasped. "He was the one who tried to take the fallen star from the Temple of Heaven. He and my master killed each other."

The young Black Fists exchanged glances, while Zheng regarded Purple Autumn through narrowed eyes.

He then turned to Leina. "I am sure the local authorities will have you tortured and executed. But I understand. You wanted to save your mother. I give you the option of fleeing Cathay forever."

The Black Fists all murmured among themselves, but he silenced them with a glare.

Tears gathered in her eyes, blurring her vision. He was letting her go.

But where? With nobody left, she had nowhere to go and no reason to live. Even if her mother had somehow survived, they would never find each other wandering a strange land. No, this was her house. Only now did she see that, only after she killed the man who had made it her home. She shook her head and pointed to her room. "I have a fatal poison. Allow me to take it."

Zheng gestured with an open hand, and followed as she went in and withdrew the crushed leaves and the messenger bird codes from her bedside table. She went back into the parlor and sprinkled it into her still-warm tea. Sipping it to savor the sweet taste, she said, "I am sorry for what I did."

Zheng nodded. "If your mother lives, I will make sure she is protected." He then pointed at the *weiqi* board and pointed. "White has lost. Because Black controls this one interior intersection. If a white piece held that instead of black, your plan would fail."

Mind spinning, Leina offered him a wry smile that took most of her energy. Each breath seemed harder to draw in. "So much rode on chance, especially after Emperor Geros pressed the attack three years ahead of schedule. In a game of *weiqi*, your idea would be cheating."

"In life, it can still be done." His handsome face blurred.

She started to speak, but her breath seized and she coughed. Hand trembling, she reached to the board and removed the piece. She mouthed, *Princess,* but the only sound was the rasp of her last exhale.

Chapter 39:
Choices

The silence made Kaiya wonder if she'd lost her hearing. The pulse of the world, so strong and steadfast just moments before, was gone. Only the fallen star in her pack vibrated and hummed, ever so slightly, and the sound vented upward into the tree canopy.

Sameer's *naga* looked grey and lifeless. Cyrus frowned, in a rare show of emotion.

At her side, Brehane's hands quivered as she chanted several guttural words. The air around them cracked and shimmered.

"Interesting, Mystic," the altivorc said. "You are drawing power from somewhere. Still, your shield never stopped me before. They say trying the same thing over and over again and expecting the same result is madness." A bolt of red buzzed out from his wand. The light fizzled and cracked in a hemisphere around them, and faded.

Brehane coughed and wobbled. "The shield can't take another hit. Scatter!"

Taking Kaiya's hand, Sameer pulled her off the path to a tree. "I can't feel the energy of the world!"

"Nor can I." Cyrus huddled behind another tree with Brehane.

The altivorc nodded at Jie. "Go. I will handle them."

With a quick bow, the traitorous half-elf raced toward the pyramid. He turned back and grinned, baring fangs. Wand spinning around his finger, he strode toward Cyrus' tree. "Give me all your pyramid dragonstones, and I will let you go."

Coming out from cover, Brehane barked several foul syllables and pointed her fingers at the altivorc. Nothing happened.

"You are powerless." The altivorc laughed.

With his back to Kaiya, he made for a vulnerable target. If only she had a weapon.

He spun and pointed the wand at her. "Which means you must have a power source." A flash of red streaked at her.

Doctor Wu stepped in front of the pulse and dropped into a low horse stance. Energy fizzled through her and into the ground. Webbed wisps of red streaked through the soil, then up the tree trunks and into the buds. The doctor staggered to one knee, her beautiful luminescent eyes fading to a light blue.

Kaiya blinked. What had just happened? It should've been her, not beloved Doctor Wu.

"Run! To the pyramid." Pressing a hand on tree roots, Doctor Wu looked up. Her eyes glimmered, feebly at first, then building. "The Altivorc King can't get past the tree canopy while the Tear of Guanyin sits at the pinnacle."

"Something that my half-elf will take care of soon enough." The Altivorc King— King?—laughed.

Kaiya gaped. She'd heard of him, of course. On the rare occasions he appeared among humans, a dozen elite altivorcs protected him. From what she'd heard, the altivorcs had a personal vendetta against Jie. Yet here she was, working for him.

"Run, fool!" Doctor Wu staggered to her feet.

Shaking the confusion from her mind, Kaiya bolted down the path. Toward Jie, who even asleep could probably kill her. She hazarded a glance back.

The Altivorc King pointed his wand at her. Then a rock popped him in the side of the head, which jerked like the lash of a whip.

"Run, Princess!" Fleet yelled from somewhere.

A hand clamped around hers. Sameer's. He pulled her along the path. Behind them, Cyrus and Brehane gave chase. The King's wand flashed again in repeated staccato buzzes, which flashed red on the tree trunks.

The edge of the grove lay close ahead. Kaiya's belly cramped. Just a few more steps. She stumbled to her knees as she reached the clearing. Her ears roared from blood coursing through her... no, from the low, primal drone of the pyramid itself. Like the Ayudra pyramid.

At her side, her friends stared up at the Tear of Guanyin. Like the Lotus Crystal she'd returned to the Temple of the Moon, it sparkled atop the pyramid in myriad rays of light blue.

Just a few degrees behind it, the nearly-full Iridescent Moon swirled in soap-bubble colors, not far from the full White Moon, with the fully-open Blue Moon forming a backdrop. The Golden Flock constellation, an omen of great change, hovered above them.

Together, the moons resembled a light blue face with two mismatched eyes, crowned with a halo. It was so beautiful that Kaiya's heart stirred from beneath the *Tiger's Eye,* and she let out a gasp.

Jie turned from where her gaze had been locked on the Tear and glared at them. Her form-fitting clothes shined dark grey, like lightning flaring along the underside of a storm cloud.

She pulled a hood over her head, leaving only a slot which revealed the bridge of her nose and the cruel glint in her eyes. The rest of her body disappeared like haze on a hot day.

"How did she get here so fast?" Cyrus exchanged glances with Brehane and Sameer. "She was just with—" He coughed as Brehane elbowed him.

Sameer stepped forward, his *naga* now glowing bright blue. "I don't want to hurt you."

"Don't you feel it?" Brehane's voice tittered in excitement. "The resonance of the world has never coursed through me like this."

"Nor me." Jie's chameleon form darted forward, her blade whirling in a blur.

Sameer engaged, their weapons never touching as they circled and stabbed and chopped in a dance of swords. It looked nothing like Jie's vicious and efficient style.

Kaiya clasped Brehane's dress. "Do something!"

The Mystic threw up her hands. "I can't. They're too fast, too close."

"How do you know the *Bahaduur* arts?" Sameer disengaged.

In that split second, Brehane chortled out several syllables and waved a hand at Jie.

Webbing shot out and entangled the half-elf. Growling, she slashed it away, but at least now she was visible.

She pulled the hood down. Her clothing returned to the same storm-cloud grey and she surged forward. Her broadsword caught Sameer in the shoulder, cutting deep. The *naga* slipped from his fingers. She drove her boot into his chest, sending him sprawling to the ground.

Brehane choked out several guttural words in the language of Shallow Magic. Glowing darts appeared and streaked toward Jie.

The half-elf spun out of the way. "You might as well surrender now," Jie cackled. She'd always had a disrespectful streak, but never had she sounded so malicious. "I will make your deaths quick."

Hand on his golden circle, Cyrus chanted a prayer in his language, calling on Athran to do something.

Anything. Kaiya couldn't tell. Tears, real tears, blurred her vision. "Why, Jie? Why are you doing this?"

Jie ignored her, instead striding toward Cyrus with her sword raised.

A shadow darted between the two. Jie's weapon clinked, stopping before it decapitated Cyrus.

Fleet. The little madaeri brandished two shortswords, twirling them like a hummingbird's wings. He snaked toward Jie with quick stabs. Sameer might be fast, but Fleet made him look almost normal. Jie backed away, losing ground.

His eyes tracking the combatants, Cyrus circled around toward Sameer. Brehane grunted out more Shallow Magic.

And here Kaiya was, useless. Pulse racing, she fought for each breath. The taste of panic sat in her mouth, she could barely contain the emotion now bubbling up from under the *Tiger's Eye*.

Yet, even with the song of the pyramid coursing through her with energy, the power of her voice still felt pent up. "Please Jie, stop." Traitor or not, if the Insolent Retainer was seriously injured…

A warm hand rested on her shoulder. Her heart must've jumped out of her chest. She turned. Lord Xu stood there, his ever-mischievous smile replaced by a grave expression.

"You said I would get my magic back." Her voice sounded petulant, like the sixteen-year-old lovestruck child she'd once been.

"You will." His stare bore into her. "You brought the fallen star. Give it to me."

Kaiya cast a glance at Jie, whose weapon went spinning to the ground. Maybe now she'd just surrender.

Fleet apparently had other ideas. His swords dragged across her body like shears, slashing through the remnants of web, yet never cutting open her clothes. Jie punched and kicked, unrelenting.

"Jie, stop." Kaiya clenched and unclenched her fists. Surely, Jie would hear reason.

Moving in a blur, Fleet jumped and drove his blade toward her face.

Kaiya's stomach leaped into her neck.

The madaeri's blade smashed through flesh and bone. Jie crumpled to the ground, motionless.

"No!" Kaiya choked on the lump in her throat. It couldn't be.

Her sworn sister was dead.

Tears welled in Kaiya's eyes. No. She'd lost both her doctor and her friend in the span of a few minutes. She started to run over.

Xu's grasp on her wrist restrained her. "The fallen star."

A friend had just died, and all he could think of was an artifact? Hands trembling, she unshouldered her pack and threw it to the ground. The flap popped open. The smooth sphere of the star shined from within.

Jie was dead. Her closest confidante, perhaps her best friend. Kaiya's chest tightened as she tried to pull out of Xu's grip.

Without releasing her, his gaze shifted up to the Tear. Xu withdrew the star and looked down at her friends. "Such a coincidence to find you all here." He turned back to her, even as she tried to pull free of his grip. "But where is Doctor Wu?"

"Here. And I have company."

Kaiya turned around to see Doctor Wu sprinting out of the trees. For someone so ancient, she ran fast. The Altivorc King loped up behind her. The doctor cleared the tree line, and the King skidded short.

Pointing his wand, he snarled. "I might not be able to get close, but I can still use this!" Energy beams zipped toward them in quick succession.

Without looking back, Xu waved a hand toward the King. The bolts crackled against an invisible barrier.

"What?" The King stared with wide eyes.

Xu turned to the King.

"Aralas!"

Aralas? Kaiya gaped. Certainly the Altivorc King must be mistaken. One too many rocks to the head, maybe. The elf angel had returned to the Heavens a thousand years before.

Xu laughed. "Of course I knew you would attempt something on the Godseye Conjunction." He held the fallen star aloft. "With all of this energy, the pyramid is very well protected, and now your minion is dead." He gestured toward Jie's body and shook his head.

The Altivorc King snarled and stomped off in the other direction.

"The other pyramids are also protected," Xu yelled at the King's back.

Kaiya's stomach clenched. This felt like another deception on top of all the others, this time perpetrated by Xu himself. "Having me bring the fallen star here had nothing to do with saving Cathay, did it?"

Xu favored her for a moment with an unreadable gaze. "What did Aralas tell your people before she returned to the Heavens?"

She looked to Fleet, who nodded emphatically. He'd asked her the same question during the escape from Iksuvius.

Kaiya closed her eyes. "Keep well the pyramids, reminders though they may be of your enslavement."

"Right," Fleet said. "If the King of the Orcs ever controls all the pyramids again, the Orc Gods will return on their flaming chariots."

"So you see, this is larger than Cathay." Xu patted her on the shoulder.

Kaiya shook her head. "The Teleri Empire and the altivorcs are allies. If they conquer Cathay, they will give the altivorcs the pyramid."

Xu pointed down into the valley below. Peng's rebellion and the imperial army faced off against each other, with Lord Wu's contingent ready to fall on Peng's flank. "The winner of this battle will have more than enough resources to defeat the Teleri."

"Not if they annihilate each other," Kaiya said. "And if Lord Peng wins, he might very well entreat with the altivorcs." Not likely, but there had to be *some* way to convince Xu to help.

"Behold!" Cousin Peng's voice carried through the night.

The dark sky above the battlefield shimmered. An undulating form of sparkling golden scales materialized. A real dragon, though far more graceful than Avarax's gargantuan form. Its eyes glowed red. Each claw had five talons, a symbol of the *Tianzi* and the Mandate of Heaven.

Kaiya gawped at it. The Guardian Dragon of Cathay, resembling all the paintings she'd ever seen. He'd only appeared a few times in history, during times of great change to anoint a new dynasty. The three hundred thousand soldiers below all sank to their knees in a ripple of kowtows.

Perhaps Lord Peng did hold the Mandate of Heaven. All of the strategizing and power struggles of the previous years had all led to this. She let out a long sigh.

Mumbling what amounted to a curse of sorts, Doctor Wu scoffed.

"Do you feel it?" Brehane pointed. "It feels like Shallow Magic. The pearl is an illusion."

Shallow Magic… a trick!

Anger welled up in Kaiya's chest, heat flaring in her face and burning off the *Tiger's Eye*. This was nothing short of sacrilege. That traitor Peng was trying to steal the Mandate of Heaven, and the sacred Guardian Dragon had fallen for his deception. "How dare he!"

"It is Lord Peng, after all." Doctor Wu snorted again, then muttered in a barely audible voice, "At least he could do the decency of getting the color right."

Gazing into the distance, Xu tapped his chin, looking a little like Tian with the gesture. He exchanged glances with Doctor Wu, then searched Kaiya's eyes. "Are you willing to sacrifice yourself for Cathay?"

She placed her hand over her belly. She bore the shame of possibly carrying Geros' twins, not to mention all the other things she'd done over the last month to ensure Cathay's safety. She nodded.

"Very well, *Dian-xia*." He turned to the Southerners. "Do you have a pyramid Greystone?"

"Whatever for?" Sameer's eyes must've been wider than tea cup saucers as they darted to Cyrus.

Cyrus clutched a pouch to his chest.

Xu's gaze lifted from the pouch. "So you do. I could take it from you, but I give you the choice. With it lies the opportunity for the princess to save her country."

The three exchanged glances. Cyrus shook his head, but then relented under Brehane's glare. He opened the pouch and withdrew a fist-sized gem, which resembled solid smoke.

"Old friend," Xu said to Fleet. "Take it and swap it with Guanyin's Tear at the pyramid's font."

Old friend? Kaiya looked from elf to Madaeri.

Fleet's mouth gaped open. "That's what the Altivorc King wants!"

"And what about our magic?" Cyrus kept shaking his head. "We will lose it, too."

"Technically, the King might be able to approach the pyramid." Xu looked back toward where the orc had disappeared. "However, I don't sense him, and with the Fallen Star and Doctor Wu, we can all have a tie to magic and can block his path."

Fleet gave a tentative nod.

Xu pointed toward the moons. "At the conjunction, swap them out. Follow me, *Dian-xia*."

Kaiya trailed Xu up the steps to the pyramid's sealed entrance. She looked at it, then at Fleet, who scrambled up the structure's side with effortless grace. She turned back to Xu. "Nobody has been in here since the War of Ancient Gods."

Xu nodded. "Aralas took this pyramid's Greystone on the day the Dwarves sacked the Temple of Tivar, and then placed a magical ward on the entrance." He pointed near the middle of the pyramid, where large gashes ripped into the smooth stone. "Do you know what that is from?"

"Damage from the Hellstorm."

"No." Xu shook his head. "You might as well know the truth. Avarax awoke during the Hellstorm. That night, he clashed with Cathay's Guardian Dragon. He left those scars in the pyramid."

Kaiya's thoughts spun. The legends and histories never spoke of such things. Avarax had awoken thirty-three years before… unless he hadn't replaced Rumiya, but had *been* Rumiya the whole time. "Why?"

"He wanted the Guardian Dragon's Flaming Pearl."

Her legs wobbled. She shot a hand out and clasped him for support. "When he took the form of the Dragon's Envoy, he told me something about the Flaming Pearl."

"I helped your ancestor hide the Pearl where Avarax could never reach it."

One shock after the other. Muscles she did not even know she had cramped her face. "The Founder?"

"No, his consort."

She took several deep breaths. Either Xu lied, or the histories she knew so well were false.

"Easy, *Dian-xia*." He placed a reassuring hand on the small of her back.

"Why are you telling me this?"

"I am going to open a portal to the Flaming Pearl." He grinned. "If you bring it back, perhaps you can win the Guardian Dragon's approval."

"Where is it?"

"So many questions." He looked up at the moons and yawned. "Great Peace Island."

Great Peace Island… where her ancestor had come from. Still, it didn't make sense. Thielas Starsong and Ayana Strongbow had whisked her all around the world with just a few words, and Xu needed a rare conjunction to pull it off?

And from what Brehane had said, the Greystone had created a magical deadspot around the pyramid in Selastyas. "How will you use magic if a Greystone blocks the pyramid's font?"

"Silly girl; you may have learned a lot about Artistic Magic, but it is still just a drop in the ocean." He pointed up. "The Godseye is upon us. You will not live to see the next time it comes."

Kaiya followed his finger. The three moons lined up, the larger Blue Moon forming the backdrop for the white, and inside the white, the smallest Iridescent Moon. The pulse of the world sounded louder and more jubilant than ever.

Xu lifted his voice in song. The world hummed around her, and the door into the pyramid swirled in a rainbow of lights. A gaping hole opened, and bright white light poured out.

It looked nothing like the inside of a pyramid.

Wind danced through the green leaves of a single cherry tree, in front of a dark stone road. And the light spilling from the pyramid entrance… was sunlight in the land beyond.

"You will be on your own in a strange land," Xu said. "Use the lessons you have learned. Listen for the Flaming Pearl's call."

"I still don't have the power of my voice."

"That could be a problem." He tapped his chin again. He then spoke a single word, and a shiny metal tuning fork appeared in his hand. "Wang Yuxiang left the

Dragon Pearl in the well of a burning temple. When you are near it, strike this on something hard."

So many things to remember. Kaiya's mind swirled; her knees felt like jelly. She took the tuning fork.

He studied her face. "Hurry. The portal will close behind you. I will open it again when the conjunction ends, in about a half-hour's time. If you are not back by then, you will be trapped there forever."

For Cathay, she would have to succeed. With a deep breath, she stepped through the portal.

Chapter 40:
Stranger

The low whir of cicadas droned in Kaiya's ears, and oppressive, humid heat hung in her lungs. She shielded her eyes from the bright sun, which seemed larger than usual.

The Iridescent Moon would help her get her bearings and measure time.

It was nowhere to be seen. Gauging the half-hour time limit would require plenty of guesswork.

She looked around, taking in the bizarre surroundings of her ancestor's homeland. If Xu was to be believed, this was indeed Great Peace Island.

It was like nothing she'd ever seen before. The smooth grey road warmed her feet through her shoes' thin soles. Perfectly square pavestones, all white with some bright flecks, lined either side. The buildings were blocky and unsightly, made of metal and stone, with windows of actual glass. Not like the beautiful stained glass the Estomari craftsmen made, but plain and clear.

A loud horn blared behind her, making her heart leap into her throat. She turned around.

A cart moving of its own accord glided toward her. A handsome man, whose fine features and skin tone suggested Eldaeri blood, leaned out from the front and yelled, "Aotsu ofu za ue, pyuboredo!"

The sounds made no sense, and she cocked her head.

He gaped. With arms covered in sleek blue sleeves, he gestured her to the stone-paved roadside.

Bowing, she moved to the side while the cart floated past her, its bottom not even touching the road. Magic, perhaps. Supposedly, as the gods' haven in this world, Great Peace Island was full of it. She stared at the man as it passed, and he stared back.

She turned around and gawked again.

A brown wooden gate with pitched tiled eaves rose before her. Though the architecture might have belonged in her own homeland, it looked ridiculously out of place with everything else around her. The plaque above, in white lettering, read *Original Mastery Temple*.

Kaiya's mouth hung open wider. This was the gate which the Founder himself had passed through, at least according to all the Imperial Family histories.

A young Cathayi man in brown pants and white shirt swept the area to the side.

She hurried over and bobbed her head. "Excuse me, I'm looking for a well."

He jumped back. Wide eyes darted around before settling on her. Strange sounds like those of the Eldaeri man's, spilled out of his mouth.

"I don't understand." She shook her head.

His eyes narrowed for a moment before he dashed off.

So rude! She turned back to the gate.

A stone obelisk at the side had some sort of inscription, a bizarre mix of the Cathay language and some other unintelligible scribble—like Xiulan's handwriting, only much uglier.

She read what she could. It mentioned her ancestor, Xinchang, though it used the symbols Zhitian, *Woven*

Field, for his surname. Something about death and fire and ruins.

"Ahr yuu oukei mihss?" a man called from behind her.

She spun around to find the cart driver. Tight blue clothes, smooth as a sharkskin she'd once seen, covered his entire body. She took several steps back.

"Ihtz oukei. Ai wount hahrt yuu." He held up both hands.

She shook her head. "I don't understand."

The man cocked his head.

Perhaps it was a waste of time. She searched for the Iridescent Moon, still not there. "I don't understand," she repeated in Arkothi, Ayuri, and finally, on a desperate whim, the secret imperial language.

His eyes and mouth widened. "How pyuboredo talk sun origin speech?"

That word again. "How do you speak the imperial language?"

His brow furrowed. "Im-Pe-Ri-Al language?"

She nodded.

"I learned in big study. Long ago, everyone speak it here." He opened his arms wide.

Wherever the big study was. Perhaps Great Peace Island had been conquered in the three hundred years since the Founder left, so much so that his language had fallen into obscurity. She forced a smile.

"So are you okay?" He reached for her sleeve and rubbed the fabric between his fingers.

Such poor manners. She pulled away. "Yes, just a little lost. I am looking for a well."

His head cocked again. "A we-ll?"

She pantomimed drawing water out of a well and drinking.

"You thirsty?"

Kaiya started to shake her head. But no, her mouth *was* dry. She nodded.

He flashed a naughty grin. "Would you like do tea?"

"I am in a hurry." She frowned. He was asking her to perform a tea ceremony, for a stranger no less.

His lower lip jutted out and he cast his eyes at the ground. "Okay. I get water." He turned back to his cart and reached inside. He withdrew the strangest clear water skin, with water visibly sloshing inside, and gave it to her. "Please."

She bowed her head in thanks and lifted the water skin to her lips. Nothing came out.

The man laughed. He extended his hand to the water skin. "May I?"

Confused, she returned it to him. With a twist of his fingers, a clear peel came off the top. He handed it back to her.

Bowing again, she took a sip. Cool and delicious.

"What is your name?" He smiled back.

"Kaia." At least, that's what it was in the imperial language.

"Well, enjoy visit Kaia. This place is kept from old times." He pointed past the gate.

"Thank you." Searching for the Iridescent Moon, still not there of course, she turned around and passed through. She glanced back to see the man staring at her, while talking to his... wrist.

He lifted his chin and waved. She turned back and looked straight ahead.

The gate opened up into a courtyard, framed by a building with thin metal columns and glass. The metal sign above was inscribed in large black letters, *Original Mastery Temple Little Study*.

It might as well have been gibberish, for all *Little Study* meant to her. Whatever the building was, it easily dwarfed the Hall of Supreme Harmony, though it did not match the architecture of all the other, even more gargantuan, structures beyond. Whoever built these enormous edifices must have had both incredible skill and a sick imagination. If not for the *Tiger's Eye* forming up, she might have vomited from the strangeness of it all.

At least the courtyard itself felt like home. The ground was paved in uneven stones, and up ahead were what appeared to be funerary tablets. In a row. A wooden signpost had a long list of strange names, all faded with time. She came closer to the row. One of the stones was marked with the name of her ancestor, though with the same incorrect characters for his family name.

As if he had died here, and not in Cathay. This outlandish place was just too disconcerting. Better to focus on finding the Dragon Pearl before the portal opened again, lest she spend the rest of her life among strangely-dressed Eldaeri who spoke broken Imperial. She closed her eyes and listened.

There. Somewhere beyond the courtyard, a low, steadfast pulse called to her, its reassuring beat reminiscent of her mother's heartbeat.

No, maybe Doctor Wu's heartbeat.

What a strange notion. Kaiya walked around the side of the building as the sound got louder, pausing only to look at another obelisk tucked into a small concave wall. *Original Mastery Temple Track* was inscribed in the single column, the symbols worn with time like the various ruins from the War of Ancient Gods.

Windows in the building slid open. Boys in high-collared black uniforms pointed at her and chattered, while girls in white blouses with red kerchiefs covered their giggles. All Eldaeri.

They'd been bloodthirsty conquerors when they arrived on the shores of Tivaralan three centuries before; maybe they'd conquered and occupied Great Peace Island since then, and wiped out all vestiges of its original culture. Though if they could build such colossal buildings, certainly they could sail across the seas and overwhelm the Teleri, Levastyans, and everyone else who stood in their way.

She shook the idea out of her mind and continued toward the source of the pulsation. On the other side of the building lay a broad field of orange-brown dirt. Boys in tight white uniforms ran back and forth. More than one paused to stare at her.

"Pyuboredo," some said.

The word didn't sound friendly. Ignoring them, she continued.

Up ahead, on the other side of the field, another concave wall surrounded a stone well. The throbbing sound came from there. Picking her way through the boys, she approached. Like the other ancient-looking places in the area, a stone obelisk bore identifying marks. *Original Mastery Temple Well*.

So this was it. Prominently displayed in such a conspicuous spot, surely the man from before knew of the well, but was too busy requesting tea ceremonies to guide her.

She peered down into its depths, from whence the pulse came. Withdrawing the tuning fork Xu had given her, she tapped it against the side of the well.

A clear tone rung out. Down in the well, something flared a gentle blue. Now how would reach it?

Several boys came up beside her. One looked down the well. "Wuht ahr yuu duuween, pyuboredo?"

She pointed down the well and pantomimed dropping something. "I lost a ball."

He squinted at her, then waved someone over. She turned.

A young woman, perhaps only a little older than her, approached. She wore a sharp black uniform like the boys in the windows, albeit with a pleated skirt instead of pants. "Mei ai herup yuu?"

"I lost a ball." Kaiya pointed back down into the well.

The woman's eyes widened. "You speak sun origin speech, but not hero speech?"

Kaiya snorted. These people thought their language belonged to heroes. Just like most of the other Eldaeri she had met.

If only Prince Aelward or Princess Alaena were here to translate for her. *Mei ai herup yuu.* If, no, *when* she saw them again, she would see if they understood the words. "Sorry, yes," she said.

The woman nodded, then turned around and yelled. A wiry young man jogged over and the two exchanged words.

He smiled at her. "I will check."

"Dangerous," Kaiya said.

He laughed. "No, it dry for thousand years. I down many times—" he gestured to the gathered boys. "—them, too. There are only rocks."

She gawked. The man bragged about violating the sanctity of a holy spot. "Look." She pointed into the well and struck Xu's metal again. The sound rung out and the blue light flashed again.

Everyone stared down the well, murmuring.

The man looked from the well to her and back again. He climbed up and over the edge, then shimmied down. "Dark! Hit again!"

Kaiya struck the clip against the well's lip. The sound rang out, clear and jubilant. Pale blue light flared up, flickering as the sound of rocks and stones shuffling and rubbing against each other echoed down below.

"Got it!"

Kaiya peered down the well. Some thirty feet down, a glowing blue ball the size of a human head cast the man's figure in blue sheen. He tucked it into his tight shirt and spider-climbed up. Time had to be running out. She searched for the Iridescent Moon—again, not there.

He emerged looking much like a pregnant woman. How she might look in several months.

If she survived this war.

He pulled the globe from his shirt. The blue light had faded, leaving a sphere caked with dirt and limestone sediment. It hummed deep in her ears, though it did not seem to bother anyone else.

The man offered it to her. "How you know it here?"

She smiled. "Mine."

"Never saw it down there before." The man took out a make-up case from his pocket. He held it up to her. Everyone else reached and held up make-up cases, bracelets, rings…

Kaiya took several steps back. They had been so helpful before, but now… perhaps they wanted to subdue her and take back the Pearl, this treasure that could possibly save Cathay.

The man held up a hand. "No. Good. Look." He presented his make-up case. In it flashed the image of her holding the Dragon Pearl. Dirt marred her complexion, and her hair looked as if birds had nested in it.

And… wait, his make-up case. It was like Xu's magic mirror. Indeed, the gathered children shouted and jostled to show her an image of herself, some projected from rings, others in the flat surfaces of their bracelets.

Whoever said the Eldaeri had no connection to magic was wrong. She pushed her way through the growing crowd of excited, shouting kids, shuffling back the way she had come. On occasion, she pulled her arm away from a child who grabbed her dress skirts. There couldn't be much more time left.

The Cathayi man from before came back, with several other Cathayi young men and women, all wearing excited expressions. They all chattered in that same strange language, but the Eldaeri cast scathing glances at them at gestured them away.

Despite the time constraint, she stopped in the courtyard, where her ancestor's grave marker stood. It couldn't be a grave marker.

No. He'd died in Cathay. It was a memorial of sort, perhaps commemorating the gods dispatching the Founder to unify Cathay. If only the entire sign made sense. She scanned her throng of followers for the woman, or either of the two men who could speak a halting version of the imperial tongue.

There. The woman waved. Kaiya beckoned her over, and she threaded a path between the kids.

"What does this say?" Kaiya gestured toward the sign.

The woman peered at it, then back at Kaiya. "Dead speech. I not learn."

"This place has history." The man who'd retrieved the Pearl sidled up to them. "A great lord cheat his boss.

Burn down old… shrine. Boss die. Many die. One thousand, two hundred years back."

Kaiya's brow furrowed. Had her ancestor been the traitor? He certainly wasn't the boss who'd died. And he'd arrived in Tivaralan three hundred years ago.

She bowed. "Thank you. I must be going." She turned back toward the main gate.

Outside the courtyard, the streets erupted in excited chatter as she exited. Lights swirled on top of another floating cart.

Eldaeri men and women in the most colorful, outlandish clothes surrounded other floating wagons. Several of the people held up shiny tubes to her. Two men in sleek, tight-fitting red and silver clothes looked at her and exchanged words. They strode with purposeful steps toward her.

"Furiz!" one yelled.

Kaiya skidded to a stop. The crowd charged toward her, past the two men, all yelling and shouting excitedly in the foreign tongue as they surrounded her. More than one shoved a tube toward her.

"Huu ahr yuu?"

"Wayrr yuu furam?"

"Wuutz za rahk?"

Kaiya's mind spun. "I don't understand. Does anyone speak the imperial language?" She looked for the moon. The portal should open soon.

"I speak!" A middle-aged Eldaeri man pushed his way to the front. Perhaps he could answer her questions.

Kaiya pointed back at the grave stones. "What does the sign say?"

"First, everyone wants to know who you are." He took her sleeve in his hands and rubbed his fingers back and forth. "You look pyuboredo, and no one has worn this material since ancient times."

These people had even worse sense of personal space than Ayuri folk. Kaiya pulled her arm back. "What is pyuboredo?"

He scratched his head. "The native people of Sun Origin. Like them." He gestured to the Cathayi, who clustered around the edges, boxed out by the Eldaeri.

That made no sense. "How do you speak the imperial language?"

"Im-pe-ri-al?" He squinted at her. "It's Sun Origin Speech. It used to be the language here. I am a teacher at the big study." He pointed off in the distance, then nodded at her. "Where are you from?"

She bowed. A teacher, even from an unknown Big Study, deserved respect. "Tivaralan."

"Where?" He shook his head.

Where indeed. Though the Tivaralan Eldaeri wouldn't admit it, rumor had it their ancestors had been criminals and exiles. Perhaps those who remained in their original homeland had never sailed west to Tivaralan.

The first man, the one who'd nearly run into her with his cart, spoke and gesticulated wildly. He pointed to the street, then up. People followed his gaze upward.

The teacher looked from the heavens to her. "They think you come from the stars."

Kaiya choked down her shocked laugh. As if she were a human angel! She shook her head. "No. Magic."

The man's jaw slackened. "What?"

The throng burst into excited chatter, everyone gesturing and turning to the street. The air shimmered, and black space opened.

The portal! People pointed and gasped.

Kaiya shouldered her way through the crowds. The portal had only stayed open for a moment when she arrived, and she had to get there now, if only to prevent any children from slipping through the ethers into a dangerous, war-torn land. The sea of people parted to make way for her.

She peered in. Xu stood there, his intense gaze locked on her. At her side, everyone gasped.

"Elestrae!" one yelled, mistaking Xu for an elf angel. It was the only word in their language she had picked out so far, and surely given the Eldaeri's mixing with elves in the past, they knew what one looked like. Others jostled to get a better glimpse.

With a frown, Xu beckoned her. She stepped toward the portal, then turned and found the individuals who had been so helpful. With a bow at the waist, she stepped backward through the portal.

The sound of cicadas and excited shouts ceased, immediately replaced by the ponderous thrum of the world's energy. The circle snapped shut, the sunlight blinking out. The sealed entrance to the pyramid stood where the door to Great Peace Island had been.

Kaiya turned to Xu. "That was Great Peace Island?"

"Yes." Xu grinned.

"In the three hundred years since my ancestor's departure, the Eldaeri conquered it."

He cocked his head. "Not exactly. I wouldn't know where to begin and explain. Now, did you retrieve the Dragon Pearl?"

Kaiya lifted it.

"Good. None worse for the wear after so many centuries." He pointed to the valley, where the fake Guardian Dragon of Cathay undulated in a circle above Cousin Peng's central banner. "The *Tianzi's* armies pay obeisance to Lord Peng as we speak. Go and present yourself before him."

Kaiya bowed low. "Thank you for your help. I will see you are well rewarded."

"Your ancestor said the same thing. Do you really think riches or power interest me?" Xu smirked. "Now go. If the Heavens smile on you, perhaps the true Guardian Dragon will reveal herself."

Herself? Xu must have misspoken, since everyone knew the Guardian Dragon was male.

Kaiya took the steps down from the pyramid entrance in twos, to where Cyrus and Doctor Wu tended to Sameer's wound.

The doctor raised her head and locked her gaze on her. Kaiya smiled, but then looked past the three to where a cloak covered Jie's body. Brehane laid the broadsword over it.

Poor Jie.

A lump formed in Kaiya's throat. Surely after travelling to the ends of the world and back, the *Tiger's Eye* must have finally faded, along with the life of the person who had put it on her in the first place.

She closed her eyes, pushing out a few tears. The energy of the world pulsed in her ears... yet still did not resonate in her heart. She came to Brehane's side and pulled the cloak back.

Fleet's sword had shattered the half-elf's pretty face from the nose up. Beyond recognition. Everything else remained unscathed, from her mouth down to her shoulder. Chest clenching, Kaiya looked up at her friends. "Where is her armor? Where's Fleet?" The scoundrel must have taken it.

Cyrus pointed up. Kaiya followed his finger's path to the pyramid. Guanyin's Tear sparkled at its top again, and Fleet now glided down the side, Greystone in hand. If not Fleet, then—

Brehane placed a hand on her chest. "I wanted to study the armor. I have never seen or felt magic like it before."

It made logical sense, but it still seemed inappropriate to leave her Insolent Retainer's body naked. She should be angry, and yet, only the logic of the choice resonated in her. The *Tiger's Eye* still held in check her emotions. She pulled the cloak back over her sworn sister's head.

Cyrus bowed. "I will ensure her remains are prepared for their final journey. She will leave this world the way she came, soul bared to Athran."

Kaiya nodded. Better that than to leave her to the carrion birds.

"Ten Thousand Years!" rang a chorus from the valley below.

With one arm in a makeshift sling, Sameer pointed down to where a sea of soldiers bowed in a ripple. "Come. You have an empire to save."

Chapter 41:
Brotherly Love

All the towns and villages Zheng Ming marched through had been devoid of enemy garrisons, or even small squads of light infantry enforcing Teleri rule.

Now, he rode his horse up to the abandoned earthworks outside of Huajing, Ma Jun at his side and an army behind him. Up ahead, the north gate stood agape. Only a small complement of Teleri soldiers defended it. Just as his scouts had reported.

Shouts, screams, and gunfire pierced the clear afternoon sky.

He pulled his horse up out of musket range and withdrew a looking glass. The Bovyans atop the gate… faced inwards. Toward the city. He passed the scope to Ma Jun. "What do you think?"

Ma Jun squinted through scope and lowered it. "If the Teleri aren't looking at us, they must be fighting someone on the inside."

Ming's thought as well. He turned to an aide. "Have the musketmen line up in ranks of three on the river bank. I will lead spearmen though the gates. If the enemy sees us, lay down volley fire."

The aide bowed and turned to relay the commands. In short order, the provincial army had deployed along the river.

Ming drew his *dao* and pointed at the gate.

His infantry surged across the bridge. Ming followed, watching. When Bovyans turned to see the commotion, his musketmen began volley fire. The enemy remained huddled low behind the wall's crenellations. Any who rose to shoot a crossbow met a barrage of muskets from both sides.

It was almost boring. By the time Ming passed through the gates, the gunfire had fallen silent, replaced by groans. Cathay soldiers crowded the square near the gates, cheering. Ming searched for a commander.

"Lord Zheng!" A young man in a uniform too big for him bowed at his waist. "Young Lord Zheng Tian told us to keep an eye out for you. He is nearby with your brother Shu. Come with me."

Ming dismounted and left his horse with an aide. "I would like to present myself before the *Tianzi*."

The messenger held his head at an angle which made it hard to see his face. "The *Tianzi* has sequestered himself in Sun-Moon Castle. No one has heard from him in weeks."

Weeks? Ming tugged his gloves off as he followed, Ma Jun in tow. "Then who is in charge?"

"Chief Minister Song is administering civilian affairs while General Tang leads the counteroffensive to retake the city."

No hereditary lords? With no one at the top, it was a wonder anything could get done. Ming cocked his head. "Who came up with such a strange idea?"

"The regent."

So a regent had been appointed, for the first time in nearly three centuries. Ming exchanged glances with Ma Jun. If the regent had left a minister and general in charge, he couldn't be all that competent. "Who is the regent?"

"Princess Kaiya."

Ma Jun's lip twitched into a grin.

If Ming's jaw hung any lower, he could probably lick the ground. "Where is she?"

"She drew the main Teleri army out of the city by fleeing south."

Ming's head spun.

Ma Jun asked, "How many Teleri occupy the city?"

"Four thousand. They control the southeast quadrant, along the White Duck Stream from the south gate to Qingjingtian Amphitheater."

So many memories. Qingjingtian was where he'd shot his friend Xie Shimin and saved several dignitaries. White Duck Stream had been where the insurgency began, with an attack on him. Ming pictured a map of the city in his mind. An assault across the stream would be difficult for both sides, depending on their numbers. "How many men do we have at our disposal?"

"Nine thousand imperial troops hold positions along the stream. Sixteen thousand Linshan provincial soldiers control the northern front to the east gate."

And fifteen thousand of his own men. Ming gritted his teeth. With a ten-to-one advantage—

"Lord Zheng!" a sultry voice called.

He turned.

A pretty girl, maybe sixteen or seventeen, batted long eyelashes at him. Wearing a plain pink dress, she looked familiar. She exposed the curve of her neck in a flirty tilt of her neck.

Now if only he could remember where he'd seen her. She was certainly too young for him to have slept with, though give it a year or so… He flashed his most charming smile. "It's been so long. My day is brighter now that you have come into it."

She pouted. "You don't remember me, do you?"

Ming tried to keep his smile enthralling, but undoubtedly looked sheepish despite his best efforts.

Her pout curved into an alluring smile. "Lin Ziqiu."

Lord Lin's daughter. No wonder. "Last time we met, you were just a little girl."

She swatted him on the shoulder in the most playful way. "No, last time was a year ago. You were about to give Princess Kaiya an archery lesson. I guess you only had eyes for her."

Ming hid a grin. If only the girl knew. The princess apparently had eyes for others, anyway.

"Well, come along now." She pointed toward a restaurant. "Your brothers are waiting for you."

Brothers? As in more than one? Ming followed her, watching the sway of her hips. She knelt at the door and bowed as she pulled it open. Ming flung his hair over his shoulder and winked as he passed through.

"Eldest Brother!" Panting, Shu rose from a chair.

At Shu's side, Tian bowed. "Eldest Brother."

The Kanin shaman and Fang Weiyong rose from a seat and embraced Ma Jun in a bizarre greeting. What was it with the natives? Not to mention Ma Jun and Fang Weiyong.

Ma Jun, in turn, wrapped his arms around Tian. "Do you have your memories back yet?"

Tian shook his head.

"I see." Ming glanced around the room. A handful of other teenagers, all dressed in plain clothes, turned their heads at angles when his gaze fell on them. Whoever they were, they didn't seem to be part of any army. He turned back to Tian. "I had expected to meet with our generals to discuss a strategy for finishing off the Teleri."

Tian gestured to the others. "My friends and I help the army. However, we don't have any say, except for the north gate."

The door closed and Ziqiu sashayed in. "Young Lord Tian urged General Tang to delay an assault on the north gate until we rescued Young Lord Shu." She tilted her chin in the cutest way toward his brother.

Ming looked around again. Someone was missing. The discourse was too normal, without a hint of sarcasm or insult. "Where's Jie?"

The silent response was awkward. The youngsters all stared at the ground. Yuha shook his head. The only sound came from outside as boots marched across the paved streets.

Tian scratched his chin. "Jie is unaccounted for. After she showed the imperial troops the secret path out of the palace, we've heard no word from her."

"How many days now?" Ma Jun asked.

Ziqiu held up four fingers.

Ming sighed. If anyone were to throttle the half-elf, it should be him. "I am sure she is all right. She is like a cockroach. It would take a lot to kill her."

Several sets of eyes glared daggers at him, including all the young people who'd avoided his gaze.

Ming sucked in a breath. "Well, I had better go meet with—"

The door slid open and a young woman slipped in. She bowed and dropped a rolled sheet of paper into Tian's hands. "An Eldaeri messenger bird arrived at Leina's house," she said.

Leina… Ming conjured an image of the exotic beauty he'd slept with on New Year's Day, just over a year ago.

Now why would a messenger bird go *there*? Tian unrolled the sheet, revealing a hypnotic combination of foreign symbols. His lips tightened as his eyes darted back and forth over the words.

"You can read that?" Ming asked.

Tian nodded. "Leina gave us the codes."

Which meant— "Leina was a spy?"

Ziqiu nodded.

Ming's heart felt like lead. It must've been her who planted the false evidence connecting him to the insurgency a year before. How gullible he'd been. "Where is she now?"

"Dead." Tian studied Ming's expression.

Ming shuffled on his feet. "So what does the message say?"

Tian looked back. "It appears the Teleri embedded a Nightblade in Peng's rebellion. He has won Peng's confidence. Peng has convinced Lord Wu to turn on the imperial army. Peng also has a secret he won't share with anyone."

Yet another betrayal. If the princess had met up with the imperial army, she'd be in danger. Ming sighed. "We need to warn her."

"Her?" Ma Jun raised an eyebrow.

"How?" Ziqiu gazed at him with adoring eyes. "The Teleri army stands between us and the princess."

Ming looked at Tian. Surely his little brother had an idea.

"We can't reach the regent," Tian said, "but we can send the emperor false information with the messenger birds."

Ma Jun grinned. "Something that will scare the Teleri into retreating."

"Or something that will get him to fight Peng first," Ming said.

Chapter 42:
Illusion of Power

Peng Kai-Long watched as the last group of imperial commanders swore their loyalty with three kowtows. Their soldiers, lined in orderly square ranks, followed suit.

"Ten Thousand Years to the *Tianzi!*" yelled General Lu.

"Ten Thousand Years!" repeated the imperial and provincial generals.

"Ten Thousand years!" droned the rank and file as they bowed in a wave from front to back. They knelt, pressed their foreheads to the ground, and stood again. Three times, each time repeating *Ten Thousand Years*. The Guardian Dragon circled above them, his red eyes and five claws gleaming as the Godseye Conjunction ended.

Kai-Long's heartbeat roared in his ears. His stomach somersaulted.

The Mandate of Heaven was his.

All without a shot fired, not a single Cathayi casualty. His genius! Years of planning, all culminating in a provincial lord's second son rising to the Jade Throne. Guns, firepowder, and a fleet of trade ships at his beck and call. Cathay would be wealthy and powerful again.

With all eyes on him, he puffed out his chest. "Men of Cathay! On this auspicious night, when the Godseye looks down on us, the Heavens have spoken. I humbly accept their mandate to bring order and prosperity to our great empire!"

The men broke out into resounding cheers.

Kai-Long raised a war fan, and the soldiers fell silent. "These are uncertain times. The Bovyan scourge tramples upon our sacred land as we speak. The infant *Tianzi* and the regents failed to stop them, and indeed let them in, either with incompetence or maybe even treason."

Jeers directed at Lord Liu Yong and Princess Kaiya erupted among the men. More than one used words reserved for prostitutes to curse her.

Kai-Long raised his fan to silence them again. Rival or not, it would not do to have the Wang royal blood—his own blood—deprecated in such vulgar terms. "I have annihilated one foreign invader; now it is time to crush another. Rest well, for at dawn we march." He chopped the fan northward, snapping it shut.

The armies roared in bloodlust. Kai-Long closed his eyes to revel in their applause. Convince a people their precious homes were under attack, and a clever man could bend them to his will. Just like his ancestor, the Founder. Once Kai-Long defeated the Teleri and consolidated his rule over Cathay, he would liberate Ankira from the Madurans and civilize the Wilds.

A hush settled over the ranks of men, their clamor falling from its crescendo. That wasn't supposed to happen, not unless he silenced them himself. Kai-Long opened his eyes. At the far end, the sea of soldiers began to part. He squinted. Several figures approached.

Cousin Kaiya among them.

Whore. Slut. Harlot. Kaiya flinched at the barely audible murmurs. Geros had whispered those insults in her ear, and now her own countrymen dared utter them.

Hurt as the words might, none stung as much as *traitor*. Not when she had sacrificed so much for the nation.

Kaiya's lip trembled as she fought back tears. Curse the *Tiger's Eye*, coming and going at the most inopportune moments! Now, when she needed to be resolute, it failed her, stripping her of her wits. The power of her voice, gone. Her dignity, torn away. All she had was some rock cradled in her arm and no idea how to use it.

Cousin Peng had won the soldiers over with some flowery words, and an illusion of a flaming pearl. The Guardian Dragon of Cathay fluttered in circles above, his ruby red eyes sparkling in the moonlight.

Certainly a great, magical being should be able to see through the deception. Hopefully Brehane would be able disperse the magic.

A reassuring hand pressed between her shoulder blades. Jie had always been the one to do that, but now, the deep pulse vibrating into her heart could only come from Doctor Wu's steadfastness. Brehane and Sameer followed several steps behind, their breaths short and shallow. Yes, they were as nervous as her.

"Don't worry," Brehane said. "I feel the magic. I can dispel the pearl illusion."

The Mystic's wobbling voice did little to inspire confidence, but Kaiya nodded. With one hand, she reached over and grasped the pole of an imperial banner. The soldier holding it bowed and released it. If at least some men recognized her legitimacy, perhaps not all was lost.

She held the banner aloft. "I—" Her voice choked until she cleared out the lump. "I, the regent for *Tianzi* Liu Yiping, demand an audience with *Lord* Peng Kai-Long."

Around her, several of the imperial troops sank to a knee, fist to the ground. Still others remained standing, their raised heads not concealing their scowls. At least in the eyes of some, Cousin Peng had succeeded in painting her as both conspiratorial and incompetent, if the combination was possible.

His voice now rose above the silence, from his place far ahead. "I thank you for your service, but as an adult *Tianzi*, I do not require a regent. Men, please escort the princess to a tent of honor."

An assassin's knife would doubtless find her throat in that tent. Kaiya straightened her back and squared her soldiers. Even without the power of her voice, she still knew how to project the image of imperial prestige. "*Jue-Ye*," she said, using the address for a *Tai-Ming* lord, "You have not made your oaths in the Temple of Heaven. You do not even hold the imperial seal. Until then, your claim might be considered… treasonous."

Though his smirk was indiscernible from the distance, it carried in his voice. "Look above, Kaiya. The Guardian Dragon of Cathay has already appeared twice to anoint me, to celebrate the defeat of a foreign invader and the unifying of our brothers in arms. Both tasks *you* failed to accomplish."

Over half the soldiers pounded the ground with their spear hafts, cheering, "Peng, Peng, Peng."

Behind her, Brehane barked several syllables in the language of Shallow Magic, setting her considerable power against whoever conjured the flaming pearl illusion. Her spell stopped on a hard grunt. Weapons rasped out of sheaths. Someone crumpled to the ground.

Kaiya spun around. Brehane sprawled in the trampled grass, her eyes staring up into her skull. A soldier raised the butt of his spear. Had she completed her spell, or had the strike to her head cut her words short? Other warriors surrounded Sameer with naked blades as he brandished his *naga*, left-handed.

And up above, the Guardian Dragon still danced in circles over Cousin Peng, still held in thrall by the fake pearl.

No, there could be no bloodshed. Kaiya lifted the banner. "Men of Cathay, stand down. Sameer, sheathe your weapon. Fleet…" She looked around. The madaeri was nowhere to be seen.

However, several of the Cathay soldiers backed off. Sameer lowered his weapon. Doctor Wu pushed through the men like a breeze through flower petals, and kneeled by Brehane. Silence fell over the armies again.

"Bring the traitor and her friends to me." Peng's snarl echoed in the valley.

Hands seized her elbows, though she cradled the Pearl as if her life depended on it. It probably did. Another soldier shoved her forward. She caught her balance and straightened again. Other men pushed forward, either to her aid or to restrain her.

"At ease." She kept her voice level and authoritative, just as her father would have. The soldiers back off, giving her space. Lifting her chin, she strode forward. The ranks of men cleared a path, though their expressions varied from anger to sympathy, lust to admiration.

Each step drew her closer to Cousin Peng, while the sounds of Sameer's and Brehane's breathing disappeared into the thousands of breaths around her.

Nobody was there to protect her if Peng decided to behead her on the spot. At least when she'd faced down Avarax, she'd had Sameer, Jie, and an army of Paladins and priestesses there to support her. Now, with Jie dead and her friends all held at the back, she only had herself to rely on.

Then again, Peng was no dragon, despite what he might think of himself. She had thwarted his plans several times. Her steps matched the beating of her heart. Firm. Resolute.

Then something pushed into the back of her legs.

She fell to her knees, prostrate before the outcrop where Peng stood gloating. Someone pulled her sash from behind, yanking her robe flaps open to her shoulders and sending Tian's pouch clattering to the ground.

With one hand holding her dress together, Kaiya dropped the Pearl and reached for the pouch. A soldier's boot stomped down and barely missed crushing her hand. The motion inadvertently kicked Xu's tuning fork, which skittered closer, just within reach.

The tuning fork, the Pearl, the dragon.

Kaiya swiped it up and tapped it to a rock. A clear sound rang out. The Pearl hummed out and glowed a faint blue through its dirt and limestone crust. Certainly that would get the Guardian Dragon's attention! She looked up.

No, the dragon still swirled in lazy circles high above Peng, its glowing red eyes locked on the fake pearl.

Stupid dragon! Kaiya struggled to stand, but a hand restrained her shoulder. Another wrenched the tuning fork from her hand. She glared back at the man, then at Peng. "How dare you? I am a princess of Cathay—"

The soldier tossed the tuning fork up to Peng, who caught it. With a furrowed brow, he turned it over in his hands. Then he looked up and jabbed an imperious finger at her. "This woman is no princess. She is nothing but a whore who slept with an enemy in order to undermine Cathay from the inside."

The gall! She tried to rise again, but her captor held on to the lapels of her gown. To stand would likely rip her dress away, baring her to three hundred thousand men.

Peng waved dismissively toward the back. "She cavorts with Southerners who do not have Cathay's best interest at heart. I offered her a place of honor, and instead, she calls my legitimacy into question." He lifted his chin to a man beside her. "General Lu, go put her with the Maduran prostitutes where she belongs."

Kaiya turned. There stood the proud general she had spurned years before, in favor of Prince Hardeep... Avarax. His stare burned with hatred. Like Geros' the first time he'd... Her chest constricted.

He marched toward her and grabbed her wrist. *Tiger's Eye* or not, anger welled inside, replacing the fear.

And with it, something sparked inside her.

Power.

A long-forgotten friend. She scowled at General Lu and sung her command: "Kneel."

The resonance of the world, so strong in this place near the pyramid, amplified by the closeness of the moons, flowed through her. Stronger than when she faced Avarax.

General Lu dropped to his knees. Soldiers behind him followed suit, rippling out in a wave of obeisance.

Peng gaped at his hand, where Xu's tuning fork now vibrated of its own accord.

Lying ignored near a bush, the Dragon Pearl hummed louder in answer. Rays of blue flared between the cracks in the covering sediment, pulsing at the same frequency as the tuning fork, the same frequency as her command.

Similar, yet different, from Avarax's gemstone. Replicating the tone, she lifted her voice in song.

With the music, her spirit soared.

The Dragon Pearl lifted off the ground, growing larger and floating higher up into the air. Everyone's gaze followed it, including hers.

But still not the Guardian's!

Peng raised both arms to the dragon. "The Guardian Dragon still recognizes me!" With a cackle, he stared down at her. "You are no Dragon Charmer." He pulled a *dao* from his sash and pointed at her. "Kill her!"

Many of the soldiers rose and drew swords or levelled spears. General Lu seized her wrist and pulled her to him. With his free hand, he covered her mouth. Kaiya struggled in his grasp.

"Drop your weapons and kneel." A loud, yet flowery female voice echoed from the army's rear.

Spears, daggers, crossbows, muskets, and swords clattered to the ground. Every last man sank to his knees. General Lu's grip went slack as he knelt. The sound washed over Kaiya like a tidal wave, compelling her to her knees as well.

An enormous chain of silvery white scales snaked through the banners and flags, whipping them with a gust of wind. Kaiya shielded her eyes and turned as the brightness surged closer. Squinting, she snuck a glance just as the dragonhead turned, revealing silvery whiskers and luminous blue eyes. Beautiful eyes, like…

The dragon swallowed up the Pearl and vaulted skyward, growing larger as he ascended. Larger and more magnificent than Peng's dragon. It wasn't possible. Unless two dragons served as messengers of the gods.

Though still smaller than Avarax, the silver dragon now dwarfed the golden one, and was far more beautiful. Long and elegant, each silver scale glistening in bright white. Spindly claws, like a willow's branches. And the hum.

Kaiya listened, trying to decipher the unique resonance of the two powerful beings. The familiar buzz of the Dragon Pearl combined with… no, it was just one sound. Come to think of it, the golden dragon had been silent this whole time, not emitting the energy pulses like Rumiya said all dragons did.

The pearl wasn't the only illusion.

The silver dragon coiled around the imposter, to three hundred thousand collective gasps. When the silver dragon pulled straight, the golden one blinked out of existence, pearl and all. The remaining dragon could only be the one true Guardian of Cathay.

While everyone else repeatedly looked up and bowed, Kaiya tore her gaze away from the spectacle and sought out Cousin Peng. Sword hanging loosely in his hand, eyes fixed upward, he staggered to his feet and backed away from the edge of the outcropping.

The Guardian Dragon pointed a talon at him. "Usurper," she—she?—said, voice echoing into the night.

A sea of heads turned to face her shamed cousin. Peng shrunk back.

The Guardian Dragon pointed a talon down at Kaiya. "The gods decree that only Wang Kaiya, daughter of the late *Tianzi*, is fit to be regent. Let her wisdom guide her in choosing the next *Tianzi*."

Kaiya's heart swelled.

Still… wisdom? Not yet twenty, she wasn't even considered an adult. Her eyes found Tian's lockpick pouch in the grass, and she picked it up. She looked up.

The Guardian Dragon swooped in graceful circles three more times, then flashed out in a majestic bloom of light more magnificent than New Year's fireworks.

"Ten Thousand Years to the regent," someone called out.

"Ten Thousand Years!" the chorus repeated. The imperial and provincial armies bowed before her, even those from Cousin Peng's own province.

Peng.

Kaiya looked to the outcropping above, where her cousin had just groveled. Now it was abandoned. He must've fled.

No, they couldn't let the traitor escape, to stir up more trouble. Not again. He couldn't have gotten far. She cleared her throat… and the magic was gone again. The *Tiger's Eye* must have locked away her emotions once more. No matter, the legitimacy conferred by the Guardian Dragon of Cathay was magic enough.

"Soldiers of Cathay," she called, bringing the men to silence. "The rebel Peng Kai-Long is hiding among us. I will reward a silver *jiao* to whoever brings me his head. Ten thousand gold *yuan* if you bring him to me alive."

Peng Kai-Long picked his way among the forest of his provincial army tents as quickly and quietly as he could. How rapidly fortunes changed. He had been just one step from the Dragon Throne, and now he huddled like a scared rat.

All because of a meddling, impossibly lucky girl, who had escaped three, no four… actually, *five* of his attempts on her life. If only he had snuffed her out years ago.

He would, if it was the last thing he ever did. Clenching his dagger, he paused by the right tent and peeked in.

The Aksumi Mystic, still maintaining his illusion as a handsome young Nanling provincial officer, was filling a pack.

Kai-Long slipped in. "You. I need your help. I can still reward you."

"With what?" The Mystic turned around with a smirk.

"I have jade and gold stashed away."

"Do you now?" The Aksumi's eyes glinted. "What do you need?"

"A disguise. One that can be maintained, like the baubles you made for me in the past." The ones he'd used to sneak Kaiya out of Sun-Moon Palace, only to have her survive the assassination he'd planned.

"I can do that." The Mystic studied him from head to toe. "What did you have in mind?"

A plan within a plan, and a contingency—just like the way he had risen from second son of a provincial lord to almost-*Tianzi*, by hijacking Chief Minister Tan's and old Hong's schemes.

He grinned. "Make me look like an old Maduran woman. Not too old." Knowing his cousin, she'd personally check on the wellbeing of the servants and prostitutes, which would put her closer to his knife.

The Mystic nodded. He produced a light bauble from his pocket and spoke a single word. The light winked out, and he dropped it to the floor. He barked out a long string of foul-sounding grunts worthy of feral dogs fighting for scraps, and the bauble flashed.

"Take it," he said.

Kai-Long snatched it up.

The man withdrew a hand mirror from his pack and held it up.

Looking into the mirror, Kai-Long suppressed a gasp. Fine lines crinkled his now-bronze skin. Coarse black hair framed a middle-aged face. Not particularly pretty, but that would prevent the soldiers from trying to take advantage of him.

"Keep the bauble with you at all times." The Mystic yawned. "Now, how about my payment?"

Kai-Long gestured toward the tent flap. "Let's go get it."

Nodding, the Mystic turned to the doorway.

Dagger in hand, Kai-Long covered the fool's mouth and slashed his throat. The Mystic clawed at his neck and choked on his words.

"Your payment," Kai-Long said. "For lying to me about summoning the Guardian Dragon."

The man's fingers went limp first, then his entire body. His illusion remained the same, which must mean he held a bauble as well.

Kai-Long patted the corpse down and was rewarded with a hard lump beneath his sash. When Kai-Long dug it out from next to the man's still-warm flesh, the body's form shimmered back to a middle-aged Aksumi male.

Kai-Long peeked out the tent. With no one around, he dragged the remains and dumped them in the closest tent.

Then he went back to the Mystic's pack and looked at the mirror. With just one of the baubles touching his bare skin, he appeared as either the young Cathay male or the middle-aged Ayuri female.

With one in each hand, he appeared as an androgynous, half-Cathayi, half-Ayuri mix. Perhaps a homelier version of Hong's concubine—yet another person who deserved retribution for her role in his downfall.

All the easier to accomplish now that he had three different disguise combinations. Now, he just needed appropriate clothes. He fished an extra uniform from the Mystic's belongings and then tucked the Cathayi bauble next to his skin.

It was time to seek out the Water Snake agent to help him with an assassination.

Chapter 43:
Race to Vengeance

Peng Kai-Long looked to where the real Guardian Dragon had just anointed his hateful cousin; a woman, no less.

Gone. Of course, in the histories, the Guardian Dragon had only made brief appearances. It didn't feed hungry mouths or reward men with treasure and women. When it came down to it, legitimacy only went as far as happy men with swords took it.

For now, it meant a level of discretion. He crept out into the night, hoping to avoid all the men searching for him. He'd taken three steps when a hand clamped down on his shoulder, sending a jolt up his spine. He turned around to meet the gazes of several Nanling provincial soldiers.

"Oh, Commander." The one who had grabbed him stepped back and bowed. The others followed suit.

Right. With the magical disguise, Kai-Long could rove with impunity among all the men searching for him. Find out who he could trust and who deserved a knife in the back. He nodded, allowing the men out of their bows.

"Lord Peng was last seen somewhere around here," one said. "Have you seen him?"

Kai-Long shook his head and pointed toward the supply tents. "Lord Peng is smart. If I were him, I would be collecting provisions."

One of the men snickered. "Lord Peng would never survive without a comfortable bed to sleep in."

Kai-Long memorized the man's face. "He is more resourceful than that. Remember, he masterfully deceived the imperials when he fled the capital and returned home to take back his province. If you do not respect your enemy, you can never defeat him. Now go check the supply tents!"

Wide-eyed, the men bowed and jogged off. With a snort, Kai-Long stalked off toward another tent. No wonder things had turned against him, saddled by such stupid men. Just outside the flap, he paused.

"May I help you, Commander?" a male voice said from behind.

Kai-Long spun around. There stood the Water Snake agent, still disguised as a messenger. Kai-Long beckoned him in.

Folding his arms over his chest, the spy narrowed his eyes. No, one of his hands went into the folds of his robe.

Kai-Long pinched the bauble under his sash and pulled it from his skin.

The agent's eyes widened. "Lord Peng."

"Yes, now come in." Kai-Long pushed through the flap.

The spy padded in after him. "What use are you to us now? I should just capture you and collect the reward the regent is offering."

"A dead woman can't fulfil a reward."

The agent shook his head. "What did you have in mind?"

Kai-Long shrugged. "You are a messenger, after all. You can get close to her. Kill her."

"Why would my clan want that?"

"Because once she is out of the way, the nation will look for leadership. I will be there to step in. When I do, your clan will be rewarded."

The spy chuckled. "I do believe a Guardian Dragon labelled you a usurper."

"It could've been yet more magic. She had a Mystic with her."

"Unconscious."

Kai-Long harrumphed. Nobody would remember all those details. "What do you have to lose? As long as the princess is regent, the Black Lotus will serve the *Tianzi*. At least with me, you have a chance."

The spy's eyes searched Kai-Long's. "Very well." He turned and slipped out of the tent.

Kai-Long followed. Now time to find General Lu. The imperial soldiers looked up to him, and he had no love for the princess. Then again, he had laid a hand on her, so he must be with the Maduran prisoners by now.

As the agent crept off in one direction, Kai-Long headed toward the Madurans, the ones he had been forced to spare as a demonstration of his leniency. Groups of soldiers still dashed about, his name on their lips.

He searched the faces in the makeshift stockade. All Ayuri males. The single Cathay guard paced outside the fencing, his gaze following his rushing comrades.

Just beyond stood the large tent for the servants and whores, unguarded. For the most part, they had been casually supervised to prevent acts of sabotage, but all had been docile and compliant.

Except the pretty noblewoman who refused to let a man touch her.

"*Jie-xia*, the prisoners are this way." General Lu's voice carried from not far in the distance.

That turtle's egg must have submitted to her, and she, in a show of magnanimity, must have forgiven his transgressions. So predictable, down to her visit to the servants and prisoners. The sound of jingling armor and heavy boots approached.

Ducking into a tent, Kai-Long swapped the magical baubles. To confirm the transformation, he withdrew the mirror. The plain, middle-aged Ayuri woman stared back at him. The voices got closer. Kai-Long dashed from the tent. To his right, the princess walked with General Lu, the halfling, and the Ayuri Paladin with his sword arm in a sling. The Mystic and doctor were nowhere to be seen.

He pushed the flap aside and slipped in. Several women gawked at him. It didn't make sense, since he should look just like one of them.

"Who are *you*?" the pretty noble said.

Of course, they wouldn't recognize a newcomer. Thank the Heavens he spoke perfect Ayuri from his years as a diplomat in Vyara City.

He opened his mouth… and then shut it. Even if he *looked* like an Ayuri crone, he would still *sound* like himself. Or would he? Not worth the risk. He pointed to his mouth and shook his head. Let them think he was mute.

An older woman—likely the one who had glared at him with such anger when he defeated the Maduran army—appraised him. "Why are you wearing *their* uniform?"

Curse the Heavens! He'd been in too much of a rush. He now pointed out of the tent and mouthed, *I lost my clothes and a soldier loaned me his*. He gestured toward a pile of clothes as he worked his arm out the uniform sleeve. *Let me borrow one*.

With a raised eyebrow, the noblewoman offered him a *sari*. Outside, General Lu's voice grew louder. They couldn't be more than twenty feet from the tent. Curses! He struggled out of the robe, revealing sagging breasts and rolls of flesh on his stomach.

How horrendous! And amazing. The magic was so… complete. Who would have ima—the bauble slipped off his skin before he caught it. His own honey tone and smooth muscle flared for that split second before returning to the Ayuri illusion.

The noblewoman narrowed her eyes at him.

The tent flap opened.

Kai-Long turned to see who it was.

General Lu froze in place, staring at Kai-Long's exposed chest. Kai-Long crossed his arms, one hand squeezing the bauble, the other reaching for his dagger caught in the folds of cloth.

"General, please wait outside. Fleet, out." The princess guided him out with just a wave of her hand. Now, it was just her.

She looked to Kai-Long. "I am sorry for the intrusion." She averted her gaze to the others. "Has everyone been well cared-for?"

With the bitch's back turned and nobody guarding her, she didn't stand a chance.

The low murmurs of Ayuri in the spacious tent reminded Kaiya of the journey to Vyara City. Meeting with dignitaries. Dancing for that buffoon Prince Dhananad. Learning Hardeep's true identity. And of course, singing to Avarax.

Perhaps the Guardian Dragon had been right: perhaps she did have wisdom, garnered from so many experiences.

Among those experiences was meeting this beautiful young Ayuri woman somewhere… but where?

A musician or dancer, perhaps.

Or maybe one of Dhananad's wives. Whoever she was, she now glared at the half-naked, middle-aged woman with such hatred. There must have been some dynamic that had developed over the weeks on the march.

One which no amount of wisdom would diffuse. It wasn't her place, either; not among foreigners who had to be somehow repatriated. Kaiya offered a nervous smile.

Then, behind her, the middle-aged woman moved in a rapid ruffling of clothes. The young woman surged forward in a blur, faster than anyone Kaiya had ever seen, besides… Paladins.

Women screamed. Kaiya's sleeve sheared with a rasp. Pain bit into her arm. She turned to see the middle-aged woman on her back, dagger in hand. The young woman stomped on the other hand with blinding speed, sending bones crunching. It sounded like glass shattered in her hand.

The woman's face disappeared, replaced by—Cousin Peng.

His expression filled with a hatred that made Kaiya shiver. Wincing at his hand, which curled at a strange angle, he staggered to his feet. The tent flap opened, and Sameer, Fleet, and General Lu rushed in.

They were too far away. Peng lunged forward with a stab.

The woman wrapped a sash around his wrist and pulled his arm to the side. With a deft twist, she plucked the dagger out of his hand.

Peng's eyes darted over the tent, his gaze pausing for split seconds over weapons, drawn and sheathed. With a sigh, he raised his hands above his head.

"May Yanluo drag you to hell, Kaiya." He spat her name.

Kaiya sighed, too. The Cathay civil war was finally over, Peng Kai-Long finally in custody—

The young woman zipped in toward him. Faster than the eye could see, the blade whispered across his body eight times in a split-second before she jumped out again. He stared as blood spurted from several surgical slashes over major arteries. He collapsed to his knees.

The woman curled her lip. "That was for every Maduran you lured into Cathay. For every prisoner you butchered in cold blood." She darted in again and yanked Peng's head back by his hair.

Kaiya held a hand up. Deserved as it might be, this was nothing short of murder. Paladins did not dispense justice this way. They needed to drag Peng before the rest of the hereditary lords for proper punishment.

"Sohini!" Sameer gaped. "What are you doing here?"

The woman looked back at him and her scowl softened. Her knife lowered. She looked… embarrassed.

That face, that expression. Kaiya sucked in a breath. The woman—Sohini—was no Paladin. She was a Golden Scorpion, *the* Scorpion who'd tried to poison her and defeated Jie.

Sohini's mouth curled into a sneer. "This is for betraying my prince." She plunged the dagger deep into Peng's throat with a sickening squish.

He crumpled into a twisted heap of *sari* and uniform, his lifeblood soaking into the tent floor.

The Golden Scorpion Sohini pushed Sameer to the side by his bad arm and flashed out of the tent. Sameer whirled around and gave chase.

Kaiya's mind spun. So much had just happened. The woman who had tried to ambush her had reappeared into her life. Then disappeared just as fast, taking Sameer with her. Cousin Peng now lay on the ground, probably dead from the brutal attack.

Fleet rolled the body over and shrugged. "Can't say he didn't deserve it."

Maybe so, but what would the army say? All of it had happened in the close confines of a tent, with only a handful of witnesses. She had promised justice, not revenge. No one would collect the reward for Peng's capture. And the Guardian Dragon and her Pearl were no longer around to reaffirm the Mandate of Heaven.

"*Jie-xia,*" a voice called from the entrance to the tent.

Kaiya turned to see a large messenger kneeling there, fist to the ground. "Speak," she said.

"The Teleri have launched an attack on Lord Wu's rear."

Chapter 44:
Dance of Heavens

Geros scanned the valley, trying to decipher the positions of the Cathayi imperial and provincial armies. The messenger birds between him and the Nightblade embedded with Peng's rebellion had ceased three days prior, and now he acted on what he had known at the time: Peng's armies faced off against the imperials, with Lord Wu's provincial army about to fall on the imperial flank.

Once Lord Wu descended, Geros had planned to lead his men to occupy that position. It would've not only provided a commanding view of the battle, but also a superior vantage point from which to engage whichever army emerged victorious… and depleted.

Yet Lord Wu had left long before the Teleri army had arrived, and from this position, it was impossible to tell if they planned to engage the Cathayi imperial troops or *join* them. He looked back at his own orderly ranks, the Bovyans showing no signs of wear after they had stolen a march on his enemies.

Past First Consuls had noted in their memoirs that he Eye of Geros allowed them to see details more clearly, and see in the dark, but he'd yet to experience it. He held his hand back to an aide. "My looking glass."

The aide thumped his fist to his chest and withdrew the scope.

Geros swiped it and took in the scene.

Peng's troops seemed to be in disarray, even though there were no signs of a battle having taken place. Strange, since Peng had proven a capable leader. Geros shifted to Lord Wu's men. They looked to be… resting?

If only he knew more. Tivar take the Nightblade for failing to maintain communication! Or perhaps they had ferreted him out.

Geros examined the imperial troops. They were breaking camp, when they should be annihilating Peng's disorganized army. On a hillside outcrop, at the close end of the imperial armies on Lord Wu's left…

Princess Kaiya.

He snapped the looking glass shut and turned back to his aide. "How many Cathayi soldiers did we count?"

The aide pointed at the groups in turn. "Lord Peng has a hundred and twenty thousand. The imperials, a hundred and fifty thousand. Lord Wu, thirty thousand."

In total, a nearly six-to-one advantage over his own forty-five thousand men. Yet none of the enemy were Bovyans, and in a pitched hand-to-hand battle, the enemy's muskets would be useless. If Peng saw the tide turn in his favor, ambition might get the better of him. Might.

For Kaiya, Geros would take that gamble.

He turned to his command team. "The Cathayi outnumber us, but their closest group is resting and the rest are not prepared. If we stretch out in thin ranks, we will be too close for them to use guns once we engage. General Tanos will attack their left-center, while General Baros falls on their left rear flank. General Kros will hold our own left flank. I will personally slide behind Baros and attack their central command."

Which was Kaiya.

General Baros gawked at him. "Your Eminence, if they see you coming, Lord Peng will be able to fall on your right and isolate you."

"Lord Peng's men are too disorganized, and he might very well turn on her… I mean, them." Another risk he would take, since this might now be his only chance to seize the princess and his unborn son. He glared at the men, who bowed their heads. "Now attack! Quickly and quietly, before they can organize."

The men all thumped their chests and hurried to their divisions.

Geros looked back at the valley, where his prize waited unawares. Soon, very soon, she would be his again.

Or he would be dead.

The energy of the world hummed in Kaiya's ears, providing a backdrop for the sounds of war. Metal clashed on metal as the Teleri smashed into Lord Wu's rear. Boots stomped, men screamed, all in a symphony of slaughter. If only she could connect to the energy, harness it into her voice, she could turn this battle into a rout. There had to be a way.

Emotions.

Enough emotions would topple the *Tiger's Eye*, hopefully for good. Kaiya conjured up memories, seeing if they would stir her feelings.

Hardeep's enchantment and Avarax's deception.

Zheng Ming's charm.

Tian treating her like dirt in their escape from Iksuvius, followed by his affection in the Wilds.

The love only she evoked in him.

The joy and rapture of making love to him.

Geros taking her.

Her father's death.

Tian's death.

Jie's death.

She was now all alone in this world. Yet, all the images and memories felt like she was reading a sterile, historical account of her life. The energy of the world remained close and torrential, but walled off, just like when Geros had collared her with the grey metal neck ring.

Hand to her throat, Kaiya looked down at the battle from the outcropping. Lord Wu's men were fleeing from the onslaught. The Teleri snaked along the provincial army's edges in the most bizarre fashion to her untrained eyes.

It seemed inconceivable that such a small force could even stand a chance against a much larger one. Beneath her, Cathayi officers scurried about, mobilizing their men to arms.

And then she saw it: the Teleri reserve slipped behind the wall formed by their forward troops. Headed where? She followed the curve of the battle lines, meandering down the mountain, along the road…

To her.

A lump formed in her throat. The reserve troop, marching double-time or perhaps faster, came for *her*. Like the Founder's victory at Narrow Barrel Valley on Great Peace Island. Facing an army twenty-five thousand with under two thousand of his own men, he had killed the enemy lord, and the opposition crumbled.

This time, they didn't plan to kill the leader. Geros undoubtedly had other plans for her.

And she had no one to protect her. Her generals and senior officers raced among the men in a vain attempt to organize them. Sameer had run off after the Scorpion. Brehane—she would be using her magic by now if she were able. Perhaps Doctor Wu was still tending her wounds. And Fleet… Fleet had disappeared yet again, after waylaying a messenger to who knows where.

As her gaze swept across the valley, something glinted in the corner of her eye. Right by her side, where she had somehow missed it.

Xu's magic mirror, the one she'd carried to Vyara City and back, rested on a folded pile of fine silk.

Instead of her reflection on its surface, several black words burned on a parchment background. The title of another book, perhaps. She read.

When a regent looks the part, her people will listen.

Never a straight answer from that elf, even in his letters. She knelt down and ran her fingers across the gold embroidered blue silk. She lifted it, revealing an outer robe with five-clawed dragon patterns stitched into it. It was beautiful. A silver-threaded sash tumbled out.

She appraised her plain travelling dress, light brown and soiled with mud, dirt, and blood. Her own sash, hastily wound back after General Lu tore it off, was creased and ratty. In whole, certainly not the bearing of a princess, let alone a regent.

She looked back at the Teleri reserve, jogging unopposed toward her position, with Geros' unmistakable gait at the head of their column.

Only a few minutes away.

It left scant time to rally her army. Cold ran up her spine. Nothing kept Geros from capturing her again. Her heart pounded in the constricted confines of her chest. Where was the cursed *Tiger's Eye* when she actually needed it?

Put on the sash and robe, Xu's voice spoke in her mind, exasperated.

Kaiya's stomach leapt into her throat. There was no sign of the elf lord. If he could see what was going on, why didn't he help?

Because if I saved the day, your people would look to me for leadership. Xu's words blew out like a long sigh. *Success or failure is on your shoulders. Now put on the clothes I made especially for you!*

What was that supposed to do? Make her appear regal in defeat? Create an extra layer for Geros to strip away?

Just do it! his voice snarled.

The elf should've just said something instead of leaving a cryptic message about fashion sense in his magic mirror.

Hands trembling, fingers stiff, she unwound her sash. Tian's pouch again tumbled out, this time hitting the rocks with a dull thud. A strange sound, really. She shook her head, trying to focus as she tore the old sash away and started wrapping the other.

She froze mid-wind. The energy of the world buzzed in her feet, resonating to her heart. Could it be?

Tentatively, she sang a single note.

The power surged through her, echoing into the night.

Soldiers from both sides froze on the battlefield and looked up at her. Geros stopped mid-stride and stared at her through his mismatched eyes.

Perhaps her fear had battered down the *Tiger's Eye*, even if she didn't feel that fright now. Still, the energy of the world coursed through her. The magic mirror's surface flashed at her feet. A Cathay marching song flickered into view, one which the slave girl Yanyan had sung during the War of Ancient Gods to mobilize Cathay slaves against their altivorc masters.

Holding the memory of Tian facing three Teleri with only a stone-headed spear, Kaiya sang.

The world's pulse vibrated through her. From where she stood, radiating out, Cathay soldiers formed up. Their unified chant and the pounding of their spear hafts on the ground followed the cadence of her voice.

Still, the Teleri lines held. Their expeditionary force scrambled up the hillside. Geros himself had closed enough for her to make out his ravenous smirk. Her song did not affect them either way, nor did she know any Arkothi songs that could evoke fear in them.

Geros was just ten paces away.

There had to be something she could do.

A word of power.

It had been so long—well, besides ordering Peng's men to kneel—since she'd used one. It had to be simple, one syllable at most, and in the Arkothi language. Even with the energy of the world welling in this spot, it might not be enough to affect so many.

Kaiya gripped the ground with her toes and straightened her spine. She sucked in a deep breath. Guanyin's Tear atop the pyramid darkened, and the Trees of Light dimmed, shrouding the battlefield in the light of the three moons alone.

"Flee." The Arkothi word rolled off her tongue and boomed. It echoed throughout the valley.

The pyramid and trees lit up again. All the energy drained out of her. Her wobbly legs unable to support her, Kaiya buckled to the ground. Tian's pouch lay near her hand, and she picked it up. Though her head and shoulders felt like a dwarf anvil, she pushed herself into a sitting position and looked to the battlefield.

The Teleri lines broke. The Bovyans threw down their arms and fled in an all-out retreat.

A rout.

Just three steps away from her, Geros took tentative backward steps before turning into a full sprint. He tripped over his feet and stumbled the rest of the way down the hillside.

Her words struggled to break free of her throat and came out only as a hoarse whisper. "Cap—capture. Capture him..."

Lord Xu materialized out of thin air. "Kaiya, come with me." He placed a hand on her shoulder, and the battlefield winked out.

Kaiya blinked. They now stood near an enormous arch, which spanned the mouth of an atoll. Her feet sunk into fine white sand. At last, after her armies had already turned the tide of the battle, he appeared.

"Sit," he said, indicating a worn boulder behind her.

She nodded and settled on the edge, letting her legs dangle over the side. Just like she had often done at Sun-Moon Palace, looking out over the lake.

Those days had been filled with uncertainty, as plotting and insurgency roiled the realm. Though Peng, the source of all the turmoil, was dead, the road ahead still felt daunting. The North lay pillaged by the Bovyans. Bridges destroyed. Ambitious lords who might not necessarily believe in or care about Guardian Dragons.

He sat down beside her and pointed to the moons, now going their separate ways. It would be three centuries before they met again in the high halls of heaven.

He patted her on the head. "The annals of history tell you the Godseye Conjunction and the appearance of the Guardian Dragon heralded in the Wang Dynasty. Let me tell you another story."

Tiger's Eye or not, Kaiya's spine tingled.

"Three hundred years ago, I sat with your ancestors under this same sky. It was not for the celebration of victory, but to mark the beginning of a new road. The next years were not easy. Warlords had undermined Yu Dynasty imperial authority for a decade before the Hellstorm, and the Long Winter would leave the people starving. Yet Wang Xinchang and Wang Yuxiang overcame the hardships and reunited Cathay."

Kaiya nodded. The histories often glossed over the process in favor of the grand story of the Guardian Dragon and the Mandate of Heaven. Still, there were more complicated stories left untold.

Xu turned her chin to meet his gaze. "Your ancestors were strangers to this land, and I daresay, not as resourceful as you. Have faith in yourself. I have faith in you. You have far surpassed my expectations."

"Expectations?"

"Remember that I once said you were born to face Avarax?"

She nodded.

"The late Queen Regent's bloodline does not easily beget scions. Your father asked for my power to help conceive his children. I gave you Yanyan's voice so you could vanquish Avarax once her ward on his power failed."

Kaiya's mind spun. How was it even possible?

"You defeated him when I could not." He grinned. "Now, you are reuniting Cathay."

Kaiya stared back at him. "Why? Why did you help my ancestors? Why do you help me? Why do you care about Cathay?"

He gazed back up at the stars. "Did you see it before? A constellation appeared above the moons just before the Godseye Conjunction. It is gone now."

"The Golden Flock." Kaiya looked. Indeed, the new stars she had seen at the pyramid had disappeared.

He pointed toward the red star, Yanluo the Conqueror. Tivar, in the language of the Orcs. "If you watched the heavens from there, you would see a very different picture. In the elaborate dance of the stars, Tivara is just one of the performers. Yet, it is one of the most important. Sometimes a stagehand must work with a diva."

A diva. Kaiya pouted like a child. Was he referring to Tivara, or her?

He laughed. "The Hellstorm, elf angels, the Altivorc King: they are all part of an intricate choreography, the push and pull of good and evil. What you do here, in undermining the altivorcs and their allies, ensures that the universe unfolds as planned."

As always, Lord Xu talked in riddles. Kaiya let out a long sigh. As if the realm wasn't enough responsibility.

Plucking the mirror from her hands, he held open the regent's robe he had made for her, the one she never managed to slip into. Indeed, her new sash still dangled from her hastily tied knot.

She threaded her arms into the sleeves. "Is it magic?"

He grinned. "You should have learned from these last few weeks that you do not always have to rely on magic."

Evasive answers yet again. She sighed. "Now what?"

Ignoring her, Xu fiddled with the mirror, and different images flashed across its face. One painting appeared.

Was that the Dragon Pearl, in someone's hands? Her hands? Or was it just a reflection? It disappeared with a sweep of his hand. He pressed the mirror to his chest and looked up. "If *I* were regent, I would worry about the remnants of the Teleri army and their capable leader."

She kept her eyes locked on the mirror. "If you were their capable leader, where would you go?"

He lowered the mirror, which now showed only a reflection. "I would hunker down in a defensible location, perhaps behind walls."

Which likely meant Huajing. Kaiya's heart sank.

Chapter 45:
Mad Dashes

Geros crumpled the messenger bird's missive. Leina insisted he bring the remnants of his army through Huajing's east gate instead of the more convenient south gate, yet left no reason why. The city's south walls rose in the distance, so close.

He looked back at the remnants of his once-proud army. Just ten thousand remained. So many had fallen on that fateful night of battle.

The rear guard of ten thousand was unaccounted for, though even faced with overwhelming numbers and superior weapons, they had stalled Cathayi pursuit for a couple of days. His current ragtag band was all that had survived eight days of forced marching with little food and constant skirmishes. The wounded had to be left behind.

He growled deep in his throat. Now, Leina wanted them to leave the highway and traipse through farmland and marsh. She should've sent supplies instead. Still, she'd proven reliable in the past. With a sigh, he beckoned his men onto the farmland.

Outside of Kaiya's carriage, long since repaired, birds screeched at each other as they competed for mates. Horses clopped, and boots marched through along the highway.

She had ridden at the head of an army too many times for her nineteen years. Hopefully, this would be the last.

She cradled the chunk of fallen star, whose steadfast throb felt comforting, even if its power seemed distant and walled-off again.

Across from her sat Brehane, now recovered from the spear butt to her head. She pulled and stretched Jie's mysterious armor while Cyrus stared out the window. Perhaps he thought about Sameer, who'd chased after the Golden Scorpion Sohini, and Fleet with him. Also missing was Doctor Wu. Kaiya had searched and searched the battlefield herself, to no avail.

In the far distance, the staccato cracks of musket fire made her heart jump. Even so, the other two showed no signs of hearing it.

Commander Zhuang rode up to the window. "*Jie-xia*, the capital is within sight."

At last. It had taken nine days, their pursuit of Geros slowed by the Teleri rear guard's defense of the central valley's final gap. "Any sign of the Teleri?

"No, *Jie-xia*." The cavalry commander shook his head. "They had a significant lead on us because of their rear guard action."

Kaiya sighed. If Geros reunited with the garrison he'd left there, they might have enough men and supplies to hold the walls and gates. "Tell General Lu to start making preparations for a siege."

Despite his earlier betrayal, the general had volunteered to lead all the assaults. He had more than proven his worth, and his soldiers adored him. Still, she'd keep a wary eye open.

Commander Zhuang said, "Our scouts reported trampled fields and boot prints up ahead."

Perhaps Geros had sent men into the fields to forage for food. Still, nothing besides radishes and leafy greens were in season. They must surely be hungry.

More musket fire pattered up ahead, though again, her companions did not appear to have heard it. She looked out the window.

Far beyond, Sun-Moon Castle and the Hall of Supreme Harmony stood out above the south walls. Had her brother survived the siege? And even if he still lived, the Guardian Dragon had entrusted her with choosing a capable *Tianzi*. As much as she adored Kai-Wu, he made a more suitable poet or teacher than ruler. Could she depose her own brother? And would the people accept that decision?

She sighed again. The *Tiger's Eye* must be weakening if she considered choosing fraternal feelings over a logical choice. In any case, the decision would need to wait until they controlled the capital.

In the distance, horse hooves pounded the pavestones.

Commander Zhuang appeared at the window again. "A messenger, *Jie-xia*, riding with the flag of the *Tianzi*."

"Send one of your men to meet with him," she said. They'd met too many spies and imposters for her to take a risk of getting too close to this messenger.

Just north of Cherry Blossom Boulevard, Ming sat astride his horse, with Tian, Shu, and Ma Jun at his side.

Waiting.

He turned his dagger over in his hands. The wait was going to kill him.

Unless Tian killed him first. His brother's hands clamped down on his. "Stop it. You are driving *us* insane."

Ma Jun nodded.

A messenger ran up and dropped to a knee. "*Jue-Ye*, the Teleri have passed through the east walls. Maybe ten thousand."

So the fake message had worked. Ming grinned at Tian. The combined forces of Linshan Province, the imperials, and his own Dongmen Province had attacked the remnants of the Teleri occupation over the last several days. Though they had captured key positions, the Bovyans still held out near the south gate. The last thing they needed was the emperor to join up with that group.

He then addressed his generals. "Wait until they are at least six blocks from the east gate before the ordering the cavalry to cut off their escape. Sound the horn when they are in position, and we will attack their flank."

"As you command, *Jue-ye*!" the soldiers all said in unison.

Ming turned to Tian. "You know what to do."

Tian crept along the rooftops as he approached the Teleri column. They marched twenty abreast along Cherry Blossom Boulevard, weapons at the ready as if they were launching an attack themselves. Ten thousand, two hundred and seven in all.

At their head, predictably, rode Emperor Geros. He was taller than the rest, with a scar on his cheek, just as Ming had said. His eyes swept back and forth, and like most people he didn't bother to look up. He pursed his lips, his stiff shoulders and jerky motions suggesting he knew something was out of place. Even still, he rode high above everyone else, an obvious and inviting target.

Taking aim, Tian fitted one of Ming's elf arrows and pulled the bowstring taut. He loosed.

A horn blared.

The Teleri kept their orderly ranks, but froze in place with their shields facing out. Geros pulled his horse up. The arrow cut right through the mount's head. As it tumbled, Geros leaped from the saddle and into the mass of Bovyans.

Tian cursed to himself. Not that he would've hit Geros anyway. It should've been Ming, the master archer, taking this shot, only he refused to climb a rooftop and get his uniform messy. At least the poor beast didn't suffer.

Provincial soldiers flooded the side streets on the northern edge of the boulevard. They stopped at point-blank range and fired into the Teleri column.

Enemy officers barked out orders, and Bovyans on the interior loaded crossbows. Those on the edges bulged out into squares to charge the side streets. One more command, and the front rows knelt and the crossbowmen shot. The last row of Cathay musketmen fired a volley, and spearmen surged forward.

They crashed into the Teleri with spears and swords. Still, the Bovyans held their line. Tian nocked another arrow, searching for Geros in the fray.

In close-range pitched battle, the Metal Men might have the advantage, despite being outnumbered two-to-one. If only musketmen could fire from rooftops!

Another horn pealed from the Teleri rear. Ming's cavalry.

And there was the emperor, taking command of his exhausted troops. Tian took aim.

"Hold the line!" Geros yelled, his heart thumping at a steady beat. "Do not let the histories say we lost to merchants, no matter how many bodies they throw against our spears!"

They sure were throwing a lot. How many in total was impossible to know without accurate intelligence, and apparently, that traitor Leina had lured them into a trap. Once they reoccupied the capital, he would be paying a visit to her home.

A high-pitched horn screeched from somewhere near the rear of his column. The feminine squeal certainly wasn't a Teleri horn, though it carried above the clanking of metal and screams of men.

Yellow flashed in his vision as the Eye of Geros warned him of danger. He involuntarily leaned his head back. An arrow zipped by his face and lodged into one of his men's arms. Geros turned to see where it had come from.

Up on the rooftop of a two-story building stood a Cathayi man, now nocking another arrow.

The Cathayi man.

The Angel of Death, whom Geros had killed once before.

Now back to claim him.

Geros cackled and snatched a loaded crossbow from a nearby soldier. How similar it was to the faceoff at the fortress in the Wilds. He took aim, just as the Angel of Death loosed another arrow. Yellow flashed in his vision.

Dao flashing, Ming smashed into the Teleri rear with the rest of his cavalry. They lumbered through the enemy's interior lines almost unopposed, hacking and slashing through crossbowmen.

While his plan hadn't worked exactly as he hoped, they were dealing a significant blow to the exhausted Teleri troops. As long as they kept this returning army from linking up with the former occupiers, they could slowly strangle and starve them out.

From astride his horse, Ming saw Emperor Geros toward the front, crossbow in hand, barking orders. Ming's free hand strayed to his bow. It would be quite a shot from this distance, but not beyond his superior archery skills, and certainly faster than wading through the Bovyans.

Not far ahead, Bovyans dropped crossbows and drew swords and spears. One Teleri at his side tried to drag him off the horse, but Ming kicked him in the face.

One of his officers sidled over. "*Jue-ye*, if we go much deeper, we will be trapped."

Ming looked to the fore, where a forest of blades awaited, and then behind him, where the Teleri swarmed around the horses. His man was right. In these close quarters, they would eventually get dragged down. It would be better to veer onto a side street.

Cathay spearmen clogged up the streets to the north of the boulevard, so he waved his sword southward. "Linshan cavalry, to me!"

They chopped a path through the Bovyans. When Ming reached the side street, he paused and glanced further up the Teleri lines. Somewhere in the mess, Emperor Geros shouted out orders.

There he was. An arrow flew down and lodged into his shoulder, just as he took a shot into the rooftops. The bolt zipped upward. Ming whipped his head to follow its path.

Tian snatched it out of the air.

Ming could only gawk at his little brother's skill.

"Protect the emperor!" a Teleri yelled. Others repeated the call until thousands of voices chanted it like a mantra. Their rectangular shields came together and their spears jutted out like a centipede's carapace. The entire column wheeled and lumbered southward down a side street.

Ming wiped sweat from his brow. Hopefully, Linshan Province's troops had succeeded in overwhelming enemy-controlled points along White Duck Stream, and could cut the Teleri off from the rest of their army.

Cheers erupted to the north and west. Cathayi cheers. They must've surrounded the emperor.

An aide rode up. "*Jue-ye*, news from the south gate. The princess has returned, bringing two hundred thousand men."

Ming stifled his grin. The Teleri numbers must have dwindled to around ten thousand in total by now, paltry compared to the imperial reinforcements. Still, it was a lot of Cathay soldiers to bring through the gate, and they might not get enough to keep the two pockets of Teleri resistance from joining the main army.

Tian ran along a street parallel to the Teleri retreat. At every intersection, he looked over to see how quickly the column of Metal Men moved.

Somewhere, behind the marching wall of shields and spears, the Teleri Emperor must be laboring with an arrow in his shoulder.

Cthayi musketmen, both provincial and imperial, stood in three-rank lines in the side streets, shooting at will. The closest rank knelt, the second stood, and the third reloaded muskets. The Metal Men took casualties at each intersection, though any man falling on the outside was immediately replaced by another.

Perhaps the emperor had already bled out, since he was no fool. It was more logical for the column to turn down a side street, crash into the thin lines of musketmen, and break out from the path where they took constant fire.

Tian looked up ahead to see a large battalion of Cathayi troops marching toward him, their banners a white ship on a black field. At their head rode a helmeted man in a black-and-white uniform and a steel breastplate. Those color, that sigil… Zhenjing Province? Why were they here?

Hurrying over, Tian bowed. "Sir—"

Two men thrust him to his knees. "Address Lord Wu of Zhenjing with proper manners."

Appropriate terms… "*Jue-ye*, the Teleri could break out of any of these streets."

Lord Wu waved him off the street. "Out of the way. Go back to your home."

Tian brushed his hands over his clothes. Of course, he wore civilian garb. Still— "If you attack them now, you can break them in two."

With a wave at his men, the commander said, "We are to cut off possible escape routes to the west, under orders from the regent herself."

The regent was in the city… He had come so far looking for her, to satisfy Yuha and his spirits. The column had come up from the south, so she must be there.

Kaiya entered the city at the head of the army, astride a horse, keeping her chin up as musket shots rang out in the distance.

Beyond the nearby rows of two-story buildings, several plumes of smoke rose above the southeastern part of the city. Teleri casualties lay strewn around the gatehouse and walls. The stench of sulphur and burning charcoal hung in the air. Though her nausea had subsided in the last couple of weeks, it threatened to rise again now.

General Tang, at the head of an imperial guard contingent, rode up and dismounted. He dropped to a knee, fist to the ground. "*Jie-xia*, thank you for coming in our relief."

She searched among his command staff. "Where is General Shan?"

"Killed at the north gate in the initial assault, before you left."

Kaiya heart sank, even through the *Tiger's Eye*. "I am sorry to hear that. General Shan had been a wise and courageous leader." She sighed, resolve firming again. "What is the Teleri army's status now?"

"Lord Zheng Ming tricked Emperor Geros into entering the city from the east, to prevent him from joining with their garrison here." He gestured to the south gate. "We recaptured the gate not long ago and have pushed them east. I have word that Lord Zheng is driving Geros south, while the rest of our armies hold White Duck Stream to prevent him from going west."

Zheng Ming... had survived Teleri capture, and the orders she'd given Jie. Kaiya nodded, even though she only had a vague idea of the map. Better to leave strategy to the professional military.

In the meantime, there was something only she could do. "General, how dangerous are the roads to the Temple of Heaven?"

General Tang looked to the east. "The Bovyans are nowhere near there right now. I will personally escort you."

Kaiya patted her saddlebag, where the fallen star hummed its unfaltering tune. One of her ancestors' first acts was to erect the temple in an auspicious location, and then place the star there. She would return the relic to its rightful place.

She turned to General Tang. "Send Emperor Geros my terms for his surrender…"

The wound on Geros' right shoulder had stopped bleeding, but it still seared with pain. Especially after the healer had applied a balm.

Each time the man tied another stitch, Geros had to hide his wince. He scanned the grassy basin and stone seating around him. It looked similar to an Estomari coliseum, except that the stands only lined one side.

Low ground to be sure, but defensible enough from the stands and also the barricades his men had erected along the side streets feeding into the plaza. The garrison had managed to meet up with them, not only bolstering their defenses but also bringing much-needed food and supplies. If they rationed everything, they could hold out a week or more until reinforcements arrived from the North.

Wishful thinking.

He laughed out loud, drawing the stares of his men, who immediately averted their eyes. No, it had been Dongmen provincial soldiers who had attacked. Either Lord Zheng had turned on him, or the son must've grown some balls and learned a little military strategy. There would be no reinforcements.

Geros pushed the healer off and stood. All his men snapped to attention.

"My friends, this is our last stand. No help is coming. But we will make them remember the day they fought the Teleri Empire. Their descendants will quiver at our name."

The men broke into cheers. Every last one of them would die for honor. Him, too. In any case, without the fallen star to give to the Altivorc King, he only had a few months before his thirty-third birthday and inevitable death soon after.

It had been a good life. His only regret was not to have conquered Cathay for Kaiya and left a stable and peaceful realm for their son to rule.

General Baros called from the top of the stone seats. "The regent has sent a request to parley. She demands our immediate surrender and Emperor Geros to turn himself in to her. The rest of us will be allowed to return home."

Geros snorted. Undoubtedly an attempt to turn the men against him, and in any other army, the terms of surrender would not be shouted out for everyone to hear. But they were Bovyans, and their response was predictable.

His men pounded on their chests. "We will fight!"

Geros grinned and strode toward the stands. It was an answer he planned to deliver himself.

Ming watched from horseback as a group of Cathay imperial officers approached the amphitheater under the flags of parley. Teleri soldiers appeared at the top of the stone amphitheater seats. Though out of earshot, he could guess what message they delivered.

Alas, the poor communication between the provincial lords and the imperial army had allowed the enemy to reach Qingjingtian Amphitheater and meet up with the garrison they had left. If they refused to surrender, they would lose, but not without inflicting devastating losses first.

He turned to his aide. "Where is the regent now?"

"Word has it she is heading to the Temple of Heaven."

"What?" Regent or not, now was not the time to pray. The Heavens rewarded those with the most guns and a better field position. Ming gestured back at his provincial soldiers, who now stood in orderly ranks along the northern end of the enemy's hastily erected wall of carts, house doors, furniture, and Heavens knew what else.

"Look." His aide pointed to the top of the amphitheater seats.

The sun gleaming off his breastplate, Geros stood tall and imposing at the top of the amphitheater's stone seats.

Ming's heart skipped into his throat. The last time he had met the Teleri to discuss terms, he had lost a battle and fallen into the emperor's hands. His hand tightened on his *dao* hilt.

"Deliver this message to the girl." Geros' voice echoed through the streets. "I will surrender only if she spreads her legs for me."

Beyond the barricades in the basins, Bovyans erupted into laughter.

Emperor Geros raised a hand, silencing them. "Otherwise we will set your precious city ablaze."

Chapter 46:
Wash Out

Kaiya listened to birds chirping in the eaves of the Temple of Heaven stupa as she approached the compound's front gates on horseback. The birds' part in spring's song echoed off the compound's elliptical walls, carrying the sound over her own horse's clopping and the sporadic musket shots in the distance.

It had been over three years since Avarax, disguised as Prince Hardeep, had brought her here to test the Dragon Scale Lute; and over a year since she'd last visited, the day Zheng Ming failed to accompany her to the temple as he'd promised. She'd been a naïve, infatuated girl, who rode off into a city on edge in hopes of nursing handsome Zheng Ming back to health.

Now, she scoffed at her younger self. If anything need be taken from that day, it was Father's prayers and the way the temple grounds magnified his voice. With the magic here, maybe she could finally break the *Tiger's Eye* for good and do something impactful in this war.

The bald, yellow-robed temple abbot shuffled forward, head bowed. "*Jie-xia*, welcome to the Temple of Heaven. I regret to inform you that the Fallen Star was stolen and—"

Kaiya withdrew the relic from her saddlebags. It pulsed in her hands as she presented it. "See it returned to its rightful spot."

The abbot gaped and bowed as he received it reverently in two hands. "Yes, *Jie-xia*. However, there is another security concern inside the temple grounds. I do not think it wise to—"

Several sets of horse hooves cantered toward her. Her honor guard clattered into defensive positions. Her own cavalry formed into a circle. Behind her, Brehane and Cyrus shuffled as they prepared their own magic. She turned.

Three cavalrymen approached, their green flags with the sun rising over twin mountains marking them as Dongmen provincial soldiers. The one in the lead rode his horse with such ease, it seemed horse and rider were one entity.

He swung out of the saddle before his mount came to a stop and dropped to knee, fist to the ground. Glossy black hair spilled out as he removed his helmet and looked up, revealing Zheng Ming. "*Jie-xia*, welcome back to the city."

Flamboyant as ever. Kaiya suppressed a smile. "Lord Zheng. I was just thinking about you."

"Oh?" With his eyebrow raised, his grin was all the more charming.

She gestured toward the Temple. "I was thinking of the last time I was here, and how you broke your promise to me."

Her men exchanged glances, and Zheng Ming's face flushed.

Brehane pushed past the men and came to Zheng Ming's side, placing a hand on his shoulder. She winked at Kaiya. "Your Majesty, if it is your wish, I will make this predatory dandy disappear."

"Perhaps later." Kaiya chuckled. "He might still prove useful."

Zheng Ming bowed. "*Jie-xia*, I have come ahead of your messengers. The Teleri refuse to surrender. In fact, Emperor Geros…" His gaze shifted to the assembled soldiers. "Emperor Geros made uh, inappropriate counter-demands."

It didn't take much imagination to guess what those were. It might be worth it, to save the city without more losses, if she wouldn't lose face among all the soldiers whose loyalty she'd gained.

Alas, the fact that she didn't bristle or blush at the suggestion showed the *Tiger's Eye* must still be in place, no matter how tenuously. She gestured to a runner. "Go to the palace and tell Chief Minister Song to come up with a plan for fighting potential fires."

She then looked to Brehane and gestured to the Temple of Heaven's gates. "Now, perhaps you would like to see one of the marvels of our capital."

"I can already feel it," the Mystic said.

Kaiya nodded toward Zheng Ming. "You will accompany me into the temple this time." An honor, for his loyalty. Not to mention that eventually she would have to marry, and he was certainly pleasant on the eyes.

He gawked, then bowed. "I do not think that would be appropriate, *Jie-xia*."

"Why not?" She raised an eyebrow. It wasn't as though he ever stood on propriety.

His eyes darted back and forth, taking in all of the assembled soldiers. "Some matters can only be discussed in confidence."

She studied his expression. He must know about Tian' death, then. Of course, Ming had already confronted his father, and surely those details would have come out. "In any case, I am setting up the army headquarters here, since it is close to the invading army. Fall in line with General Tang and the other hereditary lords." She pointed her chin toward the commanders and aides behind her.

Zheng Ming's mouth hung agape, but then he bowed. "Yes, *Jie-xia.*"

As he joined the other commanders, Kaiya gestured toward the temple guards. The abbot opened his mouth in protest, but she silenced him with a pursing of her lips. Bowing, the guards opened the double gates into the temple grounds. She dismounted, squared her shoulders, and strode through.

She stopped mid-stride. Sitting atop the three-tiered marble base, in the center of the near focus, was…

Jie? At her side stood Fang Weiyong, fiddling with acupuncture needles in Jie's shoulder while a familiar yet unfamiliar young woman stood over his shoulder.

The stranger looked up with blue eyes. Beautiful, luminous eyes, like…

Doctor Wu's.

The resemblance was uncanny. Perhaps this woman was a granddaughter—though, since no one knew how old Doctor Wu really was, this could be her great-great-granddaughter.

She beckoned. "*Jie-xia,* come."

The voice. It was Doctor Wu's.

Kaiya's mind spun. The last she'd seen the Taoist Master was before the confrontation with Cousin Peng. There was no way the aged doctor could possibly make it back to the capital first, let alone *un-age*. Kaiya took tentative steps forward, unsure if her legs could hold her. The *Tiger's Eye* must've all but faded.

A firm hand took her elbow. She turned and blinked through her misty eyes to find Zheng Ming there, as well as other soldiers trying to peel him off of her. She raised a hand and feebly gestured them off. Zheng Ming's support felt so reassuring, so… right. Even if it was wrong.

With his help, she climbed to the raised marble base where Jie sat.

No, this must be one of those bizarre dreams again. Jie was dead. Killed by Fleet.

Still, up close, the half-elf sitting there was unmistakably the Insolent Retainer, eyes closed. And beside her, a younger version of Doctor Wu.

"How?" was the only word she could manage to choke out.

Young Doctor Wu smiled. "*Jie-xia*, you know I was always looking for the secret to immortality. You helped me find it when you retrieved the Dragon Pearl." She winked.

Kaiya couldn't find words at the moment.

Doctor Wu rolled her eyes. She took Kaiya's head and pressed it to her bosom. Her heart thumped, setting the rhythm to a resolute, powerful song.

The same song as… the Guardian Dragon.

Kaiya's jaw slackened. Her mouth moved, but no words came out.

Doctor Wu, her physician for so many years, was the mythical Guardian Dragon. Who wasn't *supposed* to be a dragon in the sense that Avarax was, as much as a messenger from the Heavens.

Doctor Wu nodded. "You know the secret. Keep it that way."

With a slow nod, Kaiya turned from Doctor Wu— the Guardian Dragon—to Jie, then back to Doctor Wu. All she could do was point.

"She has lost the use of her arm, and neither my best student—" she gestured toward Fang Weiyong—"nor I can figure out why. There is nothing physically wrong, and even in this spot, where the energy of the world is strongest in the capital, we cannot heal her."

That much would make sense, except the fact Jie was dead. Words stumbled out of Kaiya's mouth. "How is she alive?"

Jie's eyes flew open. She and the two others stared at her with curious expressions.

"Fleet killed you."

Jie cocked her head and patted herself with her good arm. "I don't think so." Her tone sounded just as bitter as when they had last parted, in Dongmen. When Kaiya had given the order to kill Zheng Ming.

"I think I know what is going on," Zheng Ming said. "Jie has an identical twin."

Two? Kaiya shuddered at the thought of two insolent half-elves. Ming's sour look suggested he felt the same.

Cyrus appeared at their side. "That would explain it. I was wondering how you had made it to the pyramid so fast, after we had seen you in the Wilds."

"And you fought so differently," Kaiya said.

Jie nodded and sighed. "It's a shame. Kiri wasn't bad. I don't know why the madaeri would kill her."

"So where have you been all this time?" Ming demanded. "Tian said you've been missing for days."

Tian?

Tian was dead, unless he too had a magical twin. Kaiya's gaze swept from Jie to Ming. Surely he had misspoken, or this was one of those realistic dreams. She pinched herself, sending a flare of pain through her arm.

No, quite awake.

Jie's gaze met hers. "*Jie-xia*, your city has a rampant altivorc infestation I have been trying to eradicate."

Pulling Brehane forward, Cyrus said, "Since you can't figure out the armor, perhaps you should give it to someone it fits."

Brehane clutched her pack to her chest.

A messenger presented himself at the bottom of the dais. "*Jie-xia*, the Bovyans have set fire to the area surrounding Qingjingtian Amphitheatre."

Kaiya looked up. Beyond the Temple walls to the east, thick plumes of black wafted to the heavens. Winds typically swirled off of Sun-Moon Lake, which would carry sparks from wood building to wood building. It wouldn't be long before the entire southeast quadrant turned into a hellish conflagration.

She turned to Doctor Wu. "Legends say the Guardian Dragon controls weather and water."

"Would that the Guardian Dragon were to make an appearance," Doctor Wu said. "However, legends also say she only comes during the time of greatest need, to anoint a leader with the Mandate of Heaven."

It couldn't be. Doctor Wu, who revered life so much, would let tens of thousands perish in a fire. Kaiya plead with her eyes.

"Have you learned nothing?" Doctor Wu shooed Jie off the foci. "Stand here. Feel Mother Earth course through you. You read Xu's book on how Yanyan brought a rainstorm."

Kaiya swept her gaze around all the assembled people. Mouths agape, all the generals and officers looked from the doctor to her and back again. They probably couldn't believe a mere doctor was ordering a regent around on matters unrelated to health.

With a sigh, she strode to the focus. Sinking into a high horse stance, she gripped the marble through her shoes with her toes. The song of the world resonated in her soles and vibrated up through her legs.

Still, it stopped at her waist. The scent of burning wood drifted on the air, and she looked east. An orange gleam gathered on the horizon, like a sunrise in Hell. Pulse racing, she turned to the doctor. "The energy is there, but I can't connect to it."

"Link to it. Lower." Doctor Wu pressed her hand into Kaiya's shoulder, pushing her into a deeper stance. She then turned to the temple and yelled, "Hurry up with the fallen star."

The energy welled beneath her feet, calling to her from so close. Tears collected in her lashes. If she couldn't do this, so many people would die. Geros would win, would probably gloat at her from beyond the grave. Just like the world's resonance, taunting her.

She glanced around at all the expectant faces. Cyrus nodded at her, while Brehane smiled. Doctor Wu and Fang Weiyong, too. All of the soldiers knelt, fists to the ground. The Heavens must have a sick sense of humor to place the fate of so many people on a nineteen-year-old's shoulders.

A low pulse throbbed out of the Temple of Heaven, washing over her from all directions.

The fallen star, that was it! The energy she could borrow if that of Mother Earth refused to answer her call. On the next pulse, she sang Yanyan's rain song. Letting the frequency of Doctor Wu's heartbeat guide her, Kaiya enunciated each word.

Doctor Wu's eyes brightened ever so slightly, still pathetic compared to Avarax's eyes glowing to her song in the past. "Connect," the doctor said. "Let the song of the fallen star link with the hum of Mother Earth."

Another messenger ran up to the base and dropped to a knee. "The Teleri are pouring out of the amphitheater. They are slaughtering citizens."

The star's and earth's melodies were there, in her chest and in her lower abdomen, and yet they didn't merge. Yells and screams mingled with intermittent musket shots in the distance. The story of her failure would be written in blood.

Her shoulders shuddered, rattling at the speed of her racing heart. The *Tiger's Eye* had to be gone for her to have such reactions, yet the energy of the world remained walled-off, rising no higher than the *dantian* point beneath her navel.

"You can do it," the doctor said.

A tear rolled down Kaiya's cheek. The Guardian Dragon could do it, too, but refused. Voice cracking, she sang again, elocuting each note of the song once more. Clouds formed overhead, and a drop of rain splattered on her nose. Unless it was just another tear.

A commotion erupted near the entrance to the temple grounds. Had the Teleri gotten here so fast? Kaiya hazarded a glance. It looked like Zheng Ming in the corner of her eye, deftly avoiding the imperial guards.

"Focus!" Doctor Wu's stern reprimand drew her back to the task at hand.

The power in her was gone. She gripped her toes to the ground again and listened for the pulse. The energies were all there, but beyond her ability to use. The forces in her chest and belly struggled to meet, even though they had merged so easily and automatically in the past.

Screams grew louder. As regent, she was quickly becoming a failure, at the cost of so many lives. Her hands trembled as tears filled her eyes again.

"Let him through," Zheng Ming said from somewhere.

Cyrus and Brehane both evoked magic around her, through his uplifting prayers and her grunts and snarls. None of them helped her. Jie's forlorn sigh sounded miserable.

Kaiya was failing, and nothing in this world could save the city's southeast, and maybe more, from burning.

Arms enveloped her, warm and heartening. They lifted her out of her stance, breaking her connection with the ground, and turned her around. Her cheek pressed against coarse fabric, and the toned chest beneath. The heartbeat… so familiar. She looked up.

Intelligent dark eyes gazed back at her. The high-bridged nose and strong chin resembled Zheng Ming, but—no.

No, it was impossible.

If this was a dream, would that she never woke. If she were awake, she never wanted to sleep again.

"It's all right. You can do it." He spoke with concise economy as always, yet his words could have been an epic novel for all the affection in their warm tone.

Pulse racing, she dried her tears in his high collar. His hand ran through her hair. Her stomach flipped in twists and turns worthy of a zigzagging dragonfly.

"I can't." She placed her hand over her belly. "It's stuck. Here."

His hand covered hers, then slid down over her womb. "They need your strength." Their babies. His hand rose up toward her waist, pausing at her sash, right over his lockpick pouch.

She pushed back, just enough to reach into her sash. She pulled it out, her only memento of him. With the *Tiger's Eye*, she had kept it not for any type of emotional connection, but rather as a reminder that she had once known love. With him here, she didn't need it anymore. She looked up into his eyes and pressed the pouch into his palm.

As his fingers closed around it, a surge flowed through her body. Rising from the ground, sinking with her breath, mingling in her core. Power, like that around the Wild Turkey Island and the Temple of Shakti in Palimur, coursed from toes to fingertips. It built up, ready to explode unless…

She started to sing.

Tian looked up as a raindrop splattered onto his cheek, hopefully hiding his own tears. Several more followed, pattering in a light drizzle, then building to a downpour.

Like all the memories flooding back.

Kaiya, the Doe-Eyed Girl.

His childhood friend, separated from him by Peng Kai-Long's cruel joke. Reunited in Iksuvi to learn that she had changed.

But then they had found each other, the spirit of who they had been as children not lost in adulthood, despite the responsibilities that suppressed them. Here they were again, reunited after his death and rebirth.

His heart pounded in his chest. This was where he was supposed to be, who he was supposed to be with. He turned the lockpick pouch over in his hands, pausing each time at the flap and the awkward stitching. It weighed too much for just a set of picks.

Of course. Withdrawing his knife, he cut away the stitches on the flap and opened the secret pouch he had sewn in during their sojourn in the Wilds.

Inside hid the dull grey metal of the Teleri imperial crest.

It must've blocked Kaiya's magic all this time.

Somewhere behind him, Jie stifled a cry.

Jie could only watch the reunion she'd tried to sabotage several times over. But now, they looked so right together, the Big Brother she adored and the Sworn Sister she hated.

Oh, what could've been, with Tian.

They'd come so close, not once, but twice. Still, their love had never been allowed to blossom, thwarted by circumstance and bad timing. Now, he was with *her*. Against all odds, their hearts came together in a way his would never beat for Jie.

It was meant to be.

Her life would continue forward, without Tian in it. She wiped a tear away.

With her bad hand.

She stared at it in awe, but when she went to move it again, nothing happened. She searched the heavens through the driving rain, wondering why the gods played such evil tricks on her. With a sigh, she turned back to the fires in the east.

To duty, like she always did.

There, the flames persisted despite the downpour. The rain might've cleared some of the smoke from the air, yet still the city burned. Thousands of yells and screams erupted in a disjointed cacophony.

Jie turned back toward the hated princess at the focus. "*Jie-xia*, harder! The fires are still burning."

The princess' voice rose, angelic yet powerful.

The temple well bubbled over, spilling onto the ground.

"Wells are rising everywhere," Ming yelled from the front gate. "The stream and canals, as well."

Fang Weiyong shook his head. "Impossible. It's rained a lot, but not so much that it could raise the water level."

"The music," Doctor Wu said. "Sun-Moon Lake itself rises to salute the gods. Backflowing into the canals and streams."

Ming chuckled at the couple. Apparently, only his kid brother could melt the heart of the Ice Princess. Still, as sappy and charming as it might be, their love alone couldn't save the city.

Though perhaps a different type of magic would help.

"Come with me." He grabbed Brehane's hand and tugged her toward the entrance and the horses.

She fought back, a scowl crossing her face. "Didn't we go through this before? It's a beautiful moment, but no means no."

"No, not that." There were too many negatives to keep track of. "No, I need your help. The city needs your help. Can you ride a horse?"

Her pursed lips answered the question. Of course, they had ridden in Selastyas.

"Come on, then."

She followed him out. Ming gestured his aide off a horse, then Brehane onto it. He mounted up and spurred his mount into a gallop.

Rumor had it the princess had taken off from the Temple of Heaven on a New Year's Day, in a mad dash through the city to come visit him. Now, he might very well have been retracing her path.

Except now he had a different destination in mind. Her song reverberated in his ears, no matter how far away he galloped. Everyone else's ears, too, as soldiers, commoners, and even the occasional Bovyan wandered aimlessly, staring in the direction of the Temple of Heaven. He looked back to see if Brehane was keeping up.

They arrived at White Duck Stream, now rising nearly to street level. He followed it until they reached a famous pile of rocks—debris from an earthquake a century ago that had transformed Qingjingtian from a reservoir to a grassy basin. Water gurgled over the levee, feeding into the old streambed which the locals had since filled halfway with dirt to grow vegetables. It might take work crew days to clear the rocks, but Brehane…

He pointed at it. "Can you do something about the levee?"

Her eyes tracked from the pile of rocks to the streambed, now green with vegetable seedlings, then back to White Duck Stream. "It will wash all of the crops away."

"And the Bovyans with it."

Brehane shook her head. "The people will go hungry."

Ming threw his hands up. "Dead people won't eat at all. Plus, it's not like this one stretch feeds even a fraction of the populace."

She glared at him for a few seconds before closing her eyes and starting her chant.

Geros listened to Princess Kaiya's song, so loud she might've been standing right next to him.

But she wasn't. She never would. If only she'd come, he would've found a way to prove his love for her.

And in his anger at her refusal, he had set the city ablaze. His men almost refused, grumbling that it went against the tenets of the Last Testament of the First Geros. The Bovyan race was to bring order and build prosperity, not to wantonly destroy cities out of vengeance.

Returning from their forays into the nearby city blocks, the soldiers now gathered stoically around him, only their eyes indicating that they waited for some word of encouragement. Or maybe even absolution.

He had failed them all.

He might reach his preordained death in just a few months, but many of these men still had years to serve the Teleri Empire. He'd let his passions turn a sure future victory into a premature invasion and defeat.

Let history remember him as a fighter.

He cleared his throat so they could hear him over the pounding rain. "Bovyans! The enemy is marching on us, though the rain renders their guns useless. Defend the barricades. Let no Cathayi set foot in this basin until the last of us is dead. They shall rue the day they invited us in. Our people will celebrate our last stand. Now go, up to the barricades!"

The men broke out in cheers. They chanted his name as they sloshed in the mud toward the barriers.

Let the Cathayi come fall on Teleri spears. Let *her* know her people had died because she refused him.

Outside the amphitheater, the crackling flames fizzled. The orange-and-red glow dulled. Gurgling at the western end of the basin led to a gush of water from a gully. Filling in from the west to east, and then spilling from the rim of the basin and down the slopes, the water level rose.

His men cursed and yelled as the makeshift barricades toppled under the torrent and tumbled into the growing lake. Water rose to his knees already. Geros looked toward the stone seat tiers. Even when the water completely flooded the basin, at least those would still be dry. Better to die fighting than to flounder and drown like a rat.

He slogged through the waist-high water toward the seats. By the time he reached the slope, the water came up to his chest.

Dropping to all fours, he dug his hands into the grass and mud, yet still couldn't find purchase on the stones through the storm surge. A wood rafter tumbled down the banks and slammed into him, knocking him back.

It was all he could do to hold on to it as the water level rose. Many of his men thrashed in their heavy armor, and very few held on to weapons. Those on the stone seats shouted, beckoned, and men who had managed to climb onto floating wood paddled with their hands.

Then the princess' song ceased. The rain slowed as the clouds thinned. Sunlight lanced in ever-widening blades across the new lake. Thousands upon thousands of Cathayi musketmen lined the edge of the basin, weapons covering every angle.

"Throw down your arms," called a male voice in accented Arkothi.

Geros searched the ranks of men and found Zheng Ming astride a horse. The lordling had come of age, it appeared.

Geros growled. "Men, attack!"

The soldiers on the seats yelled out a war cry and charged, only to be cut down by volleys of musket fire. In a matter of moments, his men were either dead or incapacitated in the stands, or floating.

Ignominious defeat. The only thing that could make it worse—

"Emperor Geros," Kaiya called from where she sat on horseback at Zheng Ming's side. "You have lost."

The water's tumble sounded like applause as it receded back into the streams, sewers, and canals. Kaiya watched as Teleri gratefully accepted the ropes thrown to rescue them. Oftentimes, it took three or four of her men to subdue just one unarmed Bovyan as he came ashore.

She sighed. Behind them, the rain and rising water had doused the flames, but they would undoubtedly leave both a physical and emotional scar on the neighborhood and its residents.

The victory, in what was hopefully the last battle, had come at great cost.

Kaiya turned back to the remnants of the once-proud Teleri army. There might be only a few hundred survivors at this point, out of the fifty thousand who had joined the invasion.

Among them, Emperor Geros. Without the *Tiger's Eye* protecting her, even the sight of him sent a chill up her spine.

Still, she forced herself to look at the emperor. Though one arm hung limp, he fought against all the ropes pulling his wooden beam toward land. If only he would just let go and let the waters swallow him up. If he came ashore alive, it meant facing him.

Tian's hand found hers, from where he sat awkwardly in his saddle. It was warm, comforting, and she would lean into him now if it wouldn't send the both of them tumbling into ankle-deep water.

His gaze fell on her. "When he reaches the bank. I will kill him. For what he did to you."

Her shoulders trembled as horrifying memories of Geros' calloused hands on her surfaced. Now, here he was, coming closer to land. Closer to her. Her free hand balled into a fist so tight it might draw blood. He clawed his way to the far end of the beam.

A rope dart whizzed in and wrapped around his limp arm. Another caught around his neck. Two young men in plain clothes held the other ends of the cords. Soldiers grabbed the ropes and pulled. Geros lurched onto land, flopping like a fish out of water. Men crowded around him, seizing his arms and forcing him to his knees. Others cleared a path between him and her.

So similar to what he had done to her, in the Wilds, humiliating her before all his men. Another shudder wracked her. Tian... where was Tian? His hand had been there just a second before. She looked around, from his horse, to the crowd of her soldiers, and finally to Geros.

Tian rose up behind the emperor, yanking his hair back. A knife flashed in Tian's other hand. Just like when the Golden Scorpion had killed Cousin Peng.

Her lips moved, but no sound came out. This was nothing short of murder.

"Stop," she finally croaked, though not loud enough for her to hear her own voice. She cleared her throat. "Stop."

Tian's blade halted against Geros' neck. He looked up at her, eyes questioning. Geros' stare fell on her as well, his mismatched eyes twisting her stomach into knots.

Straightening her back and squaring her shoulders as she had done so many times in the past, she raked her gaze over the expectant faces before settling somewhere between Tian's chest and the top of Geros' head. "We will act with justice, not vengeance. Enemy generals must be accorded every respect. Confine him to the Hall of Water Spirits in Sun-Moon Palace."

Geros shook his head. "Kill me now. Better yet, allow me to kill myself."

It would be so much easier if he did. Kaiya sighed. "I have a mind to let you live what remains of your god-cursed life as a warning to others who might try to attack us."

Tian withdrew the knife from Geros' neck, stepped back and bowed. "As you command, *Jie-xia*."

What was that expression? Disappointment? Relief? Kaiya sighed. Whatever it was, they now had time to sort it out. The war was over.

Chapter 47:
Just Rewards

Kaiya fanned herself as she listened to the buzz of cicadas whirring outside the Hall of Supreme Harmony. Her belly now pushed out, with the occasional kick as a reminder of the two lives growing inside of her.

In front of her knelt a crowd of ministers and hereditary lords, lined in orderly ranks throughout the cavernous hall, and spilling out into the courtyard one hundred and sixty-eight steps below.

In the three months that had passed since the defeat of the Teleri army, she'd worked behind the scenes, helping Chief Minister Song and General Tang administer the government and military as they labored to restore stability and imperial authority throughout the realm.

Today, she would hold court as regent for the first time, where many expected her to announce her choice of a new *Tianzi*.

Beside her, the Jade Throne remained empty, which allowed her to relax in a cushioned chair at its side. The inner castle had opened months before, but her brother had never emerged, at least not publicly.

Having never wanted to be *Tianzi* anyway, Kai-Wu had been grateful for the Guardian Dragon's anointing Kaiya the decision-maker, and he let the rumor spread that he had died in the attempted coup. Today, he was enjoying a life of anonymity in Peng's province with his wife Wu Yanli. He said he wanted to be a teacher, and without a doubt, his gentle nature would serve him well in that endeavor.

Despite Lord Liu Yong's ambitions, his heir Liu Dezhen had relinquished his son's claim, probably at the urging of Cousin Kai-Hua. For the first time in seven centuries, there was no *Tianzi*.

"Take your time, make a wise choice," Doctor Wu had said a month before, with a wink. "The Guardian Dragon might very well reappear if need be."

Since the victory, she had stopped by often. Why such a powerful being had an interest in her pregnancy remained a mystery. Now, she stood toward the back with Fang Weiyong.

Kaiya pushed herself up from the chair. In front of her, the assembled lords, ministers, and generals pressed their foreheads to the ground. Many of them had served admirably throughout these trying times. Future historians might try to hail her singlehanded quelling of the rebellion and defeat of the Teleri army; for now, she'd make sure everyone got their just recognition.

"Rise," she said.

The men straightened. A thousand pairs of eyes met hers, in what would be considered impertinence if not for the awe and admiration written in their expressions. Admiration for a girl, now officially an adult at twenty years old.

She took a deep breath. "Today, because of your contributions, Cathay is once again secure. Safe from insurrection and invasion. I command you all to strive to keep it that way, through your work in the ministries, in the administration of your provinces, and in the training of your troops."

"As the regent commands." The chorus rang out, from inside the hall to out in the courtyard. Heads bowed again in a wave.

She nodded toward Chief Minister Song, who bowed. He cleared his throat and started the lengthy process of calling important ministers, generals, and lords to present themselves before her, to swear loyalty and receive their rewards.

Lord Lin's reward was generous; certainly not for his attempted declaration of independence and late help against the Teleri invasion, but rather for his daughter's role. Lin Ziqiu would serve in secret as a spy until she married the man of her choice. Kaiya suspected that man might be Zheng Ming, the only one she could not allow.

Ma Jun, with Lana and Yuha at his side, was assigned an ambassadorship to the Kanin Tribal Council, though he retained his status as imperial guard. She committed to consecrating a shrine in the Wilds, where he might pray for the repose of his comrades who died in her defense during the escape from Iksuvius. Fang Weiyong had wanted to join him, but she appointed him Chief Imperial Physician.

General Altos Di Bovyan, who had tried to protect her from Geros in the Wilds, had come at the behest of the Teleri Directori to demand that the emperor, now stripped of his title and reassigned his original name Haros Bovyanthas, be repatriated, along with the Teleri imperial crest and the Eye of Geros.

She would have liked nothing more than to give them back, since Tian suspected the crest, not the *Tiger's Eye*, had constrained her power. She offered it in return for the Teleri relinquishing their gains in the Nothori Northwest and the Wilds, and ending their breeding program in Madura—knowing well the Directori would refuse. In any case, she would ensure Cathay worked to free those countries, and Geros—Haros—would die from the curse sometime soon anyway. Before then, they would try to get as much information out of him as possible.

Cousin Peng's province in Nanling was gifted to her late imperial guard Chen Xin's cousin Lord Chen, who had nominated her as regent in the first place. Chief Minister Song's son was forgiven and assigned to the Ministry of Foreign Affairs, where his planning and spying skills could be put to good use.

Princess Alaena and Prince Aelward presented their baby girl, born in Jiangkou just before the Teleri's breaching of Huajing's wall. Kaiya gave her the Cathay name *Jin-Feng* for *Golden Phoenix*.

Cyrus had set off in search of Sameer, though Brehane had stayed behind to meet Lord Xu, as Kaiya had promised in Iksuvi. Leina's mother, whom Tian had sought out and found wandering north alone, was allowed to live in Leina's Floating World house until the end of her days.

Throughout the proceedings, Zheng Ming remained handsome and dignified, bowing as each person received their reward. He undoubtedly wondered why he had been left out when all the other *Tai-Ming* lords had been recognized. Let him guess. She judiciously avoided his gaze the whole time.

At long last, Chief Minister Song looked up from his list of names and turned to her. "That is all. Shall we adjourn, *Jie-xia*?"

The chamber broke out into low murmurs.

She stood. "I have an announcement to make."

A hush fell over all the assembled men.

"For now, the Jade Throne shall remain empty." She cradled her belly. "By laws of succession, my unborn son shall inherit." Which meant she would continue to rule as regent until he came of age, and which son… well, the lords didn't need to know about twins.

She'd expected grumbling, but the hall remained silent save for the shuffle of robes as the men pressed their foreheads to the floor. She continued, "For his valor and exploits, I will take *Tai-Ming* Lord Zheng Ming as my husband in name, and as their uncle by blood, he shall be the adopted father of my sons. He shall retain his hereditary rule over Dongmen Province and be allowed to choose his heir from what I imagine will be a long list of sons from concubines."

Cheeks pink, Zheng Ming rose from his bow and cleared his throat. "I am honored, *Jie-xia*, but if I might be so rude. Do you not plan on marrying someone?"

And by someone, he meant Tian.

She shook her head. "Let there be no question that I rule as regent, and that no one man shall influence my decisions on affairs of state."

Affairs of the heart, however, were another story. Tian had shuddered at the thought of being the regent's husband, and the social duties that came with it. She looked toward the column where his breathing betrayed his presence to her ears alone.

The old proverb asserted that those who didn't have *yuan*, destiny, could pass each other each day and never meet; while those who had *yuan* would cross oceans and mountains to be with each other.

Certainly, when neither banishment, war, nor even death could keep Tian and Kaiya apart, they were destined to be with each other.

Epilogue:
Parents and Prophecies

Cradling her two-day-old second born, Kaiya shuddered as she listened to the frantic brush strokes across rice paper inside the Hall of Water Spirits.

It wasn't that she wanted to face Geros again—the memory of what he did to her was still fresh, even after nearly a year—but, as General Altos had reminded her after his audience several months prior, there were prophecies to uphold.

A Bovyan who knew his true mother and father would end the Teleri Empire and restore the Bovyans' honor.

Her loins still ached after laboring for countless hours, and despite Doctor Fang's insistence that she stay bedridden for a month to recover, the curse could claim Geros any time now. At least she'd rested for a day.

Behind her, Tian held the smaller, weaker twin. So frail and blue he'd been, his energy sucked by a dominant twin. Doctor Fang had thought the newborn wouldn't make it to his first hour. Yet the little one was a warrior. He'd survived.

On his name day, she would call him *Yi*, for perseverance. The one of Geros' seed, she would name *Xi*, for hope. Her hope that one day, the Teleri Empire might fall. Not because of the threat they posed to

Cathay, which they no longer did, but because of the misery of the peoples they had conquered.

With a deep breath, she peered past the steel-barred door they'd installed to hold their prisoner.

Mismatched eyes wild, Geros scribbled frantically, his script growing as messy as his disheveled hair and unruly beard. A ghost of his former self, flesh hung from his bones.

A pang knotted her stomach. Despite what he'd done to her, the suffering carved into what remained of his body filled her with sympathy. Was this the curse, coming to claim him?

Some of what he wrote, in fluid Arkothi, made sense—memoirs of past glory, regrets of his last mistakes. Gibberish of the Arkothi alphabet filled other pages, reminiscent of the words she'd seen on Great Peace Island.

She cleared her throat. "Geros, come meet your son."

His brush paused, his body stilled. Slowly, he turned around, meeting her gaze. "Kaiya, you are so pale."

Behind her, Tian's hand tightened around his *dao*.

She reached back and placed her free arm on his, lest he drop his own son. "You are looking… well." A lie, certainly, but what else could she say? "Come, meet our child."

Papers clenched to his breast, Geros scuttled across the floor on one hand and two knees. He crouched by the bars, his eyes bright as he smiled.

Her stomach flipped again. The powerful, domineering man had been reduced to a dog, waiting for a treat.

Deserved? No, maybe she should've let Tian kill him seven months prior. Heavens, the curse should've claimed him by now. She held up Wang Xi and cooed. "Your father, little one."

The baby let out an adorable squeak, which made her heart race and stomach flutter. To think something so perfect could have come from *him*.

Geros reached through the bars, but Kaiya took a step back. No—even with that gentle expression, he would not be allowed to touch their son. She lifted her chin to the papers at his chest, the ones with the nonsensical alphabet combinations. "What is that, Geros?"

Blinking, he scratched his head. "My last will. Or maybe the last will of the first Geros. I'm not sure."

Ramblings of a madman. Kaiya forced a smile. "Goodbye, Geros. We will not meet again. If you need anything to keep you comfortable in your last days, be sure to let the guards know."

She turned and hobbled away, ignoring whatever the former emperor babbled.

From the threshold of the building, she caught sight of the Hall of Bountiful Harvests; where, four years before, a naïve, gangly princess' journey started when she met a dragon in man's clothing.

She leaned into Tian, and he wrapped his free arm around her. It was comforting, just like when he consoled her as a child, just like his affection in the Wilds. With him providing a reminder of who she really was, despite the image of princess and regent she projected, she would rule fairly and justly.

Jie climbed the steps to Black Lotus Temple, her first visit back in several years. The meeting with her adopted father, Master Yan, might prove interesting after what she'd learned a few months before.

The day of the regent's first audience, she'd accompanied Brehane to a meeting with Lord Xu in the Hall of Serene Reverence.

"There is no reason why your arm shouldn't work," the elf had said. Even his powerful magic had no effect.

She sighed. "It has moved on three occasions, when I wasn't even trying."

Staring at her, he pressed a finger to the center of her chest. "You must resolve something in your heart."

Tian, perhaps? She'd already given up on that. What else could there be?

"Jie!" a female voice called from the door. Princess Alaena stood there in a frilly Arkothi dress that didn't suit her, cradling her baby. "They said we might find you here."

"Aye lass," Prince Aelward said. He, too, looked handsome in his formal sailor's uniform. "We 'ad to say goodbye before we sailed home."

A handsome male elf peered around them. His eyes widened when he met her gaze. He looked at the royal couple. "This is the half-elf you were telling me about?" He turned back to her. He felt familiar.

The elf from her dream.

He had bowed, his focus never leaving her. "It seems our paths have come close, but never crossed until now. I am Thielas Starsong. And you are?"

Hair prickled on the back of her neck. No words came out of her mouth for a few seconds, probably a first. When she finally spoke, it was a squeak. "Yan Jie."

"Yan," he repeated, voice hollow. "Adopted daughter of Master Yan?"

Jie's mind had spun. Hardly anyone knew Master Yan even existed. "Who are you?"

He moved closer, arms wide. "I think you know."

"No." She had taken a step back. "You can't just appear thirty-three years after you abandoned me and my twin."

"Abandoned? Twin?" He shook his head, so violently his ears might've caught the wind and made him take flight. "No, there was only you. I had to protect you… your mother… the prophecy."

Jie's own elf ears twitched. "Prophecy?" And no twin?

Thielas' voice was almost a whisper. "A half-human girl of Aralas' blood shall slay the Orc King."

Lord Xu had choked. "Such silly tales. The elf angel was something of a philanderer, with a fetish for human women. It wouldn't surprise me if he made that up."

Everyone gawked at the blasphemy. It was hard to believe that Xu, no matter how powerful he might be, could so easily dismiss an elf angel.

"That *fetish*," Brehane had said, voice acerbic, "the nine loves of Aralas, helped win the War of Ancient Gods."

Xu scratched his chin. "Were there only nine?"

Jie had ignored the elf lord, turning instead to the other one, her supposed father. "If anything sounds made up, it's your pathetic excuse for giving me up."

Hands raised, Thielas had shaken his head. "I had to hide you, somewhere the Altivorc King would never find. Where better than your mother's people? I begged Master Yan to give you your birthright."

Jie had frowned. "He said I was left abandoned at the temple gate with a note attached to my swaddling blanket."

"And how would I find the temple gates without your clan knowing? What did the note say?"

"Master Yan lost it." That's what he'd always said.

"Since when does one of your clan lose *anything*?"

***

Which was how Jie now found herself outside the temple's gravesite, behind her unsuspecting stepfather.

Her eyes settled on an unoccupied plot for a moment, why she didn't know. Rumor had it that a Fist in the *Viper's Rest* had once been buried there and later exhumed.

It had nothing to do with her, whereas the answers she sought did. "Father," she said.

He spun around with amazing speed for his age, the clan's Black Lotus Blade in his hand. He lowered it when his gaze fell on her. "Jie. I don't think anyone has ever succeeded in sneaking up on me."

Fitting her like a second skin, Kiri's magic armor made her stealth even better, even hid her scent from the temple guard dogs. It kept her cool in the stifling summer heat, as well. Despite her frustration at his hiding the truth of her birth, his kindly eyes melted her heart. Her angry tone slipped. "Where is my birthright?"

Master Yan sighed. "You met him, then. Your father."

She nodded.

He pointed to two new grave markers. "Here lie the Architect and the Surgeon, their bodies recently returned to us. Their lives were indelibly tied to yours. Your mother was the Beauty, my daughter. You are my granddaughter by blood, though I could never tell you. Come with me."

She followed him in silence back to his study, where he opened a secret compartment built into the wall and withdrew an object bound in black cloth. He unwound it, revealing an arrow. Silver impurities veined in regular patterns through its transparent crystal point.

"Here is your birthright."

She reached… with her bad arm… and took it.

***

Jie picked her way through the wild forests of Kanin, again in search of self. She'd always taken pride in not letting destiny dictate her life, that she molded her own future; the magic arrow wrapped and hidden in her magic pouch proved otherwise. Never good at archery, she knew where to seek out a good teacher… as well as more answers.

She looked around. With her poor woodcraft skills, the forest looked more or less the same. However, the rock formation rising before her in this clearing could only be the magical pool in wild elf lands.

She lowered the hood to Kiri's… no, *her* stealth armor.

"Kala!" she yelled, removing a sealed funerary urn from the pouch. "I have Kiri's ashes."

Birds chirped and cawed. Bowstrings pulled back from all around.

Jie sucked on her lower lip. She'd never fulfill her destiny to kill the Orc King if elf arrows killed her first.

Kala's voice, familiar only in that it was a younger version of Jie's own, called out. "On your knees. Show your neck."

Kneeling, Jie bent forward and pulled the hood down further, to expose her nape.

Elf voices tittered from all around.

"Hand's up," Kala said. "Why you wear *her* armor?"

Setting the urn down, Jie raised her hands. "My friends killed her and took it. I am sorry."

"Why sorry?"

Jie's brow furrowed. "Kiri was your friend, right?"

"Still is." Kala stepped out from between two trees.

Kiri emerged, the same haunted look in her eyes, rambling in the wild elf language.

With a gasp, Jie looked down at the urn, then at the sisters. If the ashes didn't belong to Kiri... "How many sisters do we have?"

"*Vrztchkrn*. When we escape, eight." Kala held up eight little fingers, then pointed at the urn. "*She* first. *His*... weapon. Hunt *you*."

Grabbing Kala's shoulder, Kiri broke out into a tirade.

Jie shuddered. The *him* must refer to the Orc King, and the idea that her identical septuplets were out to kill her wasn't reassuring.

Still, something did make sense: people who'd claimed to have seen her all over the world, before she'd even visited. "What about the rest?"

"Slaves. Like Kiri." Kala motioned to Kiri. "*He* do bad things. Hurt them. Make sick. *He* afraid *you*."

Jie gave a slow nod. The prophecy.

No wonder Altivorcs always attacked her on sight. Still, something didn't add up. Thielas had said she was the only baby, that he'd held her in his arms. And, Kiri was clearly much younger. "*Vrztchkrn*. What are we?"

"You not *Vrztchkrn*. We *Vrztchkrn*." Kiri pointed at herself and Kiri, then stared straight at Jie. "You... you... I don't know word..."

Jie's soul might be squirming, given the weight of Kiri's stare.

"You…" Kiri cocked her head like one of the Temple dogs when they tried to understand human language. "You… our mother."

The End

Please turn the page for a short story which takes place 30 years before Songs of Insurrection. It may answer some burning questions you may have about Jie's father!

Birthright:
An Origins Short Story

Thielas Starsong held the bowstring taut, the green fletching of the arrow prickling his pointed ear. One well-placed shot would be the latest momentum change in the six-thousand-year war between elves and orcs.

Concealed behind a tree at the top of a wooded ridge, he watched as the column of two dozen tivorcs shambled along the path below. They were infamous for a lack of discipline, and their unsynchronized steps could hardly be considered marching.

Their plated shoulder and chest guards clanged in nerve-wracking cacophony, scaring wildlife deeper into the forest. Sweat on their turquoise skin glistened in blinking patches through the dappled noon sun.

A horse the size of a house, armored from head to tail-less rump, walked at the rear of the formation. It moved quietly compared to the Tivorcs. Astride it rode an altivorc, a more intelligent cousin of the Tivorcs. A prince, no less—a begotten son of the Altivorc King himself.

Straight, meticulously groomed black locks cascaded out of his crowned helmet, contrasting with the tangled hair of his minions. While the T-slotted helm protected his head, he wore only a dark tunic—an inviting target for the misinformed.

However, Thielas was well-informed: neither his magic nor his razor-sharp steel arrowhead would penetrate the cloth. Even though the orcs had lost their ability to channel magic after losing the War of Ancient Gods a millennium before, the King and his princes hoarded a handful of artifacts from before that time. Like this tunic.

The prince snarled something which Thielas, despite his century of battling the brutes, barely understood: "By the Second Sun!"

Thielas stifled a laugh, imagining the obsessive and stodgy altivorc to be appalled by his underlings' poor excuse for marching.

Don't worry, he thought, *I will end your frustration just as soon as you present me a good target.*

As if obeying a subliminal suggestion, the altivorc turned his head, exposing an eye in the helm's slit. A near-impossible shot for a human, but routine for Thielas.

Just as he was about to loose his arrow, a frail voice whispered on the winds.

It's a girl...

The urgency in the voice threw off his concentration. The arrow flew errant, jolting the Prince's head back as it plinked off the side of his helmet.

The tivorcs sank into defensive stances with growls, heads jerking this way and that to find the source of the attack. The prince himself looked straight in Thielas' direction.

He would not see Thielas.

Thielas had uttered one guttural syllable worthy of a tivorc profanity and disappeared into the ethers.

He rematerialized at the mouth of a cave, his limbs heavy and languid from the draining effect of his invocation of Shallow Magic.

Disoriented, he looked around to find the area surrounded by the straight trunks of vaulting eldarwood trees. The low-lying sun cast the wispy clouds above in a swath of red hues. He scanned the sky for the Iridescent Moon, Riyalas, which never moved from its spot in the heavens. It was high and to the south-southwest, waning to half.

Dawn. Somewhere in the mountains between Cathay and the Elven Kingdom of Aramysta.

Thielas felt his energy increase by the second, and he patted the pouch that hung over his chest. It held a rare Starburst jewel, a relic from the First Orc-Elf Wars that helped offset the fatigue of Shallow Magic.

His keen eyes were drawn to the fresh black and red blood smeared across the ground.

His heart lurched into his throat. Just a step into the cave laid a dead altivorc, a flat metal pin lodged in his eye. A young elf woman lay sprawling beside him, gutted by a horrendous slash across her abdomen. A clear orange jewel—his own beacon—sparkled just out of the reach of her lifeless fingers. Sadness yanked his racing heart back into his constricted chest, even as he buried his emotions to stay focused.

He slung his bow and drew his longsword, knowing that it would be difficult to shoot through the dense forest. Then he froze in place and listened.

Not far down a rocky path, Thielas heard the distinct cries of a newborn, high-pitched and full of vitality, almost drowning out the rhythmic jingling of metal. Looking down, he saw a trail of fresh blood heading in that direction.

As he raced through the trees, the sounds got louder. He jumped over the hacked-up body of an elf lady, lamenting that he could do nothing for her. He swerved around a pair of altivorcs, crumpled dead over a fallen tree trunk.

And then he saw them, blurs of color dancing through the trees: four altivorcs in chainmail, wielding bloodied broadswords, and a silver-haired elf maiden in a gown of starlight. Despite being a head shorter than her attackers, she held them at bay with elegant thrusts of a thin longsword.

Behind her, a human woman staggered, clutching a screaming bundle close to her chest. In the other hand, she gripped a curved, black-lacquered sword, which now served more as a crutch than a weapon.

He needed to reach her side, to save her and the elf woman.

The elf maid twisted out of the slash of one of her assailants, while simultaneously stabbing another in the neck through the narrow gap between his helmet and armor. A third altivorc met her as she finished her spin, plunging his sword into her belly.

Enraged, Thielas grunted a throaty word and the altivorc exploded in a fiery blast. Ignoring the instant fatigue creeping into his limbs, he charged into the fray as one of the attackers turned to face him. Time automatically slowed in his perception as he engaged, his enemy seemingly moving through molasses.

With this advantage, he sidestepped to his opponent's blind side, just out of the sluggish downward arc of the broadsword, and slashed across his midsection. The altivorc's armor held, and the elf had to raise his own weapon to block a slow horizontal hack.

As his enemy cocked back to swing again, Thielas flipped his sword and cut through the eye slot of his helm. A black shower sprayed from the wound as time resumed its normal pace.

Not waiting to see if the altivorc was dead, Thielas turned toward the human. She was on her knees, bent over. Beside her, her own foe lay motionless in a puddle of black, her sword lodged in its chest. The baby's cries echoed through the valley.

He looked back at the elf woman, torn between who to help first, then bounded over to the human and eased her into a sitting position. Black hair was matted against her pale, sweat-streaked face, and she afforded him a smile through wan lips. Fresh blood began to soak into the ground under her. Cooing through shallow breaths, she opened her dirty robe and brought the child to her breast.

It was then that Thielas saw the baby for the first time, her face wrinkled and flushed red. A thick shock of black hair crowned her head. Her cries stopped as soon as she latched on to the breast and suckled. *A girl...*

Behind them, the elf maid crawled forward, and Thielas tore himself away from mother and child to attend to her.

"My Lord," she whispered. "They fell upon us so fast—they came out of nowhere. We did our best to defend Meiyun. Her own male companion disappeared, probably killed first. There are still more out there."

Thielas brushed the hair out of her face and smiled kindly. He knew she would not last long, for he was far too depleted to use divine magic to heal such a horrendous wound. "Meiyun lives. You did well. I am sorry I did not get here earlier."

"It is my honor. I believe the prophecy." The woman's voice trailed off, and her eyes closed for the last time.

Thielas fought back tears as he gently laid her head down. "May Ayara take you to her bosom."

Not far in the distance, armor jangled and heavy boots crunched through the fallen eldarwood needles. He turned back to Meiyun, gauging his own strength and weighing his options.

Grief overwhelmed him when he realized a cruel fact: he lacked the energy reserves to heal her, and he did not have the dozen minutes needed to draw on the less-depleting, ritualistic Deep Magic to teleport mother and babe to safety.

Meiyun looked into his eyes. Her voice was weak, no louder than a whisper. "I am dying, Thielas. Take her. Take her to safety. My sword remembers its home. Use it. My father will ensure that she stays safe."

"I will take her to my home in Aerilysta. My sister, the queen, will watch over her."

Meiyun scowled. "Now that the handmaidens are dead, the only ones who believe the prophecy are you and the altivorcs. The elves won't protect her. My father will."

Before Thielas could rebut her, several altivorcs stormed toward them, broadswords drawn. Behind them, an altivorc who stood a head above the rest stepped forward. He was handsome, as beautiful as an elf.

In his hand he held not a sword, but a wand. It was the Altivorc King himself, clothed in the dapper uniform of a military officer going to a banquet, his head covered only by a crown. None of it would protect him from Thielas' deadly archery.

Thielas unslung his bow, and in a blink of an eye nocked an arrow. The Arrow. Silvery impurities veined in regular patterns through its transparent crystal point. There were only a dozen such arrowheads, passed down through generations of royal elves from the Elf Angel Aralas—The Hero of the War of Ancient Gods. He had said that this arrowhead could kill the Altivorc King with a single shot.

"Thielas, Thielas." The King was almost laughing. He stretched out his arms, inviting the elf to shoot. "You may have killed many of my sons, but it is not you who will slay me. Not even your esteemed grandfather could do that. You know the prophecy."

The prophecy. It wasn't worth risking such a rare relic. Thielas lowered the bow, and his eyes darted to the babe, wrapped in her mother's arms.

The Altivorc King followed his glance. A cruel smirk formed on his lips. He made a sharp motion with one hand and pointed the wand at Thielas with his other. "Kill the woman and bring the whelp to me. The elf is mine."

The king's cohorts surged forward, broadswords raised. The Great Orc uttered a harsh snarl, and a bolt of red energy exploded from the wand.

Time seemed to slow again, unbidden.

Thielas spun back, out of the line of fire, dropping his bow and taking up Meiyun's blade as he finished his turn. Another blast just barely missed him, as the horde of altivorcs closed in on the new mother and her child.

He had to get there first.

In three bounding steps, he reached Meiyun's side. He held her desperate gaze as she thrust forth the bawling babe in outstretched hands. In a decision that would haunt him forever, Thielas took the child into his free arm and uttered the single syllable that spirited them away through the corridors of magic, leaving Meiyun to face her fate alone. The vision of her last wistful smile burned in his mind's eye.

He popped back into existence in utter darkness that not even his night vision could penetrate. The cloying scent of incense assaulted him. Exhausted to the core by his repeated use of Shallow Magic, he did not have the power for the simplest of spells, a magical light. He collapsed to the ground, taking care not to harm the whimpering child in his arms.

Tears burned his eyes as reality set in. Meiyun. Dead.

As he tried to draw breath into his grief-tightened chest, his sensitive hearing picked up the almost inaudible shuffling of a dozen footsteps.

He wobbled to his feet, rocking the child in one arm while drawing his sword in another.

His blade had barely slid free of its sheath when someone twisted his wrist and knocked the weapon away. He found himself sprawled on the ground, cradling the now crying babe.

Cold steel crossed his neck in two directions, while his leg was pinned, knee twisted at a painful angle. Completely helpless, he relaxed, using what little energy he had for patting the baby.

Blinding light flooded the room, and he squinted as his eyes adjusted. Blurry, dark shapes coalesced into a dozen human male and female forms, all with black hair and honey-toned skin. They wore tight black clothes, and held weapons.

A few cleared a path to allow a man of middling years to step forward. "Starsong." He almost spat his name. "How did you find us?"

Thielas made a slow, unthreatening gesture toward Meiyun's sword.

The man made a horizontal gesture, and all of the warriors backed away. "The Black Lotus Sword. Where is Meiyun? And Feiying?"

"Young Master Yan," Thielas addressed the man, tentatively climbing to his feet. "Feiying was nowhere to be found. I assume he was killed by the altivorcs, who fell upon them unawares. Meiyun… she bid me to save her baby, to bring the girl here to be put under your protection…"

The man's face contorted, eyes narrow and jaw tight. "Her blood is on your hands. My daughter was born to rule our sect. Feiying was to be her husband. They cared for one another until you came along. I rue the day she met you. You never loved her; you just wanted to fulfill your outrageous prophecy. How did it go? A half-human girl of Aralas' Blood? Who believes such fairy tales? And now…"

The elf flinched, the ranting accusations hitting him like physical blows. Still, his heart hurt even more. "I *did* love her. It was never about the prophecy. I am sorry."

"You are sorry? Get out of my sight."

"Just give me a few moments to regain my energy and I will leave you forever."

"You will leave *her* forever, too." Young Master Yan motioned toward the babe in Thielas' arms. "She is my granddaughter, and the heir to the Black-Fist Sect now that Meiyun is dead. I will raise her as my own, and she will be protected here, for nobody—not even the King of the Altivorcs himself—will find our temple unless we allow it."

Thielas bowed his head, contrite. In that moment, he met the girl's curious gaze. She had brown eyes, large as an elf's, and even more almond-shaped from her Cathayi heritage.

His daughter.

For a few seconds, he considered keeping her, escaping through the ethers back to his homeland. Would he even survive a third Shallow Magic teleportation in such a short time?

Maybe.

However, the Young Master Yan was right. She would be better cared for here. The elves back home would always look down on the half-human, even if she were of his royal blood. And certainly, the altivorcs would look for her there. He extended his arms, his daughter in his hands. She was screaming again, even as a young woman stepped forward to receive her.

His daughter. A half-human girl of Aralas' Blood. Destined to slay the Altivorc king.

Thielas withdrew the Arrow. "Whether or not you recognize me as her father, whether or not you believe in the prophecy, this is her birthright. I beg you to give it to her one day, when she is ready to receive it."

With one last longing look at his daughter, he sang a half-minute lullaby in the musical language of Deep Magic. Her crying ceased, and her gently pointed ears perked up at the sound of his glorious voice. With the last syllable, he disappeared.

The End.

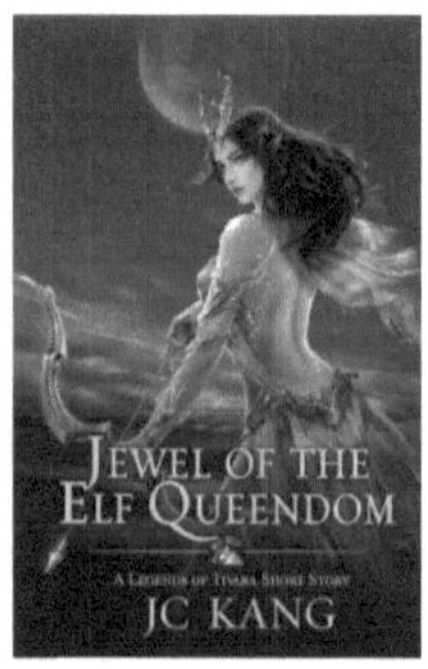

Download a free novella of Jie's adventure in her father's homeland, which takes place three months after Symphony of Fates

Appendix

Celestial Bodies

White Moon: Known as Renyue in Cathay, and represents the God of the Seas. Its orbital period is thirty days.

Iridescent Moon: Known in Cathay as Caiyue, it is the manifestation the God of Magic. It appeared at the end of the war between elves and orcs. It never moves from its spot in the sky. Its orbital period is one day, and can be used to keep time.

Blue Moon: Known in Cathay as Guanyin's Eye, it is the manifestation of the Goddess of Fertility. It sits low on the horizon. Its phases go from wide open to winking.

Tivar's Star: A red star, a manifestation of the God of Conquest. During the Year of the Second Sun, it approached the world, causing the Blue Moon to go dim.

Time

As measured by the phases of the Iridescent Moon:
Full = Midnight
1st Waning Gibbous = 1:00 AM
2nd Waning Gibbous =2:00 AM
Mid-Waning Gibbous = 3:00 AM
4th Waning Gibbous = 4:00 AM
5th Waning Gibbous = 5:00 AM
Waning Half = 6:00 AM
1st Waning Crescent = 7:00 AM
2nd Waning Crescent = 8:00 AM
Mid-Waning Crescent = 9:00 AM
4th Waning Crescent = 10:00 AM
5th Waning Crescent = 11: 00 AM
New = Noon
1st Waxing Crescent = 1:00 PM
2nd Waxing Crescent = 2:00 PM
Mid-Waxing Crescent = 3:00 PM
4th Waxing Crescent = 4:00 PM
5th Waxing Crescent = 5:00 PM
Waxing Half = 6:00 PM
1st Waxing Gibbous = 7:00 PM
2nd Waxing Gibbous =8:00 PM
Mid-Waxing Gibbous = 9:00 PM
4th Waxing Gibbous = 10:00 PM
5th Waxing Gibbous = 11:00 PM

Provinces of Cathay

Province	Ruling Family	Resources
Dongmen	Zheng	Grain, stone, guns
Fenggu	Han	Timber, rice, grain
Huayuan	Wang	Livestock, rice, wheat, lumber, firepowder, guns
Jiangzhou	Liu	Timber, wheat, silk
Linshan	Lin	Wheat, millet, timber, porcelain
Nanling	Peng	Livestock, steel, stone, gems, crossbows
Ximen	Zhao	Fishing, rice
Yutou	Liang	Fishing, rice, iron, copper, fish paste
Zhenjing	Wu	Ships, rice, fish

Human Ethnicities

Aksumi: Dark-skinned with dark eyes and coarse hair. On Earth, they would be considered North Africans. They can use Sorcery.

Ayuri: Bronze-toned skin with dark hair and eyes. On Earth, they would be considered South Asians. They can use Martial Magic.

Arkothi: Olive-skinned with blond to dark hair and light-colored eyes. On Earth, they would be considered Eastern Mediterraneans. They can use weak Mental Magic.

Bovyan: The descendants of the Sun God's begotten son, they are cursed to be all male and live only to thirty-three years of age. They are much taller and larger than the average human. Their other physical characteristics are determined by their mother's race. They have no magical ability.

Cathayi (Hua): Honey-toned skin with dark hair and eyes. High-set cheekbones and almond-shaped eyes. On Earth, they would be considered East Asians. They can use Artistic Magic.

Eldaeri: Olive-skinned with brown hair. Fine features and small frames, they are shorter in stature than the average human. In a previous age, they fled the orc domination of the continent and mingled with elves. They have no magical ability.

Estomari: Olive-skinned with varying eye and hair color. They are famous for their fine arts. On Earth, they would be considered Western Mediterraneans. They can use Divining Magic.

Kanin: Ruddy-skinned with dark hair. On Earth, they would be considered Native Americans. They can use Shamanic Magic.

Levanthi: Dark-bronze skin and dark hair. On Earth, they would be considered Persians. They can use Divine Magic.

Nothori: Fair-skinned and fair-haired. On Earth, they would be considered Northern Europeans. They can use Empathic Magic.

Acknowledgements

First, I would like to thank my wife and family for the patience they have afforded me as I pursued my childhood dream of fiction writing.

A shout-out goes out to my old Dungeons and Dragons crew: Jon, Chris, Chris, Paul, Conrad, and Julian, for helping to shape the first iteration of Tivara twenty-five years ago. Huge thanks to Brent who contributed so much backstory to the new literary version.

A gigantic thanks to my sister Laura for her spectacular job with the maps.

Thanks to the readers and writers on Wattpad for their encouragement and feedback.

Infinite gratitude to writers over at critiquecircle.com who motivated and helped me along the way. Jason, for patiently providing countless ideas. Kelly, for amazing input, character development and all the other advice. Victoria, for showing me how to layer scenes. Andy, for unparalleled wordsmithing. Ernie, for teaching me the fundamentals of fiction writing. Lindy for her sharp eye. Taylor for the numerous suggestions. Laurel, Joyce, Tracy, Traci, Larissa, Alicia, Kathyrn, and Ardyth for beta reading; and all the others who critiqued.

Finally, a huge thanks to all my readers for the encouragement you've given me. The Sisterhood of Tivara knows who they are.

Special Thanks

This special edition of Songs of Insurrection was only made possible by many generous pledges and donations.

From Patreon, I would like to especially acknowledge Elena Daymon and Samantha Mikals. I'm humbled by your support; as well as Dianeme Weidner, Spring Yang, Nicholas Klotz, Scott Engel, Mary Luu, Dexter Bradley, and Lindsay Shurtliff.

From Kickstarter, many thanks to Dyrk Ashton, Wraithmarked Creative, Zach Sallese, Dian, Ben Nichols, Rich Chang, Henrik Sörensen, Dan & Robert Zangari, Philip Tucker, Steven Hall, Jan Drake, Michał Kabza, Cody Allen, John Idlor, Kathy Jones, Nic Guinasso, Doug Williamson, Susan Voss, J. Zachary Pike, KE Sizemore, yesterspectre, Bobby McDonald, Andrew Barton, Michael Tabacchi, Emmanuel MAHE, Nicholas Liffert, A.Y. Chao, Artgor, Michael Mattson, Alexander Darwin, Krystal Xu, Caroline Atkins, Angela Engelbert, Shawna Dees, Nicolas Lobotsky, Justin Gross, Joey Hendrickson, Sarah Polk, Lawrence Wight, Eddie, Graham Dauncey, Jennifer, Virginia McClain, Christian Holt, Christopher Kranz, Leanne Yong, Kanyon Marie Kiernan, Scott Engel, Ivor Lee, Dan K, Mike Filliter, Ryan Kirk, James Yu, JC Cannon, Michelle Rapoza. Craig A. Price Jr., John Jutoy, Derek Freeman, Gerald P. McDaniel, Mat Meillier, A. Hakes, Helena Jones, Ashley, Charlie Gipson, Lapiswolf, PurpleSteamDragon, Laura E Custodio, Megan Mackie, Ashli Tingle, Stacy Shuda, Anna Lee, Don Quaintance, Anne Kinney, Jessica Stone, Stanley, Derek Alan Siddoway, Ting

Bentley, Ernesto, Gary Phillips, Dianeme Weidner, Timandra Whitecastle, Paul Cassimus, Paul, Walt Mussell, JohnYu, Chris, and Andre.

9 781970 067118